On Dublin Street

SAMANTHA YOUNG

PENGUIN BOOKS

PENGUIN BOOKS

Published by the Penguin Group
Penguin Books Ltd, 80 Strand, London WC2R ORL, England
Penguin Group (USA) Inc., 375 Hudson Street, New York, New York 10014, USA
Penguin Group (Canada), 90 Eglinton Avenue East, Suite 700, Toronto, Ontario, Canada M4P 2Y3
(a division of Pearson Penguin Canada Inc.)
Penguin Ireland, 25 St Stephen's Green, Dublin 2, Ireland (a division of Penguin Books Ltd)
Penguin Group (Australia), 707 Collins Street, Melbourne, Victoria 3008, Australia
(a division of Pearson Australia Group Pty Ltd)
Penguin Books India Pvt Ltd, 11 Community Centre, Panchsheel Park, New Delhi – 110 017, India
Penguin Group (NZ), 67 Apollo Drive, Rosedale, Auckland 0632, New Zealand
(a division of Pearson New Zealand Ltd)
Penguin Books (South Africa) (Pty) Ltd, Block D, Rosebank Office Park,
181 Jan Smuts Avenue, Parktown North, Gauteng 2193, South Africa

Penguin Books Ltd, Registered Offices: 80 Strand, London WC2R ORL, England

www.penguin.com

First published in the United States of America by New American Library,
a division of Penguin Group (USA) Inc. 2013
First published in Great Britain by Penguin Books 2013

001

Copyright © Samantha Young, 2013
All rights reserved

The moral right of the author has been asserted

Set in 12.5/14.75pt Garamond MT Std
Typeset by Jouve (UK), Milton Keynes
Printed in Great Britain by Clays Ltd, St Ives plc

ISBN: 978–1–405–91298–3

www.greenpenguin.co.uk

MIX
Paper from
responsible sources
FSC
www.fsc.org   FSC™ C018179

Penguin Books is committed to a sustainable
future for our business, our readers and our planet.
This book is made from Forest Stewardship
Council™ certified paper.

ALWAYS LEARNING   **PEARSON**

On Dublin Street

Prologue

I was bored.

Kyle Ramsey was kicking the back of my chair to get my attention, but he'd been kicking my best friend, Dru Troler's, chair yesterday, and I didn't want to upset her. She had a huge crush on Kyle. Instead I watched her as she sat beside me drawing a million tiny love hearts in the corner of her notebook as Mr Evans scribbled another equation on the board. I really should have been paying attention because I sucked at math. Mom and Dad wouldn't be happy with me if I failed a class the first semester of freshman year.

'Mr Ramsey, would you care to come up to the board and answer this question, or would you prefer to remain behind Jocelyn so you can kick her chair some more?'

The class tittered, and Dru shot me an accusing look. I grimaced and shot Mr Evans a pointed glare.

'I'll stay here, if that's okay, Mr Evans,' Kyle replied with impudent swagger. I rolled my eyes, refusing to turn around even though I could feel the heat of his gaze on the back of my neck.

'That was actually a rhetorical question, Kyle. Get up here.'

A knock at the door put a halt to Kyle's groan of acquiescence. At the sight of our principal, Ms Shaw, the whole class grew still. What was the principal doing in our class? That could only signal trouble.

'Whoa,' Dru muttered under her breath, and I looked at her, frowning. She nodded at the doorway. 'Cops.'

Shocked, I turned to look back at the door as Ms Shaw murmured something to Mr Evans, and sure enough, through the gap in the door, I could see two deputies waiting out in the hall.

'Miss Butler.' Ms Shaw's voice snapped my gaze back to her in surprise. She took a step toward me, and I felt my heart leap into my throat. Her eyes were wary, sympathetic, and I immediately wanted to back away from her and whatever it was she was here to tell me. 'Can you come with me, please? Grab your things.'

This was usually the part where the class would ooh and ahh about how much trouble I was in. But, like me, they sensed that wasn't what this was about. Whatever news was out in that hall, they weren't going to tease me about it.

'Miss Butler?'

I was shaking now from a spike of adrenaline, and I could barely hear anything over the sound of blood rushing in my ears. Had something happened to Mom? Or Dad? Or my baby sister, Beth? My parents together had taken some time off work this week to de-stress from what had been a crazy summer. They were supposed to be taking Beth out today for a picnic.

'Joss.' Dru nudged me, and as soon as her elbow

touched my arm, I shot back from the table, my chair screaming across the wooden floor. Without looking at anyone, I fumbled with my bag, swiping everything off my desk into it. The whispers had started hissing around the room like cold wind through a crack in a windowpane. Despite not wanting to know what was ahead of me, I really wanted out of that room.

Remembering somehow to put one foot in front of the other, I followed the principal out into the hall and listened to Mr Evans's door snick shut behind me. I didn't say anything. I just looked at Ms Shaw and then at the two deputies, who stared at me with a distant compassion. Standing near the wall was a woman I hadn't noticed earlier. She looked grave but calm.

Ms Shaw touched my arm and I looked down at her hand resting on my sweater. I hadn't spoken two words to the principal before, and now she was touching my arm? 'Jocelyn ... these are Deputies Wilson and Michaels. And this is Alicia Nugent from the DSS.'

I looked at her questioningly.

Ms Shaw blanched. 'The Department of Social Services.'

Fear gripped ahold of my chest, and I fought to breathe.

'Jocelyn,' the principal continued, 'I am so sorry to have to tell you this ... but your parents and sister, Elizabeth, were in a car accident.'

I waited, feeling my chest tighten.

'They were all killed instantly, Jocelyn. I'm so sorry.'

The woman from the DSS stepped toward me and

started speaking. I looked at her, but all I could see were the colors that she was made up of. All I could hear was the muffled sound of her talking, as if someone was running tap water beside her.

I couldn't breathe.

Panicking, I reached for something, anything to help me breathe. I felt hands on me. Calm, murmuring words. Wetness on my cheeks. Salt on my tongue. And my heart . . . it felt like it was going to explode, it was racing so hard.

I was dying.

'Breathe, Jocelyn.'

Those words were said in my ear over and over again until I focused on the instruction. After a while my pulse slowed and my lungs opened up. The spots across my vision began to disappear.

'That's it,' Ms Shaw was whispering, a warm hand rubbing soothing circles on my back. 'That's it.'

'We should get going.' The DSS woman's voice broke through my fog.

'Okay. Jocelyn, are you ready?' Ms Shaw asked quietly.

'They're dead,' I answered, needing to feel how the words felt. It couldn't be real.

'I'm sorry, sweetheart.'

Cold sweat burst on my skin, my palms, under my arms, across the nape of my neck. Goose bumps rose up all over, and I couldn't stop shaking. A rush of dizziness swayed me to the left and without warning vomit surged up from my churning gut. I bent over, losing my breakfast all over the DSS lady's shoes.

'She's in shock.'

Was I?

Or was it travel sickness?

One minute I had been sitting back *there*. There, where it was warm and safe. And in a matter of seconds, in the crunch of metal . . .

. . . I was someplace else entirely.

I

Scotland
Eight years later

It was a beautiful day to find a new home. And a new roommate.

I stepped out of the damp, old stairwell of my Georgian apartment building into a stunningly hot day in Edinburgh. I glanced down at the cute white-and-green-striped denim shorts I'd purchased a few weeks ago from Topshop. It had been raining nonstop since then, and I'd despaired of ever getting to wear them. But the sun was out, peeking over the top of the corner tower of the Bruntsfield Evangelical Church, burning away my melancholy and giving me back a little bit of hope. For someone who had packed up her entire life in the US and taken off for her motherland when she was only eighteen years old, I wasn't really good with change. Not anymore, anyway. I'd gotten used to my huge apartment with its never-ending mice problem. I missed my best friend, Rhian, whom I'd lived with since freshman year at the University of Edinburgh. We'd met in the dorms and hit it off. We were both very private people and were comfortable around each other for the mere fact that we never pushed each other to talk about the past. We'd stuck pretty close in our freshman year and decided to get an apartment (or 'flat' as Rhian called it) in second year. Now that we were graduates, Rhian had left for London to start her PhD and I was left roommateless. The icing on the cake was the loss of my other closest friend, James, Rhian's boyfriend. He'd run off to London (a place he detested, I might add) to be with her. And the cherry on top? My landlord was getting a divorce and needed the apartment back.

I'd spent the last two weeks answering ads from young women looking for a female roommate. It had been a bust so far. One girl didn't want to room with an American. Cue my *What the fuck?* face. Three of the apartments were just . . . nasty. I'm pretty sure one girl was a crack dealer, and the last girl's apartment sounded like it got more use than a brothel. I was really hoping my appointment today with Ellie Carmichael was going to go my way. It was the most expensive apartment I'd scheduled to see, and it was on the other side of the city center.

I was frugal when it came to my inheritance, as if spending as little of it as possible would somehow lessen the bitterness of my 'good' fortune. But I was getting desperate.

If I wanted to be a writer, I needed the right apartment and the right roommate.

Living alone was an option, of course. I could afford it. However, the God's honest truth was that I didn't like the idea of complete solitude. Despite my tendency to keep eighty percent of myself to myself, I liked being surrounded by people. When they talked to me about things I didn't understand personally, it allowed me to see things from their point of view, and I believed all the best writers needed a wide-open scope of perspective. Despite not needing to, I worked at a bar on George Street on Thursday and Friday nights. The old cliché was true: Bartenders overhear all the best stories.

I was friends with two of my colleagues, Jo and Craig, but we only really hung out when we were working. If I wanted a little life around me, I needed to get a roommate. On the plus side, this apartment was mere streets away from my job.

As I tried to shove down the anxiety of finding a new place, I kept my eye open for a cab with its light on. I eyed the ice cream parlor, wishing I had time to stop in and indulge, and almost missed the cab coming toward me on the opposite side of the street. Throwing my hand out and checking my side for traffic, I was gratified that the driver had seen me and pulled up to the curb. I tore across the wide road, managing not to get squashed like a green-and-white bug against some poor person's windshield, and rushed toward the cab with a single-minded determination to grab the door handle.

Instead of the door handle, I grabbed a hand.

Bemused, I followed the tan masculine hand up a long arm to broad shoulders and a face obscured by the sun beaming down behind his head. Tall, over six feet, the guy towered above me. I was a smallish five foot five.

I took in his expensive suit, wondering why this guy had his hand on my cab.

A sigh escaped from his shadowed face. 'Which way are you headed?' he asked me in a rumbling, gravelly voice. Four years I'd been living here and still a smooth Scots accent could send a shiver down my spine. And his definitely did, despite the terse question.

'Dublin Street,' I answered automatically, hoping I had a longer distance to travel so that he'd give me the cab.

'Good.' He pulled the door open. 'I'm heading in that direction, and since I'm already running late, might I suggest we share the taxi instead of wasting ten minutes deciding who needs it more?'

A warm hand touched my lower back and pressed me gently forward. Dazed, I somehow let myself be manhandled into the cab, sliding across the seat and buckling up as I silently questioned whether I'd nodded my agreement to this. I didn't think I had.

Hearing the Suit clip out Dublin Street as the destination to the cabdriver, I frowned and muttered, 'Thanks. I guess.'

'You're an American?'

At the soft question, I finally looked over at the passenger beside me. *Oh, okay.*

Wow.

Perhaps in his late twenties or early thirties, the Suit wasn't classically handsome, but there was a twinkle in his eyes and a curl to the corner of his sensual mouth that, together with the rest of the package, oozed sex appeal. I could tell from the lines of the extremely well-tailored expensive silver-gray suit that he wore, that he worked out. He sat with the ease of a fit guy, his stomach iron flat under the waistcoat and white shirt. His pale-blue eyes seemed bemused beneath their long lashes, and for the life of me I couldn't get over the fact that he had dark hair.

I preferred blonds. Always had.

Yet none of them had ever made my lower belly squeeze with lust at first sight. A strong, masculine face stared into mine – sharp jawline, a cleft chin, wide cheekbones, and a Roman nose. Dark stubble shadowed his cheeks, and his hair was kind of messy. Altogether, his rugged unkemptness seemed at odds with the stylish designer suit.

The Suit raised an eyebrow at my blatant perusal and the lust I was feeling quadrupled, taking me completely by surprise. I never felt instant attraction to men. And since my wild years as a teen, I hadn't even contemplated taking a guy up on a sexual offer.

Although, I'm not sure I could walk away from an offer from him.

As soon as the thought flashed through my head I stiffened, surprised and unnerved. My defenses immediately rose, and I cleared my expression into blank politeness.

'Yeah, I'm American,' I answered, finally remembering the Suit had asked me a question. I looked away from his knowing smirk, pretending boredom and thanking the heavens that my olive skin kept the blushing internal.

'Just visiting?' he murmured.

As irritated as I was by my reaction to the Suit, I decided the less conversation between us the better. Who knew what idiotic thing I might do or say? 'Nope.'

'Then you're a student.'

I took issue with the tone. *Then you're a student.* It was said with a metaphorical eye-roll. Like students were bottom-feeding bums with no real purpose in life. I snapped my head around to give him a scathing set-down, only to catch him eyeing my legs with interest. This time, I raised my eyebrows at him and waited for him to unglue those gorgeous eyes of his from my bare skin. Sensing my gaze, the Suit looked up at my face and noted my expression. I expected him to pretend he hadn't been ogling me or to look quickly away or something. I didn't expect him to just shrug and then offer me the slowest, wickedest, sexiest smile that had ever been bestowed upon me.

I rolled me eyes, fighting the flush of heat between my legs. 'I *was* a student,' I answered, with just a touch of snark. 'I live here. Dual citizenship.' Why was I explaining myself?

'You're part Scottish?'

I barely nodded, secretly loving the way he said 'Scottish' with his hard 't's.

'What do you do now that you've graduated?'

Why did he want to know? I shot him a look out of

the corner of my eye. The cost of the three-piece suit he was wearing could have fed me and Rhian on crappy student food for our entire four years of college. 'What do you do? I mean, when you're not manhandling women into cabs?'

His small smirk was his only reaction to my jibe. 'What do you think I do?'

'I'm thinking lawyer. Answering questions with questions, manhandling, smirking . . .'

He laughed a rich, deep laugh that vibrated through my chest. His eyes glittered at me. 'I'm not a lawyer. But you could be. I seem to recall a question answered with a question. And that' – he gestured to my mouth, his eyes turning a shade darker as they visually caressed the curve of my lips – 'that's a definite smirk.' His voice had grown huskier.

My pulse took off as our eyes locked, our gazes holding for far longer than two polite strangers' should. My cheeks felt warm . . . as did other places. I was growing more and more turned on by him and the silent conversation between our bodies. When my nipples tightened beneath my T-shirt bra, I was shocked enough to be plunged back into reality. Pulling my eyes from his, I glanced out at the passing traffic and prayed for this cab ride to be over yesterday.

As we approached Princes Street and another diversion caused by the tram project the council was heading up, I began to wonder if I was going to escape the cab without having to talk to him again.

'Are you shy?' the Suit asked, blowing my hopes to smithereens.

I couldn't help it. His question made me turn to him with a confused smile. 'Excuse me?'

He tilted his head, peering down at me through the narrowed slits of his eyes. He looked like a lazy tiger, eyeing me carefully as if deciding whether or not I was a meal worth chasing. I shivered as he repeated, 'Are you shy?'

Was I shy? No. Not shy. Just usually blissfully indifferent. I liked it that way. It was safer. 'Why would you think that?' I didn't give off shy vibes, right? I grimaced at the thought.

The Suit shrugged again. 'Most women would be taking advantage of my imprisonment in the taxi with them – chew my ear off, shove their phone number in my face . . . as well as other things.' His eyes flicked down to my chest before quickly returning to my face. The blood beneath my cheeks felt hot. I couldn't remember the last time someone had managed to embarrass me. Unaccustomed to feeling intimidated, I attempted to mentally shrug it off.

Amazed by his overconfidence, I grinned at him, surprised by the pleasure that rippled over me when his eyes widened slightly at the sight of my smile. 'Wow, you really think a lot of yourself.'

He grinned back at me, his teeth white but imperfect, and his crooked smile sent an unfamiliar shot of feeling across my chest. 'I'm just speaking from experience.'

'Well, I'm not the kind of girl who hands out her number to a guy she just met.'

'Ahh.' He nodded as if coming to some kind of realization about me, his smile slipping, his features seeming to tighten and close off from me. 'You're a no-sex-until-the-third-date, marriage-and-babies kind of woman.'

I made a face at his snap judgment. 'No, no, and no.' Marriage and babies? I shuddered at the thought, the fears that rode my shoulders day in and day out slipping around to squeeze my chest too tight.

The Suit looked back at me now, and whatever he had caught in my face made him relax. 'Interesting,' he murmured.

No. Not interesting. I didn't want to be interesting to this guy. 'I'm not giving you my number.'

He grinned again. 'I didn't ask for it. And even if I wanted it, I wouldn't ask for it. I have a girlfriend.'

I ignored the disappointed flip of my stomach – and apparently the filter between my brain and my mouth. 'Then stop looking at me like that.'

The Suit seemed amused. 'I have a girlfriend, but I'm not blind. Just because I can't do anything doesn't mean I'm not allowed to look.'

I was not excited by this guy's attention. *I am a strong, independent woman.* Glancing out the window, I noted with relief that we were at Queen Street Gardens. Dublin Street was right around the corner.

'Here's good, thanks,' I called to the cabdriver.

'Whereabouts?' the cabdriver called back to me.

'Here,' I replied a little more sharply than I meant to. I breathed a sigh of relief when the cab's turn signal started ticking and the car pulled over to a stop. Without another look or word to the Suit, I handed the driver some money and slid a hand along the door handle.

'Wait.'

I froze and shot the Suit a wary look over my shoulder. 'What?'

'Do you have a name?'

I smiled, feeling relief now that I was getting away from him and the bizarre attraction between us. 'Actually, I have two.'

I jumped out of the cab, ignoring the traitorous thrill of pleasure that cascaded over me at the sound of his answering chuckle.

As soon as the door swung open and I first saw Ellie Carmichael, I knew I was probably going to like her. The tall blonde was wearing a trendy playsuit, a blue trilby, a monocle, and a fake mustache.

She blinked at me with wide, pale-blue eyes.

Bemused, I had to ask, 'Is this . . . a bad time?'

Ellie stared at me a moment as if confused by my very reasonable question, considering her outfit. As if it suddenly occurred to her that she was in possession of a fake mustache, she pointed at it. 'You're early. I was tidying up.'

Tidying up a trilby, a monocle, and a mustache? I glanced behind her into a bright, airy reception hall. A bike with no front wheel was propped against the far wall; photographs and an assortment of postcards and other random clippings were attached to a board braced against a walnut cabinet. Two pairs of boots and a pair of black pumps were scattered haphazardly under a row of pegs overflowing with jackets and coats. The floors were hardwood.

Very nice. I looked back at Ellie with a huge grin on my face, feeling good about the entire situation. 'Are you on the run from the mafia?'

'Pardon?'

'The disguise.'

'Oh.' She laughed and stepped back from the door, gesturing me into the apartment. 'No, no. I had friends over last night, and we had a little bit too much to drink. All my old Halloween costumes were dragged out.'

I smiled again. That sounded fun. I missed Rhian and James.

'You're Jocelyn, right?'

'Yeah. Joss,' I corrected her. I hadn't been Jocelyn since before my parents died.

'Joss,' she repeated, grinning at me as I took my first steps inside the ground-floor apartment. It smelled great – fresh and clean.

Like the apartment I was leaving, this one was also Georgian, except it had once been an entire town house. Now it was split into two apartments. Well, actually, next door was a boutique, and the rooms above us belonged to it. I didn't know about the rooms, but the boutique itself was very nice, with handmade, one-of-a-kind clothes. *This* apartment . . .

Wow.

The walls were so smooth, I knew they had to have been plastered recently, and whoever had restored the place had done wonders. It had tall baseboards and thick coving to complement the period property. The ceilings went on forever, as they did in my old apartment. The walls were a cool white, but were broken up by colorful and eclectic pieces of art. The white should have been harsh, but the contrast of it against the dark walnut doors and hardwood flooring gave the apartment an air of simple elegance.

I was in love already, and I hadn't even seen the rest of the place.

Ellie hurriedly took off the hat and mustache, spinning around to say something to me, only to stop and grin sheepishly as she tore off the monocle she was still wearing. Shoving it aside on the walnut sideboard, she beamed brightly. She was a cheerful person. Usually I avoided cheerful people, but there was something about Ellie. She was kind of charming.

'I'll give you a tour first, shall I?'

'Sounds good.'

Striding to the door on the left nearest me, Ellie pushed it open. 'Bathroom. It's in an unconventional place, I know, right near the front door, but it's got everything you need.'

Uh . . . I'll say, I thought, tentatively stepping inside.

My flip-flops echoed off the shiny cream tiles on the floor, tiles that covered every inch of the bathroom except for the ceiling, which was painted a buttery color and inset with warm spotlights.

The bathroom was huge.

Running my hand along the bathtub with its gold claw feet, I immediately envisioned myself in there: music playing, candles flickering, a glass of red wine in my hand as I soaked in the tub and numbed my mind to . . . everything. The tub sat in the center of the room. In the back right-hand corner was a double shower stall with the biggest showerhead I'd ever seen. To my left was a modern glass bowl situated atop a white ceramic shelf. That was a sink?

I tabulated everything quickly in my head. Gold taps, huge mirror, heated towel rail . . .

The bathroom in my old apartment didn't even have a towel rail.

'Wow.' I threw Ellie a smile over my shoulder. 'This is gorgeous.'

Practically bouncing on the balls of her feet, Ellie nodded, her blue eyes smiling brightly at me. 'I know. I don't get to use it much because I have an en suite in my room. That's a plus for my prospective roommate, though. They'll get this room pretty much to them-selves.'

Hmm, I mused at the lure of the bathroom. I was beginning to see why the rent on this place was so astronomical. If you had the money to live there, though, why would you leave?

As I followed Ellie across the hall and into the huge sitting room, I asked politely, 'Did your roommate move away?' I made it sound like I was just curious, but really I was scoping Ellie out. If the apartment was this stunning, then maybe Ellie had been the problem. Before Ellie could answer, I stopped short, turning around slowly to take in the room. Like all these old buildings, the ceilings in each room were pretty high. The windows were tall and wide, so tons of light from the busy street outside spilled into the lovely room. On the center of the far wall was a huge fireplace, clearly used only as a feature and not for a real fire, but it pulled the casually chic room together. *Sure, it's a little more cluttered than I like,* I thought, eyeing the piles of books that were scattered here and there along with silly little items . . . like a toy Buzz Lightyear.

I wasn't even going to ask.

Eyeing Ellie, the cluttered room began to make sense. Her blonde hair was pulled back in a messy bun, she was wearing mismatched flip-flops, and there was a price sticker on her elbow.

'Roommate?' Ellie asked, turning around to meet my gaze. Before I could repeat the question, the furrow between her pale eyebrows cleared and she nodded, as if understanding. Good. It hadn't been that hard a question. 'Oh, no.' She shook her head. 'I didn't have a roommate. My brother bought this place as an investment and had it all done up. Then he decided he didn't want me struggling to pay rent while I do my PhD, so he just gave it to me.'

Nice brother.

Even though I didn't comment, she must have seen the reaction in my eyes. Ellie grinned, a fond look softening her gaze. 'Braden is a little over the top. A present from him is never simple. And how could I say no to this place? Only thing is, I've been living here for a month and it's just too big and lonely, even with my friends hanging out here on the weekends. So I said to Braden that I was getting a roommate. He wasn't keen on the idea, but I told him how much rent this place takes in and that changed his mind. Forever the businessman.'

I knew instinctually that Ellie loved her (obviously quite well-off) brother and that the two were close. It was there in her eyes when she talked about him, and I knew that look. I'd studied it over the years, facing it head on and developing a shield against the pain it brought me to see that kind of love on other people's faces – other people who still had family in their lives.

'He sounds very generous,' I replied diplomatically, unused to people spilling their private feelings all over me when we'd only just met.

Ellie didn't seem bothered by my response, which wasn't exactly warm with *tell me more*s. She just kept smiling and led me out of the sitting room and down the hall into a long kitchen. It was kind of narrow, but the far end opened up into a semicircle where a dining table and chairs were arranged. The kitchen itself was as expensively finished as everywhere else in the apartment. All the appliances were top of the line and there was a huge modern range in the middle of the dark wood units.

'Very generous,' I repeated.

Ellie grunted at my observation. 'Braden's too generous. I didn't need all this, but he insisted. He's just like that. Take for instance his girlfriend – he indulges her in everything. I'm just waiting for him to get bored with her like he does with the rest of them, because she's one of the worst he's been with. It's so obvious she's more interested in his cash than in him. Even he knows it. He says the arrangement suits him. Arrangement? Who talks like that?'

Who talks this much?

I hid a smile as she showed me the master bedroom. Like Ellie, it was cluttered. She prattled on a little more about her brother's obviously vapid girlfriend, and I wondered how this Braden guy would feel if he knew his sister was divulging his private life to a complete stranger.

'And this could be your room.'

We were standing in the doorway of a room at the very back of the apartment. A massive bay window with a window seat and jacquard floor-length curtains, a gorgeous French Rococo bed, and a walnut library desk and leather chair. Somewhere for me to write.

I was in love.

'It's beautiful.'

I wanted to live there. To hell with the cost. To hell with a chatty roommate. I'd lived frugally for long enough. I was alone in a country I'd adopted. I deserved a little comfort.

I'd get used to Ellie. She talked a lot but was sweet and charming, and there was something innately kind in her eyes.

'Why don't we have a cup of tea and see how we get on from there?' Ellie was grinning again.

Seconds later, I found myself alone in the sitting room as Ellie made tea in the kitchen. It suddenly occurred to me that it didn't matter if I liked Ellie. *Ellie* had to like *me* if she was going to offer me that room. I felt worry gnaw at my gut. I wasn't the most forthcoming person on the planet, and Ellie seemed like the most open. Maybe she wouldn't 'get' me.

'It's been difficult,' Ellie announced upon her reentrance into the room. She was carrying a tray of tea and some snacks. 'Finding a roommate, I mean. Very few people our age can afford somewhere like this.'

I had inherited a lot of money. 'My family is well-off.'

'Oh?' She pushed a mug of hot tea toward me as well as a chocolate muffin.

I cleared my throat, my fingers trembling around the mug. Cold sweat had broken out across my skin and blood was rushing in my ears. That's how I always reacted when I was on the verge of having to tell someone the truth. *My parents and little sister died in a car accident when I was fourteen. The only other family I have is an uncle who lives in Australia. He didn't want custody of me, so I lived in foster care. My parents had a lot of money. My dad's grandfather was an oilman from Louisiana, and my father had been exceptionally careful with his own inheritance. It all went to me when I turned eighteen.* My heart slowed and the trembling ceased as I remembered Ellie didn't really need to know my tale of woe. 'My family on my dad's side originally came from Louisiana. My great-grandfather made a lot of money in oil.'

'Oh, how interesting.' She sounded sincere. 'Did your family move from Louisiana?'

I nodded. 'To Virginia. But my mom was originally from Scotland.'

'So you're part Scottish. How cool.' She threw me a secret smile. 'I'm only part Scottish as well. My mum is French, but her family moved to St Andrews when she was five. Shockingly, I don't even speak French.' Ellie snorted and waited on my expected commentary.

'Does your brother speak French?'

'Oh no.' Ellie waved my question off. 'Braden and I are half siblings. We share the same dad. Our mums are both alive, but our dad died five years ago. He was a very well-known businessman. Have you heard of Douglas Carmichael and Co.? It's one of the oldest estate agencies in the area. Dad took it over from his dad when he was really young and started up a property development company. He also owned a few restaurants and even a few of the tourist shops here. It's a little mini-empire. When he died, Braden took it all on. Now it's Braden everyone around here panders to – everyone trying to get a piece of him. And they all know how close we are, so they've tried using me, too.' Her pretty mouth twisted bitterly, an expression that seemed completely foreign to her face.

'I'm sorry.' I meant it. I understood what that was like. It was one of the reasons I had decided to leave Virginia behind and start over in Scotland.

As if sensing my utter sincerity, Ellie relaxed. I would never understand how someone could lay themselves out like that to a friend, never mind a stranger, but for once I wasn't scared of Ellie's openness. Yeah, it might cause her to expect me to reciprocate in the sharing, but once she got to know me, I'm sure she'd understand that wasn't going to happen.

To my surprise, an extremely comfortable silence had fallen between us. As if just realizing that too, Ellie smiled softly at me. 'What are you doing in Edinburgh?'

'I live here now. Dual citizenship. It feels more like home here.'

She liked that answer.

'Are you a student?'

I shook my head. 'I just graduated. I work Thursday and Friday nights at Club 39 on George Street. But I'm really just trying to focus on my writing at the moment.'

Ellie seemed thrilled by my confession. 'That's brilliant! I've always wanted to be friends with a writer. And that's so brave to go for what you really want. My brother thinks being a PhD student is a waste of my time because I could work for him, but I love it. I'm a tutor at the university as well. It's just ... well, it makes me happy. And I'm one of these awful people who can get away with doing what they enjoy even if it doesn't pay much.' She grimaced. 'That sounds terrible, doesn't it?'

I wasn't really the judging kind. 'It's your life, Ellie. You've been blessed financially. That doesn't make you a terrible person.' I'd had a therapist in high school, and I could hear her nasally voice in my head: *'Now why can't you apply the same thought process to yourself, Joss? Accepting your inheritance doesn't make you a terrible person. It's what your parents wanted for you.'*

From the ages of fourteen to eighteen, I'd lived with two foster families in my hometown in Virginia. Neither family had a lot of money, and I went from a big, fancy house and expensive food and clothes to eating a lot of SpaghettiOs and sharing clothes with a younger foster 'sister' who happened to be the same height. With the approach of my eighteenth year, and the public knowledge that I would be receiving a substantial inheritance, I'd been approached by a number of businesspeople in our town looking to take advantage of what they assumed was a naive kid and secure an investment, as well as a classmate who wanted me to invest in his website. I guess living how the other half lived during my formative years and then being sucked up to by fake people more interested in my deep pockets than in me were two of the reasons I was reluctant to touch the money I had.

Sitting there with Ellie, someone in a similar financial situation who was dealing with guilt (although of a different kind), I felt a surprising connection to her.

'The room is yours,' Ellie suddenly announced.

Her abrupt bubbliness brought laughter to my lips. 'Just like that?'

Seeming serious all of a sudden, Ellie nodded. 'I have a good feeling about you.'

I have a good feeling about you, too. I gave her a relieved smile. 'Then I'd love to move in.'

2

A week later I'd moved into the luxury apartment on Dublin Street.

Unlike Ellie and her clutter, I liked everything to be organized around me just so, and that meant immediately diving into unpacking.

'Are you sure you don't want to sit and have a cup of tea with me?' Ellie asked from the doorway as I stood in my room surrounded by boxes and a couple of suitcases.

'I really want to get this all unpacked so I can just relax.' I smiled reassuringly so she wouldn't think I was blowing her off. I always hated this part of a burgeoning friendship – the exhausting hedging of each other's personality, trying to work out how a person would react to a certain tone or attitude.

Ellie just nodded her understanding. 'Okay. Well, I've got to tutor in an hour, so I think I'll walk instead of grabbing a cab, which means heading off now. That'll give you some space, some time to get to know the place.'

I'm liking you more already. 'Have a fun class.'

'Have fun unpacking.'

I grunted and waved her away as she flashed me a pretty smile and headed out.

As soon as the front door slammed shut, I flopped down on my incredibly comfortable new bed. 'Welcome to Dublin Street,' I murmured, staring up at the ceiling.

Kings of Leon sang 'Your Sex Is on Fire' really loudly at me. I grumbled at the fact that my solitude was being so quickly intruded upon. With a tilt of my hip, I slipped my phone out of my pocket and smiled at the caller ID.

'Hey, you,' I answered warmly.

'So have you moved into your exorbitantly overindulgent, pretentious new flat yet?' Rhian asked without preamble.

'Is that bitter envy I hear?'

'You've got that right, you lucky cow. I was almost ill in my cereal this morning at the pictures you sent me. Is that place for real?'

'I take it the apartment in London isn't living up to your expectations?'

'Expectations? I'm paying through the nose for a bloody glorified cardboard box!'

I snorted.

'Fuck off,' Rhian grumbled halfheartedly. 'I miss you and our mice-riddled palace.'

'I miss you and our mice-riddled palace, too.'

'Are you saying that as you stare at your claw-footed bathtub with its gold-plated taps?'

'Nope . . . as I lie on my five-thousand-dollar bed.'

'What's that in pounds?'

'I don't know. Three thousand?'

'Jesus, you're sleeping on six weeks' rent.'

Groaning, I sat up to pull open the nearest box. 'I wish I hadn't told you how much my rent is.'

'Well, I'd give you a lecture on how you're pissing that money of yours away on rent when you could have bought a house, but who am I to talk?'

'Yeah, and I don't need any lectures. That's the sweetest part of being an orphan. No concerned lectures.'

I don't know why I said that.

There was no sweet part to being an orphan.

Or having no one be concerned.

Rhian was silent on the other end of the line. We never talked about my parents or hers. It was our no-go area. 'Anyway' – I cleared my throat – 'I better get back to unpacking.'

'Is your new roommate there?' Rhian picked up the conversation as though I hadn't said anything about my parentless status.

'She just went out.'

'Have you met any of her friends yet? Any of them guys? Hot guys? Hot enough to haul you out of your four-year dry spell?'

The skeptical laughter on my lips died when an image of the Suit popped into my mind. Feeling my skin prickle at the thought of him, I found myself grow quiet. It wasn't the first time he'd flashed across my thoughts in the last seven days.

'What's this?' Rhian asked in answer to my silence. 'Is one of them a hottie?'

'No.' I brushed her off as I shoveled the Suit out of my thoughts. 'I haven't met any of Ellie's friends yet.'

'Bummer.'

Not really. The last thing I need in my life is a guy. 'Listen, I've got to get this done. Talk to you later?'

'Sure, hon. Talk later.'

We hung up and I sighed, gazing at all my boxes. All I really wanted to do was flop back down on the bed and take a long nap.

'Ugh, let's do this.'

A few hours later, I was completely unpacked. All of my boxes were folded up neatly and stored in the hall closet. My clothes were hung up and put away. My books were lined up on the bookshelf and my laptop was open on the desk, ready for my words. A photograph of my parents sat on my bedside table, another of Rhian and me at a Halloween party graced the bookshelf, and by my laptop on the desk sat my favorite photo. It was a picture of me holding Beth, my parents standing behind me. We were sitting out in the backyard at a barbecue the summer before they died. My neighbor had taken the shot.

I knew photos usually invited questions, but I couldn't bring myself to put those photographs away. They were a painful reminder that loving people only led to heartbreak . . . but I couldn't bear to part with them.

I kissed my fingertips and placed them gently against the photo of my parents.

I miss you.

After a moment, a bead of sweat rolling down my nape drew me out of my melancholic fog, and I wrinkled my nose. It was a hot day, and I had blasted through the unpacking like the Terminator after John Connor.

Time to try out that gorgeous bathtub.

Pouring in some bubble bath and running the hot water, I immediately began to relax at the rich smell of lotus blossoms. Back in my bedroom, I peeled off my sweaty shirt and shorts and felt a smug liberation as I walked down the hall, naked in my new apartment.

I smiled, gazing around at it, still not quite believing all the prettiness was mine for at least the next six months.

With music blasting from my smartphone, I sank deep into the tub and began to doze. It was only the growing chill of the water that nudged me to wakefulness. Feeling soothed and as content as I could be, I clambered inelegantly out of the tub and reached for my phone. As soon as silence reigned around me, I glanced over at the towel rail and froze.

Crap.

There were no towels. I scowled at the towel rail as if it was its fault. I could have sworn Ellie had towels on there last week. Now I was going to have to drip water all down the hall.

Grumbling under my breath, I wrenched the bathroom door open and stepped out into the airy hallway.

'Uh . . . hullo,' a deep voice choked out, and my eyes snapped up from the puddle I was making on the hardwood floor.

A squeal of shock got crushed in my windpipe as I gazed into the eyes of the Suit.

What was he doing here? In my house? *Stalker!*

My mouth hung open as I tried to work out what the hell was going on; it took me a moment to realize his eyes weren't on my face. They were running all over my very naked body.

With a garbled noise of distress I clamped an arm over my breasts. Pale-blue eyes met my horrified gray gaze. 'What are you doing in my apartment?' I glanced hurriedly around for a weapon. *Umbrella? It had a metal point . . . That might work.*

Another choking noise wrenched my eyes back to his, and a flush of unwanted and totally inappropriate heat hit me between the legs. He had *that look* again. That dark, sexually avaricious look. I hated that my body responded so instantly to that look, considering the guy might be a serial killer.

'Turn around!' I yelled, trying to cover up how vulnerable I felt.

Immediately the Suit held up his hands in surrender and spun slowly around, his back to me. My eyes narrowed at the sight of his shaking shoulders. The bastard was laughing at me.

Heart racing, I moved to rush toward my room to grab some clothes – and possibly a baseball bat – when my eyes snagged on a photo on Ellie's memo board. It was a picture of Ellie . . . and the Suit.

What the hell?

Why had I not noticed this? Oh yeah. Because I don't like to ask questions. Disgruntled at my own crappy observational skills, I threw a quick look over my shoulder. I was gratified to find that the Suit wasn't peeking. Skittering off to my room, his deep voice followed me, rumbling down the hall to my ears. 'I'm Braden Carmichael. Ellie's brother.'

Of course he was, I thought grumpily, patting myself dry with a towel before shoving my angry limbs through a pair of shorts and a tank top.

With my dark-blonde, brownish hair piled in a wet mess atop my head, I stormed back out into the hall to face him.

Braden had turned around; his lips quirked up at the corner now as he ran his eyes over me. The fact that I was dressed didn't matter. He was still seeing me naked. I could tell.

My hands flew to my hips in belligerent humiliation. 'And you just walk in here without knocking?'

A dark eyebrow rose at my tone. 'It is *my* flat.'

'It's common courtesy to freaking knock,' I argued.

His reply consisted of him shrugging and then jamming his hands casually into his suit pants. He'd taken his jacket off somewhere and his white shirtsleeves were rolled up to the elbow, revealing strong, thick-veined forearms.

A knot of need tightened in my gut at the sight of those sexy forearms.

Shit.

Fuckity shit fuck.

I flushed inwardly. 'Aren't you going to apologize?'

Braden gifted me a roguish smile. 'I never apologize unless I mean it. And I'm not apologizing for this. It's been the highlight of my week. Possibly my year.' His grin was so easygoing, coaxing me to smile back at him. I wouldn't.

Braden was Ellie's brother. He had a girlfriend.

And I was way too attracted to this stranger for it to be healthy.

'Wow, what a boring life you must lead,' I replied haughtily and weakly as I walked by him. You try being witty after flashing your girl pieces to some guy you barely know. I couldn't really give him much of a wide berth and had to ignore the flutter of butterflies in my stomach as I caught a whiff of the delicious cologne he was wearing.

Grunting at my observation, Braden followed me. I could feel the heat of him at my back as I entered the sitting room.

His jacket was tossed across an armchair and a near-empty mug of coffee was sitting beside an open newspaper on the coffee table. He'd just made himself at home while I was soaking in the tub, completely oblivious.

Annoyed, I shot him a dirty look over my shoulder.

His boyish grin hit me in the chest and I looked away quickly, perching on the arm of the couch as Braden sank casually into the armchair. The grin was gone now. He stared up at me with just a small smile playing on his lips, like he was thinking of a private joke. Or of me naked.

Despite my resistance to him, I didn't want him to think that my nakedness was funny.

'So, you're Jocelyn Butler.'

'Joss,' I corrected automatically.

He nodded and relaxed into his seat, his arm sliding along the back of the chair. He had gorgeous hands. Elegant but masculine. Large. Strong. An image of that hand sliding up my inner thigh crossed my mind before I could stop it.

Fuck.

I unglued my eyes from his hands to look at his face. He appeared comfortable and yet totally authoritative. It suddenly occurred to me that this was the Braden with all the money and responsibilities, a vainglorious girlfriend, and a little sister he was undoubtedly overprotective of.

'Ellie likes you.'

Ellie doesn't know me. 'I like Ellie. I'm not so sure about her brother. He seems kind of rude.'

Braden flashed me those white, slightly crooked teeth. 'He's not sure of you either.'

That's not what your eyes are saying. 'Oh?'

'I'm not sure how I feel about my wee sister living with an exhibitionist.'

I made a face at him, only just resisting sticking my tongue out at him. He really brought out my mature side. 'Exhibitionists get naked in public. As far as I was aware, there was no one else in the apartment, and I'd forgotten a towel.'

'Thank God for small mercies.'

He was doing it again. Looking at me *that* way. Did he know he was being so blatant about it?

'Seriously,' he continued, his eyes falling to my chest before climbing back up to my face. 'You should walk around naked all the time.'

The compliment got to me. I couldn't help it. The touch of a smile curled the corner of my lips, and I shook my head at him like he was a naughty school boy.

Pleased, Braden laughed softly. A weird, unexpected fullness formed in my chest, and I knew I had to break whatever weird instant attraction was going on between us. This had never happened to me before, so I was going to have to wing it.

I rolled my eyes. 'You're an ass.'

Braden sat up with a snort. 'Usually a woman calls me that after I've fucked her and called her a taxi.'

I blinked rapidly at his blunt language. Really? We were using that word already in our short acquaintance?

He noticed. 'Don't tell me you hate that word.'

No. I imagine that word can be a total turn-on in the right moment. 'No. I just don't think we should be talking about fucking when we've just met.'

Okay. That came out all wrong.

Braden's eyes brightened with silent laughter. 'I didn't know that's what we were doing.'

Abruptly, I changed the subject. 'If you're here for Ellie, she's tutoring.'

'I came to meet you, actually. Only I didn't know I was meeting *you*. Quite the coincidence. I've thought about you quite a bit since last week in the taxi.'

'Was that while you were out having dinner with your girlfriend?' I asked snidely, feeling like I was swimming against the tide with this guy. I wanted us out of this flirty, sexual place we'd landed in and into a normal just-my-roommate's-brother kind of place.

'Holly is down south visiting her parents this week. She's from Southampton.'

Like I give a crap. 'I see. Well . . .' I stood up, hoping the gesture would usher him out. 'I would say it was nice to meet you, but I was naked, so . . . it wasn't. I have a lot to do. I'll tell Ellie you dropped by.'

Laughing, Braden shook his head and stood up to pull on his suit jacket. 'You're a hard nut to crack.'

Okay, clearly I had to lay it out clear and simple for this guy. 'Hey, there will be no cracking of this nut. Now or ever.'

He was choking on laughter now as he stepped toward me, making me back into the couch. 'Really, Jocelyn . . . why do you have to make everything sound so dirty?'

My mouth fell open in outrage as he turned and left . . . having had the last word.

I hated him.

I really did.

Pity that my body did not.

3

Club 39 was less a club and more a bar with a small square dance floor beyond the alcove at the back. On the basement level on George Street, the ceilings were low, the circular sofas and square cubes that acted as seats were low, and the bar area was actually built a few levels lower, meaning drunken people had to walk down three steps to get to us. Whoever added that little design to the architect's draft had clearly been smoking something.

Thursday nights usually found the low-lit bar crowded with students, but with the semester over and the Scottish summer upon us, the night was quiet and the music was turned down as there was no one on the dance floor.

I handed the guy standing across the bar his drinks, and he gave me a ten-pound note. 'Keep the change.' He winked at me.

I ignored the wink but stuck the tip in the tip jar. We divided the money at the end of the night even though Jo argued that she and I pulled the most tips in because of the low-cut white tank tops we wore with black skinny jeans as a uniform. The tank had *Club 39* scrawled across the right breast in black French script. Simple but effective. Especially when you were as blessed in the boob department as I was.

Craig was on break, so Jo and I were dealing with the small crowd of customers at the bar, a crowd that was dwindling by the minute. Bored, I glanced down to the other end of the bar to see if Jo needed my help.

She did.

Just not in a bartending kind of way.

Reaching out to hand the customer she was serving his change, the guy grabbed Jo's wrist and tugged her over the bar so she was inches from his face. I frowned and bided my time to see how Jo would react; her pale skin grew flush and she wrenched on her arm to try to break his hold. His friends stood behind him laughing. Nice.

'Let me go, please,' Jo said between gritted teeth, pulling harder.

With no Craig around and Jo's wrist so skinny it might break, the situation was left up to me. I headed down the bar toward them, pressing the button under the bar for the security guys at the door.

'Oh, come on, sweetheart, it's my birthday. Just one kiss.'

My hand clamped down around the guy's, and I dug my nails into his skin. 'Let go of her, asshole, before I tear the flesh from your hand and nail it to your balls.'

He hissed in pain and jerked back from me, consequently letting go of Jo. 'American bitch.' He groaned, cradling the hand that was now covered in deep crescent-shaped marks. 'I'm complaining to management.'

Why did my nationality always come into play in a

negative situation? And what? Were we in some '80s brat-pack movie? I snorted at him, unimpressed.

Brian, our huge security guy, appeared behind him. He did not look amused. 'Problem, Joss?'

'Yeah. Can you please remove this guy and his friends from the bar?'

He didn't even ask why. There had only been a few occasions where we'd had people tossed out, so Brian trusted my assessment of the situation. 'Come on, fellas, move it,' he growled, and like the cowards they were, pale-faced and drunk off their asses, the three of them lumbered out of the bar with Brian behind them.

Feeling Jo tremble beside me, I placed a comforting hand on her shoulder. 'You okay?'

'Aye.' She gave me a weak smile. 'Bad night all around. Steven dumped me earlier.'

I winced, knowing how much that had to hurt Jo and her little brother. They lived together in a small apartment on Leith Walk where they took turns taking care of their mom, who had chronic fatigue syndrome. To make the rent, Jo – who was gorgeous – used her looks to get herself 'sugar daddies' to help take care of them financially. No matter how often people told her she was smart enough to do something more with her life, she was just full of insecurities. The only confidence she did have was in her good looks and their ability to snag a guy who would take care of her and her family. But looking after her mom always trumped her beauty, and sooner or later the men all dumped her.

'I'm sorry, Jo. You know if you need help with rent or anything, all you've got to do is ask.'

I'd offered more times than I could count. She always said no.

'Nah.' She shook her head and pressed a soft kiss to my cheek. 'I'll find someone new. I always do.'

She wandered away with a slump to her shoulders, and I found myself worrying about her when I really didn't want to. Jo was one of the misunderstood. She could grate on your nerves with her materialism, but humble you with her loyalty to her family. She might love pretty shoes, but they took a back burner when it came to making sure her kid brother and mom were okay. Unfortunately that loyalty also meant she'd trample over anyone who got in her way, and be trampled over by anyone willing to use her situation against her.

'I'm going on my break. I'll send Craig out.'

I nodded, even though she couldn't see me, wondering who her next victim would be. Or was that whose victim she would next become?

'It's quiet tonight.' Craig ambled toward me two minutes later with a can of soda in hand. Tall, dark-haired, and good-looking, Craig probably pulled in just as many tips as Jo and I did. He was a perennial flirt. And he was good at it.

'It's summer,' I mused, casting an eye around the club before turning my back to lean on the bar. 'It'll pick up weekdays again when August comes around.' I didn't have to explain I meant it would pick up because of the Edinburgh Festival. In August, the entire city was taken over: Tourists descended on the city, stealing all the best tables in all the best restaurants, and there were always so many of them that they made walking five steps into a five-minute journey.

The tips were great, though.

Craig groaned and leaned closer to me. 'I'm bored.' He flicked his eyes over my body with lazy perusal. 'Want to shag me in the men's toilets?'

He asked me this every shift.

I always said no, and then told him to shag Jo instead. His reply: 'Been there, done that.' I was a friendly challenge, and I think he honestly had deluded himself into thinking he'd one day conquer me.

'Well? Do you?' A familiar soft voice asked from behind me.

I whirled around, blinking in surprise to find Ellie on the other side of the bar. Behind her was a guy I didn't recognize and . . . Braden.

Blanching instantly, still mortified from yesterday, I barely noted the carefully blank expression in his eyes as he watched Craig.

Wrenching my own gaze from him, I smiled weakly at Ellie. 'Um . . . what are you doing here?'

Ellie and I had had dinner together the night before. I'd told her Braden had stopped by, but I hadn't told her about the whole naked thing. She'd told me about her class, and I could understand why she'd make such a great tutor. Her passion for art history was infectious, and I found myself listening to her with genuine interest.

All and all, it had been a pleasant first dinner. Ellie

43

had asked me a couple of personal questions that I had managed to deflect back onto her. I now knew that she was a big sister to half siblings: Hannah, fourteen, and Declan, ten. Her mom, Elodie Nichols, lived in the Stockbridge area of Edinburgh with her husband, Clark. Elodie was a part-time manager at the Sheraton Grand Hotel, and Clark was a professor of classical history at the university. It was clear from the way she talked that Ellie adored them all, and I got the impression that Braden spent more time with this family than with his own mother.

At lunch today, Ellie and I had taken a break from our own work and met in the sitting room for food and a little bit of television. We'd sniggered our way through an episode of the classic British comedy *Are You Being Served?* and bonded in the comfortable silence. I'd felt as though I were gaining surprisingly fast but steady ground with my new roommate.

But turning up at my work with her brother? Well, that was not cool. Not that she knew about my incident yesterday with Braden . . .

'We're meeting up with some friends for a drink in Tigerlily. We thought we'd stop by to say hi.' She grinned at me, her eyes dancing with mischief in a seventh-grader kind of way before she slanted them questioningly in Craig's direction.

Tigerlily, huh? That was a nice place. I noted Ellie's pretty sequin dress. It looked like something from the 1920s and screamed designer. It was the first time I'd seen her so put together, and with Braden standing next to her wearing another dapper suit, as well as their companion, Adam's, polished look, I felt a little out of sorts. Despite all my money, I wasn't used to the obviously stylish cocktails-and-crème-brûlée kind of lifestyle these guys were. Somehow disappointed, I realized I did not fit in with this crowd.

'Oh,' I answered dumbly, ignoring her questioning eyebrows.

'This is Adam.' Ellie turned to the guy behind her as soon as she realized I wasn't going to answer her silent query. Ellie's pale eyes turned dark with deep warmth as she looked up at Adam, and I wondered if this guy was her boyfriend. Not that she'd mentioned a boyfriend. The dark-haired hottie was just a little shorter than Braden, with broad shoulders that filled out his suit niccly.

His warm, dark eyes glittered at me under the bar lights as he smiled. 'Hi. Nice to meet you.'

'You, too.'

'Adam is Braden's best friend,' Ellie explained and then turned to her brother. As soon as she looked at him she burst out laughing, her giggles filling the bar like fairy bubbles as she glanced back at me over her shoulder. 'I would introduce you to Braden, but I believe you've already . . . met.' I barely heard the word 'met' over her choked laughter.

I stiffened.

She knew.

Eyes narrowed, I shot Braden a disgusted look. 'You told her.'

45

'Told her what?' Adam asked, bemused, looking at the still-chortling Ellie as though she'd gone mad.

Braden's mouth turned up in amusement as he answered Adam without taking his eyes off me. 'That I walked in on Jocelyn when she was wandering around the flat naked.'

Adam eyed me curiously.

'No,' I retorted with a bite in my tone. 'I was coming out of the bathroom looking for a towel.'

'He saw you naked?' Craig interrupted, a scowl marring his forehead.

'Braden Carmichael.' Braden stuck a hand across the bar for Craig to shake. 'Nice to meet you.'

Craig took it, seeming a little dazed. Great. Even men were charmed by him. While Braden smiled at Craig, his cheerful expression disappeared when his eyes fell on me again. I detected a slight chill in them and frowned. What had I done now?

'I have a girlfriend,' Braden assured Craig. 'I wasn't putting the moves on yours.'

'Oh, Joss isn't my girlfriend.' Craig shook his head, with a cocky grin down at me. 'Not for my lack of trying.'

'Customer.' I pointed to the girl at the other end of the bar, glad for an excuse to get rid of him.

As soon as he was gone, Ellie was leaning against the bar. 'Not your boyfriend? Really? Why not? He's cute. And he certainly thinks you're hot.'

'He's a walking sexually transmitted disease,' I answered grumpily, running a dishrag over an invisible spot on the bar, desperately trying to avoid Braden's gaze.

46

'Does he always talk to you like that?'

Braden's question brought my head up reluctantly, and I immediately felt the need to reassure him and defend Craig when I saw his cool, lethal eyes narrowed in my colleague's direction. 'He doesn't mean anything by it.'

'Oh, man, that break surely wasn't ten minutes,' Jo complained as she wandered slowly behind the bar. She reeked of cigarette smoke. I couldn't imagine why anyone would put up with a habit that made them stink so badly. I wrinkled my nose at her, and Jo instantly understood. Not taking it to heart, she just shrugged and blew me a teasing kiss as she stopped to lean against the bar across from Braden. Her big green eyes drank him in as though he were a cigarette she was trying to quit. 'And who do we have here?'

'I'm Ellie.' She waved at Jo as though she was a cute fifteen-year-old. I smiled at her. She was kind of adorable. 'I'm Joss's new flatmate.'

'Hi.' Jo offered her a polite smile before looking back at Braden expectantly.

I wasn't at all annoyed by her blatant interest in him.

'Braden.' He nodded at her, his eyes quickly returning to my face.

Okay. Really?

I was stunned.

If I were being honest, I would admit that I had been bracing myself to watch Braden turn the flirtatiousness up a notch for Jo. She was tall, model-thin, and had long thick poker-straight strawberry-blonde hair. If Braden Carmichael transformed into a smoldering flirt around me, then I had totally been expecting him to melt Jo into the floor with his charm.

Instead he'd been kind of cool toward her.

That did not make me happy in any way.

Hmm. I'd always been good at lying to myself.

'Braden *Carmichael*?' Jo asked, oblivious to his disinterest. 'Oh my God. You own Fire.'

Damn my curiosity over this guy. 'Fire?'

'The club on Victoria Street. You know, just off the Grassmarket.' Jo's eyelashes were batting a mile a minute at him now.

He owns a nightclub. Of course he does.

'I do,' he muttered and then checked his watch.

I knew that move. I used that move whenever I was uncomfortable. In that moment I really wanted to slap Jo for gushing all over him. Braden was not replacing Steven. No way.

'I love that place,' Jo continued, leaning farther over the bar to give him an eagle-eye view of her small, inconsequential chest.

Meow. Where did that come from?

'Maybe we could go together some time? I'm Jo, by the way.'

Ugh. She was giggling like a five-year-old. For some reason that giggle, which I heard every Thursday and Friday night, was suddenly very irritating.

Braden nudged Ellie as if to say *Let's go*, his expression impatient now. But Ellie was too busy murmuring to Adam to notice her brother's quiet desperation.

'What do you say?' Jo persisted.

Braden shot me a searching look that I didn't quite understand before shrugging at her. 'I have a girlfriend.'

Jo snorted, fluffing her hair over her shoulder. 'So leave her at home.'

Oh, Jesus Chri— 'Ellie, didn't you say you guys were meeting someone?' I asked loudly enough to drag her away from Adam. She needed to rescue her brother pronto.

'What?'

I gave her a pointed look and repeated the question with gritted teeth.

Finally recognizing the look on Jo's face and the one on her brother's, Ellie nodded. 'Oh, yes. We better leave.'

Jo sulked. 'Don't you –'

'Jo!' Craig called for assistance from the bottom end of the bar, where more customers had started congregating. I sort of loved him in that moment.

Grumbling, Jo shot Braden a childish pout and hurried over to Craig.

'Sorry.' Ellie bit her lip, casting Braden an apologetic look.

He waved her apology off and stepped back, gesturing like a gentleman for her to take the lead out of the bar.

'Bye, Joss.' She waved, beaming at me. 'I'll see you in the morning.'

'Yeah. Have a good night.'

I observed the proprietary hand Adam placed on Ellie's lower back as he nodded a polite goodbye my way and led her out. Was there something going on there? Possibly. Not that I would ask her about it. She'd only turn my curiosity back on me with questions about my nonexistent love life, and then she'd want to know why my love life was nonexistent. That was not a conversation I wanted to have with anyone.

My skin prickled and reluctantly I let my gaze travel back to Braden, who'd taken a step toward the bar, the polite coolness from earlier replaced with a heat that was all too familiar.

'Thanks for the rescue.' I swear his low voice vibrated all the way into my panties.

Squirming inwardly, I tried for nonchalance. 'No problem. Jo's a sweetheart, and she doesn't mean any harm . . . but she's a blatant gold digger.'

Braden just nodded, seemingly uninterested in anything Jo-related.

Silence quickly fell between us, our eyes catching, staying, locking. I didn't even realize my mouth had fallen open until his eyes dipped to stare at it.

What the hell was this?

I snapped back from him, feeling my skin flush as I glanced around to see if anyone else had caught the moment between us. No one was watching.

Why wasn't he leaving?

Looking back at him, I tried not to seem unnerved, when in actuality I was *so* out of my depth. I attempted unsuccessfully to ignore his slow, heated perusal of my body. He had to stop doing that!

When his eyes eventually crawled their way back up

to mine, I made a face at him. I couldn't believe him. He'd pretty much ignored Jo, but for me he'd turn on 'the sex.' Did he get some sick satisfaction out of tormenting me?

Stepping back from the bar with a quick grin, Braden shook his head at me.

'What?' I scowled at him.

He smirked at me. I hated when guys smirked at me. Even sexy smirks like his. 'I don't know what I like better . . .' he mused, stroking his chin in teasing contemplation, 'the naked you or you in that tank top. *D*s, right?'

What? I frowned, totally confused.

And then it hit me.

Jerk!

The asshole had just – correctly – guessed my cup size. He was never going to let me live down yesterday. I could see that now.

I threw my dishrag at him, and he laughed, dodging it. 'I'll take that as a yes.'

Then he was gone before I could summon up an epic retort that would knock him on his ass.

I swear to God, the next time we met, I'd get the last word in.

4

Lena, the heroine of my fantasy series and a badass assassin in the kingdom of Morvern, was supposed to be planning her attack on the queen's lieutenant, Arvane – a mage who was secretly having an affair with the queen's nephew and using his influence and magic to manipulate monarchical and political control. Instead Lena had begun fantasizing about stripping Ten, leader of the queen's guard, naked. Ten, who had been a blond in the first five chapters, was now dark-haired with pale-blue eyes. He was also not supposed to be the romantic hero. There wasn't supposed to be a romantic hero at all. This was about Lena!

Frustrated, I pushed away from my laptop.

Freaking Braden! He was even polluting my manuscript with his sexual toxicity.

That's it. I was giving up for today. Knowing Ellie was bringing Chinese takeout home for dinner after her research at the university, I decided to slot in some time at the gym just around the corner on Queen Street as a preemptive attack on the calories. I generally didn't care about my food intake, but I had been into sports at school and liked to keep in shape. Good thing, too, because I really liked chips, or crisps, as they were called here. Any chips, all chips – fattening, delicious, and crispy chips. My close relationship with chips was possibly the most real in my life.

I pushed out my frustration over my book into the treadmill, crosstrainer, bike, and weights until I was a sweating, jellified mess. The workout relaxed me – enough that my brain started to work again. A character started forming in my head, and she wouldn't leave me alone. Mostly because she was a lot like me. She was alone in life, independent, driven. She'd grown up in foster care in Scotland and moved to the US on a work visa and ended up falling in love . . .

The character was my mom. My mom's story had been great until it ended tragically. Everyone loves a good tragedy. Everyone would love my mom. She'd been spunky and outspoken but really kind and compassionate. My dad had adored her from the minute he'd met her, but it had taken him six months to break down her defenses. Their romance had been epic. I'd never thought about writing a romance before, but I couldn't get the idea of immortalizing my parents on paper out of my head. Flashes of memories I'd buried under a steely, cold will started passing across my eyes until the gym disappeared around me: my mom standing at the kitchen sink, washing the dishes because she didn't trust the dishwasher. My dad quietly pressing up against her back, his arms sliding around her waist and hugging her close as he whispered in her ear. Whatever he'd said had made her melt back against him, her head tilting up for his kiss. Then it flashed to my dad chasing my mom inside the house at night, the door slamming, scaring the bejesus out of me and my babysitter. My mom yelling at him for being an alpha-male douche bag. My dad growling about how he wasn't going to stand by and watch some jerk from her work blatantly flirting with her in front of him. My mom screaming that he didn't have to punch the guy. 'He had his hand on your ass!' my dad had snapped back, as I watched on in bewildered amazement. Someone had had his hand on my mom's ass in front of my dad? Idiot. 'I was taking care of it!' my mom had argued. 'Not fast enough! You're not working with him anymore!' From there the argument had escalated until my babysitter was running out of there without waiting for her payment. But I wasn't worried by the argument. My parents had always had a passionate relationship. The argument would resolve itself. And it did. My dad apologized for losing his cool but wouldn't budge on the whole not-working-with-him thing. The issue became such a big deal that my mom eventually agreed, because the jerk from her work was, well, a jerk, and I assumed there was more to the story than just what had happened that night. My mom actually moved to a different accountancy firm. Marriage was all about compromise, she'd said, and Dad would do it for her.

The memories were so clear. I could see the gold in my mom's hazel eyes, could smell my dad's cologne, could feel his arms around me, my mom's hand brushing through my hair . . .

My chest squeezed tight, and I stumbled on the treadmill, the world around me coming back, but in a pulsing of color and noise that didn't make sense. My blood was pounding in my ears; my heart rate had escalated so fast that I struggled to breathe. Pain flared up my knee, but I was barely aware of it, or of the strong hands helping me to my feet and onto solid ground.

'Focus on your breathing,' a soothing voice coached in my ear.

I followed the voice and swam through the panic, grabbing control of my breathing.

Eventually my vision cleared, the compression in my head easing, my lungs opening up. Trembling from the adrenaline spiked by the panic attack, I turned to look up at the guy who was holding on to me. His dark eyes were concerned.

'You feeling better?'

I nodded, embarrassment flooding me as I looked up to see people watching us from the machines. I gently eased from his grip. 'Sorry.'

He shook his head. 'Don't be. I'm just glad I caught you before your whole body hit the treadmill. Your knee is going to have a nasty bruise on it, though.' He gestured to it.

I glanced down and saw a tear in my sports tights, and the pain hit me. I winced, flexing my leg. 'Great.'

'I'm Gavin.' He stuck his hand out to me, and I took it politely but shook it without much energy. I was exhausted.

'Joss. Thanks, by the way.'

Gavin frowned, and I noted that he was cute, if you liked that muscly, clean-cut sporty type. And he was a blond. 'You sure you're okay? I know a panic attack when I see one.'

Flushing inwardly, I shook my head, not wanting to drag up the memories that had brought on the attack. 'I'm really fine. Just been a stressful week. But, um . . . thanks again. I'm just going to head home.'

'I've seen you here before.' He stopped me with a smile. 'I'm a personal trainer here.'

And? 'Okay.'

He smirked at my response. 'I'm just saying, I'm here. If you need anything.'

'I'll keep that in mind. Thanks again.' I gave him an embarrassed wave and took off for the locker room.

I guess the book about my mom was out.

I got home before Ellie and decided that I needed to keep moving, terrified of bringing on another panic attack. I hadn't had one of those in years. I started putting out plates in the kitchen, trying to conjure up plans in my head for the next chapter in my fantasy novel in an attempt to pretend what had happened at the gym hadn't actually happened.

And then my mind *was* taken off the panic attack. Just not by my novel.

That damn Braden intruded again.

I opened the cutlery drawer and found a bunch of crap in it that didn't belong there. Next on the list: reorganize the mess Ellie had made of the kitchen. The drawer was full of odds and ends – thread, needles, a camera, glue, double sticky tape, and photographs.

There was one of Braden leaning against a railing that looked out over water somewhere. It was a sunny day, and he had turned to the camera just in time, his eyes squinting against the light, his beautiful mouth curled up in an affectionate smile.

As I laid out the dishes, Braden's smile reminded me of his laughter, and that laughter kept echoing in my ears as it had done for the past four days since I'd seen him at the bar. All I could think about was him shirtless, with me wrapped around him like a tortilla. Just because I had written off sexual encounters, it didn't mean I wasn't a full-blooded woman who got horny just like everyone else. I had a shoc box of vibrating goodies that took care of me when I was in the mood. But since meeting Braden, I was constantly in the mood, and every now and then the thought of going out and finding a one-night stand would cross my mind.

Of course, I'd remember what it felt like to wake up in a strange bed with a strange guy on either side of me and not know what the hell had happened, and that notion instantly evaporated.

I just . . . I couldn't understand how I could be this attracted to someone. Someone I barely even knew.

The front door slammed, shaking me out of those thoughts, and I began pouring water for me and tea for Ellie.

'Hullooo,' she cooed happily as she entered the kitchen, the smell of the Chinese food triggering a series of grumbles from my stomach. 'How was your day?'

She dumped the food on the table, and I immediately began helping her put it out.

'It was fine,' I mumbled, chewing on a prawn cracker.

When we finally sat down across from each other she threw me a look of concern. 'Are you okay?'

No, I'm not okay. I went to the gym and had a panic attack in front of a bunch of strangers. Oh, and your flirtatious son-of-a-bitch brother won't get out of my head or my sexual fantasies. I'm horny, I'm pissed off, and I don't like it. 'Writer's block.'

'Oh, that's rubbish. I only know what that's like when I'm writing my research. I can't imagine how bad it gets writing a novel.'

'Beyond frustrating.'

We ate in silence for a moment or two, and I noted with curiosity how tense Ellie seemed. 'Did you have a good day?'

She gave me a wan smile just before she took a bite of curry rice. When she finished chewing she nodded. 'I'm starting to feel the pressure of being a postgrad student.'

'Ah, the joys of student life.'

Ellie murmured her agreement and then, after staring at the table in silence for a full minute, asked, 'So . . . what did you think of Adam the other night?'

The question seemed to come out of nowhere, and there was a definite coyness to it. Huh. I knew there was something going on there. 'I don't know. I didn't really get a chance to talk to him. He's cute. Seems friendly.'

A dreamy look passed over Ellie's face. No joke.

Dreamy. I'd only ever seen a look like that in the movies. The girl had it bad.

'Adam's great. He and Braden have been friends forever. If it wasn't Braden intimidating my boyfriends in high school, it was Adam.' She blushed, shaking her head. 'I followed him around everywhere when I was a kid.'

I didn't know what compelled me to . . .' Are you two seeing each other?'

Ellie jerked her gaze up to mine. 'No. Why? Did it seem that way?'

Okay. Wrong question to ask. 'A little.'

'No.' She shook her head vehemently. 'We're just friends. Anyway, Braden's always telling me what a manwhore Adam is. He'd never settle down. And he's too much like a brother to me for there to be anything . . . you know . . . *more* . . .' She trailed off unconvincingly.

I knew one thing: I would never have to worry about Ellie lying to me. She couldn't lie for shit. 'Okay.'

'So, are you seeing anyone?'

Damn. It was my fault. I'd asked a question. 'No. Are you?'

'No.' Ellie sighed. 'When was your last relationship?'

Does sex count as a relationship? I shrugged. 'When was yours?'

Ellie pursed her lips, her eyelashes dipping to cover the instantly hardened look in her eyes. A fierce wave of protectiveness rushed over me out of nowhere, surprising the hell out of me. 'Ellie?'

'Nine months ago.'

And what did the bastard do to you? 'What happened?'

'We dated for five months. He told me he worked in Glasgow for a recruitment agency. In actuality he works for a rival property development company here in Edinburgh. They were bidding against Braden for this amazing plot in Commercial Quay. Turns out he was just using me to get to Braden, to find out what Braden's bid would be so his company could outbid him. Suffice to say the relationship did not end well. He ended up with a broken nose, and Braden ended up with the plot.'

I raised an eyebrow, silently congratulating Braden on teaching the a-hole a lesson. 'Braden beat him up?'

'No.' Ellie shook her head. 'Braden doesn't fight. He hasn't in a long time. It was Adam that beat the tar out of him.'

I grinned back at her. 'I shouldn't condone violence, but . . . yay, Adam.'

Ellie laughed and then sobered. 'I'm just glad my naïveté didn't cause Braden any difficulties at work.'

I'm sure that wasn't what Braden was worried about. I didn't know how I knew that, but I did. Anyone with eyes and ears could tell Ellie was important to him. 'I can't believe someone would go to that much trouble, do something so heinous, for a plot of land.'

'Commercial Quay is really up-and-coming. Michelin star restaurants, cosmetic surgeries, stylish cocktail bars . . . Braden is building luxury flats there and they'll fetch anything from half a million to a million for the penthouse apartments. Quite the profit margin.'

I was sickened that anyone could use someone as sweet as Ellie for a damn profit margin. 'Guys suck.'

Ellie raised her mug of tea at me in agreement.

After chewing silently for a while, Ellie cleared her throat. 'I noticed a few photographs of your family in your room earlier. You know, you're welcome to put them out in the sitting room or anywhere in the flat. It's your home now, too.'

I stiffened at the mention of my family, still uneasy about having another panic attack. 'That's okay.'

I heard her answering sigh and braced myself. 'You don't really talk about them much.'

The time had come already? With Rhian it had been six weeks before she found out. Stomach churning, I pushed my plate away from me and sat back to meet Ellie's anxious gaze. We were roommates now, we got along – surprisingly well, considering how different we were – and it was time to just lay my cards on the table. 'My family is dead,' I told her numbly, no grief, no tears, nothing for her to see as I watched her cheeks grow instantly pale. 'I don't talk about them. Ever.'

I don't know what I had been expecting. Maybe because Ellie was so open and kind I thought there would be an attempt to break through my guard. But she amazed me again. 'Okay,' she answered, and I saw her struggling to hide the pity in her gaze.

'All right then.' I gave her a soft, reassuring smile, and she answered it, her shoulders relaxing.

A minute later she murmured, 'You know, you can be a little bit intimidating.'

My lips curled up apologetically. 'I know. Sorry.'

'It's okay. I'm used to Braden.'

As though he'd heard his name, Ellie's cell lit up, and his name flashed across the screen. She answered it immediately but without her usual cheer. Seems my dead family was a mood killer.

I don't know how, but Ellie managed to convince me to go out with them. I stared down at Ellie and Braden's friends, wearing a dress I'd borrowed from her wardrobe. They were seated on sofas around a low coffee table in a bar on George IV Bridge. Braden had called two hours ago asking us to meet them all there. Of course, I'd been ready an hour ago. Ellie had taken forever to get ready, and as she shot Adam a smile, I began to understand why.

'Everyone, this is my new flatmate, Jocelyn.' She turned to me. 'Jocelyn, this is Jenna and Ed.'

I'd gotten the rundown in the cab on the way there. Jenna, the cute blonde with the quirky glasses and diamond engagement ring, was Ellie's best friend and fellow PhD student. Ed, the short blond guy who made geeky stylish, was Jenna's fiancé.

'And you've met Adam and Braden.' Her smile slipped a little as she looked at the woman sitting pressed up against Braden. She had pale, almost white, blond hair, huge blue eyes, long limbs, and a full, pouty mouth. 'And this is Holly. Braden's girlfriend.'

I remembered instantly that Ellie didn't like her. From the sneer Holly gave Ellie, it was clear the feeling was mutual. I said hello to everyone, avoiding Braden's gaze and ignoring the way my heart was pounding against my rib cage just being near him and his girl-friend.

No way was I going to feel despondent about the fact that she reminded me of Jo: my complete opposite in every way.

Sitting down next to Jenna as Ellie rushed off to get us drinks, I tried to look anywhere but at the couple to my right.

'How are you settling in, then, Jocelyn?' Adam asked from across the table.

Grateful, I gave him a wide smile. 'Good, thanks. And it's Joss.'

'So you and Ellie are rubbing along well then?'

Something in his voice told me it wasn't a casual question. He was worried about my roommate. I began to wonder if Ellie's feelings might be reciprocated. 'We're getting along amazingly. She's a great person.'

My answer went over well with him. 'Good, I'm glad. So, Ellie tells me you're writing a book?'

'Oh my God,' Holly interrupted with her throaty English accent. I hated that her accent was so cool. 'Did I tell you, babe, that my friend Cheri got pub-lished?'

Braden shook his head, his eyes darting to my face. I glanced away quickly, pretending to be fascinated by Holly's news of this mysterious Cheri person.

'Cheri is my best friend from home,' Holly explained to the table just as Ellie came back with the drinks. I shimmied over to let her in beside me. 'She writes the best books.'

'What are they about?' Ed asked politely. I glanced at Jenna and saw she and Ellie were exchanging a look. I was getting that Holly was not at all well-liked among the girls.

'Oh, they're just amazing. They're about this girl from the poorhouse who falls in love with this guy who's a businessman but still has, like, an old English title . . . like an earl or something. So romantic. And her writing is just amazing. She's just amazing.'

Okay. Apparently she was amazing.

'So it's an historical novel?' Ed asked.

'No.' She shook her head in bemusement.

'Holly' – Braden appeared to be trying not to smile – 'there's no such thing as a poorhouse anymore. Are you sure it's not an historical?'

'Well, Cheri didn't say it was.'

'Then I'm sure you're right,' Adam told her congenially. Ellie's shoulders shook next to mine at the very well-disguised sarcasm in his reply. I tried to look anywhere but at Braden.

'Jenna, when's your first dress fitting, again?' Ellie asked, peering around me.

Jenna grinned impishly. 'Oh, it's not for ages. I've been banned from Mum's house because I keep going into her wardrobe to stare at it.'

'Oh?' I asked, trying to be friendly. 'When's the wedding?'

'Five months,' Ed replied, smiling lovingly at Jenna.

64

Wow. A guy who wasn't afraid to show how he really felt. It was disarming, and another flash image of my dad smiling at my mom crossed my brain. I took a drink, shoving the memory back down under all my steely resolve.

Ellie made a little squeeing sound beside me. 'You should see Jenna's dress. We're getting –'

'Oh, babe,' Holly interrupted again. 'Did I tell you about Lisa getting married in October? I told her it was a dreadful time of year to get married, but she insisted she wanted an autumn wedding. Have you ever heard anything like it? Anyway, it's some drafty castle in some place called Oban, so we'll need to arrange accommodation.'

'Barcaldine Castle.' Braden nodded. 'It's a nice wee place.'

'Maybe in the summer but not in October.'

And that was pretty much how the next hour went. Every time someone mentioned a topic, Holly took control, her loud voice carrying above the noise of the crowded bar. She made it easy to vilify her, and I knew almost immediately why Ellie couldn't stand her. Holly was loud, obnoxious, and completely self-absorbed. Worse, I got the feeling Braden was studying my reaction to her. Why did he care what *I* thought?

Needing a break from Holly's voice, a voice I'd thought charming at first and now greatly disliked, I volunteered to get the next round of drinks. I relaxed into the bar, giving the bartender my order, and enjoyed the quiet – the bar was in the back of the building, behind a wall and a corridor, away from Holly's voice.

But then *he* had to follow me, didn't he?

Heat flushed my right side as I felt him press up against me as he leaned into the bar. My nose tingled at the smell of his cologne, and those butterflies were back again.

'So . . . you're a writer?' Braden looked down at me.

It was the first time he'd asked me anything without sex in his voice. I looked up at him, taken aback by the genuine curiosity in his pale gaze. I smiled a little self-deprecatingly. I wasn't a writer yet. 'Trying to be.'

'What do you write?'

I thought about my mom and drew a deep breath, pushing the thought out. 'Fantasy.'

His eyebrows quirked a little, as though he hadn't expected that to be my answer. 'Why fantasy?'

The bartender gave me the total for the drinks before I could answer Braden, but Braden handed over money before I could even reach for my purse. 'I'll pay,' I insisted.

He waved off my offer as though I were insane. 'Well?' he asked as he took his change. The drinks sat before us on the bar but Braden didn't seem that intent on getting them back to the table.

I sighed, knowing the faster I answered, the faster I could get away from him. 'Because reality has no authority there. My imagination controls everything.' As soon as the words were out of my mouth I regretted them. A smart person would read between the lines. And Braden was smart.

Our eyes met, a silent understanding passing between

us. Finally Braden nodded. 'I can see the attraction in that.'

'Yeah.' I dragged my gaze away. Bad enough he'd seen me physically naked. I didn't need him stripping me bare to the soul.

'I'm glad you and Ellie are getting along.'

'You're very protective of her, aren't you?'

'Understatement.'

'Why? She seems a lot stronger than you think.'

His eyebrows furrowed as he thought about it. 'It's not about her strength. Maybe it's the way she looks or talks that fools people into thinking Ellie's fragile. I know different. Ellie can take the bad stuff and bounce back better than anyone I know. It's not about that. It's about making sure the bad stuff doesn't happen to her in the first place. She's too nice for her own good, and I've seen her hurt too many times by people who claimed to care about her.'

I didn't envy him that job. 'Yeah, I can see that. Ellie wears her heart on her sleeve.'

'Unlike you.'

Startled by the observation, I looked up at him warily. 'How's that?'

His eyes were searching, burrowing, trying to get inside me. I took a step back, and he inched closer. 'I've heard what Ellie had to say about you. And then there's how you are with me. You try not to give anything away.'

Back off. 'You don't either. I don't know anything real about you.'

'I'm not that hard to get to know.' He flashed me a

quick smile. 'But you ... I think you've made an art form out of deflection and self-possession.'

Stop analyzing me. I rolled my eyes. 'You think throwing a dishrag at you is an example of how self-possessed I am?'

He laughed, a deep reverberation that bumped its way down my spine. 'Fair enough.' And then he shot me *that* look again – that look that felt as though he were sliding his long, masculine fingers inside my panties. 'You look beautiful tonight.'

I flushed inwardly at the compliment. Outwardly I smirked. 'So does your girlfriend.'

Braden sighed heavily at my pointed comment and picked up a few of the glasses from the bar. 'I didn't mean anything by it, Jocelyn. It was just a compliment.'

No, it wasn't. You're playing games with me. And if we're going to be around each other all the time, I want it to stop. 'Was it? Do you talk to everyone the way you talk to me?'

'And what way is that?'

'Like you've seen me naked.'

Grinning, Braden's eyes glittered with heat. 'No. But then I haven't seen everyone naked.'

Frustrated, I shook my head. 'You know what I mean.'

I almost jumped at the warm whisper of his breath on my ear as he leaned down to murmur quietly, 'I like the reaction I get out of you.'

I pulled back. So I was a challenge? Right. I got it now. 'Just stop. You're Ellie's brother, and we're probably going to have to see each other, so I'd prefer it if you wouldn't try to make me uncomfortable.'

A scowl formed between his eyes. 'I don't want you uncomfortable.' His gaze was searching again but this time I was giving nothing away. With a deep sigh, Braden nodded. 'Fine. Look, I'm sorry. I want us to get along. I like you. Ellie likes you. And I'd like us to be friends. From now on I'll stop flirting with you, and I'll try really hard to forget what you look like naked.'

He put the drinks on the bar and held out his hand for me to shake. The look in his eyes was a new one. It was pleading, boyish, and totally endearing. I didn't trust that look at all, but I found myself shaking my head, smiling despite myself as I reached out to clasp his hand. As soon as my fingers slid along his palm, the hairs on my arms rose.

I'd thought that spark that people apparently felt when they touched someone they were attracted to was a myth reserved for chick-lit and Hollywood.

But no.

Our eyes met as heat rushed up my arm. The tingling between my legs intensified; the need in my gut moaned with want. All I could see was Braden, all I could smell was Braden, and his body was so close I imagined I could almost feel all his hard strength pressing against me. Right then I wanted nothing more than to pull him into the ladies' restroom and let him screw me hard against the wall.

Braden's hand tightened around mine, his pale eyes

darkened, and I knew . . . he wanted me, too. 'Fine,' he muttered, a dangerous quality entering his expression as he leaned down, his words puffing against my mouth, he was so close. 'I can do this. If you can pretend, I can pretend.'

I jerked my hand out of his, trying not to tremble as I reached to collect the rest of the drinks. Braden picked up the ones he'd laid down when he'd reached for that godforsaken handshake. I hated that he was right. Our attraction was nuclear. I had never known anything like it.

It made Braden Carmichael extremely dangerous to me.

And I *had* to dissemble. I shot him a careless smile. 'I'm not pretending.' I walked away before he could say anything, glad for the wall that had obscured our table's view of us. I'd have been mortified if anyone had borne witness to our interlude.

Braden sat down next to Holly, handing her a drink and Adam his. Our eyes collided for a brief second, and he gave me a mockingly polite smile before leaning back and sliding his arm around the back of Holly's chair. His girlfriend smiled at him, a manicured hand moving to rest intimately on his thigh.

'Babe, I was just telling Ellie about this Gucci dress I saw online. I was thinking you could take me to Glasgow to try it on. You'll like it. It'll be worth the money.' She fluttered her fake lashes at him.

No one needed to tell me that she meant it would be worth *Braden's* money.

Disgusted, I threw back my drink and tried to ignore them. Unfortunately, Holly didn't want to be ignored.

'So, *Josh*, how can you afford that gorgeous flat with Ellie?'

All eyes fell on me. 'It's Joss, actually.'

She gave me a shrug and a narrowed-eyed smile, and suddenly I wondered if maybe she'd caught the looks between Braden and me.

Shit.

'So?' she insisted, a little cattily.

Yeah. She'd seen 'em all right.

'My parents.' I threw back another drink and turned to Jenna to ask about her part-time job with the Scottish tourist industry.

Holly's voice cut through my question. 'What do you mean "your parents"?'

Stick a sock in it, lady! I looked at her with veiled annoyance. 'Their money.'

'Oh.' She wrinkled her nose as though she suddenly smelled something very, very bad. 'You're living off your parents' money? At *your* age?'

Oh, no, she didn't. I took another drink and then smiled at her in warning as if to say, *Don't play this game with me, sweetheart. You won't win.*

She didn't heed the warning. 'So they pay for everything? Doesn't that make you feel guilty?'

Every fucking day. 'Was it your money that bought those Louboutin's . . . or Braden's?'

Ellie choked on her laughter, smothering the sound quickly in a gulp of her drink. I patted her on the back, aiding her in her pretense. When I looked back at Holly, she was glaring at me, her face flushed red to her hairline.

Point made. Question deflected. Spoiled bitch put in her place.

'So, people can get married at Stirling Castle, huh?' I turned back to Jenna and our earlier conversation. 'I've only visited it once, but it's a beautiful venue . . .'

5

Two nights later I was soaking in the tub after a strenuous workout at the gym when I heard Ellie's whoop of joy. Raising an eyebrow at the door, I wasn't surprised by the knock that sounded on it two seconds later.

'Can I come in?' she asked with laughter in her voice.

Clearly whatever news she'd received couldn't wait. I glanced down to make sure I was sufficiently covered by bubbles. 'Sure,' I replied.

The door eased open, and Ellie stepped inside with two glasses of wine in her hands and a smug expression on her face. I took the glass she offered and grinned at her infectious good humor. 'What's going on?'

'Well' – Ellie beamed – 'after six dire months, Braden has finally dumped Holly.'

I snorted into my glass, ignoring the way my stomach flipped at the news. 'That's your exciting news?'

Ellie stared at me as if I'd said something crazy. 'Of course. It's the best news in God knows how long. Holly was the worst of the lot. You know, I think the other night at the bar was the final nail in her coffin. Braden seemed mortified by her. It's about time he dumped that self-absorbed, two-faced, money-grabbing pain in the arse.'

I nodded in agreement, thinking about his blatant flirtation with me. 'Yeah. He'd probably have ended up cheating on her or something, anyway.'

Ellie's joy instantly fled, and she scowled at me. I raised an eyebrow at her reaction. 'Braden would never cheat.'

She really did think he walked on water. I cocked my head with a cynical smirk, a look probably bordering on condescending and punch-worthy. 'Please, Ellie. He's a guy who flirts with anything that moves.'

Considering me for a moment, Ellie leaned back against the tiled walls, seeming unaware of the steam clinging to them and now most probably dampening the back of her shirt. Her celebration was apparently forgotten in the face of my negativity. 'There's one thing you should know about Braden. He would never cheat. He's not perfect – I know that. But let's just say that he would never be that cruel or dishonest to anyone. Anytime he's been in a relationship and his interest has waned and hopped onto someone new, he's been honest with his girlfriend and broken it off before starting up anything with someone else. I'm not saying his attitude isn't a little shitty, but at least he's honest.'

Curious about Ellie's surety, I took a sip of wine before asking, 'Did someone cheat on Braden?'

She gave me a sad smile. 'It's not my story to tell.'

Wow. If Ellie was being closemouthed about it, Braden really must be sore over it.

'Suffice to say, he's a serial dater. Completely monogamous but jumps from one relationship to the next. Holly lasted longer than most. I think it was because she took frequent trips down south.' Ellie then threw me a teasing, almost knowing look. 'I wonder what girl has caught his interest this time.'

I eyed her carefully. Did she know? Had she witnessed the spark between us?

'And I wonder if she'll finally be the one to knock him on his arse. He needs a reality check.'

I murmured an incoherent response, not wanting to encourage her thoughts in my direction.

'Sorry for interrupting your bath.'

'No, it's fine.' I raised my wineglass at her. 'You brought red wine. We're all good.'

'Have you ever cheated on someone?'

Whoa. Where did that come from?

'Well?'

Was this an interview to date her brother?

Staring her straight in the eye so she would know I was being deadly serious, I replied more honestly than ever, trusting Ellie not to push me too much on the subject. 'I never get close enough to anyone for that to be an issue.' My answer seemed to deflate her, and that only reaffirmed my guess that she'd been holding on to some kind of romantic notion about Braden and me. 'I don't do relationships, Ellie. I haven't got it in me.'

She nodded, her expression a little lost. 'I hope that changes for you.'

It never will. 'Maybe.'

'Okay. I'm going to leave you to your bath. Oh.' She

stopped, turning back to me. 'My mum cooks a big roast dinner on Sundays for all the family. You're invited this Sunday.'

A sudden chill descended over my warm bath, and I shivered. I hadn't been to a family gathering since high school. 'Oh, I don't want to intrude.'

'You're not intruding. And I won't take no for an answer.'

I smiled weakly, gulping down the entire glass of wine as soon as she closed the door behind her. Feeling the wine churn in my gut, I sent up a prayer for a miracle that would get me out of the family get-together.

Friday night I was running late for work at the bar. Ellie had decided to cook us dinner, and it had turned into an unsalvageable disaster. We'd ended up eating out and losing track of time as we fell into deep discussion about our work – Ellie's research and my book. Ellie had gone home to bed because of an awful headache that had come on suddenly, and I hurried to the bar. I shot Jo an apologetic look as I passed through the bar and into the staff room. I was just shoving my things in my locker when my cell rang.

It was Rhian. 'Hey, hon, can I call you back on my break? I'm late for my shift.'

Rhian sniffed down the line. 'Okay.'

My heart stopped. Rhian was crying? Rhian never cried. *We* never cried. 'Rhian, what's going on?' The blood pounded in my ears.

'I broke up with James.' Her voice cracked along with my belief.

I'd thought Rhian and James were solid. Unbreakable. *Fuck.*

'What happened?' Oh God, had he cheated on her?

'He proposed.'

Silence fell between us as I tried to understand what she was saying. 'Okay. He proposed, so you dumped him?'

'Of course.'

What was I missing? 'I don't get it.'

Rhian growled. Actually growled. 'How can you of all people not get it, Joss? That's why I'm phoning you! You're supposed to fuckin' get it!'

'Well, I don't, so stop yelling at me,' I snapped, a pang radiating in my chest for James. He adored Rhian. She was his entire world.

'I can't marry him, Joss. I can't marry anybody. Marriage ruins everything.'

And it suddenly dawned on me: We were entering our no-go area. This was about Rhian's parents. I knew they were divorced, but that's all I knew. It had to be something deeper, something worse, for Rhian to turn her back on James. 'He's not your dad. You're not your parents. James loves you.'

'What the hell, Joss? Who the fuck is this and what has she done with my friend?'

I paused. Maybe I *was* spending too much time around Ellie. She was rubbing off on me. 'Fair enough,' I mumbled.

Rhian sighed in relief. 'So you think I've done the right thing.'

'No,' I replied honestly. 'I think you're scared shit-less. But from one scared shitless person to another, I know no one's going to change your mind.'

We were silent, just breathing down the phone to each other, feeling that connection between us, that relief that there was someone else out there just as messed up.

'Have you thought about the reality of this, Rhian?' I finally whispered. 'James with someone else, I mean?'

A choked noise crackled down the line.

My heart broke for her. 'Rhian?'

'I've got to go.' She hung up. And somehow I knew she was hanging up to cry. We never cried.

Feeling a deep melancholy settle over me, I texted her to advise her to really think about things before she did anything she'd regret. For once I wished I wasn't so broken, that Rhian had a best friend who was strong and not afraid to love to hold up as an example of what was possible. Instead I was her excuse that she wasn't being irrational. I was her enabler.

'Joss?'

I glanced up at Craig. 'Yeah?'

'A little help, please.'

'Oh, sure.'

'You fancy a quick shag after work?'

'No, Craig.' I shook my head, following him out, too depressed to even banter with him.

*

Sunday rolled around before I knew it, and I was so preoccupied with my book and with Rhian – who kept avoiding my calls – and too afraid to talk to James in case he put another crack in my heart with his heartache, that I didn't have a prayer's chance in hell of coming up with an excuse to get out of dinner with Ellie's family.

Instead I was bundled into a cab with Ellie, dressed in celebration of the hot day in my Topshop shorts and a pretty olive green silk camisole. We took off for Stockbridge and stopped literally five minutes later outside an apartment that looked a lot like ours.

Inside, I was unsurprised to find the Nichols's home very much like ours, too: huge rooms, high ceilings, and a cozy collection of clutter that reminded me a lot of Ellie. Now I knew where she got it from.

Elodie Nichols greeted me with a very French kiss on either cheek. Like Ellie, she was tall and beautiful in a delicate way. For some reason I'd been expecting a French accent, even though Ellie had told me her mom had moved to Scotland when she was four.

'Ellie's told me so much about you. She said the two of you have become fast friends. I'm so glad. I was a little worried about her when she said she was taking on a flatmate, but it's all worked out nicely.'

I felt like I was fifteen again. Elodie just had that mothering way of talking down to you. 'Yeah, it has,' I answered congenially. 'Ellie is great.'

Elodie beamed, looking twenty years younger and very much like her eldest daughter.

Next I was introduced to Clark, a kind of nonde-script, dark-haired guy with glasses and a sweet smile. 'Ellie says you're a writer.'

I threw Ellie a wry smile. She told everyone I was a writer. 'Trying to be.'

'What do you write?' Clark asked, handing me a glass of wine.

We had congregated in the sitting room while Elodie checked on something in the kitchen. 'Fantasy. I'm working on a fantasy series.'

Clark's eyes widened a fraction behind his glasses. 'I love fantasy novels. You know, I'd be happy to read it before you send it off for queries.'

'You mean beta read it?'

'Yes. If you'd like?'

Remembering that Clark was a college professor and was used to grading papers, I was secretly really pleased by his offer. I gave him a small smile of gratitude. 'That would be great. I'd really appreciate it. Of course, I'm nowhere near finished yet.'

'Well, when you are, just give me a shout.'

I grinned. 'I will. Thanks.'

I was just beginning to think I'd make it through this particular family dinner when I heard kids' laughter.

'Dad!' A young boy's voice carried down the hall toward us, and then its owner appeared in the doorway. Running toward Clark, the small boy's face was lit up with excitement. I guessed this was Declan, Ellie's ten-year-old half brother. 'Dad, look what Braden got me.' He thrust a Nintendo DS and two games in Clark's face.

Clark looked at them, smiling. 'Is that the one you wanted?'

'Yeah, it's the latest version.'

Looking up at the doorway, Clark clucked his tongue in mock disapproval. 'It's not his birthday until next week. You spoil him rotten.'

I jerked around, my palms instantly sweating at the sight of Braden standing in the doorway with his hand on the shoulder of a miniature version of Ellie. The teenager was huddled close to him, her thick bangs and short haircut exceptionally stylish for such a little thing. My eyes didn't linger long on the mini-Ellie, who I deduced was Hannah. No, they slid up over Braden, drinking him in before I could stop them.

Attraction burned through my blood.

Braden was wearing black jeans and a gray T-shirt. It was the first time I'd seen him in something casual, the first time my eyes had access to his strong biceps and broad shoulders.

I felt a throb between my legs and looked quickly away, hating that he did this to my body.

'I know,' Braden answered. 'But I didn't want to have to spend another Sunday afternoon listening to Dec chew my ear off about the damn console.'

Declan just giggled, his triumphant gaze dropping to his game as he flopped down at his father's feet and started loading in a Super Mario Bros. game.

'Look what I got.' Hannah held up something that looked like a credit card. God, I hoped it wasn't.

Clark squinted at it. 'What is it?'

Hannah's eyes brightened. 'A really big gift card for the bookstore.'

'Nice.' Ellie grinned back at her, holding out her arm to her. 'What are you going to get?'

Her little sister rushed toward her, snuggling into her side as she dropped onto the couch. She flicked me a shy smile before looking up at Ellie. 'There's a new vampire series I want.'

'Hannah's a bookworm,' a gravelly voice explained right above my head.

I turned to look up at Braden standing beside the couch, looking down at me with nothing but a friendly smile. Although a little disconcerted by his changed attitude, I found myself smiling back at him. 'I see.' A swarm of butterflies awoke in my stomach, and I flinched inwardly, looking away from him. It never occurred to me Braden would be attending dinner, although it should have, considering Ellie had made it clear he was a big part of her family.

'Did you thank Braden?' Clark suddenly asked his kids, drawing my attention to them and away from the sex on legs beside me.

A couple of mumbled yeses answered the question.

'Hannah, Dec, this is my flatmate, Joss,' Ellie said, introducing me.

I smiled at them both.

'Hi.' Hannah gave me a little wave. I felt my chest squeeze at how adorable she was.

'Hey.' I waved back

'Do you like Nintendo?' Declan asked, waiting for my answer with an assessing gaze. I could tell my answer would either make us or break us.

'Oh, yeah. Mario and I go way back.'

He gave me a cheeky grin. 'You have a cool accent.'

'So do you.'

That seemed to please him, and he quickly returned to his game. I thought I'd passed.

Clark patted Declan's head. 'Son, put it on silent, please.'

Almost immediately the familiar sounds of Mario quieted and I decided that I liked these kids. Braden might have spoiled them, and looking around the home it was obvious they didn't lack for anything, but they had great manners, just like Ellie.

'Braden!' Elodie came shuffling into the room, a huge loving smile on her face. 'I didn't hear you come in.'

Braden grinned down at her and enveloped her in a tight hug.

'Did Clark get you a drink?'

'No, but I'll get myself something.'

'Oh, no, let me.' Clark stood up. 'Lager?'

'Yeah, thanks, sounds good.'

'Have a seat.' Elodie shuffled Braden down into the armchair on my right as Clark left the room. She settled onto the arm of it and brushed Braden's unkempt hair off his forehead. 'How have you been? I heard you and Holly broke up.'

Braden hadn't really crossed me as the type who liked to be mothered, but he just sat there, seeming to enjoy Elodie's attention. He took her hand and kissed her knuckles affectionately. 'I'm fine, Elodie. It was just time, that's all.'

'Hmm,' Elodie answered with a frown. And then, as if remembering I was there, she turned to me. 'You've met Joss, haven't you?'

Braden nodded, a soft, almost secret, smile curving the corners of his lips. Still, it was friendly, not sexual, and I didn't know whether to be happy or disappointed by that. Stupid hormones. 'Yeah, Jocelyn and I have met.'

I felt my brows pull together. Why did he insist on calling me Jocelyn?

The frown soon disappeared as Clark returned, and the conversation gained momentum. I did my best, answering their questions and reciprocating; however, I had never been so grateful for Ellie. She came to my rescue when her mom started asking questions about my parents, deflecting the questions easily from me to Elodie, and I sighed with relief at having escaped having to be outright rude. I thought I was doing okay. I even managed to exchange friendly, nonsexual banter with Braden.

Then we moved to the dining room for dinner.

There was just something about the laughter, all the talk and noise, as we settled around it, helping ourselves to potatoes, vegetables, and gravy to eat with the generous servings of roast chicken Elodie had put on our plates. As I poured gravy over my dinner, their chatter, their affection, the warm normality triggered memories . . .

'I invited Mitch and Arlene for dinner,' my mom said, putting out extra place settings. Dru was over for dinner since we were working on a school project together, and my dad was settling baby Beth into her high chair.

Dad sighed. 'I'm glad I made plenty of chili – as it is, Mitch will probably eat it all.'

'Be nice,' Mom admonished, with a small smile on her lips. 'They'll be here any minute.'

'Just saying. Guy can eat.'

Dru giggled beside me, shooting my dad an adoring look. Dru's dad was never around, so my dad was like Superman to her.

'So, how's the project coming along?' Mom asked, pouring us orange juice.

I shot Dru a secretive smile. It wasn't coming along at all. We'd spent the last hour gossiping about Kyle Ramsey and Jude Jeffrey. Mostly we just kept saying 'Jude' like 'Juuude' and giggling like idiots.

My mom snorted, catching the look. 'I see.'

'Hey, neighbors!' a big bellyful of joy called out as Mitch and Arlene opened the French doors, stepping inside without knocking. It was okay. We were used to their overfamiliarity since they were our only neighbors within spitting distance of the house. My mom loved their overfamiliarity. My dad? Not so much.

After a lot of greetings – Mitch and Arlene were incapable of saying hello just once – we all finally settled around the kitchen table with my dad's famous chili.

'Why do you never cook for me?' Arlene complained to Mitch after moaning a little inappropriately at her first taste of Dad's chili.

'You never ask.'

'I bet Sarah never has to ask Luke to cook. Do you, Sarah?'

My mom threw Dad a pleading look for help. 'Um . . .'

'Yeah, that's what I thought.'

'Dad, Beth's dropped her juice.' I nodded at the floor.

Since he was closest, he reached down to pick it up.

'My dad never cooks,' Dru put in, trying to make Arlene feel better.

'See?' Mitch mumbled around his chlli. 'Not just me.'

Arlene scowled. 'What do you mean, "see"? As if another man not cooking for his wife somehow makes it okay for you to not cook for your wife.'

Mitch swallowed. 'Fine. I'll cook.'

'Can you cook?' Mom asked softly, and I heard my dad choke on a piece of chili.

I hid my giggle in a swallow of orange juice.

'No.'

Silence descended around the table as we all looked at one another and then burst out laughing. Beth squealed at the noise, her tiny hand hitting her juice and sending it flying again, which made everyone laugh harder . . .

That scene was followed by another, of a Christmas dinner. Then of Thanksgiving. And then of my thirteenth birthday . . .

The memories triggered a panic attack.

First my head grew fuzzy, and I quickly lowered the gravy boat from my now-trembling hand. The skin on my face tingled, and cold sweat seeped from my pores. My heart was speeding so hard beneath my rib cage, I thought it might explode. My chest tightened, and I struggled to breathe.

'Jocelyn?'

My chest rose and fell rapidly in shallow breaths, my frightened eyes searching for the voice.

Braden.

He dropped his fork, leaning across the table toward me, a frown of concern between his brows. 'Jocelyn?'

I needed to get out of there.

I needed air.

'Jocelyn . . . Christ,' Braden muttered, shoving back from the table, intent on coming around the table to help me.

Instead, I shot out of my seat, holding my hands out to stop him. Without a word, I turned and raced from the room, running down the hall to the bathroom, where I slammed inside.

Shaking hands pushed up the window, and they and the rest of me were grateful for the rush of air that blasted over my face, even if it was warm air. Knowing I needed to calm down, I concentrated on slowing my breathing.

A few minutes later my body and mind came back to themselves, and I slumped down onto the toilet seat, my limbs all jellified. I felt exhausted again. My second panic attack.

Great.

'Jocelyn?' Braden's voice rumbled through the door.

I closed my eyes against it, wondering how the hell I was going to explain myself. Embarrassment warmed the blood in my cheeks.

I'd thought I was over this. It had been eight years. I should have been over it by now.

At the sound of the door opening, my eyes cracked open, too, and I watched as a concerned Braden stepped inside and closed the door. Briefly I wondered why he had followed me and Ellie hadn't. When I didn't say anything he came closer, dropping slowly to his haunches so that we were at eye level. My eyes searched his gorgeous face, and for once, I wished I could break my own damn rules. No relationships and no one-night stands with guys I barely knew. That meant Braden was off-limits, which was a shame, since I had a feeling he would be able to make me forget everything for a while.

We gazed at each other for what seemed like forever, not saying a word. I was expecting a lot of questions since it must have been clear to everyone, or at least the adults at the table, that I had had a panic attack. Surely they were all wondering why, and I really didn't want to go back out there.

'Better?' Braden finally asked softly.

Wait. Was that it? No probing questions?

'Yeah.' *No, not really.*

He must have read my reaction to his question in my

face, because he cocked his head to the side, his gaze thoughtful. 'You don't need to tell me.'

I cracked a humorless smile. 'I'll just let you think I'm bat-shit crazy.'

Braden smiled back at me. 'I already knew that.' He got up, holding a hand out to me. 'Come on.'

I looked at his proffered hand warily. 'I think maybe I should just go.'

'And I think you should have some good food with some good friends.'

I thought of Ellie and how warm and welcoming she'd been to me. It would be an insult to walk out of her mother's dinner, and I found myself not wanting to do anything that would alienate Ellie.

Taking Braden's hand tentatively, I let him pull me to my feet. 'What will I say?' No use pretending to be cool and collected with him now. He'd already seen me at my most vulnerable. Twice.

'Nothing,' he assured me. 'You don't need to explain yourself to anyone.' His smile was kind. I couldn't decide which smile I liked more – this one or the wicked one.

'Okay.' I took a deep breath and followed him out. He didn't let go of my hand until we reached the dining room, and I refused to acknowledge the bereft feeling in my chest as his touch fell away.

'Are you all right, honey?' Elodie asked as soon as we walked into the room.

'A little bit of sunstroke.' Braden waved Ellie's mom

off with reassurance. 'She was out in the sun too long this morning.'

'Oh.' She turned her motherly concern on me. 'I hope you at least wore sunscreen.'

I nodded, sliding into my seat. 'Just forgot to wear a hat.'

As their conversation picked up and the tension drained from the table, I ignored Ellie's suspicious glances and shot Braden a grateful smile.

6

By the end of the dinner I was a little more relaxed, although I was looking forward to getting home and being alone for a while. Determined not to be taken unawares again, I put back up that wall between my memories and me and tried to enjoy the Nichols's company. It wasn't hard. They were an easy group to like.

My plans for being alone were foiled by Braden and Ellie, who were meeting up with Adam for drinks. I tried to get out of going with them, but Ellie wasn't having it. It was like she sensed I was going home to brood or something.

After bidding the Nichols good-bye and promising Elodie I'd be back, we headed out to grab a cab to take us back to the apartment so I could pick up my purse. I only had my cell on me and was determined that nobody – as in Braden – would be buying me drinks tonight but me. The less I was in this guy's debt, the better.

As the cab drew up to the apartment, a tall, lanky figure sitting on our front stoop made my chest tighten. Heart racing, I jumped out of the cab first, hurrying over to James, who stood up, his duffel bag kicked at his feet. Large dark circles plagued his eyes, and his face was drawn and pale, the corners of his mouth tight with pain and anger.

'Just tell me one thing. Did you encourage her to leave me?'

Taken aback by the bristling anger directed at me, I shook my head numbly, taking a wary step toward him. 'James, no.'

He pointed his finger at me, his mouth twisted with bitterness. 'The two of you are so fucked-up. . . . You had to have had a hand in this somewhere.'

'Hey.' Braden stepped in front of me, calm but intimidating as he spoke to James. 'Back off.'

'Braden, it's okay.' I gazed back at Ellie, who was watching us. Silently pleading with her, I gestured at Braden. 'You two go on ahead without me.'

'I don't think so.' Braden shook his head, his eyes never straying from James.

'Please.'

'Braden.' Ellie tugged on his elbow. 'Come on. Let's give them some privacy.'

Annoyance burning in his eyes, Braden grabbed my cell out of my hand and started playing with it.

'Wha—'

He reached for my hand and curled my fingers back around the phone. 'You've got my number now. Call if you need me. Okay?'

I nodded dumbly. As Ellie dragged her brother away, I gazed down at the phone in my hand. Was Braden looking out for me? Was he concerned? I glanced at him over my shoulder. I couldn't remember the last time anyone had done something like that. It was just a little thing but . . .

'Joss?'

James's impatient voice pulled me back out of my musings. I sighed heavily, so exhausted but knowing I needed to deal with this. 'Come inside.'

Once we were settled in the sitting room with coffee, I jumped right into it. 'I told Rhian I thought she was making a mistake. I would never encourage her to leave you. You're the best thing that's ever happened to her.'

James shook his head, his dark eyes bleak. 'I'm sorry, Joss. About earlier. I just . . . I feel like I can't breathe. It doesn't seem real, you know?'

Feeling hopeless, I leaned over to rub his shoulder in comfort. 'Maybe Rhian will change her mind.'

'I thought she was over her bullshit,' he continued like I hadn't spoken. 'It's all because of her parents – you know that, right?'

'Kind of. Not really. We don't talk about that stuff.'

He eyed me with something akin to disbelief. 'You two are supposed to be best friends, but sometimes I think you do each other more damage than good.'

'James –'

'Rhian's mum loved Rhian's dad. Her dad was an emotionally stunted alcoholic prick, but that bitch loved him more than she loved Rhian. He beat the shit out of Rhian and her mum all the time. And Rhian's mum kept going back to him. Eventually he took off, filed for divorce, met someone else. Rhian's mum blamed her. Said she was a fuckup and that she'd end up just like her dad. For years she's told Rhian she was just like her dad, a disaster waiting to happen. And Rhian believes it.

'You know her mum attempted suicide twice? Selfish cow left Rhian to find her like that. Twice. And now Rhian thinks *she's* going to do to me what her dad did to her mum. I can't rationalize with her. She doesn't even bloody drink. It's all in her head! And I thought we were past it, Joss. When things got serious ages ago we went through all this, and I thought we'd beat it. That's why I proposed.' He ducked his head in an effort to hide the tears shining in his eyes. 'I can't believe this is actually happening.' He kicked the coffee table in frustration, and I barely even blinked.

My mind was off with Rhian. How could I have been her best friend for four years and not know any of this? This was way more messed up than I could have guessed. Of course, Rhian didn't know anything about my past either. I suddenly wondered if James was right. How could we possibly give each other advice when we didn't know the first thing about the other's demons?

Then it occurred to me, looking at James crying over the woman he loved, that Rhian was far less messed up than I was. She had told James everything because she'd trusted him with her issues, and she'd worked through them with him. Or she almost had.

Still, that was a huge step in the right direction.

'Joss.' James was pleading with me now. 'Talk to her, please. She listens to you. She thinks if you're happy being alone, then she'll be fine, too.'

Happy? I wasn't happy. I was just safe.

I sighed heavily, not sure what to do. 'Look, you can crash here for however long you need.'

James looked at me a moment too long, his expression unreadable. Finally he just nodded. 'I'd appreciate it if I could crash on your couch tonight. Tomorrow, I'm heading home to Mum's. Until I can get sorted out.'

'Okay.'

We didn't say anything else after that. I found a blanket in the closet and left it on the couch along with one of my pillows. I could feel James's disappointment in me every time I stepped near him, so I left him in the sitting room and closed myself in my room.

I called Ellie.

'Hey, are you all right?' she asked, the sound of music and noise in the background fading as she wandered through whatever bar she was in out onto a marginally quieter street.

No. I'm not fine. I'm pretty far from fine. 'Yeah, I'm okay. I hope you don't mind, but I told James that he could crash on the couch for the night. He's heading home tomorrow.'

'Sure thi— What?' Her mouth pulled away from her phone as she spoke to someone else. 'She's fine. He's sleeping on the couch.'

Was that Braden?

'No, I said it's fine. Braden, she's fine. Go away.' Her sigh became louder as she turned back to her phone. 'Sorry, Joss. Yeah, that's fine. Do you need me to come home?'

Do you need me to come home?

95

Was I home? Did I need her?

I barely knew her. But, like Braden, Ellie had crawled inside somehow. Exhausted by what had turned into an exceptionally emotional day, I shook my head. 'No, Ellie, I'm really okay. Stay. Have fun. Just remember there's a strange guy sleeping on your couch when you come home.'

'Okay.'

Reluctantly, she hung up and I was left staring at the wall. I was reeling. Why did I feel so off-balance? So out of control? So scared?

Why had moving to Dublin Street changed so much in so little time?

So much *had* changed, but apparently it hadn't changed enough. I was still alone. But I was alone because that's how I wanted it. Rhian, I suddenly realized, was a completely different creature altogether. She wouldn't survive alone.

I dialed her number.

She picked up just as I was about to hang up. 'Hullo?'

Jesus C, she sounded like crap. 'Rhian?'

'What do you want, Joss? I was sleeping.'

Yeah, I could just imagine that she'd spent all her time in bed since James had left. Suddenly I felt angry at her. 'I'm calling to tell you that you're a complete idiot.'

'Excuse me?'

'You heard me. Now get on the phone and call James and tell him you made a mistake.'

'Fuck off, Joss. You know better than anyone I'm better off alone. Have you been drinking?'

'No. I'm sitting here while your boyfriend lies crashed out on my couch.'

Her breath hitched. 'James is in Edinburgh?'

'Yeah. And he's heartbroken. And he told me everything. About your parents, about your mom.' I waited for a reply, but Rhian had gone deathly silent. 'Rhian, why didn't you tell me?'

'Why haven't you ever spoken about *your* parents?' she countered.

I blinked back the stinging tears in my eyes as they landed on the photograph of my family on the bedside table. 'Because they died along with my little sister when I was fourteen and there's nothing else to really say.' I didn't know if that was true or not. In fact, after the panic attacks, I had been wondering if not saying anything was the problem. I took a deep breath and told her something I had never told anyone. 'When they died, the only person I had was my best friend, Dru, and when she died a year later, I had no one. I was completely alone. I spent the most impressionable years of my life taking care of myself. There's never been concerned phone calls or people checking in. Maybe there would have been if I'd let them, but I'm used to taking care of myself and not wanting to rely on anyone else.'

After another moment, during which the only sound I could hear was the thudding of my heart, Rhian sniffled. 'I think that's the most honest you've ever been with me.'

'It's the most honest I've ever been with anyone.'

'You've just always been so self-contained. I thought

you were okay. I thought you didn't need anyone to be concerned . . .'

I settled back on the bed with my own heavy sigh. 'The point of this reluctant outpouring of all my crap isn't to make you feel guilty. I don't need anyone to be concerned for me. That's my point. Will that change one day? I don't know. I'm not asking it to. But, Rhian, when you trusted James with all your baggage, you decided that day that you were asking someone to be concerned. You were tired of being alone. Will staying with him be hard? Yes. Will fighting your fears every day be difficult? Yes. But how he feels for you . . . jeez, Rhian . . . that's worth it. And telling yourself that it's okay to run away from him and be alone just because *I'm* alone and okay with it is bullshit. I'm alone because I just am. You're alone because you made a choice. And it's the wrong fucking choice.'

'Joss?'

'What?'

'I'm sorry I haven't been a better friend. You're not alone.'

Yes, I am. 'I'm sorry I haven't been a better friend, too.'

'Is James still there?'

'Yeah.'

'I don't want to be alone. Not when I could have him. God, that sounds so cheesy.'

I shook my head, smiling, and the tightness in my chest eased. 'Yeah, it does sound cheesy. Sometimes the truth is cheesy.'

'I'm going to call him.'

I grinned. 'I'll get off the phone.'

We hung up and I lay there in the dark listening. After twenty minutes I heard my front door creak open and shut.

I found the sitting room empty, the blanket on the couch rolled up. A piece of paper lay across it. A note from James.

I owe you.

I gripped the paper tightly and walked numbly back into my bedroom to stare at the photo of me with my family. If anything, these last few weeks had taught me that it was obvious that I wasn't over losing them. I had to talk to someone. But unlike Rhian, I didn't want to talk to anyone who could use that crap against me. My therapist in high school had tried to help me, but I'd shut down every time. I'd been a teenager. I'd thought I knew best.

But I wasn't a kid anymore, and I didn't know best. And if I wanted the panic attacks to stop, I needed to make the call in the morning.

7

'So, Mystery Man is gone?' The voice scared the bejesus out of me and I jumped, the instant coffee on my teaspoon scattering onto the counter.

I threw Braden a withering look over my shoulder. 'Don't you ever work? Or knock?'

He was slouched against the kitchen doorway, watching me make my morning coffee. 'Can I get one?' He nodded to the kettle.

'What do you take?'

'Milk. Two sugars.'

'And here I was expecting you to say black.'

'If anyone is black around here, it's you.'

I made a face. 'Do you want coffee or not?'

He grunted. 'Someone's pleasant in the morning.'

'When am I anything else?' I dumped two sugars in his mug with attitude.

Braden's laughter hit me directly in the gut. 'Right.'

As the kettle brewed, I turned around, leaning against the counter with my arms crossed over my chest. I was very aware of the fact that I wasn't wearing a bra under my camisole. In fact, I didn't think I had ever been more aware of my body than I was when I was around Braden. To be honest, I'd stopped caring about my appearance and all the shit that came with it after my parents and Beth died. I wore what I liked, I looked the way I looked, and I didn't give a rat's ass what any guy thought. Somehow that seemed to work in my favor.

But standing in front of Braden, I realized I wasn't so confident about that anymore. I was curious what he thought about me. I wasn't tall and skinny like all the glamazons that surely orbited Braden's world. I wasn't tiny, but I wasn't tall. I had slender legs and a small waist, but I had boobs, hips, and a definite ass. I had good hair on the days I could be bothered to wear it down, but those days came few and far between. It was an indiscriminate color – somewhere between blond and brown – but it was long and thick with a natural curl. But my hair was so heavy it tended to annoy me unless it was up off my neck, so I rarely, if ever, wore it loose. My eyes were probably my best feature – at least that's what people told me. I had my dad's eyes. They were light gray with streaks of gunmetal in them, but they weren't huge and adorable like Holly's and Ellie's – they were almond-shaped, feline, and they were extremely good at glaring.

No. I wasn't beautiful or cute or glamorous. I also didn't think I was ugly, but worrying about being extra-ordinary had never crossed my mind before. Braden made me care . . . and that kind of pissed me off.

'Seriously, don't you work?'

He stood up from the doorframe and casually sauntered toward me. He was in another fantastic three-piece suit. Someone as tall and as broad-shouldered as he was would have probably looked more at home in jeans and flannel, especially with the messy hair and stubble, but God, he worked that suit. As he approached I found my mind wandering into fantasy land – Braden kissing me, lifting me up onto the countertop, pushing my legs apart, pressing into me, his tongue in my mouth, his hand on my breast, his other hand slipping between my legs . . .

Unbelievably turned on, I whirled around, willing the kettle to boil faster.

'I have a meeting in half an hour,' he replied, coming to a stop beside me and reaching for the kettle before I could. 'Thought I'd stop by and see if everything was okay. Things seemed tense last night before Ellie and I left.'

I watched him pour the water into our mugs, trying to decide whether or not to tell him about James and Rhian.

'Morning,' Ellie chirped, as she strolled into the kitchen, fresh awake and already washed and dressed. Her cardigan was inside out. I reached out and tugged at the label so she could see. Smiling sheepishly, she shrugged out of it and put it back on the right way around. 'So, I came home and James wasn't on the couch. Did he sleep in your room?'

Braden stiffened at my side, and I glanced up to find him frowning. He obviously hadn't considered that. I smirked, feeling smug. 'No.' I studied Ellie a moment and as my reservations disappeared over sharing the news, I realized I almost, maybe, sort of, kind of, trusted her. 'James is Rhian's boyfriend.'

'Rhian – your best friend, Rhian?' she asked, pouring herself some fresh orange juice. She settled at the table with her glass. I thought being near her as opposed to being near her brother would be a good idea, so I slipped into the chair across from her.

'He proposed, she freaked out, she dumped him.'

Ellie's mouth dropped open in horror. 'You're kidding me. Poor guy.'

I grinned, thinking about his note. 'They're going to be okay.'

'They made up?' God, she looked so hopeful and she didn't even know them.

'You're a sweetheart,' I told her quietly, and Ellie's expression melted.

'You got them back together, didn't you?' she announced with the utmost confidence in me.

Only Ellie would have that kind of assurance in someone like me. She was damnably determined to prove that I wasn't as detached as I made out. That she happened to be right on this occasion was a little annoying and a lot misleading.

'He was pissed off at you,' Braden interjected before I could respond.

I glanced over at him, still leaning against the counter, sipping his coffee as if he had all the time in the world. 'He thought I talked her into it – into breaking up with him.'

Braden didn't seem surprised by this. In fact, he

quirked an eyebrow and replied, 'Why am I not surprised?'

Ellie clicked her tongue at him. 'Braden, Joss wouldn't do that.'

'I know she wouldn't do that. But I don't think she didn't do that for the same reasons you think she didn't, Els.'

Crap. So he thought he knew me better than Ellie did. I grimaced inwardly. Maybe he did. Perceptive asshat. Unnerved, I looked away from him, sipping my own coffee and trying to ignore his gaze boring into me.

'Cryptic much?' Ellie grumbled before focusing back on me. 'You got them back together though, right?'

I owe you.

The words made me smile into my mug. 'Yeah. Yeah, I did.'

'You did?' Braden sounded so astonished by this, it was insulting.

Okay, maybe the asshat just *thought* he knew me. 'She's my best friend. I helped out. I'm not some cold-hearted bitch, you know.'

Braden flinched. 'I never said that, babe.'

I shivered as the endearment rolled over me, hitting a nerve I didn't even know I had. My words tumbled out caustically. 'Don't call me "babe." Don't *ever* call me "babe." '

My sharp tone and sudden anger caused a thick tension to fall between the three of us, and I suddenly couldn't remember why I had been so grateful to Braden yesterday when he helped me after the panic attack. This was what you got when you let people in. They started to think they knew you when they didn't know shit.

Ellie cleared her throat. 'So, James has gone back to London?'

'Yup.' I stood up and dumped the dregs of my coffee into the sink. 'I'm going to hit the gym.'

'Jocelyn –' Braden started.

'Don't you have a meeting?' I cut him off, about to stroll out of there and leave the tension behind.

'Jocelyn . . .' He sounded concerned.

I caught myself with a deep inner sigh. *You've made your point, Joss.* I didn't need to continue to be a bitch about it. Sighing outwardly, I looked up at him and offered with snarky charitableness, 'I have a travel mug in the top left cupboard if you want to take some coffee to go.'

Braden stared at me a moment, his eyes searching. He shook his head with a quizzical smile playing on his lips. 'I'm good, thanks.'

I nodded, pretending indifference to the atmosphere we'd caused, and then I glanced back at Ellie. 'You want to hit the gym with me?'

Ellie wrinkled her button nose. 'Gym? Me?'

I eyed her skinny self. 'You mean you're naturally that gorgeous?'

She laughed, flushing a little. 'I have good genes.'

'Yeah, well, I have to work out to fit into mine.'

'Cute,' Braden murmured into his coffee, his eyes laughing at me.

I grinned at him, my second nonverbal apology for snapping at him. 'Whatever. Guess I'm flying solo. Catch you guys later.'

'Thanks for the coffee, Jocelyn,' he called cheekily to me as I wandered down the hall.

I winced. 'It's Joss!' I yelled back grouchily, trying to ignore the sound of his laughter.

'So, now that we've got our introductions and all the basics over, do you want to tell me why you felt it was time to talk to someone?' Dr Kathryn Pritchard asked me softly.

Why did all therapists speak in that same soft voice? It was supposed to be soothing, but it sounded just as condescending to me now as it had when I was fourteen.

A week had passed since the morning in the kitchen with Braden, and now I found myself in a large therapist's office on North St Andrew Lane. It was surprisingly cold and modern – nothing like the cozy clutter of the therapist's I'd been sent to in high school. Plus, the high school therapy was free. This suede-and-glass chick was costing me a small fortune.

'You need flowers or something,' I observed. 'A bit of color. Your office isn't very welcoming.'

She grinned at me. 'Noted.'

I didn't say anything.

'Jocelyn —'

'Joss.'

'Joss. Why are you here?'

I felt my stomach flip and the cold sweat started, and I rushed to remind myself that anything I said to her was confidential. I'd never see her outside this office, and she'd never use my past, my issues, against me or to get to know me personally. I drew a deep breath. 'I've started having panic attacks again.'

'Again?'

'I used to have them a lot when I was fourteen.'

'Well, panic attacks are brought on by all kinds of anxiety. Why then? What was going on in your life?'

I swallowed past the brick in my throat. 'My parents and little sister were killed in a car accident. I have no other family – except for an uncle who didn't give a shit – and I spent the rest of my teen years in foster care.'

Dr Pritchard had been scribbling as I talked. She stopped and looked directly into my eyes. 'I'm very sorry for your loss, Joss.'

I felt my shoulders relax at her sincerity, and I nodded in acknowledgment of it.

'After they died, you started having panic attacks. Can you tell me your symptoms?'

I told her, and she nodded along with them.

'Is there a trigger? At least, are you aware of one?'

'I don't allow myself to think about them a lot. My family, I mean. Memories of them – actual real, solid memories – not just vague impressions . . . the memories trigger the attacks.'

'But they stopped?'

I curled my lip. 'I got really good at not thinking about them.'

Dr Pritchard lifted an eyebrow. 'For eight years?'

I shrugged. 'I can look at pictures, I can have a thought about them, but I carefully avoid actual memories of us together.'

'But your panic attacks have started up again?'

'I let my guard down. I let the memories in – had a panic attack at the gym and then at a friend's family dinner.'

'What were you thinking about at the gym?'

I shifted uneasily. 'I'm a writer. Well, I'm trying to be. I started thinking about my mom's story. It's a good story. Sad. But I think people would like her. Anyway, I had a memory – a few, actually – of my parents and their relationship. They had a good relationship. Next thing I know some guy is helping me off the treadmill.'

'And the family dinner? Was that the first family dinner you've been to since being in foster care?'

'We never really had family dinners in foster care.' I smiled humorlessly.

'So this was your first family dinner since losing them?'

'Yeah.'

'So that triggered a memory, too?'

'Yeah.'

'Have there been any big changes in your life recently, Joss?'

I thought about Ellie and Braden and our coffee morning a week ago. 'I moved. New apartment, new roommate.'

'Anything else?'

'My old roommate, my best friend, Rhian, she moved to London, and she and her boyfriend just got engaged. But that's about all.'

'Were you and Rhian close?'

I shrugged. 'As close as I allow myself to get to anyone.'

She smiled at me, a sad pressing together of her lips. 'Well, that sentence said a lot. What about your new flatmate, then? Are you allowing yourself to get close to her or him?'

'Her.' I thought about it. I suppose I had let Ellie in more than I'd intended to. And I cared about her more than I'd thought I would. 'Ellie. We've become fast friends. I wasn't expecting that. Ellie's friends are cool, and her brother and their crowd hang around a lot. I guess my life is more social now.'

'Was it Ellie and her brother's family dinner where you had a panic attack?'

'Yeah.'

Dr Pritchard nodded and scribbled something else down.

'Well?' I asked.

She smiled at me. 'Are you looking for a diagnosis?'

I raised an eyebrow at her.

'Sorry to disappoint, Joss, but we've barely scratched the surface.'

'You think these changes have something to do with it, though, right? I want the panic attacks to stop.'

'Joss, you've been in my office fifteen minutes, and I can already tell you that these panic attacks aren't going to stop anytime soon . . . unless you start dealing with your family's deaths.'

What? Well, that was just stupid. 'I have dealt with it. They died. I mourned. Now I'm trying to find a way to move on. That's why I'm here.'

'Look, you were smart enough to know that you have a problem and that you need to talk to someone about that problem, so you're smart enough to realize that burying memories of your family is not a healthy way to deal with their deaths. You haven't properly mourned them, Joss, and that's what we need to confront. Changes to daily life, new people, new emotions, new expectations – all can trigger past events. Especially if they haven't been dealt with. Spending time with a family after years of not having one of your own has broken through whatever wall you've put up around your family's deaths. I think it's possible you might be suffering from post-traumatic stress disorder, and that's not something to ignore.'

I grunted. 'You think I have PTSD, the thing that veterans have?'

'Not just soldiers. Anybody who suffers any kind of loss or emotional or physical trauma can suffer from PTSD.'

'And you think I have that?'

'Possibly, yes. I'll know more the more we talk. And hopefully the more we talk, the easier it'll become for you to think about and remember your family.'

'That doesn't sound like a good idea.'

'It won't be easy. But it'll help.'

8

I loved the smell of books.

'Don't you think that's a bit brutal for Hannah?' Ellie's soft, concerned voice asked above my head.

I smiled at Hannah, who stood an inch above me. Like her mom and sister, the kid was tall. Twisting my head around to look up at Ellie hovering behind me, my expression was incredulous. 'She's fourteen. It's a YA book.'

The book slipped from my fingers as Hannah took it before Ellie could stop her. I was spending my Sunday morning with them in the bookstore, where Hannah was having a great time spending her gift card from Braden.

Ellie seemed perturbed. 'Yes, about a dystopian world where teens kill one another.'

'Have you even read it?'

'No . . .'

'Then trust me.' I grinned back at Hannah. 'It rocks.'

'I'm buying it, Ellie,' Hannah told her adamantly, adding the book to her ever-growing pile.

With a sigh of defeat, Ellie nodded reluctantly and wandered back into the romance section. I was coming to learn she was a huge sucker for a happy ending. We'd watched no fewer than three romantic dramas this week. However, before I overdosed on another Nicholas Sparks adaptation, I was determined that tonight we'd be watching Matt Damon crack some heads as Jason Bourne.

My cell rang and I scrambled around in my purse for it, only to discover it was Rhian calling. I'd e-mailed her last night.

'Will you be okay while I take this?' I asked Hannah.

She waved me off, her nose practically pressed against the bookshelf as she scanned the titles. With laughter on my lips, I wandered away from her to answer the call in private.

'Hey.'

'Hi,' Rhian replied almost tentatively.

I braced myself.

Shit. Maybe I shouldn't have shared my news. Was she going to start treating me like a head case from now on? As in, *carefully*? Because that would be too weird. I would miss being cursed at, for one thing.

'How are you and James?' I asked before she could say anything.

'We're a lot better. We're getting there. Actually, he asked me to see someone. A therapist.'

I froze in the sci-fi aisle. 'You're kidding.'

'Nope. I didn't tell him about your e-mail, I swear. He just blurted it out. Some coincidence.' She took a deep breath. 'You really went to see one?'

I glanced around to make sure I was alone. 'I needed someone to talk to, and a professional with no personal interest in my life is the only person I trust to . . . well . . .

to talk to about what I need to talk about . . .' I frowned. Ten points for language skills on that one.

'I see.'

I winced at her tone. There was a definite bite to it. 'Rhian, I don't mean to be hurtful.'

'I'm not hurt. I just think you should talk to someone who actually cares about you. Why do you think I told James all my shit? You know, you were right before. I trusted him. And I'm glad I did.'

'I'm not ready for that. I don't have a James. I don't want a James. And, anyway, your James still wants you to talk to a therapist.'

She made a grumbling noise. 'I think he thinks if I greenlight the whole therapy thing, then I'm serious about making this work with him.'

I thought about how devastated James had been the night he came to see me. 'Then you should do it.'

'How was it? Was it weird?'

It was awful. 'It was fine. Strange at first, but I'm going back.'

'Do you want to talk about it?'

Yeah, that's why I'm paying one hundred pounds an hour to a professional, so I can talk to you. I held my sarcasm in check. 'No, Rhian, I don't.'

'Fine. You don't have to snap at me, you grumpy cow.'

I rolled my eyes. 'You know I miss your face-to-face insults. It's just not the same over the phone.'

She snorted. 'I miss someone who gets me. I called a woman on my research team a bitch – you know, in a friendly way – and she told me to go to hell. And I think she really meant it.'

'Rhian, we've talked about this. Normal people don't like to be called names. For some reason they tend to take that personally. And you are a tad bitchy, by the way.'

'Normal people are so sensitive.'

'Joss, have you read this one?' Hannah appeared around the corner of the aisle, waving yet another dystopian novel at me. I had read it. What can I say? I have a thing for dystopia.

'Who's that?' Rhian asked. 'Where are you?'

I nodded at Hannah. 'That's a good one. And there's a hot guy in it. I think you'll really like it.'

Hannah was delighted at that and clutched the book to her chest before lugging her handbasket of goodies back to the teen-fiction section.

'Joss?'

'That was Hannah.' I tilted my head at a Dan Simmons novel. Ooh, I hadn't read that one.

'And Hannah is . . . ?'

'Ellie's fourteen-year-old sister.'

'And you're with a teenager . . . why?'

What was with the tone? Her question might as well have been *And you're smoking crack . . . why?*

'We're in the bookstore.'

'You're shopping with a teenager?'

'Why do you keep saying it like that?'

'I don't know. Maybe because you've moved into an expensive flat; you're spending money you were always weird about spending; you're friends with a girl who's seen *The Notebook* fifty-five times and, like, smiles a lot; you're out for drinks with actual people on weeknights; you saved my relationship; you're seeing a therapist; and you're babysitting teens. I moved to London and you got a fuckin' lobotomy.'

I exhaled heavily. 'You know, you could just be grateful for the whole saving-your-relationship thing.'

'Joss, seriously, what's going on with you?'

I pulled the Dan Simmons novel off the shelf. 'I didn't do all those things deliberately. Ellie and I get along, and for some reason she likes having my broody ass around, and she's had a different life than what we had. She actually *likes* people, and that means I'm around them a lot.'

'Joss?'

I spun around to see Ellie standing before me, a deep frown between her eyes. A rush of concern swam over me and I bobbed my head above the shelves in panic, looking for Hannah.

'Hannah's fine.' Ellie guessed the reason for the manic head-bobbing. 'I'm stuck.' She held up a paperback with a woman in a lavish Victorian dress on the cover. A masculine pair of hands reached seductively for the laces on the back of it. There was also something about seduction in the title. In her other hand was the latest Sparks novel. 'Which one?'

Without hesitation I pointed at the bodice ripper. 'The seduction of what's-her-face. The Sparks novel would be overkill this week.'

She gestured at me with the bodice ripper and a militant nod before heading back out of the aisle.

'Seriously,' Rhian muttered down the line, 'where's Joss, and what have you done with her?'

'Joss is getting off the phone if you're done psycho-analyzing her.'

'Joss is speaking in the third person.'

I laughed. 'Rhian, get gone, okay? And tell James I said hi and, yeah, he does owe me.'

'Wait, what?'

Still laughing, I hung up on her and went to find Hannah and Ellie.

They were waiting in line to be served, and I slid in beside them, watching as Ellie stood there uncharacteristically silent and Hannah just stared adoringly down at all her books. We should have brought a backpack to hold them all.

At the checkout, I watched the clerk piling Hannah's books into weak plastic bags, and since Ellie had spaced out on me, I pointed behind him. 'Hey, could you maybe pack them into those shopper bags? These will just break.'

He shrugged lazily. 'They're fifty pence a bag.'

I made a face. 'The kid just bought a hundred pounds' worth of books, and you can't give us the bags for free?'

He waved the gift card at me. 'No, she didn't.'

'Yeah. But the person who gave her that gift card did. You're not seriously asking us to pay for something to carry them in?'

'No-o-o.' He drawled the word out like I was stupid. 'You can carry them in the free bags.'

Maybe I would have backed off if he hadn't been speaking to me in that condescending I-hate-my-job-so-fuck-customer-service manner. I opened my mouth to set him straight, but Ellie gripped my hand, stopping me. I looked up at her to see she was swaying a little, her face pale, her eyes screwed shut.

'Ellie.' I grabbed for her, and she held on to me.

'Ellie?' Hannah asked worriedly, hurrying to her sister's other side.

'I'm okay,' she murmured. 'Just dizzy. I have this . . . headache . . .'

'Another one?' This was, like, the third one this week.

Leaving the clerk to wither under my death stare, I pulled Ellie over to the side, sniping at him, 'Just pack the books into the normal bags.'

'Give them the good bags,' the girl working next to him said with a sigh.

'But –'

'Just do it.'

I ignored his irritated glare as I turned my concern to Ellie. 'How are you feeling?'

Although pale, I noted that her trembling had stopped. 'Better. I haven't eaten today. I just felt faint.'

'What about the headaches?'

She smiled reassuringly. 'Honestly, I haven't been eating enough because of my PhD. I'm feeling the pressure and I'm stressing out. I'll take better care.'

'Here you go.' The clerk held out two of the heavy shopper bags.

I muttered thanks and handed one to Hannah while keeping the other one.

'Let me.' Ellie reached for Hannah's bag.

'Oh, no, you don't.' I took her elbow. 'We're getting some food into you.'

Ellie tried to argue that she'd eat later at her mom's Sunday dinner – a dinner I had thankfully managed to talk my way out of, telling Ellie I really wanted to get a few hours of work in – but I convinced her to at least grab a snack at this cute little bistro around the corner. Hannah walked beside us with Ellie's hand on her back, guiding her through the crowds on Princes Street since she'd decided to start reading one of her books right away. I didn't know how anyone could do that – reading while walking? It gave me travel sickness.

We were chatting about the upcoming Edinburgh Festival when I saw Braden. We'd seen each other at the bar on Friday when he, Ellie, Adam, Jenna, Ed, and a few of Braden's colleagues had decided to stop by Club 39 for a drink. We hadn't really talked much, and his attitude toward me had definitely veered into the friend zone.

I didn't know if the feeling I got when he did that bothered me. But I did know I was feeling *something* when I saw him with *her*.

Braden was walking toward us, easily spotted in the crowd because of his height . . . and, well, his hotness. He was wearing dark blue jeans, black boots, and a dark gray long-sleeved thermal Henley that showcased his sculpted, broad-shouldered scrumptiousness.

In his hand was another hand.

It belonged to a woman I'd never seen before.

'Braden,' Ellie murmured, and Hannah's head popped up from her book, her whole face lighting up when she saw him.

'Braden!' she called out, and his head jerked around from smiling down at his companion to follow the voice. His smile grew even bigger when he saw Hannah.

As we approached one another, I suddenly wished I was anywhere but where I was. The little kick I got in my gut when I saw him with someone else was not fun. In fact, that kick was quite possibly the worst joke that had been played on me in a while.

I also wasn't keen on the carefully polite expression he put on his face when he saw that I was with Ellie and Hannah.

I glanced up at Ellie as we came to a stop only to find her glaring daggers at the woman with Braden. Bewildered and frankly astonished, I couldn't help but hiss her name in question.

She looked down at me, her jaw clenched. 'I'll tell you later.'

'Hannah.' Braden hugged her into his side and nodded at her bags. 'Been spending your gift card?'

'Yeah. I got loads of books. Thanks again,' she added.

'You're welcome, sweetheart.' He let her go and turned to us. 'Els, you're looking pale. You okay?'

She was still glowering at him, and I wanted to know

what the hell I was missing. 'I was feeling a bit faint. I haven't eaten.'

'I'm taking her to get some food.' I thought I should mention that, so he didn't think we were dragging her around when she wasn't feeling well.

'Good,' he murmured, catching my eye. 'Jocelyn, this is Vicky.'

Vicky and I looked at each other, our smiles polite. She reminded me a lot of Holly: tall, blond, pretty, and as natural as a freaking Barbie. Still, she was hot.

Braden definitely had a type, and I was not it. No wonder he'd stopped flirting with me. His sexual radar must have been wonky when we first met, but clearly it had been restored to order.

'Hello, Vicky,' Ellie murmured sullenly.

I couldn't help it – my eyebrows hit my hairline before I could stop them. Ellie sounded practically predatory.

I was impressed.

And definitely curious.

Braden shot his sister a quelling look. 'I had my dinner meeting last night, and Vicky was at the next table. We decided to catch up. Thought we'd grab some breakfast.'

In other words, Vicky was at the next table and they'd *hooked up*. I shrugged off the unfamiliar uneasiness that came over me. My chest felt a little sore and my stomach a little queasy. Maybe Ellie wasn't food-deprived – maybe we'd both eaten something bad yesterday.

'Nice to see you again, Ellie,' Vicky replied sweetly. She seemed nice enough.

'Hmm.' Ellie blatantly brushed her off, rolling her eyes and then skewering Braden. 'Are you coming to dinner this afternoon?'

I watched the muscle in his jaw flex. He definitely wasn't amused by his sister's attitude. 'Of course.' His eyes traveled back to me. 'I'll see you both there.'

'Joss can't make it. She has stuff to do.'

He frowned at me. 'It's just a few hours. Surely you can squeeze us in?'

In response, Vicky pressed closer to Braden. 'I'd love to have dinner, Braden.'

Braden gave her a somewhat patronizing pat on the hand. 'Sorry, sweetheart. It's just family.'

Three things happened at once: Ellie choked on her laughter, Vicky reared back like he'd slapped her, and I felt a panic attack coming on.

Feeling the fog closing in on me, I breathed through it and my confusion. 'You know what?' I took a step back from them. 'I totally forgot I said I'd drop off Jo's tips to her at her apartment. Today. Now, actually.' I waved apologetically. 'I gotta go. I'll catch you later.'

And then I got the hell out of there as fast as I could.

'Why did you run?' Dr Pritchard asked, her head tilted to the side like a curious bird.

I don't know. 'I don't know.'

'You've mentioned Ellie's brother Braden a number of times now. How does he fit into your life?'

I want him. 'I guess he's sort of a friend.' When she

just stared at me, I shrugged. 'We had an unconventional introduction.'

I told her everything.

'So you're attracted to him?'

'I was.'

She nodded. 'Back to my earlier question then. Why? Why did you run?'

Lady, if I knew that, would I be here? 'I don't know.'

'Was it because Braden was with another woman? Or because he implied you were family?'

'Both, I guess.' I rubbed my forehead, feeling a headache coming on. 'I want him to stay in the box I've put him in.'

'The box?'

'You know, the box. It's got a label and everything. It's says "Sort of Friends." We're sort of friends, but not really good friends. We hang out, but we don't really know each other. I prefer it that way. I think I might have panicked at the thought that he thinks there's more. That he thinks we're close somehow. I don't want that.'

'Why not?'

'I just don't.'

Seeming to sense my tone, Dr Pritchard nodded and didn't ask the question again. 'And your feelings regarding seeing him with another woman . . . ?'

'The only feelings I had were confusion and panic. He was with a woman he obviously has a sexual relationship and history with, and he implied somehow that our friendship was deeper than what he had with her by saying what he did to her. Like I said, that's not true. I don't want that.'

'And that's the only reason?'

'Yes.'

'So you don't want a relationship with Braden? Sexual or otherwise?'

Yes. 'No.'

'Let's talk about that. We haven't spoken about your relationship with men. You seem good at shutting people out, Joss. Has it been a while since your last relationship?'

'I've never been in a relationship.'

'Have you dated?'

I curled my lips as I remembered the so-called wonder years. 'Do you want the sordid history? Okay, I'll lay it out for you . . .'

'Did you get Jo her money?' Ellie asked quietly as she flopped down on the couch next to me.

I nodded, lying, and to purge my guilt I reached out for my coveted big bag of cookies and offered them to her. 'You want some?'

'Nah. I'm stuffed.' She relaxed back against the cushion, her eyes on the TV. 'Whatcha watching?'

'*The Bourne Supremacy.*'

'Mmm, Matt Damon.'

'Dinner okay? You feeling better?' I felt even more guilt about taking off on her like that. I was still trying to wrap my head around what exactly had happened to me in that moment.

Ellie slanted me a look. 'Mum asked after you.'

That was nice. 'Did you tell her I said hi?'

'Yes. And dinner was atmospheric. Braden was still pissed off at me.'

I smirked, looking back at the screen. 'I've never seen you like that before. It was kind of badass.'

'Yeah, well, Vicky's a slut.'

I sucked in my breath. Her normally open face was tight and stony. 'You really don't like her. Who is she?'

'She was Braden's girlfriend for a while. I can't believe he's seeing her again.'

'And . . . ?'

Realizing I meant *What the hell did she do to you?* Ellie shrugged, her face crumpling. 'I went over to see Adam about something one day, and she was there. Naked. In his bed. He was naked, too.'

I couldn't believe it. 'They cheated on Braden?'

'No.' She snorted humorlessly. 'Adam fancied her, so Braden loaned her out to him.'

Jesus C . . . 'Loaned her out?'

'Mm-hmm.'

'Does she have no self-respect?'

'Did you not hear the part about how she's a slut?'

'I can't believe Braden would do that. Just loan her out.'

'Maybe that's a bad word choice. She was actually the one who told Braden she wanted Adam. Braden didn't have a problem with it, so he let them have sex.'

Kinky, a little cold maybe, but mutual, so who was I to judge? 'So she *has* self-respect. What's the big deal?'

I tried to dig to the real source of Ellie's dislike. 'The girl likes sex.'

'She's a slut!'

Oh yeah. I definitely knew the real reason now. Adam.

'You really like Adam, huh?'

She exhaled slowly and closed her eyes tight.

A streak of pain lashed across my chest as I watched the tear roll out from under her lashes and drip down her cheek.

'Oh, honey.' I sat up and pulled her to my side, letting her cry quietly into my sweater. After a while, I reached for the half-eaten packet of cookies and handed her one. 'Here. Sugar up and let's watch Jason Bourne kick some ass.'

'Can we pretend it's Adam's ass he's kicking?'

'I'm already on it. See that guy? That's Adam, and Bourne is kicking his slutty little tushy.'

She giggled beside me, and I marveled at how someone could be so strong and yet so fragile.

9

A couple of weeks, one panic attack, and one visit to my therapist later, and there I was, struggling with my manuscript again. Usually when I was in the middle of writing my brain would wander off into fantasyland at the slightest notice, whether I was at the laptop or not. Nowadays I had to force my imagination into action. And that never worked.

With the book flagging and my anxiety dipping and diving over whether I could cut it as a writer – and worrying what the hell I was going to do if I couldn't – I decided to do what I do best: I locked it in that iron box inside of me so that I couldn't think about it, and focused on something else.

Now that the Edinburgh Festival was under way I took on extra shifts at the bar, and I hung out with Ellie whenever she asked me to. On my last visit, my therapist had encouraged me to try out family dinner again, which I managed sans panic attack – win! I also hit the gym a lot, avoiding the come-hither smiles of Gavin the personal trainer.

To Ellie's relief, Vicky disappeared out of Braden's life as quickly as she'd come into it. Not that I would have known unless Ellie had told me. I hadn't seen him since that morning on Princes Street. Work was keeping him busy – something was happening with one of his developments, and he also had this big event planned at his nightclub, Fire, at the end of the festival. This was when I discovered that Adam was Braden's architect, so when Braden was busy, Adam was busy. The few times we were all supposed to meet up – one time to see a comedian, one other time just for drinks, and the last time for family dinner – Braden had canceled, proving me wrong: He actually did work for his money.

I began to see his absence as a good thing. I was feeling more relaxed than I had in weeks, and Ellie and I had grown closer. She'd confessed everything about the whole Adam fiasco . . .

Having been in love with Adam since she was a kid, Ellie had finally plucked up the courage to do something about it after he punched out the asshole who'd set her up to get info on Braden. She went over to his apartment and pretty much threw herself at him. And because Adam was a guy and Ellie was beautiful, he'd taken her up on the offer. That was, until she was almost completely naked and on her back beneath him. Adam backed out, explaining he couldn't do that to Braden or her, and that Braden would never forgive him and he'd never forgive himself. Realizing he thought it was just a one-night-stand kind of thing, Ellie had left, quietly nursing a broken heart and a bruised ego.

I would never have guessed that stuff was between them. Ellie was supercool around him. She said she hadn't wanted things to change, so she tried her hardest to be okay about everything. I'd seen it in action – she did try hard. But sometimes something soft, something *more* would enter her expression when she looked at him. When I thought about it, there was something more in the way Adam looked at her, too. Thing is, I couldn't work out if he was just lusting after her or if his feelings ran a little deeper. I was curious as hell, but I also knew it wasn't any of my business, so I was keeping my nose out of it.

After opening up to me, Ellie had tried to talk to me again about my family, about my past.

I shut her down.

Dr Pritchard said it would take time. For now, I couldn't let go, and no matter what the good doctor said, I still wasn't sure if it was in me to let go.

'Writer's block again?'

I spun around in my seat to find Ellie standing in my doorway waving an A4 manila envelope at me.

I grimaced, closing my laptop. 'I should just get that printed on a T-shirt.'

'It'll pass.'

My only reply was a grunt.

'Anyway, I hate to ask but . . .'

'What's up?'

She waved the envelope at me again. 'Braden stopped by last night when you were working, and he left these documents. He just called to ask me to bring them to his office, because he needs them for his meeting in two hours, but I have a class –'

My stomach flipped. 'And you want me to take them to him.'

Ellie's eyes got all big and adorable. 'Please,' she begged.

Crap, fuckity, crap, fuck. Grumbling, I stood up and took the envelope from her. 'Where's his office?'

She gave me the address and I discovered it was down by the quay, which meant I'd need to get a cab to get there in time, since I had to have a shower before I left.

'I really appreciate this, Joss.' She grinned and started backing up. 'I've got to run. Catch you later.'

And then she was gone.

And I was Braden bound. Damn it. Trying to ignore the beating butterfly wings in my stomach, I huffed around, muttering under my breath as I showered and dressed. I pulled on a pair of jeans and a thin sweater as it was fairly warm outside and wearing a jacket in Scotland when it wasn't below freezing made you stick out as a tourist. No joke. A little sun came out in Scotland, and people had their shirts off.

I stared at my reflection in the mirror – very little makeup, my hair twisted up in a messy bun. The sweater was cute and showed a little cleavage, but my jeans were old and faded. Sure, I wondered what Braden thought about me physically, but I wasn't going to let that change me. I never dressed to impress anyone but myself, and I certainly wasn't going to for some guy who liked his women's legs longer, their boobs smaller, and their hair blonder.

The cab ride seemed to take forever, and, as always, I was feeling a little carsick by the time we got there after bumping down God knows how many cobbled roads. The cabdriver dropped me off at Commercial Quay, and I wandered down the man-made stream that opened out at the bottom into the water. There was a parking lot to my right and to my left a number of commercial establishments. I found Braden's office in the same building as the offices of an architect, an accountant, and a dentist. After being buzzed up – and floundering around embarrassingly in the elevator, which opened on the opposite side from the one that you got in on – I found myself in a chic reception area.

The blonde receptionist wasn't what I'd been expecting at all. She was about Elodie's age but carried at least twenty pounds more than Elodie, and she was beaming at me with a big friendly smile. Her name tag read MORAG. I'd been gearing myself up for someone tall, thin, and beautiful who would sneer at my jeans and try to have me removed from the building. Was I in the right office?

'Can I help you?' Morag was still beaming at me.

'Uh . . .' I glanced around, looking for a sign that this was Braden's office. 'I'm looking for Braden Carmichael.'

'Do you have an appointment?'

Okay, so it *was* his office. I stepped up to the desk and waved the envelope. 'He left these documents at his sister's – my roommate's – place and, um, asked her to bring them in. She couldn't, so I said I would.'

If it was possible, Morag's grin got even wider. 'Oh, how nice of you, dear. Can I take a name?'

'Joss Butler.'

'One second.' She picked up the phone on her desk and didn't have to wait long. 'I have a Joss Butler here with some documents for you, Mr Carmichael.' She made an *mmm-hmm* noise. 'I'll do that.' She hung up and smiled at me. 'Let me show you to Mr Carmichael's office, Jocelyn.'

I clenched my teeth. 'It's Joss.'

'Mmm-hmm.'

It was annoying enough that he refused to call me anything but Jocelyn, but did he really have to get other people on board? I followed the cheerful middle-aged receptionist down a narrow corridor until we came to a corner office. She knocked, and a deep voice answered: 'Come in.' I shivered at that voice and wondered for a second if I had missed it these last two weeks.

'Jocelyn for you, sir,' Morag announced as she opened the door.

I wandered in past her and heard the door shut behind me as she left us alone.

The office was bigger than I had been expecting with one large window that looked down on the quay. It was very masculine with a huge walnut library desk, leather chair, black leather couch, and sturdy bookshelves heavy with folders and hardbacks. A few metal filing cabinets were stored in the corner. On the wall above the couch was a huge painting of Venice and on the bookshelves more than one framed photograph of him with Ellie and with Adam and with his and Ellie's family. In the corner behind me were a treadmill and a weight bench.

Braden was perched on his desk, his long legs stretched out in front of him as he watched me. I felt that kick to my gut again at the sight of him and the familiar tingling between my legs. Jesus C, he was even hotter than I remembered.

Fuck, shittity fuck, shit.

'Hey.' I waved the envelope at him. *Witty opener, Joss, very witty.*

Braden smiled, and I froze as his eyes washed over the length of me, taking his time taking me in. I swallowed hard, my heart kicking up a gear – he hadn't looked at me like that since the night at the bar with Holly. 'It's nice to see you, Jocelyn. Feels like forever.'

Ignoring the flush of pleasure those words produced, I strode forward and held out the envelope. 'Ellie said you needed these pronto.'

He nodded, still gazing at me as he took the documents. 'I appreciate your bringing them down. How much do I owe you for taxi fare?'

'Nothing.' I shook my head. 'It wasn't a problem. I was just beating my head on my desk anyway.'

'Writer's block?'

'Writer's cement.'

He smirked. 'That bad?'

'So bad.'

With a sympathetic smile he stood up, bringing our bodies within touching distance. I felt the breath whoosh out of me as my head tilted back to meet his gaze. 'Sorry I had to cancel on you those last few times.'

He made it sound as though he'd canceled a date. I laughed, confused. 'O-kay.'

'I stopped by the flat last night, but you weren't there.'

'I was working. Extra shifts.' I took a step back, hoping the less proximity I had to him, the faster the heat in my blood would reduce.

I thought I saw him smile as he turned and put the documents on his desk. 'The last time we saw each other I think something I said sent you running for the hills. Or maybe someone that was with me?'

Arrogant asshole. I guffawed. 'Vicky?'

His grin was cocky now as he looked back at me. 'Were you jealous?'

Were we actually having this conversation? I hadn't seen him in two weeks and, and ... pfft! Smiling in astonishment at his egotism, I crossed my arms over my chest. 'You know, it's a wonder I managed to squeeze into the room, what with your giant-ass ego taking up all the space.'

Braden laughed. 'Well, you ran off because of something, Jocelyn.'

'One: Stop calling me Jocelyn. It's Joss. J-o-s-s. Joss. And two: You had just insinuated that I was somehow "family" after knowing me only a few weeks.'

His brow puckered as he processed this, and he leaned back against the desk again, crossing his arms over his wide chest as he thought about it. 'I did?'

'You did.'

Suddenly his eyes were searching my face and they were full of all sorts of questions. 'Ellie told me about your family. I'm sorry.'

My muscles locked, the heat he'd created evaporating as if he'd just blasted the A/C. What could I say? I didn't want him to make a big deal out of it, and I also didn't want him psychoanalyzing me. 'It was a long time ago.'

'I didn't realize I'd insinuated that. About family. But things are starting to make sense. The dinner at Elodie's . . . you running off –'

'Don't,' I snapped, taking three steps toward him. 'Braden, don't.' My voice quieted as I tried to tamp down the urge to bite at him like a wounded animal. 'I don't talk about it.'

As he studied me I couldn't help but wonder what he was thinking. Did he think I was nuts? Pathetic? Did I care? And then he just nodded. 'I get it. We don't have to . . .'

Relief washed over me, and I took a step back, only for Braden to move into me so he was almost touching me again. 'I was thinking of having a picnic on the Meadows this Saturday if it's nice out – to make it up to Ellie for not being around a lot lately. I know she misses Adam, too. Will you come?'

'That depends.' I found my way back to Snarksville in an attempt to feel less off-balance. 'Are you going to insinuate that I'm jealous of the sandwich you'll be eating?'

He burst out laughing, a full body laugh that did sweet things to my insides. 'I deserve that.' He prowled closer so that I had to step back. 'But will you forgive me and come? As a friend?' There was something deliberately sarcastic about the way he said 'friend.'

I eyed him suspiciously. 'Braden . . .'

'Just friends.' His gaze dropped to my mouth and darkened. 'I told you. I can pretend if you can pretend.'

'I'm not pretending.' Was that my voice that sounded all hot and breathy?

Braden just smirked at me like he didn't believe me. 'You know, you're really putting pressure on my acting skills.'

'Acting skills?'

'Pretending, Jocelyn.' He took another step forward, his eyes narrowed with intent. 'I've never been very good at it.'

Oh my God, he was going to kiss me. I was standing in his office in crappy jeans with crappy hair and he was going to kiss me.

'Mr Carmichael, Mr Rosings and Ms Morrison are here to see you.' Morag's voice echoed into the office from the intercom, and Braden tensed.

A strange mix of relief and disappointment flooded me, and I took an uneasy step back, turning toward the door. 'I'll let you get on.'

'Jocelyn.'

I twisted around, my eyes looking anywhere but into his. 'Yeah?'

'The picnic? Will you be there?'

The blood was still whooshing in my ears, and my body was still strung tight with anticipation for his kiss, but I shoved that all aside, remembering who he was and how much he scared me. I lifted my chin and met his gaze. 'As your little sister's roommate, yeah, I'll be there.'

'Not as my friend?' he teased.

'We're not friends, Braden.' I pulled his office door open.

'No. We're not.'

I didn't have to turn around to see his expression. I felt it in his words. Hurrying down the hall, I barely managed a quick wave to Morag before diving into the elevator that would take me away from him. What had happened? Where had the platonic, friendly Braden gone, and why was 'the Suit' back? I'd thought I wasn't his type. I'd thought I was safe.

No. We're not. Those words echoed in my head as I burst out of the office building and into the fresh air. It wasn't the words. It was the tone they'd been wrapped up in. And those words had been wrapped up in a whole lot of sexual intent.

Fuck.

10

I didn't go to Braden's picnic.

Well, I did, but I didn't.

Flabbergasted by his transformation back into 'schmexy Braden from the cab,' who couldn't take his eyes off me, I didn't know what to make of it in all my confusion. And yes, in all my scaredy-pantsishness! So I took the coward's way out and roped Rhian into helping me out of the situation – while also lying to her about why – without making it *seem* like I wanted to get out of the situation . . .

Saturday rolled by and it was a surprisingly hot day, and the Meadows – a large park on the other side of the city by the university – was crowded with sunbathers and people playing sports. Braden had managed to grab a spot in the shade. Adam, Jenny, Ed, and Braden were already there as Ellie and I approached, the sounds of laughter, kids shouting, and dogs barking creating a happy soundtrack to the scene. It was a perfect day, and the atmosphere in the Meadows was electric with contentedness. For a moment I wished I was staying.

'Uh . . .' I gazed down at the two hampers Braden had brought. They were so elaborate, I wouldn't have been surprised if he'd stolen them out of a Harrod's display. 'You call this a picnic?'

Braden had stood up when we arrived, hugging Ellie to his side and gesturing proudly at the hampers sitting on a beautiful chenille blanket. Now he looked confused. 'Yes.' He frowned at me. 'What would you call it?'

'A five-star restaurant on grass.'

The corner of his lip curled up in wry amusement. 'I had the staff at the restaurant make them up.'

'And what restaurant would that be, again? The five-star one?'

'I think she's making fun of you and all your money, Braden.' Ellie grinned at him. 'It is a bit much.'

He made a noise of disgruntlement. 'It's a bloody picnic. Sit. Eat. Shut up.'

She giggled and flopped down beside Adam, who wrapped an arm around her shoulders and squeezed her to his side. 'Nice to see you, Els.'

'Yeah, you, too.' She smiled at him but pulled away a little, causing me to raise an eyebrow. What was up with that?

'Well?'

I looked up at Braden to find him holding a hand out to me, unmasked heat in his eyes.

And Rhian saved me with perfect timing.

My cell rang and I made an apologetic face as I pulled it out of my pocket. 'Rhian, hey.' I turned and took a few steps away, not chancing that they might hear her on the other end of the line.

'I have an emergency,' she replied in a monotone. 'Abort the picnic.'

'Oh, no, you're kidding.' I played along, sounding all mothering and soothing. 'Are you okay?'

'Bloody hell, Joss, I thought you could lie,' Rhian grumbled. 'You're speaking like an alien who's heard of the human concept of "being concerned" but doesn't know how to execute it.'

I grit my teeth, ignoring her. 'Sure, I can talk. Just a sec.' I took a moment, trying to exude 'human concern' as I turned back to Braden and the gang. I had a feeling I was scowling more than frowning, but whatever. 'I'm sorry, guys, but I have to take a rain check.'

Ellie sat up, worried. 'Is everything okay? Do you need me to come?'

'No, I'm okay. Rhian just really needs someone to talk to. It can't wait. Sorry.' I chanced a glance at Braden and found he wasn't just watching me. He was *studying* me. Suspiciously. My eyes dropped quickly. 'See you later.' I walked away to their calls of good-bye and stuck the phone back up to my ear. 'I was being concerned,' I grouched at Rhian.

'Anyone who knows you knows that's not how you sound when you're concerned.'

'Well, luckily they don't know me.' Or maybe they did . . . Braden sure was looking at me funny.

'So you really don't like this Ed guy?'

I winced, remembering my lie. In an effort not to get into the whole Braden thing with Rhian, I'd lied and said that Ellie's friend Jenna's fiancé Ed was a bigot and I didn't want to be around him, but I also didn't want to hurt Ellie's feelings by saying no to the picnic. I felt bad about maligning Ed, but I didn't think it mattered too much since I wasn't expecting him and Rhian to ever meet.

'Nope, I don't.'

'You know I'm not buying it, right?'

I almost stumbled. 'Buying what?'

'You talk about Ellie all the time, Joss. I think I can safely say I understand enough about the woman to know she wouldn't be friends with a fuckin' bigot. Like I said, you can't lie for shit.'

Huh! That was so not true! 'I can lie. I am a damn good liar!'

'Oh, that's right. Yell that out while you're still walking away from them.'

Shit. I glanced around to make sure I'd put enough distance between us to not be overheard. I had. My heart slowed. 'You're a pain in the ass,' I grumbled, forgetting she'd just done me a favor.

She made a *pfftt* noise. 'You're the one who lied to me. Seriously, what's going on?'

I sighed. 'Can this be one of those things we don't talk about?'

'No.'

'Please, Rhian.'

'Have you spoken to your therapist about it?'

I frowned, wondering why she'd ask that. 'No . . .'

'Fine.' She sighed heavily. 'I won't ask about it, as long as you promise to talk to your therapist about it.

And you may lie, but I know you would never break a promise.'

'Rhian –'

'Promise.'

I shook my head. 'It's not therapy-worthy.'

'If it was worth lying to me about, then it's therapy-worthy. Sort your shit out, Joss, and promise.'

'Fine,' I agreed, but only because I knew it was Rhian's grumpy way of being a good friend.

Dr Pritchard had flowers on her desk. I smiled. She had taken note.

'You lied so you wouldn't have to spend time with Braden?'

I squirmed, wishing Rhian hadn't made me promise. 'Yup.'

'Before, when I asked you if you were attracted to Braden, you said "I was." Past tense. Were you telling the truth?'

No. 'Maybe not.'

'So you are attracted to him?'

Oh, what the hell . . . 'I've never been attracted to anyone as much as I'm attracted to him.'

The good doctor gave me a wry smile. 'Okay. But you're avoiding him even though he's made it perfectly clear that he's interested in you. Are you afraid of him, Joss?'

Honestly? 'Yes.'

'You have no intention of having any kind of relationship with him?'

'Were you not here when I told you about my past with guys?'

'That's not the same thing. For a start, you know Braden.'

'I don't want anything to do with him, all right?'

'You've just told me you're extremely attracted to this man. When you talk about him, it's clear to me that you like him, so, no, I wouldn't say you're all right – you don't want to *want* to have anything to do with him.'

'Same thing.'

'No, it's not. Why are you afraid of him, Joss?'

'I don't know,' I retorted, pissed off at the topic and at Rhian for making me discuss it. 'I just know that I don't want to start anything with him.'

'Why not?'

Jesus C, sometimes it was like talking to a brick wall with this woman. 'It would mess things up. With Ellie, with me, with him. No.'

She tilted her head to the side, her expression blank. She was good at this. 'Joss, maybe it's time to stop thinking fifty steps ahead and just let things play out naturally.'

'The last time I did that I woke up in bed with two strange guys and no panties.'

'I told you, that's not the same thing. You're not the same person, and Braden is not some stranger. I'm not telling you or asking you to do anything you don't want to do, concerning Braden or otherwise. But I am suggesting you stop predicting the future and take each day as it comes. Not forever, not even for a few months.

Try it for a few days, a few weeks even. I know it might be scary, but just . . . try.'

As I had been for the last few weeks, I was now working Saturdays at Club 39. Ellie had gotten home earlier, around dinnertime, stuffed full from the picnic and quite willing to just sit with me while I shoveled down some food before I needed to get ready for my shift.

'So, is everything okay with Rhian?' she asked, a little furrow forming between her eyebrows.

Guilt lodged in my throat. I hadn't felt too awful lying to Braden, since his three-sixty back into a predatory hottie with wicked eyes and a fuck-me smile was the sole reason I'd had to resort to lying in the first place. But lying to Ellie was a totally different ball game and it made me more than a little uneasy.

I mumbled around a mouthful of pasta, nodding and avoiding her eyes, hoping she'd get that I didn't want to talk about it.

At her answering silence I glanced up and found her watching me with curiosity. I swallowed. 'What?'

Ellie shrugged. 'Just . . . when Braden was walking me home, he said he thought maybe . . . that maybe you were lying about the call from Rhian so you could avoid the picnic.'

Jesus C, he had such an ego on him!

Never mind that he was right.

I guffawed. 'What? Because of him?'

She shrugged again. 'Was he right?'

More avoiding her eyes. 'Nope.'

'Well, just so you know, I get the impression he's planning something.'

I raised an eyebrow. 'Like what?'

She sighed, leaning back in her chair. 'With Braden you never know. I've just learned to recognize the signs. I know my brother better than he thinks I do. You're under his skin, Joss. I'm actually impressed he's been so patient. Although that probably means he's planning on doing whatever it takes to get you.'

I was surprised and couldn't pretend I wasn't. I sat back, momentarily abandoning my food. 'Under his skin? Whatever it takes?'

'As much as my brother's sex life makes me squeamish, I sometimes can't avoid hearing about it, and what I hear is that Braden always gets what he wants.'

I snorted. 'Please, Ellie, you think I'm what he wants? I'm not exactly his type. Jocelyn Butler doesn't come in Supermodel.'

Ellie looked adorably confused. 'You're kidding, right?'

'Um . . . about what?'

'You.' She pointed at me indignantly. 'You're seriously hot, Joss. Okay, you don't look like the pretty coat hangers Braden usually goes for, but you have those amazing eyes, that throaty phone-sex voice, a cup size I'd die for, and this broody standoffishness that's completely at odds with the seriously cool and funny person you are. Believe me, I've heard the guys talking. You're different, and guys being guys, they can't help seeing that as a challenge. You're hot.'

I was stunned. Was that really how these people saw me? Embarrassed, I picked up my fork, mumbling, 'Whatever.'

I could feel my roommate's smile without even looking up. 'You need a mirror.'

I shrugged.

Then Ellie grew quiet, and I found myself raising my gaze to make sure she was all right. She wasn't smiling now. 'No matter how much he denies it, Braden's interested in you, Joss. He asks me about you a lot, which he's never done before with anyone else and, believe me, I've lost at least three friends he serial-dated out of my life. I don't tell him much –'

You told him about my family.

'– because you don't say much, so of course he's even more intrigued. And like I said, Braden usually gets what he wants.'

'Please,' I huffed, 'give me a little more credit. I don't just fall into a hot guy's bed because he's used to getting what he wants. Guess what? I'm used to getting what I want, too. And what I want is *not* to fall into his bed.'

But it was like Ellie hadn't even heard me. 'If you don't manage to resist, just be careful with him, okay? He's been treated badly before, and I don't want to see that happen again.'

I heard my fork clatter to my plate as my fingers dropped it of their own accord. They were in shock, as was the rest of me. 'Wait. Are you worried about *me* hurting *him*?'

She smiled apologetically. 'You're a good person,

which makes the fact that you don't trust anyone really hard for the people who care about you. And Braden, when he cares about someone, has to know everything so he can cover all the bases and protect them. He has to be a guy people can trust. It's just who he is. If he started something with you, he'd only be hurt when you refused to let him in.'

I only sort of processed that. Mostly I just kept hearing *You're a good person, which makes the fact that you don't trust anyone really hard for the people who care about you.*

'Am I hurting you, Ellie?' I didn't want to admit how scared I was of her answer.

She exhaled heavily, seeming to weigh her words. 'At first you were. But knowing that you don't mean to hurt me helps. Do I wish you'd trust me more? Yes. Am I going to push it? No.' She stood up. 'Just know that if you ever do decide to trust me, I'm here. And you can tell me anything.'

I felt my throat close up, and I could only nod. In an effort to expel the moment, Ellie grinned down at me. 'I'm going out tonight with Braden and Adam. I was kind of cool with Adam today. It pissed him off.'

Hmm, what are you up to, young lady? 'Are you playing games with him?'

She scowled. 'Yesterday I discovered that he'd warned off Nicholas when he wanted to ask me out. So yes. I am.'

'Whoa, hold up.' I pushed my entire plate back now, totally confused. I'd met Nicholas. He was one of Ellie's friends who hung out at the apartment sometimes. He was also a tutor in her department. 'Adam did what?'

'I made some crack yesterday about not having had a date in months, and Nicholas said maybe I would have had a date if Adam would stop threatening prospective guys. I was completely confused, so Nicholas explained that he'd planned on asking me out months ago and that he'd gone to Adam for advice on where to take me.' Her jaw locked as she thought about it. 'Instead of answering, Adam warned Nicholas off, threatened him with bodily harm. Told him to stay away from me. No explanation. Just "stay away." '

I laughed in disbelief. 'And of course Adam's built and Nicholas looks like the promotions guy for *Twiglets*, so Nick backed down.'

'Exactly.'

'What the hell is Adam playing at?'

'That's what I want to know. He's messed with me, so I'm going to enjoy messing with him.'

I had to admit, I liked this side of Ellie. People thought they could walk all over her, but they were wrong. I grinned up at her. 'So the cold shoulder, huh?'

She grinned cheekily back at me, looking very much like a devilish angel. 'Full force tonight. I may even flirt with some random guy to see if that ruffles his feathers. Then I can ask him what the hell he's playing at. He was the one who didn't want to be anything more than friends.'

'Well, usually I don't condone game-playing, but in this case, he deserves it. I can't believe he's been warning off guys behind your back. I look forward to the next report, Miss Carmichael.'

Ellie laughed and hurried off to get ready for the evening, leaving me to finish dinner so I could jump in the shower before work.

Craig was on shift with me tonight along with Alistair, another bartender I'd worked with a few times before. The guys were in a fun mood, and the bar was busy. With the two of them trying their hardest to make me laugh, minutes were passing quickly and I was having a great time. Our good mood fed into the atmosphere of the club, and people had begun crowding around the bar to sip their drinks and enjoy one another's banter as well as mine and the guys'.

'I catch this cocktail,' Craig shouted down the bar to me, 'and you finally give in and shag me tonight, Joss.'

The customers tittered and laughed while I grinned back at him, pouring two Jack Daniel's and Cokes for the girls in front of me. 'No way, Tom Cruise.'

Craig had great reflexes. I would definitely lose that one.

'You're breaking my heart, darlin'.'

I waved him off, handing my customers their drinks and taking their money off them.

'What about me, Joss?' Alistair shot me a come-hither smile, but I knew he was only kidding. Alistair was happily engaged to an Irish girl who studied at Napier University. Still, he may have been loyal, but he was as big a flirt as Craig.

'Hmm, I'll think about it,' I teased back, loud enough for Craig to hear.

Craig groaned in pretend agony and pouted at the attractive girl he was serving. 'She's killing me.'

The girl giggled, her eyes bright on him. I rolled my eyes as Craig grabbed her hand and placed it on his chest. 'Feel that. That's my heart breaking.'

'Oh, man!' I rolled my eyes, cringing. 'Could you be any cheesier?'

'Of course I could.'

Alistair snorted. 'Believe it or not, that's one of his better lines.'

Craig whipped him across the head with a dishrag.

Sniggering, I passed Craig to get some rum and stood up on tiptoe to press a kiss to his cheek. That gained him a few cheers and one boo from Alistair.

Acting like idiots, we made the next hour fly by, and the tip jar filled up fast. The place got even busier, so my focus was completely on work and on my colleagues. The fact that I felt his eyes on me, then, said a lot . . .

Feeling my skin prickle, I jerked my head up and gazed out over the crowd toward the entrance; my eyes skimmed over Adam and Ellie as they followed Braden into the bar – Braden, who was walking beside a tall brunette who had her hand clamped on his arm.

Our eyes caught, and he didn't even acknowledge me. Instead he dipped his head and whispered something in the brunette's ear that made her giggle.

Something unpleasant flipped my stomach over, and I glanced quickly at Ellie. She was frowning at Braden and then scowling at Adam, brushing off his hand and striding after Braden, who had managed to convince some people sitting around a table to squeeze farther along the leather couch so that he, his mystery girl, Ellie, and Adam could sit down.

Everyone slid onto the couch except Ellie, who was now glaring daggers at them all. Adam said something to her. Ellie shook her head, looking extremely pissed off now, and Adam's face darkened. Like a whip, his hand came out and wrapped around her arm, yanking her down beside him. She struggled to get away from him, but his arm slid around her waist, his hand on her hip – a seemingly casual gesture, but his hold was clearly strong and whatever he whispered in her ear made her stop struggling.

It didn't remove the stony look from her face.

Worried, my eyes drifted to Braden, but he hadn't seen any of this. He was too busy chatting with the brunette.

Quickly, I turned away, completely unprepared for the rush of blood in my ears and the tightness in my chest.

I honestly didn't know where I stood with this guy. One minute he was giving me sex eyes and the next he wouldn't even acknowledge my presence. Well, I wasn't going to let him get to me. I served my customer and looked over at Alistair. 'I've seen some friends. Can you guys handle the bar while I get them drinks?'

'Sure thing.'

Ignoring the butterflies in my belly, I headed out onto the floor, stupidly thanking my boss for the sexy tank top he made me wear. If I had to be a little bit sweaty and held up for comparison to the brunette in the shimmery shift dress, then at least I was going to do it knowing I made that tank look good.

As I approached, Ellie's glacier-like expression melted and she smiled, relieved to see me.

'Hey, guys.' I announced myself loudly to be heard over the music. 'Can I get you drinks?'

'Oh, no need,' Adam told me with a smile. 'Darren is getting us some.' He pointed behind me, and I turned around to see a tall, clean-cut redhead waiting to push his way through the crowds to the bar.

I frowned in question. 'Darren?'

'My husband.'

The answer came from the brunette, and I looked at her in surprise, my eyes washing over her sitting next to Braden, my brain trying to make the scene in front of me and what she had just said make sense. I caught Braden's gaze, and he gave me a cool smirk, as if he knew I had assumed she was one of his Barbies. 'This is Donna. She's Darren's wife. Darren is the manager of Fire.'

Oh.

Well, I felt sheepish.

And then I caught Braden's eye again, and his smile deepened.

Ellie's suspicions from earlier played around in my brain. *Well, just so you know, I get the impression he's planning something.*

Goddamn him! He wanted me to think Donna was his date. He wanted to see relief spark in my eyes when

I realized she wasn't. And goddamn *me*, because I'd given him it.

'Nice to meet you.' I nodded at her. 'I'll send your husband back over, because he'll be standing there forever. I'll get your drinks order from him and bring it over.'

'Thanks, Joss.' Ellie smiled wanly up at me.

I frowned, hating to see her so uncomfortable. I reached out and squeezed her shoulder reassuringly, noting Adam's hand still clamped firmly on her hip. I shot him a look of warning over the top of Ellie's head that made his brow pucker in confusion. Ignoring Braden and whatever game he was up to now, I sashayed over to Darren, introduced myself, and sent him back to the others once I had the drinks order memorized.

'He's back,' Craig said in my ear, leaning around me as he shook a cocktail mix.

'Who?'

'That guy that Jo was going on about for ages after he was in here.'

'Braden.' I nodded, looking up at him. I hadn't realized how close he was standing, our faces inches apart. 'Jo wanted to make him her next sugar daddy.'

'From the feel of the daggers embedded in my back, I'd say he was interested in being someone else's sugar daddy.'

I pulled back, rolling my eyes. 'I don't need a sugar daddy, Craig.'

Craig shot a look back over at Braden. 'He bothers me. Last time he was in here he stared at you like he owned you, and tonight is no different. Something going on with you two?'

'Not a thing. I told you – I don't need a sugar daddy.'

Craig's eyes narrowed and he turned back to me, his face splitting into a mischievous smile. 'Maybe I need a sugar mama.' And then he was kissing me, one hand wrapping around the back of my neck to keep me there while his tongue slipped into my mouth and his body pressed close. Shock kept me in my place, and then the surprisingly nice feel of his lips on mine held me. Craig knew how to kiss, that was for sure. The catcalls and cheers broke through the moment, and I pulled back, pressing a hand against his chest.

'Uh . . .' I blinked, trying to figure out what was going on. 'What just happened?'

Craig winked at me. 'Just pissing off Mr Money over there and having a hot time doing it.'

I shook my head in disbelief and shoved him away, catching Alistair's grin as Craig swaggered by him, obviously pleased with himself. As I returned to preparing my friends' drinks I forced myself not to look up. I didn't want to know if Craig was right about Braden. I didn't want to acknowledge whatever feelings he might have for me and vice versa. But damn, it pleased me to know someone else had noticed his interest in me other than a hopeful, diehard romantic like Ellie. At least I knew I wasn't seeing things.

And wasn't I just a confused bundle of hormones?

Putting the drinks on a tray, I stepped out of the bar and ignored a 'Hey, sweetheart' from a customer who'd obviously caught *The Craig Show*, and I dodged around people so I could get the drinks to Ellie & Co. without spilling a drop.

'Here you go.' I put the tray on the table and started passing the drinks out.

'Uh, what was that?' Ellie asked me, her eyes round with curiosity, as she took her drink from me.

I don't know what possessed me to think that playing dumb was the way to go. 'What was what?'

Adam grunted. 'The guy with his tongue down your throat?'

I couldn't even look at Braden, because I could feel his burning gaze ... well ... burning into me. I shrugged. 'It's just Craig.'

And then I fled before they could ask me anything more.

But Craig wasn't happy with just sticking his tongue in my mouth. For the next forty minutes, he upped the flirting, kissing my neck, patting my ass, teasing me mercilessly with sex talk.

I guess my not being more upset about him kissing me let him think he could. And the truth is, I didn't do anything to make him think otherwise. I'd decided I wanted to send Braden a message.

We were not friends.

And we were never going to be anything more than not friends.

So we were ... nothing.

'Break time, Joss!' Alistair swatted me on the behind with a dishrag as he came in off his break.

I sighed. 'I'm going to take that damn thing off you if you don't stop using it as a weapon. Seriously, was that necessary?'

He grinned at me. 'What? Would you have preferred my tongue in your mouth?'

'Funny.' I swung around on my toes and strolled out of the back of the bar and into the staff area. There was a small locker room with a couch, a candy machine, and some magazines. A door to the right led into the manager's office, but Su was only in every second weekend, because she worked full-time during the week. When you closed Su's door, the noise from the bar disappeared. Head buzzing, adrenaline pumping because of Braden and Craig, I slipped inside with a can of Coke and slumped against her desk.

Encouraging Craig had been a bad idea. We'd always joked around, but tonight he'd crossed the line and I'd let him, and it was all because Braden was messing with my head. I hated the punch to my gut I'd experienced when I thought Donna was his date. I hated that he knew I'd felt something. I hated that I suspected he'd orchestrated the whole thing.

I had to find a way to let him know once and for all that nothing was ever going to happen between us.

My eyes snapped up from the carpet when Su's door opened, and I straightened, the butterflies in my stomach raging to life as Braden stepped inside and closed the door.

His eyes were calculating as they trained on my face, his features hard, clouded.

Braden looked pissed.

'What are you doing here?'

He didn't answer and my eyes did that thing again . . . lost control, running down his body, taking in the stylish black crew-neck sweater and tailored black pants. The only accessory he wore was an expensive platinum sports watch. His understated style and the fact that he hadn't shaved in a few days added up to a very hot package.

I felt that squeeze right in the bottom depths of my body, and my jaw locked. Why did he have to turn me on so much? It wasn't fair.

Covering, I took a swig of my soda. 'Well?'

'I don't like to share.'

My eyes flew to his, and if it was possible, he looked angrier than ever. In this tiny room, Braden was huge and intimidating, and the comparison between our sizes more notable. He could crush me like a bug if he wanted to. 'What?'

His eyes narrowed. 'I said, I don't like to share.'

I thought of Vicky. 'That's not what I've heard.'

'Let me rephrase.' He took a step toward me, seething. 'When it comes to you . . . I don't like to share.'

There was no time to process that. One minute I was staring incredulously up at him, the next the soda can was hitting the floor and my ass was on the desk as Braden collided with me. The heat and strength of him overwhelmed me as his large hand gripped the back of my neck and his other tugged my left thigh up, allowing him to push in between my legs and position me over the desk. His mouth crashed down on mine and the desire my body had been harboring for him for weeks took control of me. I clung to him, my hands digging into his back, my legs climbing his hips as my lips parted on an exhalation of relief that allowed his tongue inside my mouth to tease mine. The smell of him, the taste of whisky on his tongue, the feel of his warm hands gripping me tight – it . . . it all overpowered me and I made this throaty sound that I couldn't control.

His kiss wiped out any memory of Craig's.

Braden's hand tightened around my neck, and he groaned, the vibration of it surging through me, skimming down my body like hands, teasing my nipples, whispering across my belly, and sliding home between my legs. His kiss grew harder, more demanding – long, drugging kisses that stole my breath. We were panting and pulling at each other's mouths like we couldn't get deep enough, my nails scoring into his sweater as I tried to urge him closer.

When I became aware of his erection digging into my stomach I was lost. My belly squeezed, and I whimpered against his mouth, my panties drenched with arousal. The need grew hungrier as Braden's hand slid up my waist, brushing my breast and coming to a stop at the wide strap of the tank top. He broke the kiss, pulling back only an inch to gaze into my eyes. His own were dark, his lashes lowered over them, his lips bruised. I felt two of his fingers slide under my strap and lower it, tugging the left side of my top down so that my bra was visible. His gaze never left mine as he repeated the process with my bra strap.

Cool air hit my naked breast and my nipple puckered up invitingly. Braden's eyes dropped to it, and I felt his hand glide up to cup me. He caressed it, his thumb brushing over my nipple, and I gasped as it tightened and a bolt of lust shot between my legs. He looked back at me. 'You like that, babe?' he murmured, his eyes returning to my mouth. 'Do you like my hands on you?'

Well . . . yeah!

'Or' – his head dipped and his lips brushed softly against mine – 'will any man's do?'

It took a moment for those words to penetrate, and when they did I squashed the hurt and drew back in anger, my arms falling from around him to yank my bra and top back up.

'Fuck you,' I snapped and tried to push by him, only to have him press deeper into my legs, his hands grabbing hold of my wrists to stop the fists that were about to fly at him.

'What the hell was that out there?' he fumed at me, but he was definitely still turned on, his hard-on digging into me, making my own body go to war with my head.

'None of your business, that's what it was.'

'Are you fucking him?'

'None of your business!'

He made a low, irate sound under his breath and tugged on my arms. 'Considering I want to fuck you, it is my business. And considering you definitely want to be fucked by me, I think it's in your best interests to answer me.'

'You are an arrogant, egotistical asshat, you know that!' I raged, determined that this alpha-male douche bag was not going to control me. 'I wouldn't have sex with you if you were the last man on earth!'

It wasn't the most original comeback. I knew that. And it was definitely the wrong thing to say.

With my hands still pinned, Braden kissed me again, nipping angrily at my mouth, rubbing his hard cock against me in torment. My body keened and my lips fell open to let him in. I tried to put up the pretense of a struggle, but my body was far more interested in getting laid than in having control over the situation.

'Are you sleeping with him, Jocelyn?' he murmured sexily, his lips trailing lush kisses along my jaw.

'No,' I breathed.

'Do you want to sleep with him?'

'No.'

I was vaguely aware of the grasp around my wrists disappearing and my hands – with a mind of their own – reaching for purchase against Braden's taut stomach.

'Do you want me to fuck you?' he growled in my ear.

I shuddered hungrily. *Yes!*

Instead of telling the truth, I shook my head, trying to maintain some kind of control.

And then his hand was cupping me between my legs, two fingers rubbing hard against the seam of my jeans. Excitement flooded me in a torrent of shivers. 'Oh God . . .' I moaned, trying to press closer.

His lips brushed mine, and I reached for something deeper, something wetter, but Braden pulled back. 'Do you want me to fuck you?'

Anger exploded over me, and my eyes snapped open to glare at him. 'What the hell do you think?'

I tugged his head down, our lips crashing together as I pulled out of him what I wanted. His arms encircled my waist, pressing our bodies together as our mouths fed hungrily on each other. Impatience raged between us, and Braden's strong hands slid their way down my back and under my butt, lifting me easily. My body understood what he wanted, and my legs automatically wrapped around his waist as he turned around and took two steps to press me against the wall, his erection rubbing against the V of my jeans as his hips thrust into me. Satisfaction and need slammed through me, and I gasped against his mouth, silently begging for more.

'Oh, fuck – sorry!' Alistair's startled voice penetrated the fog, and I jerked back from Braden, my chest rising and falling rapidly as I tried to catch my breath.

I gazed at Alistair in horror as reality returned.

What. The. Hell.

Oh fuckity, fuckity, fuck fuck fuck! I sucked at self-control! 'Shit,' I breathed out.

Alistair's confused gaze flew between me and Braden before coming back to me. 'Break's over.'

I swallowed past the panicked lump in my throat. 'I'll be right out.'

As soon as he was gone, I felt the room close in on me. I was still wrapped around Braden. I unwrapped my legs, and Braden lowered me to the ground. As soon as my feet were stable, I pressed a hand to his chest, pushing him back. 'I need to get back to work.'

Gentle fingers grasped my chin and forced my gaze up to his. His expression was like granite, determined, controlled . . .and completely at odds with his swollen mouth and mussed-up hair. 'We need to talk.'

About my complete lack of control and willpower? 'I don't have time right now.'

'Then I'll come over tomorrow night.'

'Braden –'

His grip on my chin tightened, quieting me. 'I'll come over tomorrow night.'

This was not happening. How could I let this happen? 'Braden, I don't want anything to happen between us.'

He raised an eyebrow, clearly unconvinced. 'Tell that to your damp knickers, babe.'

I narrowed my eyes at him. 'You are such a dick.'

He grinned and leaned down to brush a soft kiss across my lips. 'I'll see you tomorrow.'

I grabbed ahold of his sweater, stopping him from leaving. 'Braden, I mean it!'

Chuckling, he patiently uncurled my fingers from his sweater and stepped back. 'I have a proposition. I'll come over tomorrow to discuss it.'

Argh! Was he deaf? 'Braden –'

'Good night, Jocelyn.'

'Braden –'

'Oh.' He turned back to me when he reached the

door, and his expression hardened. 'I'll be waiting until the end of the shift to put you and Ellie in a taxi. I see you flirting with that wanker again, and I'll knock his teeth out.'

And then – *poof!* He was gone.

I took stock for a moment, unable to believe what I'd just allowed to happen. But my lips were throbbing from those desperate kisses, my cheeks burning from the scrape of his two-day-old beard, my heart racing, and my panties (or knickers) definitely wet.

Worse . . .I was still so freaking turned on I had half a mind to shut the door and finish what he'd started myself.

Tomorrow this had to end. If Braden could so completely take me over like that, there was no way I could go any further with this.

Maybe I should move out.

My chest ached at the thought of leaving Ellie and the apartment on Dublin Street. No! I could do this. I could put the arrogant jackhole in his place.

I nodded, standing up on my feet, only to wobble a little.

I rolled my eyes. Why the hell did he have to be the human version of a sexually charged nuclear weapon? Grumbling, I put myself back together as much as I could and headed out to the bar, ignoring Alistair's quizzical looks, Braden's burning gaze, and Craig's attempts at flirting.

I liked Craig's teeth where they were, thank you very much.

11

My keys clattered against the walnut of the sideboard in the hallway, the first loud noise to break the silence between me and Ellie. After a busy night at the bar my head was usually buzzing, and it took me a few hours to unwind before I could head to bed, but tonight it was worse. I could still feel Braden on my mouth, on my breasts, between my legs. I could still smell and taste him, for God's sake. And I'd pretended I felt none of this as he'd done as promised and seen Ellie and me into a cab after my shift. In fact, I didn't say a word to him.

I didn't say a word to anyone.

Alistair and Braden were the only two who knew why. Craig watched me in confusion for the rest of the night, probably wondering where my good mood had gone, and I avoided Ellie's eyes. I avoided them in the bar, I avoided them out on the sidewalk, I avoided them in the cab, and I was avoiding them now. Kicking off my shoes, I kept my back to her, and then left her in the hall as I moved through to the kitchen to get a glass of water.

'Are we not going to talk about it, then?' Ellie asked quietly, following me.

I looked at her over my shoulder, pretending ignorance. 'Talk about what?'

She threw me a look of exasperation. 'About the fact that Braden was seething over your kiss with Craig, that he followed you into the staff room and didn't come back for twenty minutes, and that when he did come back he looked like he'd been mauled by a woman who'd been locked in an empty room without a vibrator or a man for ten years.'

I couldn't help it. I burst out laughing at the visual.

Ellie was not amused. 'Joss! Seriously, what's going on?'

The laughter died on my lips. 'He kissed me. We stopped. It's not happening again.'

'Braden won't back off if he thinks you're interested.'

'I'm not interested.' *I'm so interested.*

'I think you are and I —'

'Ellie.' I whirled around, my nerves stretched to the max. 'Just stop, okay? Please. I don't want to talk about this.'

She looked like a kid who'd had her favorite toy taken away. 'But —'

'Ellie.'

'Fine.' She sighed.

In an effort to take her mind off it, I leaned back against the counter with a concerned quirk of my right eyebrow. 'So what was up with you and Adam tonight?'

'I'm like you. I don't want to talk about it.'

Yeah right. 'Ellie . . .'

Her pale eyes narrowed unhappily. 'Okay, so I want to talk about it. Damn it, how can you be so good at keeping things to yourself?' She pouted. 'It's really hard.'

I grinned and shook my head. 'Not for me.'

She stuck her tongue out at me and slumped wearily into a kitchen chair. 'I'm knackered. Tonight was exhausting.'

'Hence the crabbiness?'

'I'm not crabby.'

'You're a little crabby.'

'Well, you would be too if you'd had to put up with Adam tonight.'

I slipped into the seat beside her, wondering if I should hit the gym harder this week in preparation for kicking Adam's ass. 'What happened, honey?'

'He's confusing me.' Ellie grimaced, eyeing me sadly. 'He keeps saying that we're just friends, but he acts like we're not. Braden's so wrapped up in you, he didn't even notice Adam's behavior tonight, and Adam used that to his advantage.'

'I did notice him getting all possessive on your ass, pulling you down beside him and all that.'

'Possessive? The harder I tried to be cool toward him, the more he got in my space. And then when Braden was with you, I called him on it. I asked about Nicholas and why he was acting so weird . . .'

'And what did he say?'

'That Nicholas wasn't good enough for me, and if I'd stop acting like a petulant child, he'd stop being overbearing.'

Guy was good. I laughed humorlessly. 'Nice way of sidestepping the actual question, huh?'

'Well, you'd know all about that,' she grumped.

I snorted. 'Meow.'

Ellie groaned. 'Oh, God, Joss, I'm sorry. I'm acting like such a bitch.'

'I find it charming. Really.'

She giggled and shook her head, her eyes drooping tiredly. 'You're crazy.' She stood up. 'But I love you.' She yawned as I froze at her words. 'I need my bed. We'll talk in the morning, try to make sense of Adam's nonsense, yeah?'

But I love you. 'Uh . . . yeah,' I replied, dazed.

'Night.'

'Night.'

But I love you . . .

'Come on,' I begged Dru. 'It'll be fun. Kyle will be there.'

Dru eyed me doubtfully. 'I totally embarrassed myself at the last kegger, Joss, and that didn't involve having to wear a bikini.'

I rolled my eyes. 'We all embarrassed ourselves at the last kegger. That's kind of the point. Come on. Nate will be there, and I really want to hang out with him tonight.'

'You mean hook up with him?'

I shrugged.

'Joss, maybe we should sit this one out. We've been going to a lot of parties lately.'

Grinning, I hooked an arm around her neck and drew her to my side. 'We're kids. We're supposed to party.' I need to party. I need to forget. *'And I don't want to party without you. I'll tell you what — I'll even upchuck on a JV cheerleader for you.*

That way, no matter what you do, I'll still have committed the most treasonous act of the evening.'

Dru laughed, hugging me close. 'You're crazy . . . but I love you.'

The walls closed in on me as my chest squeezed tight. I wheezed, trying to draw a breath.

I was dying.

The panic attack lasted longer this time, those words refusing to allow me to focus.

Eventually I struggled through to reality, pushing the memories back and allowing my body to relax.

When it was over, I wanted to cry, but crying would only make me weak. Instead I stood up on shaky legs and trod the memories into the kitchen tiles. By the time I'd changed and slid into bed, I could pretend it was all forgotten.

'You had another panic attack?' the good doctor asked softly.

Why had I mentioned it? We'd have to talk about *her*, and there was nothing Dr Pritchard could say to change what I had done. 'Yeah, it doesn't matter.'

'It does matter, Joss. What triggered this one?'

I stared at my feet. 'My friend.'

'Which one?'

My best friend. 'Dru.'

'You haven't mentioned Dru before.'

'No.'

'Why did Dru trigger a panic attack, Joss?'

My eyes slowly lifted to hers, raw pain burning

through me. 'Because she died.' I sucked in a deep breath. 'And it's my fault.'

I woke up just before noon and was immediately blasted by memories of the night before. Memories of Braden and the taste of what was possible between us. In an effort to forget, I spent lunch talking in circles about Adam with Ellie and fighting off the nerves that kept zinging in my belly every time I thought about Braden's promise to come see me that night.

I was just getting ready to head in for a bath when Ellie's phone beeped. She cursed as she scrolled through a message.

'What?' I asked lazily as I put away our lunch dishes.

'Braden's been pulled into the office again; he's missing another family dinner. I'll have to put up with twenty questions from my mum asking if he's all right.'

I ignored the disappointed pang in my chest. If Braden was working tonight he wouldn't be coming over after all. I should be freaking rejoicing. 'Your mom really looks out for him, huh?'

'Well, Braden's mum is a selfish, vain, money-grabbing witch who flitted in and out of his life whenever it suited her. He hasn't seen her in years. So . . . yes. My mum looks out for him because his own mum doesn't.'

How could his mother not care about him? He was Braden Carmichael, for Christ's sake. 'That's unbelievable. I can't imagine doing that to my own kid.' *Not that I'll be having any.*

Ellie gave me her sad eyes. 'Braden looks a lot like our dad. Braden's mum, Evelyn, really loved him. He ended things with her abruptly. Settled some money on her. When she told him she was pregnant, he said he'd look after Braden, but he didn't want anything to do with her. When she looks at Braden, all she sees is the man who broke her heart, so she's never been very loving. Ever. Braden spent the school years at home in Edinburgh with a distant but controlling father, and his summers flying around Europe watching his mum hook up with rich idiots who didn't have time for kids.'

My heart ached for little boy Braden.

And I made the mistake of letting it show on my face.

'Oh, Joss . . .' Ellie breathed. 'He's okay, you know.'

I don't care. I jerked back from her soft expression. 'I don't care.'

Her lips pinched together, but she didn't say anything. Instead she stood up, and when she walked by me she squeezed my shoulder.

I stared at the sink, as a disquiet settled over me. I wasn't ready to let anyone in yet, but my mask kept slipping whenever Ellie or Braden was around.

I grabbed my phone and headed into the bathroom to soak in the tub and drown it all out with some tunes, but as I was getting undressed my phone rang.

Braden Calling.

I stared openmouthed at the screen, trying to decide whether or not to answer it. I let it ring until voice mail picked up.

It rang again.

And I just stared at it again.

Two minutes later, as I sank into the tub, thinking I'd escaped, Ellie banged on the bathroom door. 'Braden says pick up the phone!'

My phone rang, and I closed my eyes. 'Fine!' I yelled back and reached for it. 'What?' I answered.

His deep chuckle rolled over me seductively. 'Hello to you, too.'

'What do you want, Braden? I'm in the middle of something.'

'Ellie says you're in the bath.' His voice was low. 'Wish I was there, babe.'

I could almost feel him there. 'Braden. What. Do. You. Want?'

He gave a huff of amusement. 'Just thought I'd call to let you know I can't make it tonight.'

Thank you, Jesus!

'I'm having a problem with a few suppliers on this development, and it's put us back a few weeks. I don't know when I'll be free this week, but I guarantee that the moment I get some time, I'm coming to see you.'

'Braden, don't do that.'

'After last night, there's no denying the promise of what's between us. I'm not backing off, so rather than coming up with a new defense – which I'm sure I'd find highly entertaining – just give in, babe. You know you're going to eventually.'

'Have I mentioned how annoying and arrogant you are?'

'I can still smell and taste you, Jocelyn. And I'm still fucking hard.'

My stomach flipped and I squeezed my legs together. 'God, Braden . . .' I breathed without thinking.

'I can't wait to hear you say that while I'm inside you. See you, babe.'

And after *that* parting line, he hung up.

I groaned, my head falling back against the tub.

I was so screwed.

12

You know how on those nature shows, when the cute little meerkat is strolling along on its four cute little meerkat legs to get back to her burrow, where all her little meerkat politics, drama, and family await her, and then this big-ass eagle comes swooping over-head . . . ?

The smart little meerkat runs for cover and waits that big-ass eagle out.

Some time passes, and the meerkat finally decides that the eagle got bored and went off to scare the crap out of some other cute little meerkat. So the meerkat crawls out from her hidey-hole to carry merrily on her way.

And just when that little meerkat thought she was home free, that big-ass eagle swoops down and catches her in his big-ass claws.

Well . . . I know exactly how that little meerkat feels . . .

Braden didn't call again, or text or e-mail. I spent the next few days keeping busy, fighting with my manu-script, erasing chapters that an eighth grader could have written, cleaning the apartment from top to bottom, and taking advantage of the distraction that was the

Edinburgh Festival with Ellie. We hit the Theatre Big Top in the Meadows to catch the show *The Lady Boys of Bangkok* – and damn, were those some pretty boys – went to the Edvard Munch exhibit out in the west of the city at the Scottish National Gallery of Modern Art, and we bought cheap tickets to see this young up-and-coming comedian who was stuck in a dingy room in the dated Student Union building on the university's main campus. Being in the Union brought back a lot of memories of Rhian, James, and I hanging out in there. I tried to let myself enjoy the crowds of the festival, the tourists, the smells of coffee and beer and hot food everywhere. Peddlers on the sidewalk, selling their wares – jewelry, posters, random mementos, flyers everywhere.

I'd also paid a traumatizing visit to my therapist and spoken about Dru for the first time.

Yeah. I didn't want to think about it.

Suffice to say, by the time Thursday rolled around, I'd managed to convince myself that Braden had only been playing with me. After all, if he'd been serious, he would have at least texted me to make sure I hadn't forgotten him, but nope. Nothing. *Nada.*

I'd changed my shifts at work from Thursday and Friday nights to Friday and Saturday nights, so I was free to hang out at home tonight. When Ellie told me she was staying with her mom because she felt like hanging out with her family, I stupidly didn't think anything of it. I was unprepared. I was relaxed, thinking Braden had forgotten about me.

I stuck my stupid head out of my stupid hidey-hole. That's when Braden swooped in like a big-ass eagle.

The apartment was silent except for the sitting room, where I was curled up in an armchair, sipping from a glass of wine and watching Zack Snyder's *300*. I realize now what a bad idea that had been. All those rippling muscles and the languid side effect of the wine ... I blame it all for what happened next.

'You know, you should really lock the door when you're home alone.'

'Shit!' I jumped, spilling wine all over my jeans. I shot out of the chair, glaring at Braden, who stood in the doorway looking unamused. What did he have to be pissed about? His favorite jeans hadn't just gotten ruined! 'Jesus C, Braden, for the last time, would you freaking knock!'

His eyes dropped to my stained jeans before flicking back to my face. 'If you promise to lock the door when you're home alone.'

I grew still, taking in his serious expression. Was he ... concerned about me? I frowned and dropped my gaze as I put my almost-empty glass on the coffee table. 'Fine,' I murmured, unsure of what to do with that.

'Ellie's gone for the night.'

My eyes shot to his face, and I found him watching me intently. He was wearing a suit, but he looked a little rumpled, like he'd been working for hours and had come to see me without making a pit stop at home. My stomach flipped as realization dawned. 'Did you orchestrate that?'

The left side of his mouth quirked up. 'For future reference, Ellie can be bought with a box of champagne truffles.'

I was going to kill the traitor.

Especially because Braden looked so damn good. That, and the fact that the costume department for *300* had done a number on my libido, caused the hormonal wreck that stood before Braden. I willed myself to take Dr Pritchard's advice and stop thinking fifty steps ahead. I told myself all the time that I was living life in the present because planning a future was just so terrifying. But while I lived my life in the present, I constantly worried about what awaited me tomorrow, and I think the good doctor was suggesting I take my own damn advice and live for today.

But with Braden?

It was too dangerous. I already knew I didn't want a relationship with him.

'I take it you weren't expecting me?' Braden asked as he settled himself on the couch.

Not wanting to appear intimidated, I slipped back into my seat on the armchair. 'No. I managed to convince myself through wishful thinking that we were done with whatever that was that happened before . . .'

He shrugged out of his jacket. 'You mean when I dry humped you against a wall?'

My jaw locked with irritation. If he'd been a character in a book, I would have hated his dirty mouth. As it was, my body loved his dirty mouth. No need to tell him that. 'You know, Braden, I've watched you over the last few months and you're such a gentleman to everyone but me. What's with that?'

'I want you in my bed. Gentlemen are boring in bed.'

Good point. 'Gentlemen are gentlemen in bed. They make sure you're having a good time.'

'I'll make sure you're having a good time and that you're okay with everything that we're doing. I just won't be well mannered about it.'

Stomach flip, belly squeeze. 'I thought we already discussed this. You and I are not happening.'

He frowned at me, leaning forward, his elbows on his knees and his hands clasped together between them. His shirtsleeves were rolled up again. It was like he knew what that did to me. 'We haven't discussed anything.'

I sighed heavily. 'Braden, I like you. I do. Yeah, you're an overbearing ass and you say whatever is on your mind without filtering out the filth, but you seem like a good guy and you're a good brother to Ellie.' Our eyes caught, and I almost flinched at the pang of attraction that zinged across my chest. 'Ellie has become a really good friend and I love living with her here. I don't want to mess that up. And I don't want to be in a relationship. With anyone.'

He looked at me so long in silence, I didn't know if he was ever actually going to respond. I had just decided it might be best to leave the room and Braden to his thoughts, when he relaxed back against the couch. His eyes darkened. I knew that look. *Uh-oh*. 'Good thing I'm not proposing a relationship.'

It was safe to say I was completely confused. 'Well, what are you proposing?'

'Just sex.'

What? 'What?'

'You and me. Just sex. Whenever we want. No strings attached.'

'Just sex,' I repeated, feeling the words roll around my mouth and brain. *Just sex.* Sex with Braden whenever I wanted with no strings attached. 'What about everything else? Ellie, the apartment, the whole gang hanging out?'

Braden shrugged. 'None of that has to change. We'll be friends who hang out and have sex with each other.'

'And what would we tell people?'

'It's nobody's bloody business.'

I tilted my head, exasperated. 'I meant Ellie.'

'The truth.' He eyed me carefully. 'I don't lie to my sister.'

'She won't like it.'

Braden chuckled. 'I don't give a flying fuck if Ellie likes it or not. In fact, I'd prefer it if my wee sister stayed clear of my sexual business.'

'That'll be kind of hard since the person you want to have sex with lives with her.'

That didn't bother him in the least. 'Your bedrooms are on opposite sides of the flat. And you can always visit my bed in my flat.'

Hmm. Braden's apartment. I was curious to see it.

No! No, stop it! 'I can't.'

'You can't, or you won't?' His eyes narrowed dangerously.

Stomach flip, belly squeeze. I closed my eyes. I could feel his body pressed against mine, feel his tongue stroking mine, and his hand gentle but firm against my breast. Oh God. My eyes flew open and I found his gaze had softened on me. 'Just sex?'

I could tell he was trying to stifle a smile, like he knew he was winning. 'Well . . . almost.'

What? 'Almost?'

'I need someone to accompany me to business dinners and whatever inane social events Morag has scheduled me to appear at. It would be nice to go with someone who wasn't expecting a marriage proposal or a diamond necklace at the end of the night.'

'That's not just sex. That's like an arrangement. Like the arrangement you usually have with all those Barbies you date. Which brings me to why me? Braden, you've got a lot of money and you're not exactly hard on the eyes – although I doubt you need me telling you that and giving you something else to be a cocky bastard about – so why not go out and get one of those tall, skinny blondes who will jump at the chance of jumping you?'

Surprise flashed across Braden's face, and he dipped his head down. 'One: because they need me to care about them. They want me to talk about my feelings, and they want me to buy them shit. *We're* talking about taking that out of the picture, which works for both of us. And two: seriously?'

I frowned. What did he mean by 'seriously'?

'Well' – he shook his head, grinning now – 'you always surprise me.'

'How's that?'

'I just assumed you knew how sexy you are. Apparently you don't.'

Wow. I flushed inwardly and rolled my eyes at him, like his words hadn't penetrated my armor. 'Whatever.'

My blasé response didn't deter him. He was determined to answer my question. 'No, you don't look like my usual woman. And yes, I like long legs. And yours are short.'

I glowered at him now.

Braden grinned. 'And yet they still gave me a semi-hard-on in the taxi when you were wearing those little shorts. And again when you wore them at Elodie and Clark's.'

My mouth dropped open. 'You're lying.'

He shook his head, enjoying himself. 'You've got great legs, Jocelyn. An amazing smile when you use it on occasion. And fantastic tits. And yeah, I usually date blondes. But you're a blonde. I think.' He laughed when my glower turned into a full-on glare. 'Doesn't matter about the color. You never wear it down, and I can't get the thought of you beneath me, and that hair spread out across my pillow while I move inside you, out of my head.'

Oh. God.

'But I think mostly it's your eyes. I want something from them no one else gets.'

'And what's that?' I asked, my voice low, almost hoarse. His words had affected me as deeply as any aphrodisiac.

'Softness.' His own voice had deepened in the highly sexual atmosphere. 'I want them soft the way a woman's can be only after she's come for me.'

I gulped inwardly. Outwardly, I tilted my head to the side with a wry grin. 'You're good with the words. I'll give you that.'

'I'm good with my hands. Will you let me give you that?'

I laughed and his answering grin was wicked and beautiful. I sighed and shook my head again. 'It sounds like more than just sex, Braden. You're asking for companionship. That's complicating things.'

'Why? It's just two friends going on a few dates and having sex afterwards.' He sensed my unmoving doubt on that one, because he shrugged. 'Look, when have I ever gotten serious about a woman? I want you. You want me. It's hanging over what should have been a perfectly nice friendship, so let's just deal with it.'

'But adding date nights into it? Doesn't that extend the time period on this thing?'

I thought I saw a flash of annoyance in his eyes, but it was gone with a flicker of his lashes. 'You want to put a time period on it?'

'A month.'

And then he grinned, realizing I was giving in.

Shit. I *was* giving in.

'Six.'

I snorted. 'Two.'

'Three.'

We stared at each other, and as if it suddenly occurred to us that we were talking about how long we were intending to explore a sexual relationship, the already hot tension between us burned deeper, and the air thickened. It was like someone had lassoed a rope around the two of us and was tugging and tugging, trying to draw us closer. An image of us in my bed, naked and writhing, flashed across my mind and my body instantly responded. Panties sufficiently damp, my nipples joined the party and tightened – visibly. Braden's eyes dropped to my breasts and started to smolder before they returned to my face.

'Done,' I murmured.

His next question was unexpected but practical. 'Are you on the pill?'

I'd had irregular, heavy periods, so I was on the pill to stop that. 'Yes.'

'Have you been checked?'

I knew what he meant. And after my last sexual encounter and not remembering what the hell had happened, yeah . . . I'd been checked for STDs. 'Yes. Have you?'

'After every relationship.'

'Then I guess we're good to go.'

The words were barely out of my mouth before Braden was standing above me, his large hand reaching out for mine, his face determined, serious. His eyes blazing.

'What? Now?' I squeaked, totally unprepared.

He cocked an eyebrow. 'You want to wait?'

'I just . . . I thought I'd have time to get ready.'

'Get ready?'

'You know . . . perfume, nice lingerie . . .'

With a grunt of amusement, Braden took hold of my wrist and hauled me out of my chair. My small body slammed into his, and his arms came instantly around me, holding me to him. A hand slid down my hip and around to my butt. He squeezed it lightly and pressed me against him, his erection hard against my belly. I stifled a moan, tilting my head back to meet his eyes. They glittered down at me. 'Babe, nice lingerie is for seducing a man. I'm already fucking seduced.'

'Okay, but –'

His mouth cut me off, crushing against mine, his tongue seeking immediate entry. His kiss was deep and wet and it said *This isn't a date – this is sex.* That was fine by me. I groaned and slid my arms up around his neck, and Braden took that as my acquiescence.

One minute my feet were on the ground; the next I was in Braden's arms, my legs around his waist, my hands in his hair as we kissed and bit and nipped and licked at each other's mouths, learning the taste and feel of each other.

'Fuck,' Braden responded, the word vibrating against my lips.

No time to complain about him leaving my mouth – I felt the air blow through my hair, and we were moving into the hall, down the hall, into my bedroom, and then

I was falling. I hit the mattress with a surprised 'oof' and stared up at Braden indignantly. 'Was that necessary?'

'Strip,' he answered gruffly, unbuttoning his shirt with quick, nimble fingers.

My sex clenched. My jaw did, too. 'Excuse me?'

He stopped what he was doing and leaned down over me, his hands on either side of my hips on the mattress, his face in mine. 'A second proposal: When we're fucking, you don't argue with me.'

'Bu—'

'Jocelyn,' he murmured in warning.

My eyes dropped to his mouth, the mouth I wanted back on mine. If that meant not arguing during sex, fine. I'd just argue with him when we weren't having sex. 'Why do you insist on calling me Jocelyn?' I made sure my tone wasn't argumentative, just curious. Because I *was* curious.

His lips touched mine, soft, gentle, and he pulled back, those pale-blue eyes of his bright with heat. 'Joss is a girl's name. Possibly a tomboy's name.' He smirked. 'Jocelyn, on the other hand, is a woman's name. A really sexy woman's name.' He pulled back. 'So strip, Jocelyn.'

Okay. He could call me Jocelyn.

I sat up and lifted the hem of my shirt, pulling it up and over my head. I threw it across the room and took a moment to watch Braden strip out of his own shirt. It dropped to the floor and I followed it before letting my eyes travel back upward. I smiled in anticipation at the sight of the hard-on tenting his pants, and then my mouth went dry as I took in his naked torso.

Braden worked out. Like, *really* worked out.

The waist of his pants hung low, showing off his flat stomach and the sexy V-cut of his muscles there. I bit my lip. I wanted to touch him. My eyes followed his six-pack up to a strong chest and broad shoulders. And it was all nicely wrapped up in unblemished golden skin.

'Fuck, Jocelyn.' I looked up and found his gaze blazing even brighter than before. 'If you keep looking at me like that, this is going to be over far sooner than I'd like.'

Hmm. I liked that. I liked that I had power over him. 'Well, we can't have that.' I grinned saucily and reached around to undo my bra. The cold air hit my naked breasts as I dropped the bra off the side of the bed, and this time I was treated to Braden's perusal.

His eyes drifted from my chest to my face, and suddenly he looked a little angry. I stiffened in surprise. 'Do you know what it's been like for me since that day in the flat? Sitting across from you in bars, at dinner, knowing that underneath all the attitude is every man's fucking fantasy.'

Oh, he was good.

His eyes narrowed as he reached for the buttons and zipper on his suit pants. The zipper slid down loudly. 'I'm going to make you pay for making me wait to have you.'

The throbbing between my legs got worse. *Sounds good.*

I reached up and unwound my hair, letting it fall

around my shoulders in all its glory, shivering as the need in Braden's eyes sharpened. 'Fine,' I agreed huskily.

I don't know which one of us got our pants off faster after that, but one minute I was trying to take back some control with all my sexy attitude and hair, and the next minute I was pantyless, on my back, my breasts pressed against Braden's chest, my thighs spread open to accommodate him between my legs . . . and I was staring up into his eyes, breathless with anticipation.

'What are you waiting for?' I murmured.

His gave me a wry smile. 'For you to back out.'

I huffed in annoyance. 'I'm naked, aren't I?'

'So? You have been before.'

'Braden!' I hit his shoulder as he chuckled softly, and his laughter caused his lower body to move – that long, thick, delicious cock of his sliding down over my belly and back up again.

I gasped at the pulse of pleasure the teasing action caused, and Braden groaned in answer, his lips falling on mine. I'm sure the kiss was meant to be slow, sexy, tormenting. It started out that way. But weeks of fore-stalling this moment had made us both a little impatient. The kiss grew aggressive, bruising, my hands gripping tight to his hair, his hands kneading my waist, my ribs, my breasts. My breasts were particularly sensitive, and when his thumb brushed my nipple, my hips jerked against him.

'You like that, babe,' he murmured, not really asking as the answer was obvious. His lips trailed kisses down my jaw and neck, my hands slipping out of his hair to his shoulders as he stopped at my right breast. He placed a soft, deliberate kiss to the rise of it, and I swear I stopped breathing. Another kiss. Another.

'Braden . . .' I begged.

I felt him smile against my breast just before I felt the wet heat of his tongue against my nipple as his lips closed around it, drawing it in deep. A sharp lance of lust shot through my sex. 'God, Braden!'

He did the same to the other breast, and I found myself tilting my hips into his, more impatient it seemed than even he was. Then again, it had been longer for me.

'Babe,' his voice rumbled above me as his hand slid down to my hip, stilling me. 'Are you wet for me yet, Jocelyn?'

Yes. God, yes. 'Braden . . .'

'Answer me.' I could feel his hand moving downward, felt the graze of his fingers high on my inner thigh, teasing me. 'Tell me you're wet for me.'

When I thought about this afterward, I couldn't believe I wasn't embarrassed by his question or his demand. Or how turned on I was giving in to that demand. I'd never had a lover speak dirty to me during sex, but it was working for me. 'I'm wet for you,' I whispered against his mouth.

Satisfied, he kissed me, a deep, exploring kiss, and his tongue slid over mine as his fingers traveled an inch higher. I jerked at the first touch of them brushing against me. No one else's fingers had been down there in a while. In response, Braden's kiss grew harder, his touch gentler. My lips broke from his in a moan as he slid his thumb against me, finding my clit and pressing down on it.

'Baby, you're so fucking wet,' he groaned, his head falling to the bed beside mine, his lips on my neck as he removed his thumb from my clit. Before I could voice my protest, he slid two thick fingers slowly inside my channel. My knees fell open as I reached for more, my hands clinging to Braden's naked back as I surged up for that *more*.

'More,' I pleaded.

And he gave me more, thrusting his fingers in and out of me. He rose up on his other arm to look down at my face as he worked me toward orgasm.

'Yes,' I sighed, feeling it coil and tighten.

And then his fingers were gone.

'What –'

'You're not coming until I'm inside you,' he told me, his features taut with need as he pinned my hands to the bed. 'I want to feel you come around me.'

Well, I wasn't going to argue with that.

I held on to my sigh of pleasure at the feel of his throbbing cock at my entrance. He rubbed against me teasingly, and I wanted to grab his ass and force him inside. But he held tight to my wrists, grinning as if he knew exactly what I was thinking. As torture, he circled his hips, teasing me more.

'Braden,' I growled impatiently.

This only made him laugh. 'What, babe?'

'If you don't hurry up, I'm backing out.'

'Well, we can't have that.' He thrust hard inside me,

and I whimpered, stiffening at the flinch of discomfort I felt as my body struggled to accept his size.

Braden's whole body tensed, his eyes dark. 'Are you okay?'

I nodded, exhaling as my body relaxed around him.

His grip on my wrists loosened, but he didn't let me go. Instead he nudged forward tentatively, his jaw locking, his eyes closing as if he was in pain. 'Jesus, Jocelyn,' he breathed hoarsely. 'You're so fucking tight.'

I lifted my hips, urging him to move, feeling the pleasure start to coil again, feeling full of him and desperate for satisfaction. 'It's been a while.'

His eyes flew open. 'How long?'

'Braden . . .'

'How long?'

I sighed. 'Four years.'

'Babe.' He dipped his head and kissed me lightly, and when he pulled back, his cocky grin was in place. He surged deeper inside me, his hands moving up from my wrists so his fingers could tangle through mine. Like this, he held me as he gently moved inside me, taunting me toward climax and then yanking me back.

'Harder,' I gasped.

His lips skimmed my ear. 'Ask for it, Jocelyn.'

'Braden, harder. Fuck me harder.'

I raised my hips, and Braden slammed back into me. I cried out, my neck arching. He groaned against my ear as he thrust hard, our bodies so focused on reaching climax that his hands let go of mine. He cupped my ass, tilting me higher so that his cock could slide deeper.

'Come for me, babe,' he ordered roughly.

I nodded, feeling the pressure in my body build. I was almost there. 'Braden, Braden . . .'

His hand slipped between my legs and his thumb massaged my clit in beautiful circles.

'Oh God!' I cried out as he wrenched the orgasm out of me, my sex tightening and pulsing around his cock.

'Fuck.' His eyes widened as he stared down at me, watching me as I came long and hard. I closed my eyes, desperate to break the connection between us in that moment, and I felt Braden's head drop to the crook of my neck as he shuddered, his deep grunt as he came inside me making me spasm against the wet heat of his release.

He relaxed into me, his breath hot on my neck. My muscles felt warm and gooey, my thighs resting against the tops of his. We smelled of fresh sweat and sex, and I was still pulsing around him.

Wow.

Best. Sex. Ever.

Braden kissed my neck and raised his head, his features soft with postcoital satisfaction. 'Jocelyn,' he murmured before he kissed me slowly, wet and deep. When he pulled back, he slid out of me carefully, rolling onto his side, his hand stroking tenderly across my belly as he did.

I stared at him, wondering a lot of things.

Had it been just as earth-shattering for him? He'd come hard, too, so I hoped so.

And what happened now? Why was he just lying there, staring at me?

I looked up at the ceiling, unnerved by that soft look in his eyes. 'Um . . . thanks.'

Feeling the mattress shake, I turned my head on the pillow to find Braden laughing at me.

'What?'

He shook his head, clearly amused at me for some reason. He leaned over and pressed another kiss to my mouth. 'You're welcome.' He grinned, his thumb brushing my lower lip. 'And thank you. Fucking great sex, babe.'

I burst out laughing. From relief. From hysteria. From disbelief.

I'd just had sex, phenomenal sex, with Braden Carmichael. And I was pretty sure we were going to do it again sometime. And I wanted to.

But on my terms. 'I'm going to clean up.' I got out of the bed, unabashed by my nudity since he'd made it perfectly clear that he liked what he saw. As I strolled casually down the hall to the bathroom, I hoped Braden knew what 'I'm going to clean up' really meant: By the time I got back to the bedroom, his ass better be dressed and ready to leave.

But when I got back from the bathroom, his ass was still lying in bed, waiting for me.

I threw my hands to my hips, a scowl furrowing my brow. 'What are you doing? Shouldn't you be dressed?'

He flashed a taunting smile my way. 'Do you know how sexy you are right now?'

I rolled my eyes. 'Braden.'

At my warning tone, his smile disappeared, and he sat up. 'I'm not leaving yet.'

'But you *are* leaving?'

He didn't respond verbally. Instead he reached over and grabbed my hand, hauling me onto the bed. Damn, he was strong.

'Braden,' I grumbled as I found myself lying on my side with his arms around me.

He kissed my forehead. 'You smell good.'

Uh, what?

I glanced up from under my lashes to see that he had closed his eyes.

Was he serious? Did he think he was sleeping with me?

I wriggled out of his hold and turned over, shimmying away, my back to him, hoping he'd take my hint. No such luck. Seconds later his strong arm was around my waist, his hand flat against my stomach, and my body was sliding back across the sheet, colliding with his.

His arm tightened around me, his front hot against my back. I felt the shivery soft touch of his lips against my shoulder. 'Night, babe.'

Stunned, I lay there in silence for a moment.

This was not what I'd been expecting. Not at all. It certainly didn't scream *We're sexual partners only!*

And it felt good.

And scary.

'Are we . . . spooning?' I asked loudly, trying to insert bite into my tone and failing.

I felt the huff of his breath on my neck. 'Go to sleep, babe.'

Uh . . . no!

As if sensing my imminent escape, Braden pulled me even tighter against him, pushing his leg between mine, hooking it around one of them. 'Go. To. Sleep.'

Such a bossy a-hole.

'Spooning was not in the terms of our agreement.'

He ignored me. After a minute or two of silence I heard his breath even out. He really was going to sleep! I tried to wiggle but his muscles just flexed in warning, and I wasn't strong enough to get away.

So I lay there, waiting.

I was wonderfully exhausted by all the amazing sex, and sleep sounded like heaven, but I was determined that I was not falling asleep in his arms. That was just a little too . . . relationshipy.

Forcing myself to stay awake, I lay in his arms for half an hour, until I felt his body completely relax. Biting my lip to stifle any heavy breathing that may have been caused by the exertion of having to move like a ninja, I lifted his arm as gently as possible and moved my leg out from under his.

I froze.

I swore I thought I heard his breathing change.

I listened carefully, relaxing at the sound of even breaths.

Stealthily, silently, I shifted away from him, hovering near the edge, my legs slowly descending to the floor. My butt was just off the bed when I found myself tugged back with such force, I bounced off the mattress with a choked scream.

My heart pounded against my ribs as Braden expertly rearranged me, moving so fast, I was underneath him in seconds, my wrists pinned above my head and his body straddling mine.

He did not look happy. 'Will you go to fucking sleep?'

I glared up at him. 'Not with you in my bed. This was not part of the deal.'

'One: I bought the bed. Two: It's just sleeping, Jocelyn.'

I ignored the bed comment since it was true. 'No. It's spooning. You said it was just sex. No spooning. We fuck, we have fun, you go home. That's the deal.'

He studied me intently for a moment and then lowered his head until his lips were almost touching mine. 'We fuck, we have fun, and then we spoon. I don't go home. I don't go home because sometimes in the middle of the night I wake up, and when I wake up, I want to fuck. And for some baffling reason, the person I want to fuck is you. Now, I'm only going to say this one more time: Go to sleep.'

He let me go only to fall at my side and tuck me back against him.

Spooning.

I clenched my jaw. 'And what if I don't want to be woken up so you can have your way with me?'

He pressed his face into my neck, and I felt him smile against my skin. He kissed me and pulled back. 'Why don't I give you a preview of what I intend to do in order to wake you up?'

And then I was flat on my back again as Braden kissed his way down my body. Knowing how sensitive I was, he stopped at my breasts, one hand playing with my nipple, his mouth sucking on the other. I sighed, lighting up for him, the fight totally forgotten. Already I was growing wet for him again, my hips restless. And he knew that, too. Lifting his head from my breasts, he kissed between them and followed an invisible line down my torso, dipping his tongue in my navel, and moving farther down, his lips skipping across the soft, quivering skin of my lower belly.

He pushed my thighs apart and then his mouth was on me.

I whimpered as his tongue licked me, playing with my clit. I was panting by the time his fingers joined in. My hands glided through his hair, tightening, urging him closer as he masterfully spurred on my climax, licking and finger-fucking me into a frenzy.

'Braden,' I moaned when he withdrew his fingers. I was so close. So goddamn close . . .

And then he was thrusting them back inside, in and out, in and out, his tongue working its magic on my clit.

'Braden!' I exploded against him as he wrung every inch of that orgasm out of me. My body shuddered with more spasms as he crawled back up beside me.

Okay, that one had been just as out-of-this-world-amazing as the last one he'd given me.

I lay there panting, staring at the ceiling in dazed wonder until Braden appeared above me again. He didn't say a word, but when he leaned down and kissed me, letting me taste myself as he flicked his tongue against mine, I felt like the depth of that kiss was saying it all for him.

He'd made his point.

My useless limbs didn't protest when I found myself in his arms again.

Spooning.

' 'Night, babe,' his voice rumbled in my ear.

' 'Night,' I mumbled, my eyes fluttering closed.

Then it was lights-out.

13

I was lying there, staring at my ceiling, feeling the twinge between my legs and the ache in my muscles when I moved.

I'd had the best sex of my life last night.

With Braden Carmichael.

And then we'd spooned. I frowned at that, my head turning on the pillow to eye the empty spot beside me on the mattress. I didn't like the idea of spooning being part of the deal, but since it came with added benefits, I was going to swallow my discomfort and deal with it. Especially since Braden had done the right thing and left without waking me.

That screamed *just sex!*

This could work. I could do this.

The sound of a cupboard shutting in the kitchen drew me out of bed, my heart picking up speed. Was Ellie home? And then my eyes fell to the end of the bed. Braden's shirt. He'd picked it up off the floor. I checked my alarm clock. Eight o'clock.

Shit. He was still here. What was he doing here? Didn't he have work? Irritation niggled its way into my blood, and I could feel my cheeks getting hot as I hopped out of bed, digging out a tank top and pajama shorts. On the move, I twisted my hair into a messy ponytail and went to deal with him.

I stopped short at the kitchen doorway and felt that all-too-familiar squeeze of lust. Standing pouring milk into two mugs of coffee, Braden was hot. He had pulled on his suit pants but was of course shirtless. The muscles in his broad shoulders moved as he did, and I couldn't help but remember how good they felt moving underneath my hands.

'Two sugars, right?' he asked before looking over his shoulder with a small smile.

That smile hit me in the chest like a punch. It was intimate. It was affectionate.

It hurt like hell. My expression hardened. 'What are you still doing here?'

'Making coffee.' He shrugged, adding the sugar and stirring.

'Don't you have work?'

'I have a meeting in a few hours. I have time for coffee.' He smiled again as he crossed the kitchen to hand me my drink, my hand wrapping around the hot mug just as his mouth came down on mine. Addicted to the taste of him, I kissed him back. It wasn't a long kiss. Short but sweet. When he pulled back I was scowling.

Braden sighed and took a sip of his coffee before asking, 'What now?'

'You're still here.' I turned on my heel and headed into the sitting room, tucking my feet underneath me as I curled into the corner of the couch. Braden sank into the armchair and I tried not to ogle him. My scowl deepened. 'And you're shirtless.'

His mouth quirked up at the corner as if he knew exactly what the sight of him half-naked did to me. 'I need coffee before I can function, and since I was making coffee for myself, I thought I'd make one for you.'

'Surely you can function enough without coffee to call a cab?'

'And we need to talk,' he added.

I groaned and took a big gulp of hot coffee. 'About what?'

'About your shifts at the bar, for one thing. I might need you to accompany me on weekend nights. Any way you can see about having your shifts changed?'

I answered with a saccharine smile.

Braden raised an eyebrow. 'Is that a yes or a no?'

'That's a big fat *hell no*. Braden, I'm not changing my schedule for you.' I shrugged. 'Look, I'll meet you halfway at best. If you have somewhere you want me to be and you give me plenty of notice, I'll make a shift swap.'

He nodded. 'Sounds good.'

'Is that it? Are we done?'

His eyes narrowed, and I felt a sudden change in the air. Braden leaned forward and I leaned farther back into the couch even though there was a coffee table between us. 'Stop treating me like a one-night stand you can't get rid of, Jocelyn. It's getting on my last nerve.'

I was seriously confused. 'You said this was just sex.'

'I also said we were friends and you agreed. Are you this rude to all your friends?'

'Sometimes.' He gave me a warning look, and I exhaled heavily. 'Look, I just don't want this to get complicated. Don't you think spooning and then making me coffee in the morning is a little . . .'

'A little what?'

'Ugh.' If he was going to be obtuse about it, I was giving up. 'I don't know.'

Braden put his mug down and stood up, coming toward me slowly. My eyes followed him half warily, half lustfully, my gaze trailing up his six-pack to his throat. I really wanted to kiss his throat. He sat down, close, his arm reaching along the back of the couch so that I was caged in. 'I've never done this before. I'll bet that you haven't either. So let's play it by ear. No rules. No preconceived ideas of how this should be. Let's just do what feels natural.'

'You're wrong,' I muttered. 'I have done this before.'

To my surprise, I watched Braden's expression change instantly from soft to hard. The look he gave me was unfathomable as the muscle in his jaw ticked. I felt like he was trying to bore inside me, but I couldn't look away despite how uncomfortable it felt. 'Done this before?' he asked softly.

I shrugged. 'There was nothing in the deal about sharing our sexual histories. Suffice to say, I know what I'm talking about. And there is no spooning or coffee in the morning in these kinds of deals.'

'Done this before?' he repeated. 'I thought you said you hadn't had sex in four years. That would make you eighteen the last time you had sex.'

Oh, I saw where he was going with that. I narrowed my eyes. 'So?'

'When I was eighteen, most of the girls I knew thought they were in love with whoever they were shagging.'

'And?'

Braden shifted closer, trying to intimidate me. 'So when have you done this before?'

'That's none of your business.'

'Fucking hell, Jocelyn, can you not answer one personal question?'

Anger blazed through me. I knew it. I freaking knew it. 'That's it, we're done. This was a complete mistake.' I moved to get up but found myself tackled back onto the couch, flat on my back with Braden lying over me. I stared up at him in disbelief. 'You are such a caveman!'

An all-too-familiar pissed-off Braden breathed dragon fire on me, his face inches from mine. 'We're not done. We've barely even started.'

I shimmied under him but that only concluded in him pressing his hips deeper into mine, and that only led to him hardening against me, and that only led to my skin flushing as my panties grew damp. *Shit!* 'Braden, this isn't going to work. I'm not your girlfriend. You said no touchy-feely emotional crap.'

He bowed his head, his shoulders shaking. He gazed down at me from under his long lashes, laughing incredulously. 'You are not like other women.'

'No,' I answered honestly, 'I'm not.' He shifted again, getting comfortable on top of me, and I felt the brush of his hard cock teasing me between my legs, my thighs opening involuntarily. I bit my lip to stifle a gasp, and Braden's eyes flashed hungrily. 'Stop it,' I breathed.

'Stop what?' he circled his hips again, rubbing against me and causing another spike of heat between my legs.

'Braden.' I pressed my hands against his chest. 'Seriously.'

'We're friends,' he whispered against my mouth. 'Friends can ask questions. Now, who did you let fuck you?'

Fine. If that's what he wanted . . . 'Quite a few guys. I don't remember most of their names.'

He froze, pulling back to study me. I saw the tick in his jaw again. 'What the hell does that mean?'

Whoa! Was he angry? I glared at him, my defenses up. 'I don't do relationships, Braden. I told you that. But I like sex and I used to like to party. Alcohol doesn't make for a loving relationship.'

He was silent a moment as he processed this. In fact, he was silent so long, I knew what he was thinking. And I felt ugly and worthless. I pushed against his chest again. 'You can get off me now.'

But he wouldn't budge. He shook his head, his expression clearing as his eyes returned to mine. 'Four years,' he replied quietly. 'You hadn't had sex for four years. Since you came here, I'll bet. What changed?'

'That's another question.'

Braden's expression darkened to something so scary I was finally, truly intimidated. I tensed underneath him, holding my breath as his pale eyes fired ice chips at me. 'Did someone hurt you, Jocelyn?'

What? *Oh my God* . . . I relaxed as I realized what conclusion he'd drawn. 'No.' I reached up and soothed a hand across his cheek, hoping it would erase that look in his eyes. 'Braden, no. I don't want to talk about it, okay?' I explained gently. 'But no one hurt me. I was wild. And then I stopped being wild. However, I wasn't lying last night. I've been checked and I'm clean. And anyway, I'm sure you've been with a lot more women than I've been with guys, and I'm not judging you.'

'I'm not judging you, Jocelyn.'

'Oh, you were so judging me.'

'I wasn't.'

'You were.'

He sat up, his arm banding around my waist to drag me up with him, and then his other arm came around my waist so that I was smooshed up against his hot, naked chest. My palms fluttered uneasily onto his pecs, as he stared down at me with this intense look in his eyes. 'I don't like to share,' he murmured.

He'd said that before. Something twisted in my chest, a mixture of exaltation and unease. 'Braden, I'm not yours.'

His arms tightened. 'For the next three months you are. I mean it, Jocelyn. No one else touches you.'

My body completely ignored my mind as it screamed *Run, run, run!* and I felt my breasts swell and my nipples harden at that growl of warning. 'You're being an ass,' I told him hoarsely, my eyes betraying me as they dipped to his mouth.

'I wasn't judging you,' he continued as though I hadn't said anything, skimming soft, teasing kisses along my jaw to my ear. 'In public, you're Joss Butler. Cool, self-possessed. In bed, you're Jocelyn Butler – you're hot, babe. Uncontrolled. Needy. Sweet,' he breathed. 'I like that I know that. I don't like the fact that other men do, too.'

Maybe I was just so turned on that I forgot who we were and what this was supposed to be, but I found myself in an unusual moment of honesty. I leaned down and kissed his throat, loving the way he arched his neck to let me. My hand slid up his chest, across his shoulder and curled around his neck. I nipped and licked and kissed my way back up to his mouth, and then I pulled back, so ready to have him inside me, it wasn't funny. 'They were boys, not men. And just so you know . . . they never got what you got last night from me. They never got it, because they never gave me what you gave me. Not even close.' I brushed my lips across his and glanced up to meet his eyes, smirking at him. 'There. That's a little more air you can blow into your ego.' My grip tightened around his neck. 'But it is the truth.'

I waited for him to say something, anything. Instead the color in his eyes grew dark with desire, and I was crushed to him. His lips demanded I open my mouth and I did, allowing the deep, possessive kiss, trying to steal breath from him since he held me so tightly that mine was gone. In less than a minute I was under him. In less than another minute I was naked, and in less than another he was moving inside me and proving once again that sometimes I really could be needy and sweet.

I strolled into the bedroom, dressed in the tank and shorts again, and I watched as Braden buttoned up his shirt. He grinned at me over his shoulder. 'Making sure I'm really going?'

I shrugged, feeling a lot more relaxed now that he'd given me two spectacular orgasms. 'We'll play this by ear.'

His grin deepened. 'This is going to be easy if all it takes is sex to change your mind.'

I gave him an exasperated look. 'Braden. I'm serious. We'll play this by ear, and while we're sleeping with each other, we agree not to sleep with other people. But we also agree, no pressing each other for answers to questions we don't want to answer.'

After a while of just gazing at me, Braden finally nodded. 'Agreed.'

'Okay. Agreed.'

'I better get back to my flat, shower, change.' He pressed a quick kiss to my lips, his hand coming to rest on my waist. 'I'll see you tonight.'

I frowned. 'No. I'm working tonight.'

'Yeah. Adam, Ellie, and I will stop by.'

'No, you won't.' I shook my head. Not after last time. And, truthfully, I needed some space from him.

Braden's brow furrowed. 'Why not?'

'I'll be working. No distractions.'

'You working with Craig?'

I grimaced. 'Yes.'

His grip on my waist tightened. 'He kisses you and –'

'You'll knock his teeth out.' I nodded, rolling my eyes. 'Yeah, yeah, I already got the macho-Scotsman memo. Nothing will happen. I promise. But you're not coming tonight.'

'Fine.' He shrugged in overly casual agreement. 'Then I'll be here when you get back.'

Okay. I almost nodded my agreement before my brain went, *Wait! No! No, no, no!*

'No!' I replied a little more loudly than I'd meant to.

Braden did not look amused. 'Not even twenty-four hours in, and this arrangement is already exhausting the fuck out of me.'

'Well, you've given me four orgasms. That oughta take it out of a guy.' I grinned saucily.

My deflection didn't work. 'I'll be here – tonight.'

'Braden, seriously, don't. This is all really new. I need some space.'

'*Babe.*' He leaned down and pressed a tender kiss to my forehead, and I relaxed. See, he could be agreeable and willing to compromise sometimes. 'We've only got three months. There's no time for space.'

Or not.

'I'll be tired after my shift.'

'Not in the morning, you won't be.'

'Then come over in the morning.'

With a weary sigh, Braden nodded. 'Fine.' He pulled me to him, lifting me off my feet so that he could give me a searing, wet kiss he knew I wouldn't forget in a hurry. And once he'd settled me back, dazed, on my feet, he left the apartment without even a goodbye.

'Do you think I'm nuts?' I made a face, bracing myself for Dr Pritchard's answer.

'Because you've agreed to make yourself sexually available to Braden?'

'Yeah . . .'

'Joss, you're a grown woman. These decisions are yours to make. Do *you* think you're nuts?' She smiled softly as she asked.

I laughed humorlessly, as I thought about Braden and everything he made me feel. 'I think it's the best way to deal with the attraction between us. This way it doesn't become a huge mess that concludes with me having to move out. Neither of us wants a relationship. We're both consenting adults. We both know the rules. I would never agree to anything more, so it works out well. We use each other until we get bored. No hard feelings. No mess. No moving.'

'But you could have just walked away from Dublin Street. Put Braden out of your life for good rather than come to this agreement with him. Why didn't you?'

I frowned, thinking that was obvious. 'Because of Ellie. She's my friend.'

Dr Pritchard nodded carefully, taking this in. 'So you're willing to explore something with a man who you previously said scared you because of how he made you feel, and you're willing to do this because of your friendship with his sister?'

'Yes.'

'So you're willing to care about Ellie ... but not about Braden?'

Wait. No. What? 'That's not ...' I trailed off, feeling my chest tighten. 'Ellie's a friend. That doesn't mean anything. I like her. I don't want to lose her, but that doesn't mean anything.'

Dr Pritchard sighed, for once looking a little irritated. 'You know, Joss, this process will go a lot smoother if you stop lying to yourself.'

I took a deep breath, focusing on opening up my lungs. 'Okay.' I nodded. 'I care about her. She's a good friend and a good person.'

'And yet, you tell yourself all the time that you care about no one. That you will never care enough to get close.'

'It's not like she's my family,' I bit out, desperate to make my point, to make her see how I saw things. 'It's not the same thing.'

She cocked her head to the side in that way I hated. 'Are you sure about that? I think from everything you've told me, Ellie treats you like family.'

'You're twisting what I said.' I shook my head, feeling that familiar headache. 'I care about people. I never said I didn't. I care about Rhian and James, and yeah, I care about Ellie.'

'So why won't you let yourself care about Braden?'

I looked at my feet. 'It's just sex,' I muttered.

'But there's no guarantee that's true, Joss,' Dr Pritchard answered quietly. 'No one can predict how you'll feel about Braden by the time the three months are up. Or how he'll feel about you. And considering what you've told me – that your feelings for Braden scare you – I suggest you think on that carefully.'

'The way I felt for him *sexually* scared me. It's intense. But I can deal with it. It's just sex,' I repeated stubbornly, and somewhere deep down, buried inside my iron box, there was a voice trying to get out, telling me I was willingly sticking my head in the sand.

'So, is it true you're banging Braden Carmichael?' Jo asked loudly as I poured my customer a pint of Tennent's.

The customer caught my answering glower and grinned sympathetically as he took his drink. 'Why don't you say that a little louder, Jo? I don't think the people in the back heard you.'

'Alistair caught them.' Craig waggled his brows suggestively as he reached past me for a bottle of Baileys. 'Said he was practically in your knickers.'

Alistair had a big mouth.

I shrugged indifferently at the two of them and took my next customer's order.

'Oh, come on,' Jo complained. 'I had my eye on him. I want to know if he's off the market.'

Ignoring the flash of anger I felt at that, I shot her a cold smile. 'You can have him when I'm done.'

Jo's mouth fell open. 'So it's true? You're sleeping with him?'

Apparently so, although the sleeping thing hadn't

originally been part of the deal. The son of a bitch had snuck that in. I raised an eyebrow at my colleague, refusing to get into the details.

Her face fell. 'You're not going to dish the dirt?'

I shook my head and leaned over the bar to take another order.

'Kin ah hae a mahjito, Jack in Coke, a boatil eh Miller . . . aw, aye, in, eh, Stace wahnted a cosmo. Dae ye dae cosmos?'

Luckily, working in a bar for four years in Scotland had given me plenty of practice in understanding not only the thicker accents, but the drunken thicker accents.

In translation: Can I have a mojito, Jack and Coke, a bottle of Miller . . . oh, yes, and, uh, Stace wanted a cosmo. Do you do cosmos?

I nodded and reached down to the fridge for the Miller.

'Is he good?' Jo was suddenly in my face again.

I sighed wearily and brushed past her to start making the cosmo.

'Is it exclusive?' Craig called down the bar. 'Or can we still shag?'

'What do you mean "still"?' I scoffed.

'Is that a no?'

'That's a hell no.'

'Oh, come on, Joss,' Jo begged. 'I've heard he's an effin' stallion in the sack, but that's secondhand gossip. Give me firsthand.'

'Tell you what,' I mused. 'Why don't I give you first finger?' I flipped her off. Yeah, I know, not the most eloquent or mature response, but she was really starting to bug me.

Jo scowled. 'You're no bloody fun.'

'Guess I'm not.'

The atmosphere in the bar was nowhere near as warm and electric as it had been last weekend. Jo was pouting, Craig didn't seem to know how to act around moody me, and I was, well, moody, because I was stuck inside my own head.

I couldn't get the memories of last night and this morning out of my mind, and if I was honest with myself, I was irritated and uneasy at the fact that I was actually looking forward to seeing Braden tomorrow. I *was* trying to worry less about my decision to get into this arrangement with him. I wanted to just enjoy myself. It was just taking me time to relax into it.

It helped that Ellie was being cool about the whole thing. I guess I didn't know what to expect from her, but I thought there would be more disapproval than there had been.

She'd walked into the apartment earlier that day to find me at my laptop. I'd discussed my idea to write a contemporary novel based loosely on my mom and dad with Dr Pritchard, and she thought it was a good idea. Therapeutic even. However, I'd yet to start it – fear gripped me tight every time I'd laid my fingers against the keys. Writing it would mean opening up all the memories, and I didn't know if I could handle the inevitable panic attacks. The good doctor said the idea was to get to a point where the memories no longer caused panic attacks, and she thought the writing might be a nice way to ease me into that.

After Braden left, I'd managed to write the first page. I was staring at that incredulously, astonished that I'd actually put words down, when Ellie got home and immediately stopped by my bedroom.

She grinned knowingly at me as I turned in my seat to greet her. 'So . . . how are you?'

I wasn't one to get easily embarrassed, but I have to admit it was a little awkward to know Ellie knew I had had sex with her brother. I made a face. 'Is this going to be too weird for you?'

'You and Braden dating?' She shook her head, her eyes bright. 'No way. I think it's great.'

Uh-oh. I cleared my throat, remembering that Braden didn't want to lie to her. 'Actually, Ellie, we're not really dating. It's more of a physical thing.'

Ellie seemed surprised. 'You mean like friends with benefits?'

Actually, I prefer the term 'fuck buddies.' Ellie would never say the word 'fuck,' though. 'Pretty much.'

She crossed her arms over her chest, her expression curious. 'Is that what you want?'

I nodded. 'You know I'm not looking for a relationship.'

'And Braden?'

'The whole arrangement was his idea.'

Ellie rolled her eyes. 'Braden and his damn arrangements.' She heaved a sigh of exasperation. 'Well, if it's what you both want, then fine. Just as long as it doesn't affect you and me, I'm cool with it. It's completely unromantic but whatever.'

I smirked at her. 'I promise we'll be fine. So we're cool?'

Her smile in return was adorably lopsided. 'We're cool.'

To prove that we were cool, we spent the afternoon together, wandering Princes Street and colliding with little bundles of tourists here and there who stopped repeatedly to take photographs of majestic Edinburgh Castle. It loomed high on its rock, creating a surreal clash of modern meets medieval . . . and some chaos, since the tourists taking the photographs didn't give a crap where they stopped or how many people stumbled into them in their abrupt need to capture the wonder of it. For a few hours, we were in and out of every clothes store in the city center, trying to find a dress for Ellie to wear on her date that night. That's right. *Date*. She'd met some guy named Jason in Starbucks; he'd asked her out, and she'd said yes. She said he was cute, but I got the feeling this had more to do with sticking it to Adam.

Still, I was a little worried for her. This was her first date since the Adam fiasco, and she seemed really nervous when she left. Although I was pretty preoccupied with my anxiety over the whole Braden situation, I couldn't help feeling curious about Ellie's date, and wondered how it was going.

I was such a killjoy at work later that evening. For the first time in a while, I was desperate for my shift to end so that I could go home and overthink things in the comfort and quiet of my own home.

The bar closed at one in the morning. After cleanup, I got home around two. When I stepped into the apartment, I saw light from under the sitting-room door. It seemed Ellie was still awake. Wanting to make sure she was all right, I pushed the door open quietly and drew to a complete halt.

The only light lit was the floor lamp at the back of the couch and lying in the peaceful gloom, his body sprawled on the couch, his feet dangling over the edge because of his height, was Braden. His eyes were closed. He looked so young with his lashes fanned across his cheeks, his features slack with relaxation as he slept. It was weird seeing him like that. Usually I felt the eight-year age difference between us. He was more mature, together, responsible, and decisive. But lying there, he could be mistaken for my age. He was way less intimidating like this, and I liked it. A lot.

Open on the table was a black folder, a couple of documents loose from their plastic pockets. Braden's suit jacket was draped across the armchair, his leather shoes were on the floor next to the coffee table, and an empty mug sat near all the paperwork.

He'd come here to work?

More than a little bemused, I backed quietly out of the room and closed the door. I'd thought he and Adam would have been out on a Friday night.

'Hullo.'

I whirled around to find Ellie standing in the kitchen

doorway, still wearing the pretty peach summer dress she'd bought for her date, although she was sans the high-heeled gold sandals that made her legs go on forever. I followed her into the kitchen and closed the door behind us so our voices wouldn't travel and wake up Braden. 'How was your date?'

Folding her arms over her chest, Ellie leaned back against the counter with a very displeased expression on her face. Uh-oh. 'Not good.'

'Oh God, what happened?'

'Adam happened.'

'Okay. Explain.'

'Braden called me earlier to tell me he had to work late again tonight, but Adam was free and was wondering if I fancied grabbing something to eat, maybe catch a movie afterward. I told Braden to tell Adam I had a date with Jason.'

'Right . . . ?'

Ellie's face flushed, her pale eyes sparking angrily. 'He called me five times during the date.'

I tried to choke down my laughter and only kind of succeeded. 'Adam did?'

'Whatever Jason got from the five one-sided conversations, he said that I clearly had "stuff" going on, and he was looking for something uncomplicated. And then he left.'

'Wait.' My look was castigating. 'You didn't pick up every time Adam called, did you?'

She flushed again, this time from embarrassment. 'It's rude to ignore someone.'

I huffed, 'Ellie, be honest. You love that the idea of you being on a date with some other guy is driving Adam crazy.'

'He deserves a little torture.'

'Wow. You are so much more bloodthirsty than I'd thought.' I grinned. 'It's brilliant, Ellie, it is. But how long are you planning on keeping this up? It must be exhausting. Wouldn't it just be easier for you both to sit Braden down and explain to him that you have feelings for each other? He'll just have to accept that.'

'It's not that simple.' Ellie bit her lip, staring dazedly at the floor. 'It could ruin Adam and Braden's friendship. Adam would never take that risk for me.' She shook her head sadly, and I felt a pang in my chest for her. Adam needed a serious wake-up call. 'Speaking of' – she glanced up at me with a curious furrow between her eyebrows – 'I came home a few hours ago and found Braden here doing his work. Said he was waiting for you. Aren't you going to wake him?'

Well, considering I told him to give me some space tonight, no. He can get a crick in the neck for his trouble. 'No. He looks wiped. And I'm wiped. He should have gone home.'

Ellie's eyes were teasing. 'He must have enjoyed himself last night if he's eager to see you again so soon.'

I snorted. 'Do you really want to have this conversation about your brother?'

She thought about it and wrinkled her nose. 'You're right. Boo.' She pouted. 'You date a guy and I can't even have girly talks with you about it.'

I laughed softly. 'If it makes you feel any better, I'm

not exactly the girly talking kind of person. And Braden and I aren't dating. We're just fucking.'

I was rewarded with a prudish pursing of her lips. 'Joss, that's so unromantic.'

I pulled the door open quietly and winked at her. 'But hot.'

Leaving her to make *that's gross* faces, I headed into the bathroom and got ready for bed. I was out as soon as my head hit the pillow.

14

The niggling face of consciousness nuzzled against mine, and as I woke, I became aware of a heavy weight across my waist and the fact that I was unusually warm. I realized that the heat was what had awoken me. If I was to take a cue from the heaviness of my eyes and their reluctance to open, it was too early for me to be awake and I should probably fall back asleep.

But that heavy weight across my waist felt familiar.

Forcing my eyes open, I looked at the bare chest lying inches from my face.

Okay, what?

Wake up! My sleepy, sore eyes traveled up that chest to a face and reality slowly but surely sunk in. Braden was in my bed.

Again.

It took me a moment to remember coming home last night and finding him asleep on the couch. I'd talked to Ellie, cleaned up in the bathroom, and then hit the hay.

Clearly sometime during the night Braden had crawled into bed with me.

That was so not the deal.

With a huff of annoyance I pushed against his chest

with all my might. And by all my might, I mean I rolled him right off the bed.

His large body hit the floor with a painful-sounding thud, and I leaned over to see his eyes fly open, bleary and confused as to why he was looking up at me from his sprawled position on the floor. Did I mention he was completely naked? 'Jesus Christ, Jocelyn,' he complained, his voice hoarse from sleep. 'What the hell was that?'

I smirked down at him. 'That was me reminding you that this is just sex.'

He pushed up onto his elbows looking sexy as hell with his mussed hair and belligerent expression. 'So you thought you'd deposit me from your bed?'

'With style.' I nodded, smiling sweetly.

Braden nodded slowly as if accepting that I was in the right. 'Okay . . .' He sighed . . .

. . . and then I strangled a squeal of fright as he lunged upward, his strong hands gripping my upper arms as he dragged me down onto the floor with him. 'Braden!' I yelled, as he rolled me onto my back. And then he did his worst.

He started to tickle me.

I squealed like a girl, wriggling and laughing as I tried to evade his attack. 'Stop it!'

His grin was wicked and determined, and he was fast and strong, dodging my kicking legs and still managing to pin me to the floor *and* tickle me. 'Braden, stop!' I could barely breathe from laughing so hard and from exerting so much energy to get away from him.

'Can I trust that I can lie next to you in the future without fearing stealth attacks while I'm sleeping?' he asked loudly over the noise my breathless, half-choking, half-giggling self was making.

'Yes!' I promised, my ribs starting to hurt now.

He stopped and I took a deep breath, relaxing into the floor beneath him. I winced. 'This floor is hard.'

His eyes narrowed. 'Yeah, tell that to my arse.'

I bit my lip so I wouldn't laugh. I failed. 'Sorry.'

'Oh, you look sorry.' His mouth quirked up at the corners as he placed his hands on either side of my head and braced himself above me, nudging his knee between my legs. 'I think maybe I should punish you anyway.'

My body responded immediately to the look in his eyes, the tone of his voice. My nipples pebbled, and as I bent my legs, spreading them open, I felt the pulse of my sex telling me I was ready for him. I ran my fingers over his six-pack before sliding my hands around to clutch his lower back. 'You want me to kiss your tushy all better?'

Braden had just been about to kiss me, but he pulled back. 'That's such a weird word.'

'So is "knickers." What the hell are knickers?' I pushed away a memory of a similar conversation with my mom – many similar conversations, in fact, during which I'd teased her about some of the weird words she used. I focused on Braden's eyes to push her out of my mind.

He grinned down at me. 'Okay, admittedly, "panties" is a sexier word than knickers. But you've got to admit that "pants" is a terrible word for trousers.'

I scrunched my nose up. '"Trousers" is such a fussy word. Like "whilst." You all say whilst a lot.'

Braden made a face. 'What Scottish people have you been talking to?' His voice deepened as his melodic accent got upper-crusty and kind of English-sounding. 'My woman was arguing pedantically about British words *whilst* I was trying to fuck her.'

I burst out laughing, smacking his back as he grinned cheekily down at me. 'You started it with the whole tushy thing, Mr Dar—' 'I sucked in my breath as his hand slid sensually down my waist, around my back, and down under my shorts and panties so he was cupping my bare butt. He jerked me upward, pressing his hard cock against me. I gasped as everything tingled – my scalp, my nipples, my sex. The atmosphere between us changed instantly.

We didn't speak as Braden pulled back onto his knees, his erection throbbing. I sat up, my eyes still on his as I reached out and wrapped my hand around him. The fire in his eyes flared as my grip tightened and I slid my hand down the hot silk of him. His hand wrapped around mine – I thought at first to guide me, to show me what he liked – but instead he took my hand in his and forced it behind my back, dragging me up to his mouth. His lips were soft, gentle at first, but I wanted more. I flicked my tongue against his, deepening the kiss into something wild, lush, and wet. God, the man could kiss. I could still smell his cologne on him, feel the gentle abrasion of his stubble against my cheek, and I could taste what being with me did to him. I'd never known that someone's desire for me could be so powerful. But his was. It drove me over the edge and made me forget everything else.

Braden's lips reluctantly parted from mine, and he let go of my hand, shifting back a little to trail his hands along the waistband of my shorts. I leaned back on my elbows, giving him better purchase, and I watched, my belly a flurry of excited butterflies, as he slowly pulled my shorts and panties off and threw them over his shoulder. Helping him out, I lifted my camisole off and stretched back, naked, for his perusal.

The sex was different than it had been the day before. Braden's touch was more deliberate, more patient, almost reverent, as he pressed me onto my back using his body, positioning himself between my legs. He cupped my breasts in his hands, holding them up to his mouth, his lips and tongue taking turns to slowly enflame my body.

'Braden.' I sighed, clutching at the nape of his neck, my own neck arching, my breath faltering as he drove me toward release with just his mouth wrapped around my nipple.

He lifted his head, his hand gliding between my legs. Pleasure shot through me as two fingers slipped inside me. 'So wet,' he murmured, eyes bright. 'Tomorrow after family dinner you're coming back to my place and I'm going to fuck you in every room, in every way I can.'

My eyes flew to his, my chest rising and falling rapidly at his words.

'I'm going to make you scream there since you can't here,' he promised softly, and I realized this was also a reminder to be quiet, since Ellie was down the hall. 'But right now, I'm going to enjoy watching you bite your lip.'

And I did. He pushed inside of me and I swallowed a cry by biting my lip, holding on for dear life as his earlier slow gentleness disappeared, his groans and grunts against my neck sexy as hell as he pounded me into orgasm.

I felt a little more relaxed for my bar shift on Saturday night. Braden did me a favor and gave me space – he, Ellie, Jenny, Ed, Adam, and a couple more of their friends I didn't know so well headed out for dinner and drinks. I was invited to the dinner part of the evening, but I didn't feel ready to be in a social situation just yet with Braden, and like I said, I wanted some space.

When I got home from work he wasn't there, and when I woke up, I was alone.

Even Ellie gave me space.

That meant I actually did some writing. In fact, I wrote a whole chapter of my contemporary novel, and it only took one panic attack. But the attack was so short, it barely counted, and once I got past the initial panic, I was able to deal with the memory of my mother telling me how scary it had been to come to the States alone but how liberating it had felt to do it. Best of all, I knew that feeling. I could write that feeling well. And I did.

'You know, you should have a typewriter.'

I spun around in my computer chair at the sound of the familiar voice. I gazed up at Braden, who was lounging in my doorway in jeans and a T-shirt. It was raining outside. He really should have had a sweater on. Or a *jumper*. Another weird word we'd discussed when he was dressing to leave me yesterday. What the hell was a jumper, anyway? My mom had never been able to give me an answer that made sense, and Braden had just smiled at me like he thought I was cute. I was never cute. 'A typewriter?'

He nodded, eyeing my laptop. 'Just seems more authentic, no?'

'Well, my mom promised to buy me one for Christmas, but she died before she could.'

I froze.

My heart sped up as my words echoed back at me.

Why had I told him that?

Braden's gaze sharpened at my reaction, and then he shrugged. 'You'd only end up with a bunch of wasted paper if you had a typewriter.'

He was giving me an out. My smile was a little weak as I replied, 'Hey, I have good typing skills.'

'It's not the only thing you're good at.' He grinned lasciviously as he wandered into the room.

'Oh, you have no idea.'

He chuckled, and I thought he was coming over to kiss me. To my surprise he walked around the bed to my bedside table and picked up the photograph of my parents. 'This your mum?'

I looked away, my shoulders tensing up. 'Yeah.'

'You look like her, but you've got your dad's coloring. She was beautiful, Jocelyn.'

Pain dug its claws into my chest. 'Thanks,' I mumbled, getting up, my back to him as I headed toward the door. 'So, what are you doing here?'

I heard his footsteps quicken behind me and felt his arm come around me, his palm flat on my stomach as he pulled me back against him, my head resting on his chest. I was quickly getting used to Braden's tactility. The man liked to touch me. All the time. I'd have thought it would have been harder to get accustomed to, as I wasn't really an overly affectionate person, but Braden didn't really ask me whether I wanted to be hauled into his arms every five seconds.

And the truth was, I didn't really mind it.

Another surprise.

His breath whispered across my ear as he bent his head to murmur, 'I thought I'd come by and pick you and Ellie up for family dinner. Make sure you turned up. Wouldn't want you to miss the after-dinner dessert at my place later.'

I relaxed as we returned to familiar ground, turning my cheek to catch his lips with mine. 'Wouldn't want that either.'

'Okay, gross.' Ellie's voice broke us apart. She stood

before us in the hallway. 'Could you close the door when you're friends-with-benefiting each other?'

I pulled out of Braden's arms. 'What are you, twelve?'

She stuck her tongue out at me and I laughed, swatting her playfully on the ass as I passed her to get my shoes. I was just shoving my feet into my favorite boots when someone's cell rang.

'Hullo,' I heard Braden answer and turned around to watch him walk into the hall past Ellie. He had his serious face on. 'What? Now?' He sighed, running a hand through his hair as he shot me a look. 'No. It's fine. I'll be there soon.' He slipped his phone into his back pocket with a frustrated groan. 'That was Darren. Family problems. He can't do his shift today at Fire, and I've got a Sunday delivery coming in, as well as a guest deejay tonight, and he can't get anyone who knows what they're doing to cover for him. I have to take care of it.' His eyes held mine for a moment and I saw the frustration deepen.

'You're missing another family dinner?' Ellie grumbled. 'Mum's going to love that.'

'Tell her I'm sorry.' Braden shrugged regretfully, eyes still on me. 'Looks like tonight is out.'

Oh, yes. His plans for me at his apartment. I felt a strange mixture of relief and disappointment as I grinned at him. 'Oh, well.'

'Don't look too disappointed.' He threw me a sardonic smile. 'We'll just have to arrange some time this week.'

'Um' – Ellie stepped between us – 'can you not schedule whatever this is that's going on between you in front of me, please?'

Smirking, Braden leaned down and gave Ellie a quick peck on the cheek. 'Els.' And then he walked past me. 'Jocelyn.' He gave my hand a squeeze, his thumb trailing softly along the back of my hand before he let go and kept walking right on out the front door.

I stared after him, even once he was gone. What had that been? The hand thing? I looked down at my hand, the skin still tingling from where he'd caressed it. That hadn't felt very friends-with-benefitsy.

'Just sex.'

'What?' I looked up at Ellie, who was staring at me incredulously. 'What?' I repeated.

'Just sex.' She shook her head and grabbed her jacket. 'If you two want to believe that, then it's none of my business.'

Ignoring her and the ominous churning in my gut, I shrugged into my own jacket and followed her out the door.

'What are you doing here?'

I'd collided into Ellie's back in the doorway of her mother's sitting room, so I didn't know whom she was asking – accusingly – that question.

'Your mum invited me.'

Ah, Adam. I peered around Ellie to see him sitting on Elodie and Clark's couch with Declan beside him.

They were watching soccer together. Clark was in his armchair, reading the newspaper. Clearly not a soccer fan.

'My mum invited you?' Ellie strode into the room, her arms crossed over her chest. 'When?'

'Yesterday.' Elodie's voice trilled behind us, and we turned to see her and Hannah walk in carrying glasses of soda. 'What's with the attitude?'

Ellie glowered at Adam, who grinned back up at her, unrepentant. 'Nothing.'

'Adam, you're missing it.' Declan pulled on the sleeve of Adam's light-blue sweater, which did great things for his body. No wonder he and Braden got laid so easily. Together the two of them were like a *GQ* ad.

'Sorry, bud.' He gave Ellie a teasingly solemn look. 'Sorry, can't talk. We're watching the football.'

'Better watch you don't get a football rammed up your arse,' Ellie muttered under her breath, but both Adam and I heard her. He laughed, shaking his head as he turned back to the screen.

'What's funny?' Elodie smiled sweetly, completely unaware of the tension between her daughter and Adam as she handed everyone a glass of Coke.

'Ellie said a bad word,' Declan replied.

Okay, so I, Adam, *and* Declan were the only ones to hear.

'Ellie, he hears everything,' Elodie complained.

Ellie scowled, throwing herself onto an armchair. I thought it was best to give her some support since Adam being here had clearly thrown her for a loop, so

I perched beside her on the arm of the chair. Ellie sighed. 'I'm sure he's heard worse at school.'

Declan grinned at his mom. 'I have.'

Clark sniggered into his paper.

Elodie shot her a husband a suspicious look before turning back to Ellie. 'That's no excuse to speak that way in front of him.'

'I just said arse.'

Declan snorted.

'Ellie!'

She rolled her eyes. 'Mum, it's not a big deal.'

'It really isn't,' Declan agreed. 'I've heard *way* worse.'

'Why did you say arse?' Hannah asked serenely from the other couch.

Clark choked on a laugh as he turned a page of the paper, still refusing to look up.

'Hannah!' Elodie spun around to glare down at her. 'Young ladies don't use bad language.'

Hannah shrugged. 'It's just arse, Mum.'

'I was calling Adam an arse,' Ellie explained to her little sister. 'Because he is an arse.'

Elodie looked like she was about to explode. 'Would everyone stop saying arse!'

'I know.' I blew out an exaggerated breath of exasperation. 'It's called an ass, people. *Ass.*'

Clark and Adam burst out laughing, and I shrugged apologetically at Elodie, smiling sweetly at her. She rolled her eyes and threw up her hands. 'I'm going to check the dinner.'

'Do you need help?' I asked politely.

'No, no. My *ass* can handle itself in the kitchen, thank you very much.'

Chuckling, I watched her leave and then looked down at Ellie with a teasing grin. 'Now I understand why you don't curse a lot.'

'So why is Adam an arse?' Hannah persisted.

Ellie stood up, shooting the man in question a dirty look. 'I think the question is: When isn't he an arse?' And then she stormed off after her mother.

Adam's gaze followed her out of the room, his eyes no longer laughing. He turned back to me. 'I messed up.'

Understatement of the year. 'I guess you did.'

I could feel Clark's eyes on us as Adam sighed, and when I looked over at Ellie's stepdad, I could see he wasn't amused anymore. His gaze was burning into Adam with a million questions, and I got the impression that he was putting two and two together.

Time to divert his attention. 'So, Hannah, did you read the books I recommended?'

Her eyes lit up as she nodded. 'They were amazing. I've been looking up more dystopian books since.'

'You've got Hannah reading dystopian novels?' Adam asked with surprise, smiling at me.

'Yes.'

'She's fourteen.'

'Well, these are written for fourteen-year-olds. Anyway, I was taught *1984* when I was fourteen.'

'George Orwell,' Clark muttered.

I grinned. 'Not a fan?'

'Hannah's reading *Animal Farm* for English,' he said, as if that explained it.

Hannah was smiling, a little twinkle of devilment in her eyes that reminded me of Ellie. 'I'm reading it out loud to Mum and Dad so they can help me.'

In other words, she was torturing her mum and dad for fun. She and Ellie really were full of surprises. Angels with dirty faces, as the saying goes.

A few minutes later we were sitting around the table, Ellie and Elodie bickering unintelligibly.

'I just said you looked pale.' Elodie eventually sighed as she took her seat with the rest of us.

'Which translates into "you look like crap." '

'I never said that. I asked why you're pale.'

'I have a headache.' She shrugged, her shoulders tense, her lips and brow pinched.

'Another one?' Adam asked, his eyes narrowed on her.

What did he mean, another one? 'You've had more than one?'

Adam looked angry now, his concern for Ellie bordering on majorly pissed off. 'She's had a few. I've told her to get checked.'

Ellie glowered back at him. 'I was at the doctor's on Friday. The doctor thinks I need glasses.'

'You should have made an appointment weeks ago.'

'Well, I made it this week!'

'You don't take care of yourself. You're running yourself ragged at the university.'

'I do take care of myself. In fact, I was taking care of

myself on Friday night, but someone ruined my down-time.'

'He was an arse,' Adam countered.

Elodie cleared her throat meaningfully.

Adam held up an apologetic hand. 'He was a butt.'

Declan and Hannah giggled. Maybe I did, too.

'You don't even know him. And thanks to you, I never will.'

'Stop changing the subject. I told you to make an appointment with the doctor's office weeks ago.'

'You're not my dad.'

'You're being a child.'

'I'm being a child. Listen to you – *he was a butt*. What the hell, Adam? You're making my headache worse.'

He frowned and lowered his voice. 'I'm just worried about you.'

Oh, he was worried about her, all right. I tilted my head to the side, watching him. God, he was looking at her like James looked at Rhian.

Was Adam in love with Ellie?

I stifled the urge to throw my fork at him and tell him to man up. If he cared about her, he should just *be* with her. What was so difficult about that?

'I would think you of all people would understand what was so difficult about that.' Dr Pritchard frowned at me.

And I would know this . . . how? 'Um . . . what?'

'You cared about Kyle Ramsey.'

I felt the knot in my stomach appear as it always did when I thought about him. 'He was just a boy.'

'Who you didn't want to care about because of Dru.'

Shit. She was right. I hung my head in my pain. 'Then Adam's doing the right thing, isn't he? Braden would just get hurt. Like Dru did.'

'You didn't kill Dru, Joss.'

I drew in a breath. 'I wasn't the bullet, no. But I was the trigger.' I looked the good doctor in the eye. 'It's still my fault.'

'One day, you're going to realize that it wasn't.'

Ellie and Adam acted as our entertainment at Sunday dinner at Elodie's, and I was kind of exhausted from watching them by the time we got home. Ellie disappeared into her room, still not feeling well and still pissed, and she didn't come out.

I, on the other hand, sat at my computer and started to write.

My phone beeped, and I picked it up to find I had a text message from Braden.

I forgot how nice and big my office desk is at the club. I definitely need to fuck you on it.

I shook my head, my lips curled upward as I text back: *Luckily for you, I can work with nice and big.*

I got an instant text back. *I know ;)*

For some reason, Braden texting me a winky face made me grin like an idiot. For someone who was seriously intimidating when he wanted to be, he was also incredibly playful.

So when do you want to schedule office desk sex? Let me know so I can pencil you in. My sex calendar is filling up pretty fast here.

When he didn't reply after five minutes, I bit my lip, remembering how serious he'd been about the whole not-sharing-me thing.

I texted him again. *It was a joke, Braden. Lighten up.*

I didn't think he was going to reply and was trying not to worry that I'd said the wrong thing – this whole fuck-buddy thing wasn't quite as stress-free as I'd been led to believe – when my phone beeped five minutes later.

Hard to tell with you sometimes. Speaking of hard . . .

I was caught between laughing and scowling but decided it was best to let it go, since he was back to joking again. I texted back: *wood floor?*

No . . .

. . . hardback book?

Think more anatomical . . .

I laughed out loud, quickly texting him back. *Last text. I'm working on my novel. I'll see you and your hard cock on your nice, big office desk for sex later.*

Good luck with the writing, babe. x

The kiss freaked me out.

Better to pretend it was a smiley face. Just a smiley face . . .

My phone rang in the middle of my freak-out. It was Rhian.

'Hey,' I answered breathily, still thinking about the little kiss and what it meant.

'Are you okay?' Rhian asked warily. 'You sound . . . weird.'

'I'm fine. What's up?'

'Just checking in. We haven't spoken in a while.'

I took a deep breath. 'I'm screwing Ellie's brother. How are you and James?'

15

Braden was the master of the dirty text message. Sometimes he was subtle . . . Other times, well – *I can't wait to be inside you again, babe. x* – not so much.

Buried with work, Braden was AWOL over the next few days. If I was a different kind of girl, I might have been freaking out that he'd disappeared after we'd had sex, but in all honesty, I enjoyed having that time away from him to breathe. We'd only just started our arrangement and already it felt like it'd been weeks. By Tuesday afternoon, his text messages were starting to get to me. As in . . . they were turning me on. It was amazing how for four years I had been fairly okay without sex. I saw to myself and got by. However, having sex with Braden had reawakened my appetite. An apparently never-ending appetite. I wanted food all the time. And only Braden's food would do. Of course, I didn't confess this to Rhian, even though she had a bunch of questions about the guy who'd managed to pull me out of my four-year dry spell. I told her he was hot. That the sex was hot. The rest of the conversation consisted of her repeating, 'I just can't believe it.'

Yeah, that wasn't very flattering.

Telling Rhian about the hot sex only made me hungrier. That's why I found myself at the gym. Again. I'd already been there the day before. By pounding my feet into the treadmill, racing the exercise bike, and rowing the hell out of the rowing machine, I hoped to burn out all the sexual tension inside of me. It didn't really help.

'Joss, right?'

I looked at the guy who had stopped by my treadmill. Ah. Gavin. The personal trainer who had been flirting silently with me for the past few weeks, ever since the incident on the treadmill. 'Yeah?' I asked casually.

Gavin smiled sweetly at me, and I groaned inwardly. One: Clean-cut pretty boys weren't my type. Two: I already had my hands full with a Scotsman. I didn't need another one. 'Back again so soon?'

Yeah, he was watching me. That wasn't creepy at all. 'Uh huh.'

He shifted on his feet, clearly unprepared for my less-than-enthusiastic response to his barging in on my Operation Relieve Sexual Frustration Caused by a Missing-in-Action Braden Carmichael. 'Look, I was just wondering if you maybe fancied getting dinner together sometime.'

I stopped the machine and stepped off as gracefully as I could considering I was sweaty and icky. I gave him a platonic smile – you know the one: the pressing together of the lips with no teeth showing. 'Thanks. But I'm already seeing someone.' I left before he could respond, smiling as I realized that at least the arrangement with Braden had some positives. Not counting multiple orgasms.

After I showered and changed, I left the gym, dodging Gavin, and as soon as I turned on my phone I had a text from Braden.

Make yourself available Thursday night. Business dinner. Put on a nice dress. I'll pick you up at 7.30pm. x

I rolled my eyes. It hadn't even occurred to him that I might not be free. Bossy bastard. I texted back: *Only because you asked so nicely.*

Annoyed, I strode down the sidewalk clutching my phone tightly in my hand. I'd have to talk to him about his tendency toward obnoxiousness. My phone beeped, and I stopped, still scowling. A scowl that fell away at his one-word text: *Babe. x*

I could hear him say it with a teasing smile in his voice and I shook my head, grinning in exasperation. Jackhole was too damn charming for his own good.

Not that I had much to go on about the business dinner – who we would be dining with or where we would be dining – but I did know that I didn't have a dress that would do. So for once I decided to use my money for something frivolous and headed into Harvey Nichols on St Andrew Square. After two hours of trying on dresses – some of which cost more than my monthly rent – I finally decided on a classy but sexy Donna Karan dress. In the silhouette of a calf-length pencil dress, the silver-gray jersey material clung to every curve. A drape twisted from the right shoulder to the left hip, adding a touch of elegance to what would normally be just a sexy/casual dress. Adding in a ridiculously expensive black clutch purse by Alexander McQueen with the signature gold skull clasp – I thought the skull appropriate – and black leather platform pumps by Yves Saint Laurent, I looked hot. In fact, it was the hottest I'd ever looked. And the most I'd ever spent on one outfit. Ellie was enraptured over it.

Ellie could be enraptured over it all she wanted. I was nervous about *Braden's* reaction.

Turns out I hadn't needed to be.

Well – depends on how you look at it.

Thursday night, I was standing in the sitting room with Ellie, sipping a glass of wine while I waited on Braden. I'd left my hair down, and it fell down my back in loose natural curls that Ellie had oohed and aahed over, begging me to wear my hair down all the time. Nope to that. I didn't really do makeup, but I'd put on some blush, mascara, and a deep scarlet lipstick that took the outfit up a notch.

Our front door opened and shut, and my stomach flipped.

'It's me,' Braden called. 'I've got a cab waiting so we sh— 'He stopped speaking as he entered the sitting room, his eyes frozen on me. 'Fuck.'

Ellie giggled.

I squinted an eye at him. 'Is that a good "fuck"?'

He grinned. 'Well, you're that, too, babe.'

'Euch.' Ellie made a choking sound. 'Gag me.'

Ignoring her, Braden sauntered casually toward me. He was wearing a simple but elegantly cut black skinny suit with a slim velvet lapel, white-gold cufflinks, and a dark silver-gray shirt that matched my dress perfectly. His skinny tie was bloodred, like my lipstick. We had unknowingly coordinated.

He looked yummier than I did, though.

His eyes scanned me from head to toe, and by the time they came back up to my face they were blazing. 'Come with me.' He grabbed my wrist, and I just managed to hand Ellie my wineglass before I was hauled down the hall in shoes I'd had to practice walking in, and dragged into my bedroom.

He spun around, hooking an arm around my waist and tugging me toward him.

'You have got to stop doing that,' I complained.

'Babe, you look . . . let's just say, if there wasn't a taxi waiting to take us to the restaurant for our reservation, you'd be on your back right now.'

Overconfident much?

'In fact . . .' he murmured, squeezing my waist, his eyes dipping to the low neckline of the dress.

'Braden.'

He jerked his eyes back to mine. 'You look beautiful, Jocelyn.'

My stomach flipped again, and I smiled softly. 'Thank you.'

'But you need to put your hair up.'

'What?' I touched my head, scowling up at him. 'Why?'

To my utter bewilderment, Braden's eyes narrowed dangerously. 'Just do it.'

I made a *pfft* noise and pushed against his chest, stepping out of his hold. 'Not unless you tell me why.' My hair looked good. He would not make me think otherwise.

'Because' – his voice was low, a deep purr he reserved for the bedroom; hence why I felt it all the way down in my panties – 'I like being the only man who knows how beautiful your hair is. How gorgeous you look with it down.'

Something nudged inside my chest. An almost-ache spread. Outwardly, I smirked. 'How very Victorian of you.'

Braden's narrowed eyes began to glower. 'Jocelyn,' he warned.

I threw my hands up. 'Are you serious?'

'Deadly.'

'Braden –'

'Jocelyn.'

I stopped, my hands on my hips as I searched his face. It was implacable. My God, he was serious. With a huff of disbelief, I crossed my arms over my chest. 'I don't take well to orders, Braden.'

'I'm not ordering you. I'm asking.'

'No, you're demanding.'

'I just don't want you to wear your hair down.'

'Fine.' I cocked my head to the side as my eyes deliberately perused the length of him. 'I don't take orders, but I do make deals. The hair goes up, but you owe me a favor in return.'

He flashed me a wicked smile. 'Sounds good, babe.'

'Oh, I didn't say the debt would be sexual in nature.'

His grin only widened. 'So what are we talking about here?'

'Well, that's the thing.' I sidled over to him, pressing up against him with a smile. 'You won't know until you know.'

Braden's head dipped toward mine, his lips almost brushing my mouth. 'Deal.'

'Brave man.' I laughed and stepped back. 'You also look really good tonight, by the way.'

'Thank you,' he murmured, his eyes still eating me up.

'Well, you better tell the cabdriver we'll be out in ten minutes. I need to fix my hair.'

I managed to style my hair up into an elegantly messy bun, bid a good night to Ellie, whose eyes were all teary at the sight of us together – I don't think she'd quite grasped the concept of fuck buddies yet – and slid into the cab before Braden. When he got in, he gave the cabdriver our destination. It was Braden's French restaurant, La Cour, the one he'd inherited as part of his father's businesses, and it was situated on Royal Terrace near the Regent Gardens. I hadn't been there before, but I'd heard great things about it. As Braden settled back, he settled in close to me and reached for my hand.

For the entire cab ride I stared at his large, masculine hand in mine, fighting the urge to pull away from his touch. It wasn't because the hand holding wasn't nice. It was nice. Too nice.

Too *more*.

This was supposed to be just sex. But there he was . . . holding my hand.

I barely even noticed we'd pulled up to the restaurant before Braden was paying the cabdriver and helping me down out of it.

'You're quiet,' he murmured, as he laced his fingers through mine again to lead me inside.

I didn't answer that. 'Who are we meeting?'

But before he could respond, the maître d' appeared with a huge grin on his face. 'Monsieur Carmichael, we have your table waiting, sir.'

'Thank you, David.' Braden said his name with the French pronunciation, and I wondered if the guy was really French or if it was all part of the restaurant's image. The restaurant itself was opulent elegance. It was modern rococo with black-and-silver patterned gilt-framed chairs, deep red tablecloths, black glass candelabras, and clear crystal chandeliers. The restaurant was packed.

David led us through the tables to a cozy one in the east corner, far away from the bar and kitchen access. Like a gentleman, Braden held my seat out for me, and I couldn't remember if anyone had done that before. I was so focused on the gesture and the sensual brush of his fingers against my neck as I sat that it took until Braden was also seated and ordering wine for me to notice that we were seated at a table for two.

'Where are the others?'

Braden flicked me a casual glance as he took a sip from the cold glass of water the waiter had just poured. 'What others?'

What others? I gritted my teeth. 'You said this was a business meeting.'

'Yes, but I didn't say what business.'

Oh my God. This was a date! No way. First the bossiness, then the hand-holding . . . no. No, no, no. I pushed my chair out, about two seconds from shooting up to my feet when Braden's next words froze me in place.

'You try to leave, I'll tackle you.' Even though he wasn't looking at me when he said it, I could tell he was deadly serious.

I couldn't believe he'd tricked me into this. With a sullen expression, I pushed my chair back under the table. 'Asshole.'

'Just for that, I expect you to wrap that dirty mouth of yours around my cock tonight.' He narrowed his eyes at me.

I felt the impact of those words as they pebbled my nipples and soaked my panties. Despite my body being completely turned on, *I* was floored. I couldn't believe he'd just said that to me in a fancy restaurant where anyone might overhear. 'Are you kidding?'

'Babe' – he gave me a look that suggested I was missing the obvious – 'I never kid about blowjobs.'

The sound of someone choking brought my head up. Our waiter had descended on us just in time to hear those romantic words, and his rosy cheeks betrayed his embarrassment. 'Ready to order?' he croaked out.

'Yes,' Braden answered, obviously not caring that he'd been overheard. 'I'll have the steak, medium rare.' He smiled softly at me. 'What are you having?' He took a swig of water.

He thought he was so cool and funny. 'Apparently sausage.'

Braden choked on the water, coughing into his fist, his eyes bright with mirth as he put his glass back on the table.

'Are you okay, sir?' the waiter asked anxiously.

'I'm fine, I'm fine.' Braden waved the waiter off, his voice a little hoarse as his eyes pinned me to my seat. He shook his head, his lips twitching with amusement.

'What?' I shrugged innocently.

'You're sexy as fuck.'

The waiter was now staring at us openly, his head bobbing between us, waiting on what scandalous thing would be said next. I smiled up at him and closed my menu. 'I'll have the steak, too. Also medium rare.'

He took the menus from us and hurried off, probably to tell all the other waiters what he'd heard the restaurant owner say to his date. Grimacing, I kept that look on my face as I slid my gaze back to Braden. 'You know, the whole point of this arrangement was that you didn't have to buy me a fancy dinner to get laid.'

The sommelier approached with the red wine Braden had ordered, and we were both silent as he poured a little out for Braden to taste. Satisfied with it, Braden gestured for the sommelier to proceed. As soon as he was gone, I lifted my glass and took a fortifying sip.

I could feel Braden's eyes burning into me.

'Perhaps this is the friends part,' he replied softly. 'I want to spend time with my friend, Jocelyn.'

While that was nice . . . 'That's how things get complicated.'

'Not if we don't let them.'

He must have seen the doubt on my face, because next thing I knew, his fingers were on my chin, gently lifting my face to his. 'Just try it tonight.'

I could feel his touch like a shiver across my skin. I'd had him inside of me. He'd given me quite a number of orgasms. I knew the smell, taste, and touch of him. I thought that would be enough. That it would be over. But looking at him, I realized it wasn't anywhere near over. This attraction, this need – whatever the hell it was – it had only just caught fire, and neither of us was ready to call out the fire department just yet. 'Okay.'

In response, he brushed his thumb over my mouth and smiled at me with his eyes before letting go.

And then we were two friends spending time together. We talked about all the usual stuff: music, movies, books, hobbies, friends. We made each other laugh. We had fun. But it was all little things. Braden was careful to make sure that he never asked anything he knew I wouldn't answer. And when I stumbled over a question because it related to the past, he cracked a joke and changed the subject. This was a smart man.

We were just finishing up dessert when a sultry voice

with an accent as melodic as Ellie's drifted across our table. 'Braden, honey, I thought that was you.'

My eyes lifted to the woman who was standing by our table and was now dipping down to kiss Braden's cheek, giving him an eyeful of her small but perfectly formed breasts. Her dress was red, daring and as sultry as her voice. She gave me a bright smile as she drank me in.

'Aileen. How are you?'

She grinned and stroked his cheek affectionately. 'Better for seeing you.'

Oh, hell. I tried not to shift uncomfortably as an inexplicable tightness lodged in my throat. This was an ex-girlfriend. Awkward.

'How's Alan?'

Who the hell was Alan? *Please be her husband.*

'Oh.' She waved the question off with a grimace. 'We're separated. I'm here with a very charming date.'

Well, go back to him, lady, so we can get on with our date.

Shit! Not a date! Not a date!

Braden smiled and turned around to nod at me. 'Aileen, this is Jocelyn.'

'Hi.' I smiled politely, not really sure how to converse with an obvious ex. As I looked the tall blonde glamazon over, I was convinced more than ever that I was the opposite of Braden's usual type.

Her eyes assessed me. After a second she smiled and looked back at Braden. 'Finally, a girl who doesn't look like Analise.' She touched his shoulder affectionately again. 'I'm glad for you.'

'Aileen . . .' Braden pulled back, his jaw clenching.

Analise? My eyebrows were raised in question. Who was Analise?

'Still sore, I see.' Aileen tutted and took a step back. 'I guess we all are about spouses. Takes time.' She waited for someone to say something, and then, as if suddenly realizing that she was intruding on our dinner, she laughed, a little embarrassed. 'Anyway, I better get back to Roberto. Take care, Braden. It was good to see you. And nice to meet you, Jocelyn.'

'You, too,' I murmured, trying to hide the fact that it felt as though someone had rammed the table into my gut. Spouses? I sucked in a breath, a shot of adrenaline kicking my heart into a riot as Aileen sashayed away, having no idea she'd caused tension between me and Braden.

My lips felt numb. 'Wife?'

'Ex-wife.'

Why did I feel betrayed? That was stupid. Or was it? He'd said we were friends. And Ellie . . . Ellie was my friend, and she hadn't told me Braden had an ex-wife. Did it matter?

You haven't told him anything, Joss.

No, I hadn't. But I also hadn't been married.

'Jocelyn . . .' Braden sighed, and I lifted my eyes to see that his expression was like granite. 'I would have told you about Analise eventually.'

I waved him off. 'It's none of my business.'

'If that's the case, why do you look shell-shocked?'

'Because I'm surprised. I got into this with you

248

because you were a serial dater. Not a one-woman kind of guy.' I touched a hand to my chest. What the hell was that pain in there?

He ran a hand through his hair and then sighed heavily again. The next thing I knew, he had hooked a leg around my chair leg and was pulling me toward him, until our shoulders were almost brushing.

I stared up at him questioningly, lost for a moment in his beautiful eyes.

'I got married when I was twenty-two,' he began softly, quietly, his eyes studying me as he explained. 'Her name was Analise. She was an Australian postgrad student. We'd only been together a year before I proposed, and we were only married for two. The first nine months were great. The next three months, rocky. The last year, hell. We fought a lot. Mostly about my inability to let her in.' He swirled his wineglass, dropping his gaze. 'And when I think about it, that was true. Thank fuck.' His eyes came back to me. 'The thought of handing her – someone as vindictive as her – all my personal crap . . .'

'Like putting ammunition in her hands,' I murmured, understanding completely.

'Exactly. I believe you work hard to make a marriage work. I didn't want to give up. But one day, not too long before my father passed away, he called me and asked me to check a property we were trying to sell on Dublin Street. Not Ellie's and yours,' he added quickly. 'He told me there had been a complaint about dripping water in the downstairs flat, so I went along to check.' His jaw clenched. 'I didn't find a leak, but I found Analise in bed with a close friend of mine from school. My dad had known. They'd been going behind my back for six months.'

I closed my eyes, feeling pain for him echo in my chest. How could anyone do that to him? To *him*? When I opened them, his gaze was soft on me, and I reached for his arm, squeezing it consolingly. To my surprise, his mouth quirked up into a smile. 'It doesn't hurt anymore, Jocelyn. Years of retrospection took that away. What I had with Analise was superficial. A young man's dick leading him astray.'

'You really believe that?'

'I know that.'

I frowned, shaking my head. 'Why would you buy a property on Dublin Street again?'

He shrugged. 'Analise may have fucked off back to Australia once I divorced her and made sure she left with nothing, but she'd still tainted the city I loved. I've spent the last six years creating new memories all over the city, building over the mess she left behind. The same is true with Dublin Street. The flat you're in was a mess. A shell on a street poisoned with betrayal. I wanted to create something beautiful in place of all the ugliness.'

His words sank inside me so deeply I couldn't breathe. Who was this guy? Was he real?

He lifted his hand to my face, his fingers gliding softly along my jawline and curving down my neck. I shivered. Yes, he was real.

And for the next three months he was mine.

I stood up abruptly, grabbing my clutch. 'Take me back to yours.'

Braden didn't argue. His eyes flared with understanding. He left a tip, grabbed my hand, and we were out of there and in a cab before I knew it.

16

I had no clue where Braden lived and was surprised to be let out of the cab at the university on the walkway that led down to the Meadows. Situated above a café and a little express supermarket was a modern building hosting luxury apartments. We rode the elevator to the top, and Braden let me inside his duplex penthouse.

I should have known.

The place was amazing, to say the least, but it definitely looked like a guy lived there. Hardwood floors everywhere, a huge chocolate-brown suede corner-unit couch, a wall-mounted fire with a black glass surround, a huge wide-screen TV in the corner. A partition wall separated the sitting room from the kitchen and its matching island. The kitchen itself was clearly top of the range, but it was finished in a cold stainless steel and looked like it had never been used. At the back of the apartment were stairs leading up to what I guessed were the bedrooms.

It was all the glass that made it so cool. Floor-to-ceiling windows on three sides offered views of the city, and French doors led out from the sitting room onto a huge private terrace. I'd discover later that upstairs on the opposite side of the building, the master bedroom had floor-to-ceiling windows and another terrace, giving this penthouse a three-hundred-and-sixty-degree view of the city.

The view at night was spectacular. My mom had never done the city justice when she tried to describe it to me. I felt an ache rip across my chest as I stood in the middle of Braden's sitting room staring out at the world, in pain, and wondering how often Braden did the same thing.

'You haven't said a word. Are you okay?'

I turned to face him, knowing in him I'd find the temporary cure. 'Do you to want to fuck it out?'

Braden smiled slowly, bemused, causing another twist of attraction in my gut. 'Fuck it out?'

'All the bullshit. What she did. What he did. Every soulless bitch that wanted something from you.'

His expression changed immediately, becoming hard, unfathomable, as he took a step toward mc. 'Are you saying you don't want anything from me?'

'I want this. I want our arrangement. I want you' – I sucked in a breath, feeling my control slip – 'to fuck it out of me.'

'Fuck what out, Jocelyn?'

Couldn't he see it? Was my mask really that good? I shrugged. 'All the nothing.'

He was silent for a moment, his eyes searching.

And then I was wrenched into his arms, his hold tight at my nape as his mouth fell on mine. It was a desperate kiss. Whether it was his desperation or mine, I didn't know. I just knew I'd never been kissed so deeply, so hungrily. It wasn't about finesse. It was about trying to sink ourselves inside each other.

Braden broke the kiss, his chest rising and falling hard as he tried to catch his breath. I stared up at him, already deep in a sexual fog, as he cupped my face gently in his hands and pressed a soft kiss to my mouth, his tongue just flicking mine teasingly. When he pulled back, his hands whispered down my arms and he turned me around slowly with his hands on my waist. I stood with my back to him, my breath stuttering as his fingers reached for the side zip of the dress. His touch was so hot, I could feel the heat through the material. The only sounds in the room were that of our excited breathing and the sharp *zip* of the zipper as Braden slid it down excruciatingly slowly, his fingers brushing my skin as he went. Once it was unzipped, he glided his hands back up my arms to the straps of the dress and just as slowly peeled them off my shoulders. Done, he gripped the material at the hips and tugged the dress down until it pooled at my feet.

'Step out,' he whispered hoarsely into my ear.

Pulse racing, I lifted my heels and stepped out of the circle of the dress, the movement making me realize how embarrassingly wet I already was. Braden lifted the dress off the floor and draped it across his couch. When he came back I felt his hand stroke the soft skin of my buttocks. Did I mention I'd bought new lingerie, too? I was wearing black lace from Victoria's Secret. The panties cut high across my butt cheeks so that more skin was showing than not, and the bra was cut low so that my cleavage looked hot in the dress.

I shivered as Braden continued to caress me, his fingers sliding down the crease of my backside and then entering me from behind. I moaned, arching back into him as he pulled his fingers out and then slid them back in.

'Braden.'

He withdrew only to clasp me by the hips and press me back against him, his erection digging into my backside as I still had on the heels. 'That's all it takes to make me hard,' he told me softly, his lips brushing my ear. 'You – saying my name.'

My chest tightened, and I didn't know how to reply. I didn't want to talk. I just wanted to feel.

As if he sensed that, he turned me around and stepped back, his eyes taking me in, in my sexy new underwear. 'Gorgeous. But I prefer you naked.' His eyes dipped to the shoes and they sparked. 'Those can stay on.'

I reached behind me to unfasten my bra, but Braden was back in my space, his hands stopping mine. He shook his head and I dropped my arms. 'Just wait.' He moved away from me. I stood there in nothing but my underwear and heels, and watched as Braden slowly and tortuously undressed. Wearing nothing but his suit pants, his chest and feet bare, he grinned at me, his eyes smoldering with intent. I didn't care what the intent was. I just wanted him inside me already.

But Braden wasn't done. With an arm around my waist, he brought me into his body, the bare skin of my stomach touching his torso, my naked legs brushing his pants, my breasts pressed against his naked skin. I felt a tug as his other hand made quick work of taking out all the pins that were holding my hair up, and seconds later it was tumbling down my back in a riot of messy curls. I watched his eyes flare and for once thanked God for all my hair, if this was the kind of reaction it got from Braden. His hand tightened in it and he jerked my head back, his lips hovering over my exposed throat. I held my breath, my skin overheated, my legs trembling, my hands gripping his shoulders as I waited. I felt the tickle of his mouth on my skin, another kiss, a barely there butterfly brush, and I found myself making a noise of frustration.

Braden's breath huffed against my throat and then his mouth was pressing there, his tongue flicking softly against my skin as he trailed hot kisses down, down, until he hit the rise of my breasts. Cold air blew over me as he tugged down the bra, my nipples tight and begging for his mouth. His lips closed around me and I jerked my hips into his, his hard cock digging into me, the need there coiling into wildness. 'Braden, please,' I begged, my back arched toward his mouth. My hand brushed down his chest, smoothing over his hot, hard skin, to cup him through his pants.

His breath faltered and he pulled back, his own hips leaning into my touch as he rubbed himself against my hand. 'Fuck,' he murmured, his eyes closing briefly before flashing back open with fire in them. 'I can't wait.'

I nodded, my belly squeezing with anticipation, my panties absolutely drenched with it. Braden undid my bra in seconds, his large hands taking a moment to cup my breasts. I felt him grow even harder against me.

That's when his slow, torturous control really snapped. I was tugged toward him as he moved back toward the door, where a high side cabinet was positioned against the wall, and then I was spun around, pushed none too gently into it, his front at my back. My breath was coming out in frantic puffs now as I gripped ahold of the unit. Braden's hands came around to squeeze my breasts, forcing my body back into his as his tongue flicked my ear. 'I'm going to take you like this. It's going to be hard, Jocelyn, hard and rough. You ready?'

I nodded, my heart spluttering a little.

My panties were gone, whipped down my legs, and I stepped out of them, kicking them to the side. The heat of him at my back, the sound of the zipper on his pants sliding down, sent a bolt of pure lust through my sex, and my nails dug into the cabinet in anticipation.

He splayed a hand across my belly, tugging me back and up so that I was bent over, my arms flat on the unit and bent at the elbow. He slid a finger inside me. 'Babe,' he murmured smugly, 'you're soaked.'

I made a guttural *get on with it* sound, and he chuckled in response an instant before he slammed his cock inside me. I cried out at the deep invasion, my back bowing, but Braden gave me no time for reprieve. He slid out a couple of inches and thrust back inside, the cabinet solid beneath my weight as I relaxed into it. The apartment filled with the sound of our heavy breathing, our groans and grunts, the wet slap of flesh as he fucked me hard into oblivion. His fingers dug into my hips as he pounded into me from behind, groaning as I pushed back into him in perfect but rough rhythm. My panting got louder, spurring him on, and he reached up to pinch my nipples as his hips continued to jerk against me. That was the trigger.

'Braden!' I screamed, an orgasm to beat all others exploding through me, my sex squeezing and pulsing around his cock as he continued to ride me to his own climax.

He came with a deep groan, his mouth on my shoulder, his hands gripping my hips even tighter to his as he rocked up into me, shuddering as he came.

My limbs were no longer working. The only thing holding me up was Braden.

After a while, he slipped out of me carefully, but still I winced. He hadn't taken it easy on me. As if he sensed that, he held me tight. 'Are you okay?'

No. I was freaking awesome. 'That was amazing,' I breathed, falling against him.

His laugh was low, almost a purr. 'You're telling me.'

I found myself turned around to face him and gently lifted onto the cabinet, Braden hitching my legs up around his hips, my hands resting on his chest as he locked eyes with me. I felt something shift in his expression as he looked at me, something that made my breath catch. He caught the sound with his mouth as he dipped his head to kiss me slowly, languorously. Tenderly.

Sometimes words aren't needed for you to know a

change has come upon you. You can share a look with a friend that cements a deeper understanding between you, and thus a stronger bond. A touch with a sister or brother or parent that says *I'm here, no matter what* and suddenly someone who was just a relative, a person whom you love, turns out also to be one of your best friends.

Something happened there with Braden when he looked at me, when we kissed.

It wasn't just sex.

I needed to get out of there.

He pulled back, his lip quirked up at the corners as he brushed my hair back from my face. 'I'm not done with you yet.' And then he kissed me again.

I stayed there, wrapped around him as we made out. It was a real, honest-to-goodness make-out, and, like teenagers, we were at it for at least ten minutes. My body warred with my emotions. I didn't want to give up what was between us. It was addictive, seductive. But I didn't want anything more than what we were able to give each other physically. *I should leave.*

I couldn't leave.

I understood now what people meant when they referred to someone as their drug.

That meant I'd just have to redefine the night. Sex. It was just sex.

Decision made, I pulled back and licked my swollen lips before I scooted off the cabinet and kicked off my heels. 'I have an apology to make,' I reminded him, lowering myself to my knees.

Eyes lidded, Braden gazed down at me. 'For what?' he murmured as his semi-hard cock rose into a full-blown hard-on.

I grinned. 'For calling you an asshole.'

He laughed, thick laughter that choked off into a groan as I wrapped my mouth around him.

Even though Braden had pressed a remote that drew blinds across the windows, which took up most of the wall in his bedroom, the morning sun still shone brightly into the room, waking me. I turned my head on his pillow and saw that the clock said seven thirty. I knew Braden wasn't beside me, because usually his heat woke me, plus I could hear the shower running in his en suite.

The rest of last night flashed back. The restaurant. Finding out about his wife. Aching for him. Coming here. The wild sex against the cabinet. Me going down on Braden, him returning the favor. A naked tour of his duplex that ended in his bedroom. Still feeling weird, I'd shoved him onto his back on the bed and kissed and licked my way up his amazing body before taking him inside me. The plan was to ride him back a few hours to where we had been before.

Braden had other plans.

As I came, he'd flipped us over and drove into me over and over, his eyes gazing down into mine. I wanted to close them like last time. But I couldn't.

I closed them now with a soft groan.

This was so getting complicated, and as cowardly as

it might have been, I just couldn't face Braden in the light of day after the intensity of the previous evening. I slipped out of the huge oriental-style bed and scurried quietly from the room, jogging downstairs to my clothes. I hurried into my underwear and dress, stuck my feet into the shoes even though they hurt, and grabbed my clutch. I let myself out, my heart thumping hard against my chest as I guiltily made my way out into the fresh air. Not really in the mood to do the walk of shame, I hailed a cab at the top of Quartermile and didn't relax until we were pulling onto Dublin Street.

I was just putting my key in the door when I got the text.

Whatever the fuck that was, don't do it again. We'll talk.

I exhaled heavily, exhausted by the prospect.

Judy Garland was singing at me, telling me the sun was shining and to come on, get happy. There was nothing wrong with a little Judy Garland, but right then I wanted Gene Kelly to come back on the screen and dance for me. I'd showered off the sweat and sex from last night, changed into jeans and a hoodie, and curled up on the couch to watch old movies. If I'd tried to sit down at my laptop and write, I would only have gotten lost in my very confused and messed-up thoughts. So I was numbing my mind with musicals and my big Old Hollywood crush, Gene Kelly.

I had just made myself a sandwich when I heard the front door open. My heart stopped for a second until I heard light footsteps. Ellie. I breathed a sigh of relief.

'Hey.' Ellie smiled down at me as she strolled into the room. 'Back from the optician's.'

I put Judy on mute. 'How'd it go?'

'Apparently I need glasses for reading and watching the TV.' She wrinkled her nose. 'I don't really suit glasses.'

I doubted that. Ellie could wear a trash bag and still look cute. 'When do you pick them up?'

'Next week.' She grinned suddenly. 'So? How was dinner?'

'Your brother tricked me. It was just us two.'

Ellie snorted. 'Typical Braden. Did you have fun, though?'

'Other than meeting an obvious ex-girlfriend of Braden's, who seemed perfectly pleasant, if a little clue-less, as she inadvertently told me about Braden's ex-wife, then, yeah' – I shrugged nonchalantly – 'we had fun.'

Ellie gasped, and anxiety clouded her pale eyes as she stood up and walked over cautiously to sit next to me. 'I would have told you, Jocelyn, but Braden wanted to tell you himself. And it's personal for him. I wish I could explain, but it really is his business.'

I waved her off. 'It's okay. He told me about Analise. How she cheated on him.'

Ellie's eyebrows drew together. 'He told you?'

Was he not supposed to? 'Yeah.'

She sat there for a moment, seemingly frozen, and then something in her eyes softened as she smiled at me. 'He told you.'

Oh God, she was getting romantic ideas in her head again. 'Stop.'

'What?' Her eyes grew huge with pretend innocence.

I made a face. 'You know what.'

Before Ellie could respond our front door opened and slammed shut. Heavy footsteps tread down the hall toward us.

'Oh, crap,' I muttered, ignoring Ellie's questioning eyes.

The door to the sitting room swung open, and there he was in his suit, leaning against the doorjamb, his expression blank.

'Hey, Braden.' Ellie greeted him weakly, sensing the sudden danger in the air.

'Afternoon, Els.' He nodded at her and then pinned me to the couch with his lethal blue gaze. 'Bedroom. Now.' He turned on his heel and left me to follow.

I sat there gaping.

'What did you do?' Ellie whispered worriedly.

I shot her a look. 'I snuck out of his place this morning.'

Her eyebrows rose. 'Why?'

Already feeling inexplicably guilty, my guilt transformed quickly into anger. 'Because that's what fuck buddies do,' I snapped, jumping off the couch. 'And he needs to stop ordering me around.'

I stomped – yes, stomped – into my bedroom and slammed the door shut behind me, chest heaving with indignation. 'You need to stop ordering me around.' I pointed my finger at him.

The blank expression he'd been wearing as he stood at the bottom of my bed was quickly replaced by displeasure. That was putting it nicely. He was pissed. 'You need to stop acting like a fucking head case.'

I drew in a sharp breath. 'What the hell did *I* do?'

He looked incredulous, throwing his hands up in disbelief. 'You snuck out of my flat like I was some drunken lay you were ashamed of.'

He couldn't have been more wrong. I crossed my arms over my chest – a protective measure – as I shook my head, refusing to meet his gaze.

'You want to disabuse me of that notion and tell me exactly why I got out of the shower this morning to find you'd buggered off?'

'I – I had stuff to do.'

Braden grew scarily quiet. 'You had stuff to do?'

'Yup.'

'I thought you were more mature than this, Jocelyn. I guess I was wrong.'

'Oh, don't pull that crap,' I replied irritably. 'I'm not the one getting my *knickers* in a twist because my *fuck buddy* didn't stick around for a cuddle in the morning.'

At the flash of something in his eyes, I felt my stomach drop. The look was gone as fast as it appeared, and his features hardened against me. 'Fine. It's done. Forget about it. I need you to get the Saturday two weeks from now off. I've got DJ Intrepid, a famous deejay from London, playing at Fire for Freshers' Week.' His voice sounded detached, empty, and all that distance was directed at me. I didn't like it. 'I want you there.'

I nodded numbly. 'Okay.'

'Okay, then. I'll text you later.' He strode toward me and I waited tensely for his next move. He didn't even look at me. Just reached for the door and brushed past me.

He didn't kiss me good-bye.

I felt sick. Now who was making things complicated?

Dr Pritchard took a sip of water and then cocked her head at me once I stopped talking. 'Has it occurred to you that you may be developing deeper feelings for Braden?'

I sighed heavily. 'Of course it has. I'm not stupid.'

'And yet you're determined to stay in this arrangement with him, fully aware that this might become more to you and still championing its end?'

My smile was definitely without humor. 'Okay . . . maybe I'm a little stupid.'

I know I'm hardheaded. I get that about myself. I know I have issues a mile long, and I know those issues aren't going away anytime soon. But living these last few months on Dublin Street, with a little help from the good doctor, I have been able to see myself in a different light. I had been convinced that I had no real attachments in this life, because that's the way I wanted it. Slowly but surely, I was coming to terms with the fact that Rhian and James were attachments, and Ellie was definitely an attachment. I might not want to care about them, but I did. And with caring comes all kinds of crappy stuff . . . like remorse.

I apologized to Ellie for snapping at her. She, of course, accepted graciously.

But all Friday I was plagued by guilt, and I kept seeing Braden's face flash before my eyes. That guilt brought back some bad shit, and I found myself locked in the bathroom, Friday afternoon, seeing myself through a pretty awful panic attack.

I'd realized something. Something terrifying.

It might just be sex with Braden, but that didn't mean I hadn't formed an attachment to him.

I might not *want* to care about him, but I did.

That's why, as I was leaving for work, I sent him a text that said something I had never said to a guy before.

I'm sorry x

You have no idea how fast my pulse was racing after I added the kiss. One little kiss, and my hands were shaking.

Craig and Jo were not happy with me that night. I messed up a couple of orders, spilled half a bottle of Jack, and then knocked over the tip jar into the spillage, getting a couple of notes wet. When I checked my phone on break and still hadn't received a text back from Braden, I gave myself a good talking-to.

I could not turn into an inept idiot because some guy hadn't accepted my apology. I had shown some real growth sending that text. I nodded angrily to myself, and if he couldn't see that, then fine! To hell with him. I was Joss Butler. I took shit from no man.

I returned to work feeling defiant and determined,

and I managed to do my job without any more incidents. I explained away my clumsiness, telling the guys I'd had a migraine but was feeling much better. They swallowed that since I started joking around with them like normal, doing what I had always been good at and shoving my feelings down under the iron box inside of me.

We finished up the night, and Jo and Craig kindly offered to let me go early since I 'hadn't been feeling well.' I wasn't going to argue. I grabbed my stuff, said good-bye to Brian at the door, and headed up the steps to George Street.

'Jocelyn.'

I spun around and found Braden standing on the sidewalk by the club. My stomach was back to churning again. We stared at each other silently for a minute until I found my voice. 'You were waiting on me?'

He smiled a little as he approached. 'Thought I could walk you home.'

Relief I wasn't willing to admit to for too long poured over me, and I grinned up at him. 'Does that walk happen to conclude with us naked in my bed together?'

His laughter was low, rough, and it floored me as always. 'That's what I had in mind, yes.'

I took a deep breath. 'I'm forgiven for being a bitch, then?'

'Babe.' Braden reached out to stroke my cheek, clearly having forgiven me.

I tugged on his jacket, pulling him closer. 'I think you should show me who's boss, anyway.'

His arms wrapped around my waist, and I found myself snuggled up against him. 'I thought you told me I was to stop bossing you around.'

'Well, there are special circumstances when I'd allow it.'

'Oh? What would those be?'

'Any that result in me coming.'

He grinned, squeezing me closer. 'Why do you have to make everything sound so dirty?'

I laughed, remembering those were the words he'd used the day he'd walked in on me naked. God, it felt like a lifetime ago.

17

With a lot of sex and laughter that weekend, Braden and I closed the breach between us. I worked, Braden worked, and then on Sunday Elodie and Clark took the kids to St Andrews for the day, so Ellie, Braden, and I hung out with Adam, Jenna, and Ed. It was the first time Braden and I had been out in a social situation with other people since starting our arrangement. I knew as soon as we walked into Ed's favorite pub on the Royal Mile for lunch that everyone was now aware of our arrangement. Jenna stared at us like we were a science experiment, and Ed had this stupid little-boy grin on his face. Adam actually winked at me. I swear to God I would have fled the premises if Braden hadn't anticipated my reaction and grasped my arm to pull me forward. Once they realized that nothing had really changed – we weren't a couple, there was no hand holding or fondling, and our chairs were, in fact, pretty far apart – everyone just acted normal. We had a great lunch, a few beers, and then hit the movies together. In the theater, Braden did seat us alone in the row behind the others, and okay . . . there may have been fondling in the dark.

We didn't see each other on Monday, so I actually managed to write another chapter of my book and squeeze in a visit with Dr Pritchard. That was fun.

Tuesday, Braden took his lunch break in my bed. Wednesday he got caught up with work, so I didn't see him at all. I spent the night with Ellie, enduring a teen romance that actually made my teeth hurt it was so sweet. I insisted that for the next movie night, we watch something or someone get maimed by an action star, or put on a Gene Kelly movie.

'You're such a boy.' Ellie wrinkled her nose as she chewed on chocolate buttons.

I glanced away from the sickly sweet romance to look at her across the room. She was sprawled over the couch, covered in chocolate wrappers. How did she not put on weight? 'Because I hate cheesy romance?'

'No. Because you'd rather watch someone get pummeled than declare his love.'

'True.'

'Boy.'

I made a face. 'I think Braden would disagree.'

'Ugh. That was mean.'

I grinned wickedly. 'You called me a dude.'

She turned her head on a cushion to look back at me. 'Speaking of . . . not that I wanted to notice – I can't help my exceptional observational skills – but you seem to be doing whatever you guys are doing on Braden's schedule. You okay with that?'

It wasn't that I hadn't noticed that myself. But, seriously, how could I argue with it? I 'worked' from home, and Braden worked all the time. When I did work, it was on two of the only nights Braden was free. 'He's a busy guy. I get that.'

Ellie nodded. 'A lot of his girlfriends resented it.'

'I resent being called his girlfriend,' I warned her teasingly.

'I never called you his girlfriend. I just meant ... Actually, you know what? I don't know what I meant, because you two boggle my mind.'

I could tell she was getting ready to work her overly romantic self into a conniption over me and Braden, so I quickly changed the subject. 'You haven't said much about Adam lately.'

My roommate's face fell, and I wished I'd picked another subject to move on to. 'We've barely spoken since that Sunday at Mum's. I think he realized he was sending mixed signals, so he's just completely backed off.'

'I didn't notice anything weird between you last Sunday when we were hanging out.'

'That's because you were in Braden Land.'

I guffawed. 'Yeah, okay.'

Ellie shook her head. 'Delusional numpty.'

That was a new one. I couldn't remember Rhian or James ever calling me that. 'Did you just call me a numpty?'

'Yup. A delusional one.'

'What, may I ask, is a numpty?'

'A person demonstrating a lack of knowledge of a situation; a silly person; an idiot; a dumbass. A delusional numpty: Joss Butler and her stupid, idiotic, blind misconception of the true nature of her relationship with my brother, Braden Carmichael.' She glowered at me, but it was an Ellie glower, so it didn't really count.

I nodded my head. 'Numpty. Good word.'

She threw a cushion at me.

When Thursday rolled around and I got a text from Braden telling me he couldn't make it that night, I have to admit to a teensy bit of disappointment. I couldn't admit to being hugely disappointed, because I'd stuffed that emotion inside my iron box. He was in the final stages of closing a deal on the development he'd been working on that summer, so I understood. But it didn't mean it didn't suck.

I dug deep and wrote the entire day away, amazed and gratified that I'd managed to write a few more chapters without having to open up the memories that would be sure to send me back into the bathroom with a panic attack. Although, admittedly, I hadn't had one of those since the epic attack last Friday.

Thursday night, with no Braden to keep me busy, I eased my pain with a Denzel Washington marathon. Ellie gave up two movies in and went to bed. A few hours later, I was out.

I woke up as I felt the world drop beneath me. 'What?' I mumbled, my eyes trying to adjust to the dim light.

'Shh, babe.' I heard Braden's low voice above me, and I realized I was in his arms. 'I'm putting you to bed.'

I sleepily wrapped my arms around his neck as he carried me toward my bedroom. 'What are doing here?'

'Missed you.'

'Mmm,' I mumbled, burying deeper into him. 'Missed you, too.'

A second later, I was out.

One minute I was dreaming the world was flooding, the water rising inside our apartment with no way out, my panic growing deeper and deeper as the water crept up toward the ceiling, leaving me awaiting imminent death, when a bolt of lust shot between my legs and I looked down to see a gorgeous merman's head there. The water drained away in an instant, and I was flat on my back with the faceless merman, who was now just a man, and he was licking away at me with gusto.

'Oh God,' I breathed, sensation ripping through me and pulling me with it into consciousness.

My eyes flew open. I was in my bed. It was morning.

And Braden's head was between my legs.

'Braden,' I murmured, relaxing against the mattress, my hands sliding into his soft hair. He had the most magical tongue.

My hips jerked as he sucked at my clit, his tongue circling it, his fingers sliding inside me. I lost control of my breathing, my heart pounding in my ears, and I was coming around his mouth in seconds.

Talk about a wake-up call.

My muscles sank into the bed as Braden crawled up my body, his eyes smiling down at me as he braced him-self above me. I could feel his hard-on rub against my wet center. 'Morning, babe.'

I caressed his waist, scoring my nails lightly across

his skin in a way I knew he liked. 'Morning to you, too. And what a happy morning it is.'

He laughed at my goofy grin and fell off me to lie at my side. I turned to check the clock, but my eyes caught on the object on my desk. I bolted upright, staring at it, wondering if I was actually seeing correctly. I felt Braden at my back, and his chin came down on my shoulder.

'Do you like it?'

A typewriter. A shiny black old-fashioned typewriter sat on my desk beside my laptop. It was beautiful. It was just like the one my mom had promised to buy me. The one she didn't buy me because she'd died before she could.

This was an amazing gift. A thoughtful, beautiful gift. And it was more than sex.

I felt the pressure on my chest before I could do anything to stop it, my brain fogging up as if it also was too full. The tingles exploded across my skin as my heart galloped out of control.

'Jocelyn,' Braden's worried voice penetrated the fog, and I reached for his hand to reassure him. 'Breathe,' he murmured in my ear, his hand squeezing mine, his other on my hip, holding me to him.

I breathed in and out in rhythm, taking back control, letting my lungs open, my heart rate slow, my brain unfog itself. Exhausted, I leaned back into Braden's chest.

After a minute or two, Braden spoke. 'I know you don't want to talk about why you're having these panic attacks, but . . . do they happen a lot?'

'Sometimes.'

He sighed and my body moved as his chest moved. 'Maybe you should talk to someone about them.'

I pulled away from him, unable to look at him. 'I already am.'

'You are?'

I nodded, hiding behind my hair. 'A therapist.'

His voice was quiet. 'You're seeing a therapist?'

'Yeah.'

My hair was brushed back behind my ear, his fingers gliding along my jaw to turn my face to his. His eyes were kind, concerned. Understanding. 'Good. I'm glad you're talking to someone, at least.'

You're beautiful. 'Thank you for my typewriter. It's beautiful.'

Braden gave me an uneasy smile. 'I didn't mean to cause a panic attack.'

I kissed him quickly, reassuringly. 'That's my bullshit – don't worry. I love it. It was really thoughtful.' And more. To push out the *more*, I grinned devilishly, my hand sliding down his stomach to grasp his cock. It hardened instantly. 'I can't accept it, however, without giving a gift in return.'

Just as my head descended Braden stopped me, grasping me by the upper arms to pull me back up. I frowned. I knew he wanted it. He was throbbing in my grip. 'What?'

His expression had changed so quickly, his eyes becoming dark, his features hardening to granite. 'You go down on me because you want to, not because of the typewriter. It was just a gift, Jocelyn. Don't go fucking it up in your head and twisting it into something else.'

I let this sink in, and finally I nodded. 'Okay.' I squeezed him a little harder, and his nostrils flared. 'Then I'm going down on you in return for you going down on me.'

Slowly he let me go and rested back on his elbows. 'That I can work with.'

'The book is coming along, then?' Dr Pritchard asked, seeming pleased.

I nodded. 'I'm getting there.'

'And the panic attacks?'

'I've had a few.'

'When did those occur?'

I told her, and when I finished, she lifted her gaze, and there was something in it that I didn't understand. 'You told Braden you were seeing me?'

Oh, hell, had that been the wrong thing to do? It had just slipped out. I didn't know why . . . 'Yeah, I did.' I pretended like I didn't care one way or the other if telling him was the right thing to do.

'I think that's good.'

Wait. What? 'You do?'

'I do.'

'Why?'

'Why do *you* think I do?'

I made a face. 'Next question.'

*

276

I saw Braden nearly every day after that morning. We spent the next week hanging out. Ellie, Braden, Jenna, Adam, and some girl whom Adam had brought along as a date stopped by the bar on Saturday night before dragging Braden to a nightclub. He seriously hated clubbing, which had brought me to ask him why he owned a nightclub. His reply was that it was good business. When he was being dragged out of the bar for the nightclub, I gave him a sympathetic smile. I was not at all surprised to find later that he'd escaped the club to come pick me up. Sunday was dinner at Elodie and Clark's, which consisted of Declan and Hannah bickering, Clark ignoring said bickering, and Elodie making the bickering worse. Ellie, in an effort to forget Adam's date last night, complained constantly that she didn't think the lenses in her glasses were right, and no one noticed anything different about me and Braden. Thank God. Elodie's head would explode if she knew what was going on between us.

Monday night Braden had come over after he'd gone to the gym – we had memberships at different gyms, for which I was thankful; I needed to focus when I was exercising – and we'd hung out with Ellie; then Braden had stayed the night. Tuesday night I went on my first official required business dinner. A real one this time. What I hadn't known was that Braden was selling his French restaurant and keeping the contemporary, upmarket Scottish seafood restaurant he owned down by the shore. It was a private sale to a business friend. A private sale, but the local media had still found out and written a piece on the established La Cour changing hands, speculating over the reason for Braden's selling it.

'It's too much,' Braden had explained after asking me to accompany him to the dinner, which was really just a celebratory thing between him and the guy who'd bought it. 'The nightclub has become a much bigger success than I was expecting, the estate agency is always pulling me into some problem or another and away from the property development, which is what I enjoy, and I'm just spread too thin. La Cour was my dad's. There's not anything about it that has my stamp on it. So I sold it.'

We met Thomas Prendergast and his wife, Julie, at Tigerlily. I wore a new dress and tried to be as charming as possible. Well, charming in the only way I knew how. Thomas was older than Braden and much more serious, but he was friendly and clearly respected Braden. Julie was like her husband – sedate, quiet, but friendly. Friendly enough to ask personal questions. Personal questions Braden helped me deflect.

I rewarded him well for that later.

Overall, the dinner was nice. Braden seemed more relaxed now that he didn't have La Cour resting on his shoulders, and for some reason I found that him being relaxed made me relaxed. We hung out at his apartment Wednesday night, mostly because we had to be quiet at my apartment and that took some of the fun out of the sex. So we had sex loudly on the couch, on the floor, and in his bed.

Replete, I lay in the tangled sheets, staring at his ceiling. His bedroom was as contemporary as the rest of the duplex. Low, Japanese bed, wardrobes built into the walls so they didn't take up space. An armchair in the corner by the window. Two bedside cabinets. Nothing else. He needed some pictures, at least.

'Why don't you talk about your family?'

My whole body tensed, the breath whooshing out of me at the question I was completely unprepared for. I twisted my head on my pillow to stare at him incredulously. He wasn't looking at me warily, like he was waiting for me to freak out. He just looked determined. I sucked in my breath and looked away. 'I just don't.'

'That's not really an answer, babe.'

I threw up my hands. 'They're gone. There's nothing to talk about.'

'Not true. You could talk about who they were as people. What you were like as a family. How they died . . .'

I struggled for a moment with my anger, trying to hold it in. He wasn't meaning to be cruel – I knew that. He was curious; he wanted to know. It wasn't unreasonable. But I'd thought we understood each other. I'd thought he understood me.

And then I realized that he couldn't possibly understand. 'Braden, I know your life hasn't been easy, but you can't possibly understand how messed up my past is. It's shit. And that's not a place I want to take you.'

He sat up, pushing his pillow against the headboard, and I twisted onto my side to look up at him as he looked down at me, a pain in his eyes I had never seen before. 'I understand messed up, Jocelyn. Believe me.'

I waited, sensing more on the horizon.

And he sighed, his eyes drifting over me to look out the window. 'My mum is the most selfish woman I've ever known. And I don't even know her that well. I was forced to stay with her during the summer holidays, traveling around Europe, living off whatever sad fuck she'd managed to manipulate into being with her. During the school year, I lived with my dad in Edinburgh. Douglas Carmichael could be a harsh, distant bastard, but he was a bastard who loved me, and that was more than my mother ever did. And Dad gave me Ellie and Elodie. Elodie was the one thing I had issues with my father over. She's a sweet person, a good woman, and he never should have chased after her and treated her like all the others. But he did. At least she ended up with Clark, and Ellie ended up with a brother who will do anything for her. My dad was neglectfully affectionate with Ellie, nothing more. With me he put on the pressure. And I was an asshole kid who rebelled against following in Daddy's footsteps.' He huffed at himself, shaking his head. 'If we could only go back and knock some sense into those kids we once were.'

If only.

'I started hanging around the wrong people, smoking pot, getting drunk, and getting into a lot of fights. I was angry. Angry at everything. And I liked to use my fists to get rid of that anger. I was nineteen and dating a girl from a rough area here. Her mum was in prison, her dad gone, and her brother was a junkie. Nice girl, bad home life. One night she turned up at my door, and she was just a hysterical mess.' His eyes glazed over as he remembered, and I knew instinctively that what he was about to say next was going to be beyond awful. 'She was crying, shaking, and she had vomit in her hair. She'd gotten home that night and her brother was so off his face on smack that he raped her.'

'Oh my God,' I breathed, feeling physical pain for this girl I had never met, and for Braden for having had that happen to someone he cared about.

'I lost it. I didn't give myself time to think. I tore off, running the whole fucking way to his place on adrenaline alone.' He stopped, his jaw clenched tight. 'Jocelyn, I beat him within an inch of his life.' He looked down at me, his expression remorseful. 'I'm a big man,' he whispered. 'I was, even as a teenager. I didn't realize my own strength.'

I couldn't believe he was telling me this. I couldn't believe this had happened to him. Braden, who I had thought lived in a world of elegant dinners and fancy apartments. Apparently he'd been in another world for a little while. 'What happened?'

'I left, made an anonymous call for an ambulance, and told her what I'd done. She didn't blame me. In fact, when the police found him, we covered for each other. Her brother was a well-known junkie, there were no witnesses, and they just assumed it was drug-related. He was in a coma for a few days. The worst bloody days of my life. When he woke up, he told the police he couldn't remember who'd attacked him, but when I walked in with his sister, she told him what he did.'

Braden's voice hitched a little. 'He started to cry. It was probably the most pitiful sight I've ever seen, him crying and her just staring at him with hatred in her eyes. She left. He promised me he wouldn't tell the truth about what had happened. He said he'd deserved it, that I should have killed him. There was nothing I could do for either of them. I never saw him again. My relationship with her fell apart when she turned to drugs to deal with what happened, refusing my help. Last word I heard a few years back was that she'd OD'd.'

I pulled myself up beside him, my whole body aching for him. 'Braden . . . I'm sorry.'

He nodded and turned his head to gaze at me. 'I've never been in a fight since. Lifted my hands to no one. My dad and I buried a lot of shit after that. He was the only other person who knew the truth, and he helped me turn everything around. I owe him.'

'I think we all do.' I smiled sadly, brushing my fingers along his jaw as it sunk in that he'd trusted me with this.

Me.

Oh God.

Did I owe *him* somehow? Or wasn't it like that? He'd trusted me because he knew I wouldn't tell anyone; he knew I wouldn't judge him.

It occurred to me as I lay there beside him, feeling pain for him, that I knew he would never tell anyone anything I shared with him. He would never judge me. I heaved a sigh and dropped my hand, my stomach twisting as I fought with myself. 'Dru.' Her name just fell off my lips before I could even think about it.

Braden's body tensed with alertness. 'Dru?'

I nodded, my eyes on his stomach rather than his face. Blood rushed in my ears and I clutched the sheets to stop my fingers from trembling. 'She was my best friend. We grew up together and when my family died, she was all I had left. There was no one else.' I swallowed hard on the memories. 'I was a mess after . . . wild. I dragged Dru to parties we were too young to be at, did things we were too young to do. It was a little over a year after . . . and there was this kegger down at the river. I was on this path of picking guys off, some to just make out with or, if I was drunk enough, then to do other stuff, and Dru was trying to get up the confidence to ask Kyle Ramsey out.' I huffed humorlessly. 'Kyle used to drive me crazy. He was always bugging me, but after . . . well, other than Dru, he was the only person I sat down and talked to about everything. He was really a good kid. And I liked him,' I confessed softly. 'I really liked him. But Dru had had a crush on him forever, and I was no longer the girl he used to have a crush on. She didn't want to go that night. But I convinced her that Kyle would be there, and I forced her to come along.

'It was about halfway through the party, and I thought Dru was off talking to Kyle while I was flirting with the captain of the football team, but Kyle was suddenly there, asking to speak with me. We walked off for some privacy, and he started to say all these things. How I was better than what I was doing with all those guys. How my parents would be so upset if they could see me like that.' I took a shuddering breath on that confession. 'And he told me that he cared about me. That he thought he could really love me. I didn't think. I just let him kiss me, and before I knew it we were getting pretty hot and heavy. He stopped before it went too far and told me I didn't have to sleep with him to keep his interest. That he wanted me to be his girlfriend. And I told him that I couldn't be, that Dru was crazy about him, and I couldn't do that to her. We talked in circles for a little while until I decided I needed to get drunk or something to get away from all the teen drama, but when I went out into the main party one of Dru's friends told me I was a backstabbing slut. And I realized that Dru had found out about my making out with Kyle.'

I closed my eyes, seeing the image of her standing by the rope swing, the hatred in her eyes so intense. 'I found her farther down the river, drunk off her ass. She was trying to get onto this old rope swing that swung you out over the water, but it was frayed and unused and the current that night was bad. I begged her to come back to the party and talk to me, but she just kept shouting that I was a traitor and a whore.' I looked up at Braden to find his sad eyes on me. 'She swung out on the rope before I could stop her, and it snapped. She screamed for my help as the current took her, and I didn't think – I just shot into the water after her. But Kyle had been behind us, and he came in after me and was a far stronger swimmer. Rather than let me get to her, he tugged me back to the rocks. Dru's body washed up down the river. She was gone. And I never spoke to Kyle again.'

'Baby,' Braden murmured, reaching for me.

I held my hand up to warn him off, shaking my head, my eyes furious. 'I killed her, Braden. I don't deserve sympathy.'

He looked shocked. 'Jocelyn, you did not kill her. It was a tragic accident.'

'It was a series of events caused by my actions. I'm to blame.' He opened his mouth to talk and I placed a gentle hand over his lips. 'I know it's not rational. I *do* know that. But I don't know if I'll ever get to a point where I don't blame myself. However, I'm trying to live with it. Telling you is huge. Believe me.'

Braden hauled me across the bed and up into his arms, his hand at the nape of my neck. 'Thank you for trusting me.'

I cupped his cheek in my hand and sighed wearily. 'I think we need to have sex now.'

His brows drew together. 'Why?'

'To remind us of what we're doing here,' I replied, my tone meaningful.

Braden's eyes narrowed. 'No,' he told me gruffly, squeezing my nape. 'I'd have sex with you for anything else but that.'

Surprised, I found for once I had no reply, and Braden didn't wait on one. He pressed a hard kiss to my mouth and then slid down the bed, pulling me with him. He tucked me into his side and leaned over to switch off the light. 'Go to sleep, babe.'

Shell-shocked by the night's events, I lay there listening to him breathe before exhaustion finally claimed me.

'How do you feel now that you've told Braden about Dru?'

My gaze slid from the postgraduate degree framed on Dr Pritchard's wall to her face. 'I feel scared, but relieved at the same time.'

'Scared because you told someone other than me?'

'Yes.'

'And relieved . . . ?'

I shifted in my seat. 'I'm perfectly aware that I keep things from people, and I know that it isn't brave, but it's how I handle things. When I told Braden, the world didn't end. I felt brave for once. And that was kind of a relief.'

18

I would be sticking my head in the sand if I didn't say things changed between me and Braden after that night. We grew closer. Sharing-looks-and-understanding-what-they-meant kind of closer. And we spent a lot more time together. I decided not to think about the future. Right then I was having amazing sex with a great guy who also happened to be a friend. I didn't want tomorrow. I knew what was waiting for me in tomorrow, and what was waiting was an inevitable mess. Everything was a lot nicer in the present.

Saturday rolled around before I knew it, and it was Braden's guest deejay night at Fire, kicking off the first week of university starting up. I wasn't particularly looking forward to crowds of freshmen, but neither was Braden, and he had to be there to show respect to this famous deejay I had never heard of. So Ellie, Adam and I were doing him a favor. I made the mistake of going shopping with Ellie and Hannah that afternoon for an outfit and allowed myself to be talked into buying a minidress. I had never owned a minidress. It was simple, turquoise blue, with a high neck, and was backless to just below my waist; the hem sat a good few inches above my knees – definitely shorter than anything I'd ever worn in public before.

Okay, so there were those green-and-white-striped shorts, but the dress was definitely more risqué.

I piled my hair up on top of my head, wore my makeup a little heavier – I let Ellie do it – and put on a pair of ankle-strap suede wedges that were the same color as the dress. Ellie was, as per usual, stunning in a gold shift dress and spaghetti-strap sandals.

We were meeting Braden at the club, which was probably a good thing, since he took one look at me upon my arrival and scowled. The four of us were standing in his office, the music from the club pounding all around us. My hands flew to my hips at his expression. 'What?' I snapped.

His eyes traveled the length of me and returned with a glitter of danger in them. 'What the hell are you wearing?'

I narrowed my eyes. 'What the hell is *your* problem?'

Ellie cleared her throat. 'I think she looks nice.'

Braden cut her a warning look.

Though I was hurt by his response to what I thought was a pretty hot dress, I shrugged like I didn't care. 'Let's get a drink.' I spun on my heel and took satisfaction in the sound of Braden inhaling sharply. He'd caught a look at the back of the dress.

I heard footsteps following me out as I wound my way through the fairly quiet club. We were early and people were just starting to show. Fire's main floor was huge and split on two levels. Four long, curving steps separated the bar and a small dance floor, which had sofas and tables around it, from a larger floor space.

Black walls with twinkle lights surrounded the upper level, and down on the main space, the edges of the room were broken up with paper flames lit up from the back. A huge modern chandelier molded into flickering flames hung from the ceiling and added drama to what was an otherwise understated club. Customers came into the club from the level below, where one staircase led them up here and another led them downstairs to two more levels. The first lower level hosted a smaller lounge and dance floor, and the basement level hosted a cocktail bar.

I didn't even make it to the stairs that would lead me up to the bar when I was tugged back against Braden's chest. His hand slid down my waist and gripped my hip tight as he bent to murmur in my ear, 'You look good enough to eat – that's my problem.'

I tilted my head back to look up at him, feeling stupid that I hadn't realized he was having a caveman moment. 'Oh.' I grinned now, a little smugness creeping into my voice. 'Well, good thing you're the only one who's getting under this dress, huh?'

He smiled predatorily, clearly only somewhat appeased, but he nodded, giving me that one. 'Fair enough. Go join Ellie and Adam at the table I reserved for you. I'll have drinks sent over.'

'Where are you going?'

'I have friends arriving, as well as the local media. Have to be seen for a bit. I'll be over soon.'

I nodded and turned around, making my way up the stairs and over to Ellie and Adam, who looked like they were having a pretty heated conversation. I was about to spin around to head elsewhere when Adam looked up and slid purposefully away from Ellie, his eyes telling me to sit my ass down. I threw him a *you're an idiot* look and sat down on Ellie's other side. 'Braden's having drinks sent over,' I told them. 'I didn't realize he had other friends appearing tonight. I thought it was just us and random people.'

'No.' Ellie pursed her lips, clearly in a bad mood now. 'Some of his exes as well as his previous friends-with-benefits girls love clubbing. He invited them and a few of his guy friends.'

She might as well have just punched me. I stiffened, stunned that Braden had invited ex-girlfriends tonight. And he had previous friends with benefits? He'd told me he'd never done that before.

'Ellie.' Adam shot her a reproachful look. 'What are you playing at?'

Confused, she shook her head at him, and he nodded toward me. Ellie turned to look at me, and whatever she saw on my face made her go pale. 'Oh, crap, Joss, I didn't mean anything. I mean, those girls don't mean anything . . .'

'Let's get drunk,' I suggested loudly.

Adam eyed me carefully. 'I don't think that's a good idea. Let's just wait for Braden.'

But waiting for Braden turned into a longer plan than we could stand. For a while I watched through the dim light of the club as it filled to the brim, and witnessed girl after girl flirting with him as he grinned back at them like an idiot, piling on their drinks.

Unused to the sharp spike of jealousy I was feeling, I shrugged on supercool pre–Dublin Street Jocelyn, and headed out onto the dance floor. Ellie was with me for a while, and Braden stopped by to see how we were. I waved him off with a brittle smile, and before he could question it, he was pulled away by another guest. Then Ellie was gone, and I searched the crowds for her, only to spy her at the bar, eyeballing Adam, who was flirting with some girl I didn't recognize. Men. I shook my head angrily. Assholes.

Maybe I was a little drunk.

I was just about to go to the bar and ask for water when I felt a cool hand on my bare back. I turned, surprised to find Gavin the personal trainer smiling down at me.

'Joss.' He grinned, still touching me. 'It's nice to see you again.'

I'll admit that the huge smile I gave him was more about my being pissed off at Braden for getting me to take the night off work and then ignoring me for most of it than my being glad to see him. 'Gavin, hey.'

He whistled as he drew his gaze down my body, and I noted the slight sway of his own. He was definitely drunk. 'You look stunning.'

I smiled again. 'Thank you.'

'What are you doing here tonight?'

'Uh . . . I know the owner.'

His eyes narrowed, and he nodded slowly. 'I see.'

'What about you?'

'Well, I'm here to dance. With you.'

I laughed outright. 'Oh, smooth.'

'I do try. Why do –'

Smack!

Gavin's hand was ripped away from my body, and I watched in horror as he crumpled to the floor, blood trickling down his nose. I glanced up at Braden, who was shaking out his already-swelling fist, his chest heaving with fury as he glared down at Gavin. The crowd had parted around us, watching, and I felt Adam and Ellie sidle up to us. 'What the hell was that?' I choked out, loud enough to be heard over the music that had been turned down a notch when the crowd had ooohed at Braden's punch.

Braden shot me a dirty look. '*That* is Gavin. The friend who fucked Analise. Why the hell were you talking to him like you know him?'

My mouth fell open as I turned to look at the personal trainer, watching as he got back on his feet. Shock and disgust warred within me. 'He's a trainer at my gym. He helped me once.' I glanced back up at Braden. 'I swear, I didn't know.'

Gavin snorted and we looked back at him. He was wiping the blood from his nose and grinning at Braden. 'Looks like you moved on to better things, Bray.' His eyes scanned me now, sleazy and probing. 'Here's hoping history repeats itself, because I've wanted between her legs for fucking weeks. How about it, Joss? You fancy shagging a real man?'

Braden was like lightning. One minute he was at my side and the next he had Gavin on the floor, his fist pounding into him again and again. Adam darted past me and started to pull him off, the security appearing through the crowds to pick up a bloodied Gavin and hold him back.

Adam's grip on Braden was tight as the two faced off. Braden pointed threateningly at Gavin. 'You stay the fuck away from her,' he snarled.

Gavin wiped at his face again, wincing. 'Christ, you never hit me when I banged your old lady, Bray. Tease you about your latest skank, and I'm down in seconds. Is her pussy made of gold or something?'

Braden growled and lunged for him again, but one of the bartenders helped Adam to hold him back. 'Get him out of here,' Adam ordered the security. Then his eyes narrowed on Gavin. 'I see you out on the street, I'll knock your teeth through the back of your skull.'

Gavin made a face at Adam's threat and let the security manhandle him out of the club.

I stared in astonishment at Braden, not really even registering Gavin's horrible words. Braden had hit someone. Over me? After just telling me he hadn't hit anyone since he was nineteen, he'd hit someone. Over me. Or had it been about his ex-wife?

I struggled to process it, the blood still whooshing in my ears.

Braden jerked Adam's hands off him.

'You all right, bud?' Adam asked him.

Instead of answering, Braden's eyes slid to me. His arm shot out and he grabbed my wrist, pulling me as he spun around and started making his way toward his office. I shot a wide-eyed look over my shoulder at a worried Ellie but didn't stop the momentum for fear I'd go over on my ankle.

I was hauled into the office with a sharp tug, and I tottered up against Braden's 'nice and big' office desk as the door crashed shut behind us. Very deliberately, Braden turned the lock.

I waited, unnerved by this scary fire-breathing caveman-on-crack version of Braden as he strode menacingly toward me. 'First you wear that dress so every man in this club wants to screw you. Then you start flirting with the man who fucking betrayed me,' he hissed into my face.

I pushed against his chest to no avail, my own anger rising. 'Hey!' I retorted. 'One: Back off the dress. I like it, so suck it up. And two: I didn't even know who he was!'

If it was even possible his face got a whole lot cloudier. I shivered, trying to step back, but the desk was in my way. 'And yet you were still flirting with him!'

He'd never yelled at me before, and I flinched back, intimidated and pissed off in equal measure. I shoved harder at his chest, but he only leaned into my hands like a damn cement block. 'Me?' I huffed incredulously. 'You ask me to take the night off for this, and then I find out you've invited all your previous fuck buddies and girlfriends, and you spend the entire night flirting your ass off with more than one of them! What is this, Braden?' I felt the anger dissolve into hurt and with it my voice grew quieter. 'Is this me getting laid off early?'

I watched some of the fury melt from his expression, his hands coming up to grip my hips tight to his. My breath stuttered at the feel of his erection rubbing against me, but I wasn't surprised. There was something electric between us, and it was really confusing being this angry and this turned on all at the same time. 'Babe, that wasn't anything out there.' His voice was low, his head bending toward mine. 'I wanted a big take tonight, and a lot of those girls like to party and have a lot of friends who like to party. That's all it was.'

'And the flirting?'

He shrugged. 'I didn't even realize. I didn't mean to hurt you.'

I scoffed, needing to hold onto a little bit of dignity. 'You didn't hurt me. I can't be hurt by you.'

At my scathing tone, Braden's mouth hardened – the anger was back. I found myself pushed roughly against the desk as Braden grasped the backs of my thighs and lifted my legs, pressing in between them as he shoved the hem of my dress up to my waist. I clutched at him for balance, the desk cold against my backside. 'Don't fucking lie to me, Jocelyn.'

I tried to push at him, but he only pressed deeper, his right hand leaving my leg to unbutton his slacks. I was panting now. 'I'm not lying.'

I felt his cock nudge against my sex as he leaned in to whisper in my ear, 'You're lying.' He kissed my neck.

Then he surprised me by taking a shaky breath. 'I'm sorry for hurting you.'

I could only nod unsurely, feeling out of control of the entire situation.

'Babe.' He pulled back, his eyes blazing now with something I didn't understand. 'I hit him,' he said hoarsely, and I suddenly realized the look was disbelief. 'I hit him. Seeing him with you . . . I hit him.'

Because of me. I cupped his face in my hands, suddenly not afraid of him. 'Don't,' I whispered across his lips. 'Don't do that to yourself.'

He crushed my lips beneath his at the exact same moment that he tore my panties off, his tongue thrusting into my mouth hungrily as his cock thrust hungrily inside me. I gasped at the sudden invasion, arching my back as he gripped me high by the back of the thighs and pounded into me over and over, my cries of pleasure filling the office, his grunts muffled in my neck. 'Jocelyn,' he growled, trying to bury himself deeper. 'Lie back,' he demanded.

I did it instantly, falling back, the bare skin revealed by the dress pressed against the cool wood. At this angle, Braden lifted my legs higher, which allowed him to slide in harder, deeper. I writhed on the desk, my lower body completely in Braden's control. The torture was exquisite, and the orgasm tore through me in record time.

Braden wasn't done. As I came down off my orgasm, I watched him watch me as he ground into me, chasing his own climax. I could feel another orgasm building. When Braden came, he threw his head back, his teeth gritted, the muscles in his neck straining as his hips jerked against me. The feel of him coming inside of me, the image of his face in release, was the sexiest thing I'd ever seen, and I cried out, my sex pulsing around his cock as I came again.

'Jesus.' Braden watched me, hunger in his eyes.

Finally my muscles relaxed, and I closed my eyes, trying to catch my breath.

He was still inside me when he apologized softly, saying, 'I was a dick tonight.'

'Yeah,' I murmured.

He squeezed my hip. 'Am I forgiven?'

I opened my eyes and smiled, amused. 'I already accepted the two orgasms as an apology.'

Braden didn't laugh like he normally would have. Instead he nudged his semi-hard cock a little farther inside me until I could almost feel it kissing my womb, and he muttered, 'Mine.'

I blinked, not sure I'd heard right. 'What?'

'Come on,' Braden sighed, pulling carefully out of me and tucking himself back into his pants. He gently eased me up off the table and grimaced as he picked up my torn panties.

'Now I'm walking out of there in this dress without any underwear on, caveman.' I grinned saucily.

Braden closed his eyes at the thought. 'Fuck.'

19

The next few months were a blur of Braden. After the night at Fire he had still been pretty raw about the whole Gavin thing, but I did my best to convince him that the guy deserved to be punched, and more important, that losing his temper in that moment did not a make him a bad guy. I discovered more from Adam about Gavin. Apparently they'd all been friends since elementary school, but as they'd gotten older, Gavin had turned into a bit of an asshole. He was sly, sometimes caustic, horrible to women – a shit-stirrer as Adam called him – and a liar. Braden had had this stubborn sense of loyalty to him because they'd been friends for so long. That was until the guy had screwed his wife. As I reiterated all these things to Braden, I think I finally got through, and a few weeks later I watched the grim contemplation gradually disappear.

Of course I canceled my gym membership after Braden persuaded me to join his, where I discovered that part of the reason he had those sexy broad shoulders and narrow hips was because he swam after every workout. Somehow, more often than not, I ended up working out with him and taking that swim, too. Somehow, in fact, we invaded each other's lives almost completely. We took turns staying at each other's apartments on weeknights whenever we could; we both were pretty content to just hang out and watch TV or listen to music, but we also had fun throwing in trips to restaurants and the movies, or grabbing a few drinks with friends. At least twice a month we had some kind of event that involved Braden's work. I'd even ended up mentioned in an entertainment article for the local paper as Braden's regular plus one and latest woman. I tried not to let it get to me.

Braden tried to make it to Club 39 on Fridays and Saturdays, and that meant Ellie and Adam and whoever else was with them that night were there too. Braden told me he liked to watch me work, that it was sexy, but Ellie pronounced that he was marking his territory in front of my colleagues and customers.

All I knew was that he was with me as much as he could be and that meant he made sure he was at the bar a lot. And it didn't bother me.

In fact, I missed him when he was gone. Our arrangement hadn't turned out the way I'd expected it to at all – the arrangement actually kind of fell apart. And somewhere along the way I'd stopped caring, as long as it meant I could be with him without any scary questions about the future.

We were in my room; Braden was going over Adam's drawings for a new development, which were spread out all over my bed. I was at my typewriter working on chapter fifteen of my novel, and I was happy with it so far. In all honesty, I was really excited about where the story was going. The characters felt more real than any

I'd written before, and I knew it was because they were based on my parents. I was staring at my notes, trying to work out if the line of dialogue I'd written in this scene was appropriate for my main character. The more I thought about it, the more it didn't feel true to her, and I was trying to think how to change it without changing the point she was attempting to make. I was so lost in thought, I didn't even realize Braden was watching me, so I jumped, startled, when he spoke, my heart lodged in my throat at his words. 'It's Jenna and Ed's wedding next week, and the end of the terms of our arrangement.'

I froze.

I already knew that. I'd been dreading him bringing it up.

'Why haven't you brought it up?' Dr Pritchard took a sip of water. 'The three months are nearly up. Don't you think you should discuss it?'

I tilted my head to the side. 'Don't you think I've come a long way in five months?'

'You've definitely opened up, Jocelyn. But I still think you haven't fully dealt with your family's passing. You still won't talk about them.'

'I know you think that. But what I'm saying is that five months ago I had a best friend I knew nothing about and who knew nothing about me. I didn't like getting involved too deeply in people's lives, and I was determined to surround myself with casual acquaintances.' I grinned in relieved disbelief. 'Ellie and Braden changed all that. Especially Braden. He's . . .' I shook my head, still not able to really believe it was true. 'He's my best friend. Three months ago I was determined to just have sex and then end this thing. But he's a part of me now. He's in deeper than anyone else, and I have no idea what to expect from that or from the future. I don't really want to think about it. However, I do know that I'm not ready to lose my best friend again.'

'You should discuss this with him, Joss. He needs to know this.'

I frowned, anxiety gripping me at the thought. 'No. No, I'm not doing that. If he wants this to end, then fine, but if it ends, it'll be easier if only I know the truth.'

Dr Pritchard sighed. 'Why? So you can bury that truth along with all the others?'

You're such a buzzkill. 'You're such a buzzkill.'

She laughed. 'Only because I don't bury the truth.'

'Always have to have the last word, huh?'

I turned slowly to face him. 'Yeah, it is.'

Braden pushed the paper off his lap and gave me his entire focus. 'How do you feel about it?'

'How do *you* feel about it?'

His eyes narrowed. 'I asked you first.'

I sighed, little ants of uncertainty swarming in my gut. 'What are we, five?'

'Well, are we?'

I stared into his stubborn eyes. 'Braden.' I didn't even mean for it to come out as a plea, but it did.

'I could answer this one easily, Jocelyn – we know

who's more open here out of the two of us – but I'm not going to. I want, for once, to know how *you* feel.'

'What do you mean "for once",' I snapped. 'You get more out of me than most people, buddy.'

He flashed me a quick, cocky, and far too attractive grin. 'I know, babe. Tonight I want more.'

I don't think he realized it, but right then he'd made the first play. He wanted more. So, with some confidence, I shrugged casually and turned back to my typewriter. 'I don't mind if we tear up the agreement.'

He was silent behind me as I waited. Finally, he said, 'What if I suggested we stop pretending we're fuck buddies, too?'

A slow smile spread across my lips, and I was thankful he couldn't see it. 'Yeah,' I answered with a good amount of boredom. 'I could work with that.'

Did I mention Braden could move fast?

Papers went flying as he lunged across the bed to grab me by the waist and haul me off my chair onto the mattress. Startled, I laughed up at him as he pressed his body into mine. 'When will you quit throwing me around like a rag doll?'

His grin was unrepentant. 'Never. You're so tiny I do it without really meaning to half the time.'

'I am not tiny,' I replied indignantly. 'I'm five-five. There are tinier people, believe me.'

'Babe, I'm almost a whole foot taller than you. You're tiny.' He bent his head to brush my lips with his. 'But I like it.'

'What happened to your love of the long-legged bimbo?'

'It was replaced by my love for great tits, great sex, and a smart mouth.' He kissed me deeply, his tongue tangling with mine deliciously. Wrapping my arms around his neck, I sank into the kiss like always, but for once my mind wasn't just on the kiss . . .

In a roundabout way . . . had that been some kind of declaration of love?

I gasped at the thought but luckily timed that gasp to when Braden stuck his hand down my pants, so he never realized I was freaking out.

I told myself that's not at all what he'd meant and shrugged it off, just enjoying each day with him as they came. A few days later I was in the kitchen taking a coffee break from the novel when Ellie sauntered in. She was home today, grading papers.

She smiled slyly as she slid into the seat opposite me.

I quirked an eyebrow in suspicion. 'What?'

'I just got off the phone with my big brother.'

'And?'

Ellie made a face. 'He told me you're going to the wedding together.'

'And?'

'Joss.' She threw a tea biscuit at me and I dodged it. 'When were you going to tell me?'

I glanced down at the violent biscuit now littering our floor. 'Tell you what exactly?'

'That the arrangement between you and Braden is over? It is, right? You're dating now?'

Dating? That word was a little labely. I refused to be labeled. 'We are seeing each other.'

Ellie squealed and I flinched back. 'Oh, this is fantastic! I knew it, I knew it!'

'I wish I knew what you knew,' I replied in bemusement.

'Oh, come off it. I knew from the start Braden was acting differently about you.' She sighed with absolute contentment. 'Life is good. It'll be even better with a cup of tea.'

'You need to refill the kettle.' She nodded and headed over to it, and as I watched her I thought about Adam. 'Adam's got a date. Are you taking one?'

Her shoulders stiffened a little as she carried the kettle to the sink. 'I'm taking Nicholas.'

'Ooh, that should be fun,' I murmured, thinking about the possible drama once Adam found that out.

A crash brought my head up as Ellie cursed, her face scrunched up. I rushed over to see that she'd dropped the kettle into the sink and was clutching her right arm. 'You okay?' I asked, confused as to what had happened.

Her face was pale. She nodded, her lips pinched. 'Just a cramp in my hand from marking all those papers.'

'You dropped the kettle.' It wasn't the first time she'd been working so damn hard her hand had cramped up. 'You need to go easy and take more breaks. You work too hard.' Ellie looked so worried I felt my heart flip. 'Els, are you okay?'

She gave me a wobbly smile. 'Stressed.'

'Take a nap.' I rubbed her shoulder soothingly. 'You'll feel better.'

'Hey, gorgeous.'

I spun around on my heels and grinned at Braden, who was standing all sexy in a black contemporary tux. He and Adam had decided to forgo wearing traditional kilts since November in Scotland was 'Baltic,' as they said. 'Hey, handsome.'

'Did I tell you how much I like this dress?' He strolled in casually, his hands reaching for my hips to pull me close. 'It's a good dress.'

It was amethyst satin and hugged my figure, showing a little cleavage and a little leg. It was a dress that teased, and Braden enjoyed being teased. I pressed a familiar kiss just under his jaw, my favorite place to nibble. 'We better go before we're late. Is Ellie ready yet?'

'No. And I can't sit out there alone with Nicholas.' Braden grimaced.

I wrinkled my nose. 'That poor guy is so boring.'

Braden groaned and buried his face in my neck. 'My sister needs her head checked,' he mumbled into my skin, and I laughed silently, stroking his hair.

'Ellie will be fine.'

Braden pulled back, suddenly all bristly and growly. 'He's not good enough for her.'

I shrugged, picking up my clutch and coat. 'I'm not good enough for you, but that hasn't stopped *you*.'

He grabbed my hand tightly, scowling at me. 'What?'

'I'm ready!' Ellie bounced into my room in a designer fifties-style dress with a white, pale yellow, chocolate, and teal print. She had on a silk petticoat underneath and wore a white wool coat that cost more than my entire outfit. I smiled. She looked so pretty. 'Joss, you look great. Taxi's waiting.' She took my hand and dragged Braden and me out into the hall, where the unfortunately monotonous Nicholas was waiting for us.

I was just glad I didn't have to answer for that insanely stupid slip-up back in the bedroom.

The entire wedding – ceremony and reception – was held at the Edinburgh Corn Exchange, an events venue that hosted everything from weddings to rock gigs. It was a pretty old building with Greek columns, but it wasn't spectacularly beautiful and neither were its surroundings. But the ceremony room was beautiful, and the reception was just breathtaking. Everything was white and silver with ice-blue lights. It was a winter wonderland for a winter wedding.

Braden had wandered off to talk to Adam, who'd so far spent most of the wedding ignoring his very pretty date and glaring at Nicholas. Why he was glaring at Nicholas when Ellie had left the poor guy to his own devices, to flutter around to everyone like the social butterfly she was, I had no idea. But if looks could kill . . .

I shook my head. He needed to get a clue already.

'Joss.'

I glanced up from sipping champagne to find Elodie standing over me. She and Clark were at the next table,

306

and I glanced past her to see Clark in deep conversation with an older guy I didn't know. Who was I kidding? I hardly knew anyone there. I smiled up at Elodie, who looked gorgeous in sapphire blue. 'Hey, how are you?'

She gave me a *you know how it is* smile and slid into the empty seat next to me. By now, of course, she'd cottoned on to the fact that Braden and I were seeing each other – especially because he wasn't subtle about it and Declan had caught him kissing me in the kitchen at a Sunday dinner weeks ago. He'd said, 'Ugh, yuck,' and then proceeded to enlighten the entire family.

'Braden seems really happy.' Elodie grinned over at him across the room. I noted that a pretty and very tall blonde had joined him and Adam, and tried not to narrow my eyes like a jealous tiger. 'I don't think I've ever seen him this happy.'

I felt an ache of warmth ripple across my chest, but I didn't know what to say.

She looked back at me, her eyes kind but serious. 'I think you're a lovely girl, Joss. I do. But I also think you're incredibly difficult to get to know. I don't know why, but you have such a guard up, sweetheart. It's high and nearly impenetrable.'

I felt the color drain from my face.

'I think of Braden as a son. A son I love very much. What Analise did to him broke my heart. He shouldn't have to go through that again. Or worse.' She looked again at him and then back to me. 'With you, I think it'll be worse.'

'Elodie . . .' Words failed me.

'If you don't feel about him the way he feels about you, end it now, Joss. For his sake.' And then she stood, patted my shoulder in her mothering way, and headed back over to the husband that she adored.

'Babe, you okay?'

I glanced up, my heart still banging in my chest, to find Braden standing over me, his eyebrows creased with concern. I nodded, still speechless.

He didn't look convinced. 'Come on.' He took my hand and drew me to my feet. 'Come dance with me.'

La Rocca's 'Non Believer' was playing. It was a favorite of mine. 'You dance?'

'Tonight I do.' I let him lead me onto the dance floor and buried into him as he held me close. 'Your heart is racing. Did Elodie say something to you?'

Just the truth. She was right. I should walk away. I breathed him in, not able to picture a moment without him in my life.

So I was selfish. I snuggled closer. I couldn't walk away. But if I hurt him? Oh God, the thought of hurting him ripped me apart. Ripped me so totally that I knew I cared more for him than I did for myself.

I was in deep.

I felt my breath hitch. Reading the change in me, Braden squeezed me closer and murmured, 'Breathe, babe,' in my ear. I wasn't having a panic attack, just a freak-out, but I didn't say anything, enjoying the calm as he stroked my back soothingly.

'What did she say?' His tone was hard. He was mad at Elodie.

I shook my head, reassuring him. 'She just men-tioned how important family is. It wasn't her fault.'

'Babe,' he whispered, stroking my cheek.

'You want to get me drunk?' I asked, trying to lighten the mood.

Braden snorted, sliding his hands sensually down my back to the curve of my hips. 'I don't need to get you drunk to have my way with you.'

'Oh, you are so lucky I like the whole caveman thing, Braden Carmichael.'

20

I don't know why, but I didn't tell the good doctor about any of that. I coveted that piece of me, held it close, as I tried to figure out what exactly I was going to do with it. I still had no plan, but I didn't let it get in the way of enjoying my time with Braden. I'm thankful for that, because little did I know, only a few weeks after the wedding, during the first week in December, everything would change.

While Ellie worked at the kitchen table, Braden and I lounged in the sitting room, the lights low, the Christmas tree lights glittering at the window. Ellie had insisted we put the tree up on the first. She was a Christmassy girl. It was a cold December night, a Wednesday, and we were watching a Korean revenge movie called *A Bittersweet Life*. I was into it, but it seemed Braden's mind was elsewhere.

'Do you fancy going to the German market this Saturday?'

I'd already been last Saturday with Ellie, but I loved the German market, and I'd be with Braden, so, yeah, I was up for that. Edinburgh at Christmastime was magical, even to a nonbeliever like me. White lights were wrapped around all the trees in Princes Street Gardens.

A German market with all these amazing smells and pretty gifts and weird sausages set up camp on the west side of the gardens by the Royal Scottish Academy, and on the east side, by the Scott Monument, was a fairground with a huge Ferris wheel that lit up the night sky. There was nothing quite like walking that street on a crisp winter's day at dusk.

'Sure,' I replied, and smiled over at him. I was lying sprawled out on the couch, and Braden was lounging at the end of it.

He nodded. 'I was thinking in February we could take some time off work. A long weekend maybe. I've got a cabin in Hunters Quay and it looks right over the Holy Loch. It's pretty nice. Peaceful. Not to mention there's an amazing Indian restaurant in Dunoon, which is just across the Loch.'

It sounded awesome, especially considering I'd been in Scotland for over four years and hadn't gone farther than St Andrews. 'Sounds great. Where is it exactly?'

'Argyll.'

'Oh.' That wasn't the Highlands, was it? 'Isn't Argyll in the west?'

As if he read my mind, Braden grinned. 'It's the western Highlands. It's beautiful, trust me.'

'You sold me at the Loch,' I exaggerated the *ch* sound like he did. 'Just tell me when, and I'm there.'

At that, Braden looked affectionately amused. 'Sex and holidays.'

'Uh, what?'

'I'm making a list of things that make you agreeable.'

I scoffed, pushing my foot into his leg. 'And all you got is sex and vacations?'

'The length of the list is not my fault.'

'Are you saying I'm disagreeable?'

He raised an eyebrow. 'Woman, how stupid do you think I am? You really think I'm answering that? I want to get laid tonight.'

I pushed him harder. 'Watch it, or you might get laid to rest.'

Braden threw his head back and laughed.

Scowling but not really meaning it, I turned back to the movie. 'You're lucky you're good in bed.'

'Oh.' He grabbed at my foot. 'I think you keep me around for other reasons.'

I slanted him a look out of the corner of my eye. 'Right now, for the life of me, I can't think what those reasons are.'

Braden tugged harder on my foot, raising his fingers toward it. 'Take it back or the foot gets it.'

Oh hell, no! I yanked at my appendage. 'Braden, no.'

Deaf to my warning, he started to tickle me, his grip tightening as I laughed breathlessly and kicked out, trying to get free.

He wouldn't stop.

Ruthless!

'Braden,' I panted hysterically, attempting to shove at him with my arms but struggling as he continued his war on my feet. I laughed harder, ribs aching, and then . . . horror.

I broke wind.

Big-time.

Braden immediately let go of my feet, his loud, rumbling laugh filling the room, laughter that only deepened when I lost my balance from kicking out at him and then being abruptly let go, and fell off the couch with an undignified thud.

Mortified as he collapsed against the couch belly laughing at my fart and then my fall, I grabbed a cushion and launched it at him from my position on the floor.

Of course this only made the idiot laugh harder.

I warred between feeling humiliated that I'd farted in front of him – something you just didn't do in company – and laughing, as his was so infectious. 'Braden!' I whined. 'Shut up. It's not funny,' I huffed, my lips caught in part smile, part grimace.

'Oh, babe.' He tried to catch his breath, wiping a tear from the corner of his eye as he grinned down at me. 'That was definitely funny.' He held out a hand to help me up.

I slapped it away. 'You're such an immature a-hole.'

'Hey, I'm not the one who just let off.'

Oh God, it was so awful. I groaned, falling onto my back and covering my eyes with my hands.

'Jocelyn.' I felt his hand on my knee and heard the amusement in his voice. 'Babe, why are you so embarrassed? It was just a fart. Brilliantly timed, I might add.'

I sucked in the mortification. 'Oh my God, shut up.' He chuckled again and I furiously snapped open my eyes. 'You're enjoying this!'

'Well, yeah,' he gave a huff of laughter, his eyes bright. 'I've never seen you embarrassed before. Even when I walked in on you naked you gave me attitude and acted like you didn't care. That *you're* mortified by a fart is really quite adorable.'

'I am not adorable!'

'Oh, I think you are.'

'I am cool and self-possessed,' I argued. 'Cool and self-possessed people do not break wind. You, in particular, are not supposed to know that I break wind!'

His lips twitched. 'I hate to tell you this, babe, but I already knew that you broke wind. Part of the human condition and all that.'

I shook my head defiantly. 'We should just end it now. All the mystery is gone.'

Braden was laughing hard again as he reached down to pull me up by the waist. I was in the middle of letting him help me when a crash and thud sounded from the kitchen. Our eyes flew to each other, our laughter dying.

'Ellie?' Braden shouted out in question.

Silence.

'Ellie!'

When she didn't call back, my worried gaze met his, and I jumped to my feet. Braden had already let me go to run through the apartment.

'Ellie!' I heard him cry out, and the fear in his voice had me picking up speed.

The sight that greeted me in the kitchen shocked me. I stood frozen, watching as Braden kneeled on the floor, his hands hovering over Ellie, whose body twitched in convulsions, her eyes fluttering rapidly, her mouth slack.

'Ellie?' Braden's pale face snapped up to me. 'Call nine-nine-nine. I think she's having some kind of seizure.'

I rushed out of the room, adrenaline making my hands shake and my coordination clumsy as I grabbed for the phone on my bedside table and dropped it. Fumbling, I cursed, utter fear choking me as I hurried back into the hall as the operator picked up. 'Emergency, what service do you require? Fire, police, or ambulance?'

'She just passed out.' Braden sat next to her, helpless, as her body went limp. 'I don't know what to do. Fuck, I don't know what to do.'

'Ambulance.' I heard the line go on hold and then two seconds later the ambulance control room picked up. 'My roommate,' I spoke breathlessly into the phone, panicking because Braden of all people was panicking. 'We heard a crash and rushed into the kitchen, and she was convulsing and now she's unconscious.'

'What telephone number are you calling from?'

I rattled it off impatiently.

'What is your exact location?'

Trying not to get angry at the robo-speak of the woman on the end of the line, I rattled the address off, too.

'Is this your roommate's first seizure?'

'Yes!' I snapped.

'What age is your roommate?'

'Twenty-three.'

'Is she breathing?'

'She's breathing, Braden, right?'

He nodded, his jaw clenched as he watched me.

'Okay, can you move your roommate into the recovery position as a precaution?'

'Recovery position,' I repeated to Braden and watched as he immediately, gently rearranged her.

'The ambulance is on its way. Please keep any pets out of the way of the ambulance crew when they arrive.'

'We don't have pets.'

'Okay. Please stay on the line until the ambulance arrives.'

'Braden,' I whispered, still shaking, 'what's going on?'

He shook his head as he brushed Ellie's hair off her face. 'I don't know.'

A noise drew us up.

A noise from Ellie.

I rushed over to them, falling to my knees to bend over her. Another groan escaped Ellie's mouth as her head turned slowly. 'Wha . . .' Her eyes flickered open, dazed with confusion as she saw us hovering over her. 'What happened?'

Despite regaining consciousness, the paramedics took Ellie away in the ambulance. Braden and I jumped into a cab to follow them to the Royal Infirmary of Edinburgh. Braden called Elodie and Clark, and then he called Adam. After we arrived there was a lot of standing around and no one was really telling us anything, and when Elodie, Clark and Adam arrived, there had still been no word.

'We left the kids with our neighbor,' Elodie whispered, fear in her eyes. 'What happened?'

Braden explained as I stood silently by, my mind racing over all the worst outcomes. Being in the hospital was freaking me out, and I just wanted Ellie to come out and tell us everything was okay. I didn't think I could handle anything else.

'Ellie Carmichael's family?' a nurse called and we all stampeded toward her. She stared at us wide-eyed. 'Are you all immediate family?'

'Yes,' Braden answered before Adam or I could respond.

'Come with me.'

Ellie was waiting for us, sitting up with her legs dangling off the side of a bed in the ER. She gave us a typical little-girl Ellie wave, and my heart lurched in my chest.

'What's going on?' Elodie rushed to her side, and Ellie grabbed at her mother's hand reassuringly.

'Ellie's family?'

We turned to find a fortysomething, bookish-looking doctor hovering over us. 'Yes,' we all said in unison, at which Ellie cracked an exhausted smile.

'I'm Dr Ferguson. We're sending Ellie up for an MRI as soon as it becomes available.'

'An MRI?' Braden's features grew taut as he glanced back at his sister. 'What's going on, Els?'

Her eyes were filled with trepidation as she took us all in, our worry blasting out at her. 'I haven't felt right for a while.'

'What do you mean "felt right"?' Adam asked impatiently, crowding her, his bristling, angry intimidation making Ellie flinch.

'Adam.' I pulled on his shoulder to get him to ease up, but he just shrugged me off.

'I think the doctor was wrong about me needing glasses,' Ellie admitted quietly.

Dr Ferguson cleared his throat, obviously feeling he should come to his patient's rescue. 'Ellie has told us she's been dealing with headaches, numbness and tingling in her right arm, a lack of energy, some lack of coordination, and today she had her first seizure. We're just sending her up for an MRI to see if we can find anything that might explain Ellie's symptoms.'

'Numbness?' I muttered, glancing at her arm, images of her squeezing it, shaking it, flooding over me. The amount of times she'd told me she had a headache. *Fuck*.

'I'm sorry, Joss. I just didn't want to admit I was feeling so rubbish.'

'I can't believe this.' Elodie sagged against Clark. 'You should have told us.'

Ellie's lip trembled. 'I know.'

'When will the MRI be ready?' Braden asked, his voice low and demanding.

Dr Ferguson didn't seem to be intimidated. 'I'll take Ellie up as soon as it's free, but there are a few patients booked in before her.'

And so the waiting began.

21

After hours and hours of waiting, Ellie had an MRI and was sent home. They told us we'd receive the results as soon as possible but this still meant up to a two-week wait. In the end we waited ten days, and those ten days were awful. A kind of blank numbness fell over us as all the worst outcomes raced through our heads. I went to see Dr Pritchard but couldn't even bring myself to talk about what was going on with me. It was a quiet session.

The whole ten days were a quiet session – the three of us sitting in the apartment, taking calls from Adam and Elodie, but not really saying much else. There was lots of tea and coffee making, takeout, and television. But no discussion. It was like the fear had put a lockdown on any meaningful conversation. And for the first time since we'd started seeing each other, Braden and I shared a bed without having sex. I didn't know what to do for him, so I let him take the lead. When we did have sex, it was slow and gentle. When we didn't, Braden would roll me onto my side and wrap an arm around me, pulling me back into him, his head resting next to mine. I wrapped my own arm over his, hooked my foot around his leg and let him fall asleep against me like that.

*

Dr Ferguson called and asked Ellie to come in to speak with him.

That was bad. That sounded bad. I stared at Ellie after she got off the phone and everything I'd been holding in, controlling, just burst apart at the seams. I saw the fear in Ellie's eyes, but I was so consumed by my own, I couldn't say anything to her that would help, so I didn't say anything at all. Braden accompanied her to her appointment, and I waited in the apartment – the big, cold, silent apartment – staring at the Christmas tree, unable to believe that Christmas was only ten days away.

The two hours they were gone I had to sit my ass on that iron box of mine to keep the lid closed. Or I wouldn't have been able to breathe.

When I heard the apartment door open, everything felt lethargic, like I was moving underwater, struggling slowly against the weight. The sitting-room door opened, and Braden walked in, his face so pale and his eyes so glazed that I knew before I even looked at tear-streaked Ellie. I knew what fear felt like when it was pulsing from a person; I knew how grief could thicken the air, how it could slam into your chest and cause pain through your whole body. Your eyes, your head, your arms, your legs, even your gums.

'They found something. A tumor.'

My eyes flew to Ellie, and she shrugged at me, her mouth trembling. 'They've referred me to a neurologist, Dr Dunham at the Western General. I've got to go in and speak with him tomorrow about everything. About the next step. Whether it requires surgery. Whether it's malignant or not,' Ellie finished.

This was not happening.

How had I let this happen?

I took a step back, confused, angry, disbelieving that this was happening again.

It was all my fault.

I'd let them in, I'd broken my rules, and I was back at square fucking one!

Shit.

Shit!

SHIT!

But the terrified screams echoed only in my head. I gave Ellie a stoic nod. 'You'll be fine. We don't know anything yet.'

But I knew. I knew. I was a curse. I knew I couldn't be this happy. I knew that something bad would happen. What had I done to Ellie?

Ellie? I hurt for her. I wanted to take away her fear. I wanted her to be okay.

But I didn't do any of that.

Instead I shoved her inside my iron box. 'I've got my shift at the bar tonight. I'm going to get in some gym time before then.' I nodded at them robotically and made to move past them.

'Jocelyn?' Braden grabbed my arm, his eyes full of apprehension and fear. And disbelief at my attitude. He needed me.

I didn't want to need him.

I tugged my arm back gently and gave him a brittle smile. 'I'll see you both later.'

And then I walked out, leaving them alone with their fears.

I didn't go to the gym. I went to Edinburgh Castle before it closed. The walk up the Royal Mile to Castle-hill was brisk and frosty, the cold biting into my cheeks, my lungs seeming to work extra hard against the winter air. Once I crossed the drawbridge, I paid for my ticket, and then strolled under the stone arch and took the pebbled walkway that swept upward on the right. I headed up the main thoroughfare and turned right to the castle walls. There I stopped, standing by Mons Meg, one of the world's oldest cannons, and together we stared out over the city. Even in the slightly misty frost, the city was breathtaking from here. I'd paid the not-so-inexpensive entry fee to the castle just for this view. And I guess for the majesty of it all. It was where I believed I could find a little peace, and I did this whenever I panicked about never, ever finding the long-lasting peace I sought. Today I needed this.

Blazing through the last few months, burying my head in the sand, pretending there weren't conse-quences to loving people, had gotten me where I was. Only six months of making the change into the 'new me' and the floor had been ripped out from underneath me again.

That kind of thinking was selfish.

I knew that.

Ellie was the one suffering, not me.

But that wasn't true either.

Ellie Carmichael was one of a kind. She was sweet, kind, sort of goofy, funny, big-hearted . . . and my family. The first family I'd had since losing my own. I felt protective of her; I hurt when she hurt; I thought about her happiness and what I could to do to make her life better. Not even my relationship with Rhian was as close.

I was almost as close with Ellie as I had been with Dru.

And now I was going to lose Ellie as well.

I sunk down to the ice-cold stone ground beside the cannon and wrapped my arms around my body in an effort to choke out the pain. It occurred to me that if I rewrote it all in my head, then maybe I wouldn't feel this way. Maybe Ellie and I weren't that close. Maybe we never had been. If that were true, then losing her would be okay.

I jumped suddenly at the sound of my cell ringing. Stomach leaden with dread, I pulled it out and exhaled in relief when I saw it was Rhian calling.

'Hey,' I answered hoarsely.

'Yo, bitch,' Rhian called down the line, sounding surprisingly chipper. 'How's it hanging? I'm just calling to let you know that James and I are flying into Edinburgh in three days and then heading through to Falkirk to stay with his mum over Christmas. We're going to nip in to see you before we get the train, so I need your address, hon.'

Awful timing. 'Things are kind of weird at the apartment at the moment. Can I meet you for coffee instead?'

'Jesus, Joss, you sound like hell. Is everything okay?'

I don't want to talk about it over the phone. 'I'll explain when I see you. Coffee?'

'Yeah, okay.' She still sounded worried. 'The coffee shop in the bookstore on Princes Street. Three o'clock Tuesday.'

'See you then.' I hung up, my eyes scanning the view and then traveling upward to the white clouds with their pale bellies and grumpy faces. It was just a vast array of weightless, floating fluff. Their bellies weren't dark or heavy.

Without the weight, there would be no rain.

Jo grabbed me before I could take my next customer's order and tugged me all the way back into the staff room. Her hands flew to her hips, her eyebrows drawn together. 'You're acting really weird.'

I shrugged, enjoying the blanket of numbness I'd found and promptly wrapped around myself. 'I'm just tired.'

'No.' Jo took a step forward, her face etched with concern. 'There's something going on here with you, Joss. Look, I know we're not really close, but you've always been there for me when I go on and on about my problems, so if you need to talk to me, I'm here.'

I don't want you to be there for me. 'I'm fine.'

She shook her head. 'You've got this, like, dead look in your eyes, Joss. You're scaring the crap out of me and

Craig. Has something happened? Did something happen with Braden?'

No. And it's not going to. 'No.'

'Joss?'

'Jo, it's really busy out there – can we not do this?'

She flinched and then bit her lip uneasily. 'Okay.'

I nodded and spun on my heel, heading back into the bar to get on with it. I saw Jo sidle up to Craig and whisper something to him. His head whipped around to stare at me.

'Joss, what the fuck is going on with you, sweetheart?'

I flipped him off as an answer.

Craig shot Jo a look. 'I don't think she wants to talk about it.'

To my utter shock, Braden was waiting outside of Club 39 for me. My shift had whipped by in a blur. I couldn't even remember doing anything, so it took me a moment to come out of the fog and recognize him. He stood leaning against the wrought-iron railing, unshaven, staring down at the ground in grim contemplation, his hands shoved into the pockets of his smart double-breasted wool coat. He turned as I stepped up onto the sidewalk, and I almost flinched at the sight of him. His hair was more unkempt than usual, his eyes dark and bloodshot.

For a moment, I almost forgot that everything we'd had these last few months no longer existed. It was buried within the iron box inside me. I crossed my arms over my chest, frowning up at him. 'Shouldn't you be with Ellie?'

Braden's gaze was probing as he looked down at me. My heart hurt. He looked so young and vulnerable. I didn't like seeing him like that. 'I gave her a little whisky. She cried herself to sleep. I thought I'd come get you.'

'You should have stayed with her.' I made to walk past him, and he grabbed my arm tightly, almost painfully, hauling me to a stop.

When I looked up at him, he looked less vulnerable and more pissed off. This was a Braden I recognized and, strangely, felt easier to deal with. 'Like you should have stayed this afternoon?'

'I had stuff to do,' I replied blankly.

His eyes narrowed as he pulled my body into his. Like always, I had to tilt my head back to meet his gaze. 'You had stuff to do?' he asked in furious disbelief. 'You had a fucking friend who needed you. What the hell was *that*, Jocelyn?'

'I don't know what you're talking about.'

He shook his head slowly. 'Don't,' he whispered hoarsely, dipping his head so our noses were almost touching. 'Don't do this. Not now. Whatever shit you're spinning in that head of yours, stop. She needs you, babe.' He swallowed hard, his eyes glimmering in the streetlights. 'I need you.'

I felt that familiar choking in the bottom of my throat. 'I didn't ask you to need me,' I whispered back.

I saw it. The hurt flickered across his face before he quickly checked himself. Abruptly he let go of me.

'Fine. I don't have time for your multitude of emotional issues. I have a wee sister who may or may not have brain cancer, and she needs me, even if you don't. But I'll tell you something, Jocelyn' – he stepped forward, pointing a finger in my face, his own hardened with anger – 'if you don't see her through this, you'll hate yourself for the rest of your life. You can pretend that you don't give a shit about me, but you can't pretend Ellie means fuck all to you. I've seen you. Do you hear me?'

He hissed, his hot breath blowing across my face, his words cutting through my soul. 'You love her. You can't sweep that under the rug because it's easier to pretend she means nothing to you than it is to bear the thought of losing her. She deserves better than that.'

I closed my eyes in pain, hating that he could see so deep inside of me. And he was right. Ellie deserved better than my cowardice. I couldn't hide from what I felt for her because everyone had seen it and under-stood it. *She* had seen it and understood it. How could I desert her when I was the one who'd let our friendship happen? For her, I would have to be brave, even if it took everything I had left. 'I'll be there for her,' I found myself promising. I opened my eyes, hoping he could see my sincerity. 'You're right. I'll be there for her.'

Braden squeezed his eyes closed, exhaling heavily. When he opened them, there was a tenderness in them again that I told myself I hadn't missed for the last five minutes. 'Jesus. We lost you there for a few hours. What are we going to do with you, Jocelyn Butler?' He reached an arm out as if to pull me close to him, and I dodged it, stepping back.

'You should go home and get some rest. I'll see to Ellie tonight.'

Braden tensed, his eyes searching my face again, his jaw clenched. 'Jocelyn?'

'Just go home, Braden.' I turned to leave, but he grabbed my hand.

'Jocelyn, look at me.'

I tried to tug my hand loose, but he wouldn't let go, and it took everything within me to harden my features as I glanced back to face him. 'Let go, Braden.'

'What are you doing?' he asked, sounding as if he'd swallowed sandpaper.

'We'll talk about this later. Now is not the time. This is about Ellie.'

Looking dangerous now, dangerous and determined, Braden glowered at me. 'Don't even think about breaking up with me.'

'Can we talk about this later?'

Instead of answering, Braden yanked me hard against him and crushed his mouth over mine. I could taste the Scotch and desperation on his tongue as his hand held my head against his, the kiss deep, wet, and bruising. I couldn't breathe. I pushed against his chest, making a noise of distress, and he finally let me go. Well, his mouth did. His arms still bound me tight.

'Let me go,' I whimpered, my lips swollen and sore.

'No,' he breathed harshly. 'I'm not letting you do this

to us. I don't believe for a second I don't mean anything to you.'

You don't have a choice. 'I can't do this with you.'

'Why?'

'I just can't.'

'Then I don't accept that.'

I struggled in his arms, glaring up at him. 'If I break up with you, you have to accept it!'

Fire-breathing Braden appeared almost instantly. 'No, I fucking don't!'

'Hey, you all right there?' A drunk guy drew our attention, and we jerked our heads around. He was squinting at me and Braden locked together, and it suddenly occurred to me that we were arguing on George Street on a Friday night where there were still people around to hear us.

'We're fine,' Braden told him calmly, still not letting me go.

The drunk guy looked at me. 'You sure about that?'

Not wanting this to descend into a fight – the last thing Braden needed right now – I nodded. 'We're cool.'

The drunk eyed us again, and then, deciding we could work it out ourselves, he turned around and started to hail a cab.

I glared back at Braden. 'Let me go.'

'No.'

'You can't caveman your way out of this.' I couldn't meet his gaze as the pain and the lies bubbled up out of me. 'I care about you, Braden. I do. You're my friend. But this has gone on too long.'

'You're afraid. I get it.' He bent to murmur comfortingly in my ear. 'I know why you ran today, and I know why you're running now. But shit happens, babe – there's no protecting against it. You also can't let it take over your life and rule your relationships with people. We need to enjoy the time we have, however long it's going to be. Stop running.'

You should have been a therapist.

I tried to let my body relax, and I ignored the horrendous churning in my stomach. 'That's why I'm ending it. Life is short. We should be with the people we love.'

Braden froze against me, and I waited, breathless, hoping for the strength to continue the lie. He slowly pulled away from me, his eyes hard as he gazed into mine. 'You're lying.'

Yes. I'm lying, babe. But I won't survive you. And worse, you won't survive me. 'I'm not. I don't love you, and after everything you've been through, you deserve someone who loves you.'

His arms fell away from me, but not even as if he meant to let go. He looked shocked. I think he was in shock. I took the opportunity to step back from him, afraid if I stayed close, I'd eventually let go of my steely resolve and tell him that I was such a goddamn liar and I didn't want him to ever let me go.

But I'd been selfish enough for one day.

'You love me,' he argued, his voice soft, low. 'I've seen it.'

I gulped and forced myself to meet his eyes. 'I care about you, but there's a big difference.'

For a moment, I wasn't sure if he was going to say anything, and then his eyes dulled, and he gave me a sharp nod. 'All right then.'

'You're letting me go?'

He curled his upper lip, his expression painfully bitter as he took a step back from me. 'Apparently . . . I never had ahold of you.' He turned sharply and without another word began striding down the street into the dark.

Braden never once looked back and that was a good thing.

If he had, he'd have seen Jocelyn Butler crying real tears for the first time in a long time, and he would have known that I'd lied. And lied big. For anyone who saw me knew they were watching a heart in the process of breaking.

'I don't think that's the healthiest thing you've ever done, Joss. Do you?' Dr Pritchard asked quietly, her brows drawn together.

'It was the best thing I've ever done.'

'Why do you think that?'

'If I tell Braden the truth, that I love him, he will *never* back down. He's tenacious like that. And then he might spend the rest of his life with me.'

'And that would be a bad thing?'

'Well, yeah,' I responded irritably. 'Did you not hear what I did to Ellie and him? I am so terrified of losing again that I pull shit like that.'

'Yes, but you're aware now that that's what you do. That's a step in the right direction.'

'No it's not. I have issues a mile long, and I can't promise that I won't do that to him over and over again. That's not fair to him. Braden's trust was broken once before by a woman he thought he loved. If I'd stayed with him and kept pulling that crap, I'd be breaking his trust over and over again. And he doesn't deserve that.'

Dr Pritchard cocked her head to the side. 'That's not up to you to decide. Surely that's up to Braden to decide. And you don't know for sure if you would keep pulling that crap, as you say. Being with Braden might help you through it. He might help you.'

'It didn't help. Being with him didn't help.'

'He talked you into being there for Ellie, and you have been. I'd say he helped.'

Stubborn determination gripped me. 'I'm not telling him the truth. What I'm doing is best for him.'

'What I'm trying to say, Joss, is perhaps you should stop being a martyr. Perhaps what Braden thinks is best for him is having you in his life. And perhaps he's willing to work through your anxiety and deal with your mile-high defenses.'

'Maybe you're right.' I nodded, my eyes blazing as I tried to lock out the hurtful thought of a future with Braden. 'Maybe I am a martyr. And maybe he would.

But he deserves better than that struggle. He deserves to be content in his relationship, the way my father was with my mother. And if their love has shown me anything, it's that Braden's right. Life is too damn short.'

Once the rain starts falling, it doesn't stop just because you tell it to. I guess it stops in its own time. My tears, like the rain, kept falling as I made my way home through blurry vision. In truth it's difficult to describe a broken heart. All I know is that unimaginable pain – this throbbing, sharp ache that almost incapacitates you – centers in your chest and radiates out. But there's more than the ache. Denial lodges itself in your throat, and that lump is its own kind of pain. The affliction of heartbreak can also be found in a knot in your stomach. The knot contracts and expands, contracts and expands, until you're pretty sure you're not going to be able to hold down the vomit.

I somehow managed to hold on to at least that much of my dignity.

As soon as I got back to the apartment, through the pain of throwing away Braden came fear. I stared down the hall at Ellie's bedroom door, and I had to stop myself from going back on my promise not to run from her.

Instead I did the opposite.

I kicked off my boots, shrugged out of my coat, and crept silently into her darkened room. In the moonlight shining through her window, I saw Ellie curled up in a protective ball on her side. I made a move toward her and the floor creaked under my foot, and Ellie's eyes flew open immediately.

She gazed up at me, her eyes round with wariness.

That hurt.

I started to cry harder, and at the sight of my tears, a tear slid down Ellie's cheek. Without a word, I crawled into her bed and right up beside her as she turned onto her back. We lay side by side, my head on her shoulder, and I grabbed her hand and held it in both of mine.

'I'm sorry,' I whispered

'It's okay.' Ellie's voice was hoarse with emotion. 'You came back.'

And because life was too short . . . 'I love you, Ellie Carmichael. You're going to get through this.'

I heard her breath hitch on a sob. 'I love you, too, Joss.'

22

That's how Braden found us the next day – lying with our heads tucked into each other, holding hands, sleeping with dirty, tearstained cheeks like two little girls.

He didn't wake me. In fact he didn't even look at me.

I woke up because he was shaking Ellie awake.

'What time is it?' I heard her ask sleepily.

'It's past noon. I've made you some lunch.' The sound of his voice might as well have been a fist punching through my chest. My eyes opened with difficulty, crusty from the salt of my dried tears and swollen from the worst crying jag I'd had since losing Dru. Braden was bending over Ellie, brushing her hair back, his eyes bright with love. They were also still bloodshot and had dark circles underneath.

He looked like hell.

I would still bet I looked worse.

'I'm not hungry,' Ellie whispered.

Braden shook his head, a no-nonsense expression on his face. 'You need to eat. Come on, sweetheart, time to get up.'

I watched as Ellie took his large hand and he pulled her gently up off the bed and onto her feet. Still holding on to her, he led her out, her linen pants wrinkled to the max, her shirt twisted around her body, and her hair a wild mess. She looked like someone whose life had just been upended. I hurt so badly for her. I couldn't even look at Braden, because the pain I felt for him was indescribable.

'Joss, you coming?' Ellie looked back over her shoulder at me.

And for her, I nodded. Even though I didn't want to be anywhere near Braden.

You know what was worse? He couldn't even be outright petty about the breakup. Sure, he couldn't look at me and wouldn't talk to me, but . . . he'd made my damn lunch, too.

Ellie and I sat at the kitchen table eating the tasty scrambled eggs and toast while Braden stood leaning against the counter sipping coffee. Ellie didn't catch on to the quiet between us at first, because she was stuck inside her own head and silence at this point didn't seem unusual.

I'll tell you how unselfish that girl is: With everything she was going through, she still noticed what was going on with her brother and me. And a lot sooner than I'd expected her to. It was our fault – we weren't exactly subtle about it. I got up to put my plate and mug in the sink, and Braden moved to the other side of the room. I then moved to get some orange juice out of the fridge, and Braden moved back to the sink. I moved near the sink to get a glass out of the cupboard, and Braden moved back to the fridge. I moved to the fridge to put the juice back, and he moved again to the sink.

'What's going on?' Ellie asked softly, her brows drawn together as she watched us.

We mumbled a couple of 'nothings' back at her.

'Guys?' Ellie looked paralyzed. 'Did the doctor call?'

Our heads jerked over to her and immediate remorse settled over us. 'No.' Braden shook his head. 'No, Els. We've got the appointment with Dr Dunham later this afternoon, just as planned.'

'Then why are you two acting strangely?'

We stared at her impassively, but one of us gave something away, something big, because after a minute of searching our faces, Ellie's fell. 'You broke up.'

Braden ignored her. 'Els, you should get in the shower, brighten yourself up a bit. You'll feel better.'

'Because of me?' Ellie stood up, her eyes round. 'You broke up because of me?'

I chanced a look at Braden, but he was staring solemnly at Ellie. Like me, he hadn't wanted to add any more weight to her shoulders. I turned back to her. 'No, Ellie. Not because of you. This had nothing to do with you, and it's done. We're okay. Don't worry about us. We're getting you through this minus the drama.'

Her expression hardened, her chin jutting out mulishly. 'You're clearly not talking to each other, though. What happened?'

Braden sighed. 'She doesn't love me, and I think she's an untrustworthy, cold bitch. Now get in the shower.'

Since he wasn't facing me I didn't bother to mask the

pain I felt at his words. *Untrustworthy, cold bitch. Untrustworthy. Cold. Bitch. Cold. Bitch. Bitch. BITCH.*

I also forgot that Ellie *could* see me until her eyes turned dark with sympathy.

'Braden,' she whispered, soft admonishment in her voice.

'Shower. Now.'

Her eyes came back to me, worried. I couldn't believe she was worried about me at a time like this. 'Ellie, shower.'

'You're worse than my parents,' she murmured humorlessly, but deciding she'd rather not face off with two of the most tenacious people she knew, she headed out of the kitchen, leaving us alone in a thick, awful silence.

Finally Braden spoke. 'You left some of your shit at my place. I'll drop it off this week.'

He had stuff in my room, too. 'I'll get your things together for you.'

It should be noted that at this point we were leaning against opposite ends of the kitchen counter, talking to the wall in front of us and not at each other.

Braden cleared his throat. 'You came back for her?' Was that hope in his voice?

'Well, sometimes untrustworthy, cold bitches keep their word,' I answered stiffly, taking a sip of my juice.

Braden grunted and slammed his mug down on the counter. 'She doesn't need your charity or your fucking guilt.'

Fuck.

Shit, fuckity, shit, fuck.

Clearly Braden had taken the night to let his anger simmer and boil over. I braced myself, trying to be understanding and not hurt him any more than I already had. 'She doesn't have my charity or my guilt.'

'Oh, so I was right last night, then.' Braden nodded. 'Unlike me, she has your love.'

'Braden . . .' I choked out. I'd expected him to be like he always was. Braden was stoic, intimidating, immovable, and cool. Not vulnerable and bitter and angry. Basically he was being a dick at a really inappropriate time. Then again, I'd dumped him hours after he learned his little sister might have cancer, so who was the bigger dick? 'You don't love me either, Braden.'

His eyes flashed before casting down my body and back up again, in a cold perusal that sent horrible shivers through me. His gaze came back up to mine and it was as pale as ice. 'You're right. I don't love you. I'm just annoyed I have to look for a new arrangement, especially when the old one wasn't half bad in bed.'

I'd say I was a pretty good actor, but any more of his verbal assault and I was going to crumble under the pain. I turned away quickly so that he wouldn't see what his words did to me. 'I'd hoped that we could still be friends, but clearly you don't want that. So can we just agree to not talk to each other unless we have to for Ellie's sake?'

'If it were up to me, for Ellie's sake, I'd kick your arse out and tell you never to darken our doorstep again. But Ellie doesn't need that right now.'

Shock drew my head up and I gazed at him incredulously. 'Are you kidding?'

He crossed his powerful arms over his chest and shook his head. 'No. I can't trust you. You're fucked up. I don't think Ellie needs that.'

'Last night you wanted me here for Ellie.'

'I've had time to think about it. If I could, I'd get rid of you. But that would just cause Ellie more pain. She doesn't need that right now.'

'You could do that?' I was almost wheezing. 'Just throw me out of your life?'

'Why not? You did it to me last night.'

'No. I broke up with you. I didn't throw you out of my life.' I glared at him. 'But if I had known how little I really did mean to you, I probably would have.'

'Oh.' Braden nodded. 'That's right. You don't love me, but you care about me.' He shrugged. 'Well, I could give a shit about you.'

I locked my jaw, trying so hard to hold in the tears.

'As a matter of fact, I fucked someone else last night.'

You ever had a shotgun bullet blast through your stomach? No? Me neither. But I have a feeling what I felt when Braden said that would be similar to being blasted by a shotgun. And, really, not even the best actress in the world can mask that kind of pain.

I physically flinched at his words, my body jerking back, my knees almost giving out, my eyes wide, and my mouth open in horror. And then the worst happened. I began to cry.

Through my tears I saw Braden's lips pinch together,

and he took two steps toward me, his whole body bristling. 'I fucking knew it,' he hissed, still coming toward me.

'Don't touch me!' I yelled, not able to bear the thought of him being near me now.

'Don't touch you?' He snarled, his eyes sparking violently. 'I'm going to kill you!'

'Me?' I turned, grabbed a plate off the dish rack, and spun around, letting it fly at his head. He ducked, and it smashed against the wall. 'I'm not the one who fucked someone two seconds after we broke up!'

I reached for a glass to throw, but Braden was on me, his strong hands pinning my wrists to my sides, his body pressing mine against the counter. I struggled viciously, but he was too strong.

'Let me go!' I sobbed. 'Just let me go. I hate you. I hate you!'

'Shh. Shh, Jocelyn,' he said soothingly, bending his head into my neck. 'Shh, don't say that,' he begged against my skin. 'Don't say that. I didn't mean it. I lied. I was angry. I'm a fucking idiot. I lied. I was with Elodie all night. You can call her and ask – she'll tell you the truth. You know I would never do to you what was done to me.'

His words penetrated my hysteria, and I stopped struggling – and started trembling. 'What?'

Braden pulled back to show me a pair of pale-blue and very sincere eyes. 'I lied. I wasn't with anyone else. There hasn't been anyone else since we got together.'

My nose was all choked up from crying so much, so

I sounded like a five-year-old when I murmured, 'I don't understand.'

'Babe' – the tenderness was back in his voice, although I could still see the annoyance in his eyes – 'I was pissed off last night when you broke up with me, so I just walked away. I went to Elodie's because I knew she'd be awake worrying about Ellie, and I wanted to see if she was okay. She knew something was wrong with me as soon as she let me in. I told her what had happened and she told me what she said to you at the wedding, and she also told me that when she said that to you, you looked like you'd been slapped. And after, when we were dancing, she realized she was wrong about you.'

He let go of my wrists to slide his hands into my hair, tilting my head back so I couldn't look away. 'I spent last night going over and over the last six months in my head and I *know* that you're lying to me. I know you love me, Jocelyn, because there's no fucking way I can be this much in love with you and not have you feel the same way. It's not possible.'

My heart pounding, I tried to swallow down the fear clawing at my throat. 'So what the hell was this morning?'

He squeezed my nape and bent his head closer to mine, his eyes definitely still dark with anger. 'You're not untrustworthy, you're not cold, and you're not a bitch. You have . . . issues. I get that. We all have issues. But once I realized you were lying to me, I began to understand why. You think you never gave yourself

342

away with me. You think you have time to backpedal and pretend nothing happened between us, because that way, if anything ever happens to me, you can tell yourself that you don't care and you don't feel the pain.'

Oh my God, he was a goddamn psychic now.

'You're also bloody good at pretending you don't feel anything. I thought if I could hurt you this morning, I might get the proof I needed that you were lying.'

I pinned him with a look that said I wanted to rip his balls off. 'So you told me you had slept with someone else?'

He nodded gently and brushed an apologetic kiss across my lips. 'Sorry, babe. I did it to get to the truth . . . but if I'm honest, I mostly did it to hurt you the way you hurt me last night.' His eyes filled with remorse. 'I'm really sorry. I never want to put that look on your face again or ever make you cry, I swear. But the truth is, you did cry. You cried because the thought of me doing that to you ripped you apart. You love me.'

I tried to gather my thoughts, my panic sending them scattering. There was too much to deal with, too much to discuss, and it all had to be later because Ellie needed us. 'One: That was the shittiest thing in the world to do. Two: We can't do this right now.'

'We're not leaving this kitchen until you admit you love me.'

'Braden, I mean it.' I pushed at him sternly, and he let me go, although he didn't step back. 'I'm still broken up with you. I'm not changing my mind.'

His eyes looked to the heavens, and I watched him

wrestle with his patience. Finally his gaze cut back to me, and I could see the muscle in his jaw twitching. 'Why not?' he bit out.

I wouldn't explain it to him. He'd just find some way to argue around it, and I just . . . no! 'Because I just won't. Now, we have a long day in front of us and a possibly even longer few months, so just . . . let it go.'

'Okay.' Braden threw up his hands and stepped back. I was just about to sigh with a small kind of relief when he spoke again. 'For now.'

Oh hell. 'What?'

He grinned at me, and it was a weary grin aiming for boyish wickedness, but he was too tired and worried to reach it. 'I love you. You're mine. I'll kill any bastard who tries to take you from me. So, here's how it's going to go: Ellie comes first, but while we're taking care of her you can be as pigheaded as you want and pretend that we're broken up. I'll even let you. But I'm also going to be here every day, showing you what you're missing.'

My cheeks were still wet, my eyes swollen, and I knew I must look a mess, but right then I didn't care. Part of me was overwhelmed and in awe. The other half of me was scared shitless. And holding on to both of their leashes was my headstrong persistence. 'Are you insane? I'm not changing my mind.'

'Yes, you will.' Braden sighed. 'We're going to need each other through this. All of us. But if you can't do that, then I'm going to play hardball. I'm going to do whatever it takes. Some of it will frustrate you, some of it will turn you on, and some of it will hopefully really piss you off.'

'You *are* insane.'

'No.' We spun around to see Ellie standing in the kitchen doorway in her bathrobe, wearing a small, exhausted but determined smile. 'He's fighting for what he wants.'

'He's not the only one.' I heard Adam's voice as the front door opened and shut, and Ellie turned in the doorway to look out into the hall.

We waited as his footsteps approached and then he was there beside her.

Christ, he looked like hell. I'd never seen Adam unshaven before, and he was wearing a ratty old T-shirt, a parka, and jeans that had seen way better days. He had dark circles under his eyes to rival Braden's, and desperation was etched in every molecule of his expression.

Adam took Ellie's hand and brought it to his lips, his eyes closing as he pressed his mouth to her skin. When he opened them I saw tears shimmering there and felt my throat close up. I watched Ellie's breath catch as he tugged on her hand and pulled her into the kitchen with him to face Braden. All of sudden Adam looked a little sick. 'I need to tell you something.'

Braden crossed his arms over his chest, frowning as he took in the two of them standing close together. 'Go on.'

Adam seemed to brace himself, but I saw determination in his eyes and I admired that. 'You're like a brother to me. I would never do anything to hurt you.

And I know I haven't been what a brother would consider good material for his wee sister, but I love Ellie, Braden. I have for a long time now, and I can't *not* be with her. I've wasted too much time as it is.'

Ellie and I held our breath as the two best friends faced off.

Braden's eyes went to Ellie, his expression not giving anything away. God, he could be an intimidating a-hole when he wanted to be. 'Do you love him?'

Adam looked back at her, and she squeezed his arm. With a small smile she turned to her brother. 'Yes.'

Braden shrugged and reached casually over to the kettle to turn it on. 'About bloody time. You two were giving me a headache.'

My mouth fell open along with Adam's and Ellie's. Not once in the entire time we'd been dating did Braden let on that he knew what was going on with Adam and Ellie. That sneaky bastard.

'You really are a know-it-all pain in the ass,' I announced, brushing by him rudely. I stopped quickly at Ellie and Adam to say, 'I'm happy for you.' And then I hurried down the hall to the bathroom to get away from Braden and his perceptive, growly, inflexible ass.

I heard Braden's soft, scratchy laugh, his delicious voice echoing in my head as he countered, 'She loves me, really.'

23

Ellie hadn't wanted a huge fuss made about the appointment at the hospital, so she'd decided to allow just Elodie and Clark to take her to meet with the neurologist. I was a little surprised that the appointment was on a Sunday, but Braden had swooped in and used some sweet talk – more like he growled and pulled some strings as he knew someone on the hospital board – to get the neurologist to see Ellie as soon as possible.

Elodie and Clark had picked her up, dropping Hannah and Declan off with us, and taken Ellie away an hour ago. Braden and Adam didn't leave. The five of us sat in the sitting room, staring at the clock, staring at our phones. I got up to pee. Braden made some more coffee. Adam didn't move once.

Two hours later, Hannah was tucked into my side; Braden was watching Declan, who'd fallen asleep in the other armchair; and Adam had his eyes closed so tight with worry that Hannah even noticed and reached across to squeeze his hand. Adam shot her a grateful smile, and I kissed her soft hair, my heart hurting because she was just as much of a sweetheart as the one we were all worried about.

The front door opened.

We all shot to our feet. Well, not Declan. He woozily woke up and kind of fell onto his feet.

Elodie entered the sitting room first, but I couldn't gauge her expression. I glanced behind her to see Clark with his arm around Ellie's shoulders, and I swear to God I had to keep myself from bursting into tears.

'What happened?' Adam moved toward her and Clark immediately let Ellie go.

Ellie sunk into Adam's side and smiled tremulously. 'Let's sit. I'll explain.'

'I'll make us all some tea.' Elodie nodded and headed back out of the room as we all sat, our butts right on the edges of our seats.

Ellie heaved a deep sigh. 'Good news is that my tumor is actually a big cyst with two small tumors on it. It's sitting on the surface of the top right side of my brain, so they can remove all of it. Dr Dunham thinks that in all likelihood the tumors are benign. He thinks the cyst has been there a long while and that it's just gotten slowly bigger and needs to come out for obvious reasons. I'll have surgery in two weeks' time, and they'll send the tumors off for biopsy.' Ellie smiled, her lips trembling a little. 'I'm a little scared about the surgery, but Dr Dunham was really confident and said that the risk in this kind of surgery is, like, two percent, and the possibility of one of the tumors being cancerous is really very small.'

At once, we all let go of our breath, relief cascading over us in a huge wave that almost knocked us off our chairs. Braden rushed Ellie before anyone else could,

348

squeezing her up into his arms until she told him she couldn't breathe, and while he did that Clark reassured Declan, who was still a little sleepy, that Ellie was going to be okay. Braden finally let his little sister down with a loud smack of a kiss on her forehead, and before she could even catch her breath Adam was on her, kissing her right on the mouth in front of everyone. A real kiss, too. Ballsy.

'Well, it's about time,' Clark said with a sigh.

Ellie laughed against Adam's mouth at that one. Obviously she was just now realizing I'd been right all along. She and Adam had been anything but subtle these last few months.

'What's funny?' Elodie asked, bustling back into the room.

I took that opportunity to haul Ellie into my arms. 'Worst twenty-four hours in a very long time, my friend.'

She pulled back to look at me. 'I'm sorry I put you through that.'

'Why are you apologizing? This isn't your fault. I'm just sorry you have to go through all this.' I sighed heavily and then looked at the tea and coffee Elodie had brought into the room. I gave her an apologetic look as I said, 'I don't think that's strong enough.'

She raised an eyebrow at me. 'Do you have anything stronger in the house?'

'Not really.' I glanced at Ellie. 'But there is the pub just a few doors down from us that we've never been into yet. Maybe it's time. I think there's a possibility they'll have something stronger.'

'Strong sounds good to me,' Ellie said.

'And me,' Clark agreed.

'We have the kids,' Elodie complained.

I grabbed my purse, which had been sitting on the coffee table. 'They're allowed into a pub if they're with an adult. They can have a Coke.'

Elodie didn't look too sure.

I smiled reassuringly. 'It's just one drink. A celebratory drink at that.'

'Clark can have a drink. I'll drive us home,' Elodie said, relenting, and we grabbed our things to leave.

Elodie and Clark shuffled the kids out first. Adam had his arm around Ellie, and she was tucked in close to him, looking amazingly happy for someone who had major surgery coming up in a few weeks' time. Then again, for over twenty-four hours we'd all been convinced she had cancer only to discover she probably didn't . . . and of course she finally had Adam right where she wanted him.

That left me and Braden to trail at the back, and I got the first taste of what he'd meant earlier. His fingers brushed my lower back to guide me out the door, and it was so deliberate it wasn't funny.

He knew I was sensitive there.

I tried to hold back the shiver as I turned to lock the apartment, but Braden got in my way, so that when I turned I collided with him.

'Sorry.' He smirked, moving slowly so my breasts brushed against his chest.

I felt my nipples harden and flinched at the heat that

pulsed between my legs. My look was scathing. 'Sure you are.'

Braden laughed softly as I leaned down to lock the door, and then I felt his shadow fall over me. I glanced up to my right to see his hand pressed against the door near my head. I twisted around to look up at him, only to find he'd cocooned himself around me. 'Need a hand?'

I narrowed my eyes into slits. 'Back off before I turn your balls into a key ring.'

I could tell he was trying really hard not to laugh. Unfortunately, not hard enough. 'Babe, you've got to know when you say shit like that, it just makes me love you more.'

'You sound like a very bad villain or stalker right now.'

'I don't care how I sound, as long as it's working.'

'It's not working.'

'A few more days and it will.' He brushed a quick kiss across my cheek and then abruptly pulled away before I could kill him.

'Come on, guys,' Ellie called to us from farther up the sidewalk. Elodie, Clark and the kids must have already gone inside. 'What's taking so long?'

'Jocelyn was just begging for sex, but I told her it was a highly inappropriate time for it,' Braden answered loudly, causing passersby to chuckle at him.

Furious at him for so many reasons, I rushed down our stoop toward them. 'That's okay, sweetheart,' I answered just as loudly. 'I have a toy that does a better job of it anyway.' With that I slammed into the pub, where he couldn't hound me in front of the kids.

And although immature – and yes, highly inappropriate considering the reason we were going for a drink – I couldn't help but feel satisfied that I'd finally got the last word in.

I admit it. I was a big fat coward.

I didn't meet with Rhian and James on Tuesday like I'd promised. Instead I e-mailed her, explaining Ellie's situation and that I didn't want to leave her alone at the moment. If Rhian thought it was weird I couldn't take just two hours out of the day to see her, she didn't let on. If she thought it was weird I was e-mailing her instead of calling her, she didn't let on.

The truth was, I barely saw Ellie over the past few days because Adam had practically moved into her bedroom and the two of them only came out of there for snacks and bathroom breaks.

I didn't want to see Rhian and James. *That* was the truth.

And why?

Because not too long ago I had spewed crap down the phone to Rhian about not running from James just because she was afraid of what the future might hold for them, and I really wasn't in the mood to get a lecture from Rhian about breaking up with Braden and being a total hypocrite.

My story with Braden was entirely different. It was. Really.

Okay – I was just scared. No. Terrified. And I had every right to be. I just had to look at the way I'd reacted to Ellie's situation to know that Braden would be in for a tough, neurotic life with me. Plus, my life had been so much calmer without him in it. I had rarely worried about anything, my emotions had been pretty stable, and I'd had, if not peace, then quiet. Being with Braden was tumultuous and really, when I thought about it, exhausting. Take out the amazing sex and all that I was left with was a bunch of ugly emotions. Worry – that he might get bored and stop liking me. Jealousy – I'd never been the jealous girlfriend before meeting Braden, but now my claws got all sharp any time I saw a woman flirting with him. Fear for him – as if I didn't have enough to worry about for myself, now it freaking mattered to me whether he was happy and healthy. And it mattered more. That just was not cool.

I liked pre-Braden Joss.

She was spunky and cool and independent.

Post-Braden Joss was kind of a mushy asshat.

It didn't help matters that Braden had kept to his word. He turned up at the apartment any chance he could, and even though I told him that Ellie was preoccupied, he still hung around.

'I was washing the dishes, and the sneaky bastard crept up behind me and wrapped his arms around my waist. And kissed me. Right here.' I pointed angrily to my neck. 'Can I not have him committed or something?'

Dr Pritchard snorted. 'For loving you?'

I drew back, shaking my head in disgust. 'Dr Pritch-ard,' I admonished softly, 'whose side are you on?'

'Braden's.'

It was a Thursday night, two days after Christmas, and I was covering for a colleague at the bar. Ellie's surgery was in three days.

I'd had an exhausting week of dodging Braden and, whenever she came out of her room, trying to calm Ellie down about her surgery. Dodging Braden wasn't so easy. Even though Darren, his manager at Fire, had quit because his wife was pregnant and she demanded he get a normal nine-to-five, Braden got him a job as a manager in one of the city hotels that a friend owned. Even though that meant training his new manager, Braden had still found time to come around and bother me. There was the sink incident – to which I may have overreacted because it reminded me of a memory I had of my parents – the scene in which he walked in on me having a shower to ask me where the television remote was, the time he ate his lunch in the kitchen without a shirt on – he said he'd 'accidentally' spilled coffee down it and had to put it in the wash – and there were the many, many moments when he just looked at me for no good reason at all. I swear to God he was wearing on my panties. I had been this close to just giving in when he started to back off a little.

Of course I wouldn't have given in anyway.

Because I could see the big picture.

He'd started the cooldown a few days before Christmas, and was even on pretty good behavior when we had Christmas dinner with Ellie's family. The only awkward moment came when we had to exchange gifts. We'd both bought our gifts a while ago, and they were more meaningful than what two mere friends would have given each other. Braden had managed to get me a signed copy of my favorite book by my most favorite author. How he pulled that off, I don't know. Oh, and did I mention the stunning diamond tennis bracelet? Uh-huh. I got him a first edition of his favorite book, Hemingway's *The Sun Also Rises*. It was the most elaborate gift I'd ever bought, but it was worth it to see the way he smiled at me when he opened it.

Shit.

Fuckity, shit, fuck.

Maybe I expected him to up the ante after that, but Braden seemed to do the exact opposite and just . . . disappear.

I wondered if it was a new tactic.

So I was on alert when he didn't show up with Ellie and Adam on Thursday when I was covering a shift. He'd dragged them into the bar the week before when I'd picked up extra shifts, after Ellie demanded I get out of the apartment – I think I had been hovering – and he'd sat on the sofa across from the bar, in my direct line of vision, dividing his time between watching me and flirting with pretty girls. I was guessing this was the pissing-me-off part of his promise.

So I was surprised he wasn't there Thursday.

Ellie was still awake when I got home from work.

She came out of her room and closed the door softly behind her. 'Adam's sleeping,' she whispered, following me into the sitting room.

I grinned at her over my shoulder. 'No wonder. You must have worn that poor boy out.'

Ellie rolled her eyes at me and slumped down onto the couch beside me. 'It's not really like that. Well . . . kind of.' She blushed, her eyes bright with happiness. 'Mostly we're talking a lot. Sorting things out. All those misunderstandings. Apparently he's been in love with me for a while.'

'Oh, you don't say.'

'Funny.'

'Speaking of funny, Braden didn't turn up at the bar tonight.'

His sister eyed me carefully. 'His new manager needed help. Were you disappointed he wasn't there?'

'No,' I answered quickly. Probably too quickly. Damn it, I missed pre-Braden Joss. 'I just noticed a lack of ego in the room and thought, hey, where's Braden?'

Ellie didn't laugh. She gave me a motherly look of disapproval. 'Braden's right. You're in love with him. So why are you giving him the runaround? Are you enjoying his chasing you? Is that it?'

I raised my eyebrow at her. 'Those tumors have brought out the snarkiness in you, huh?'

She made a face.

'Too soon for tumor jokes?'

Her eyes narrowed.

'Is there never a time for tumor jokes?'

'Never, Joss. Never.'

I winced. 'Sorry. That was mean.'

'No. Mean is using my tumors as a tool for deflection. I love you to bits, Joss, but I love my brother, too. Why are you doing this to him?'

'I'm not doing this *to* him. I'm doing this *for* him.' I turned to her, my eyes sincere as I tried to make her understand. 'I don't handle bad things very well. I'm not proud of it, but it's true. Look how I just walked out on you when you needed me. When Braden needed me.'

'But you came back,' she argued. 'You were in shock, but you've been here every second since.'

'Braden talked me into it,' I confessed. 'He had to shake some sense into me. And as he did that I realized that I can't protect myself or the people around me from bad stuff happening. And apparently bad stuff follows me around, so it's probably going to happen again sometime. When it does, I can't guarantee I won't go off the deep end, and I just can't do that to Braden. His life would be unstable with me, and after that bitch cx-wife of his put him through hell, he deserves someone who can give him peace.'

'Joss, you're talking as if you're some mental case. You're not. Your only problem is that you won't face what happened to your family and start dealing with it.'

I slammed my head back against the couch. 'You sound like Dr Pritchard.'

'Who?'

'My therapist.'

'You're seeing a therapist? How did I not know this?' She slapped her hand across my arm.

'Hey.' I winced, pulling away from her.

'This is what I'm talking about.' Ellie was angry, her eyes flashing just like Braden's did when he was pissed off. 'I'm your best friend, and you didn't tell me you were seeing a therapist. Does Braden know?'

'Yes,' I answered like a sullen teenager.

'Well, that's something, at least.' She shook her head in disbelief. 'You have got to start dealing with your family, Joss. I think if you do that, everything else will start to feel not so big and overwhelming. And you'll realize you can take each day at a time with Braden. You don't have to protect him from being with you. He's a big boy, and clearly he knows a lot more about you than I do, and miracle of miracles he still wants to be with you.'

'Funny. You really do sound like Dr Pritchard.'

'In all seriousness, Joss, I think you need to stop playing around.'

'I'm not playing.' I studied her carefully, though, catching something in her face. 'What? What is it? What do you know?'

She took a minute, almost as if she wasn't sure she should say whatever it was that was on her mind. Suddenly I got this awful feeling in the pit of my stomach.

'Adam and I went out for lunch today.'

'I know. I was in here, staring at a manuscript I haven't touched in days.'

'Well.' Ellie couldn't meet my eyes. 'We met Braden for lunch and he brought the new manager of Fire with him.'

'And?'

Her eyes flicked up to mine, and I tensed at the concern in them. 'His new manager is Isla. Isla is a five-foot-ten, stunning blonde who also happens to be smart and funny.'

I think I felt my heart plummet into my stomach.

'Joss, they seemed into each other.' She shook her head. 'I didn't want to believe it, but they were flirting, and Braden was . . . was very attentive. They seemed . . . close.'

Jealousy is a horrible thing – the pain of it is almost as consuming as heartbreak, and I would know, because I was feeling both at the same time. I felt like someone had ripped open my chest with his bare hands, removed my heart and lungs, and replaced them with a bunch of rocks. I stared at the Christmas tree, my mind whirling. This was why he hadn't been around lately.

'Joss?' Ellie touched my arm.

I looked at her, determined not to cry. I gave her a sad smile. 'I guess I was right all along, then.'

Ellie began to shake her head.

'No, this is good.' I stood up, needing to be alone. 'I broke up with him because he deserves to find someone decent and normal. And now I don't have to feel guilty about it, because I was right all along. He doesn't love me. You're not *into* someone else after just

359

breaking up with the love of your life, right? This is good.' I moved toward the sitting-room door and heard Ellie scrambling out of her seat.

'No!' Ellie hissed. 'That's not what it is, or why I told you.' She followed me into the hall, but I wasn't really listening since I had a lot of blood rushing in my ears. 'Joss, I told you so you'd stop messing around and just be with him again. Listen, I may –'

I slammed the door in her face.

'Joss.' She banged on it.

'Night, Els!'

'Shit,' I heard her mutter, and then her footsteps faded away.

I tried. I really did. But when I curled up in my bed, I couldn't stop the tears.

24

'Ellie's surgery is tomorrow.'

Dr Pritchard nodded. 'You're nervous?'

I nodded, my stomach churning. 'Her surgeon has great credentials and he's really confident that this is fairly straightforward for brain surgery, but I'm still worried.'

'That's only natural.'

I exhaled slowly, the exhale turning into a small smile. 'I'm booked on a flight to Virginia at the end of January. I'm flying out there after Ellie's two-week recovery at home.'

Dr Pritchard's eyebrows hit her hairline. 'Oh? What prompted this?'

Ellie's bravery and Braden's moving on. 'Braden's met someone, just like I wanted him to. But Ellie is really the one who gave me the courage. She's been really brave about everything, and we were sitting talking last night, and there she is with this huge surgery ahead of her and she's worrying about *me*, worrying that if I don't start facing up to my past, I'll never get better.'

Dr Pritchard gave me a sad smile. 'Ellie convinced you in one conversation to do what I've been trying to get you to do for almost six months?'

'I guess you needed to be diagnosed with something

scary and be really brave about it so I'd feel like the worst kind of coward.'

'I'll need to add that to my repertoire.'

I laughed, that laughter trailing off into a tense silence. 'I'm scared,' I finally admitted. 'I have my family's things in storage. I'm going over to visit their graves and maybe finally do something about all that stuff.'

'You never told me you kept all of their things.'

'Yeah. Put it in storage and pretended like it didn't exist.'

'This is a really good step you're taking, Joss.'

'Yeah. I hope so.'

She frowned now. 'Braden's met someone?'

I ignored the pain. 'It's what I wanted.'

'Joss, I know you told yourself that, but still, it can't be easy to see him with someone new so soon. Especially after chasing you and promising you that he wouldn't give up.'

'It just proves me right. He doesn't love me.'

'And he's definitely seeing this new woman? There's no misunderstanding?'

'Not according to Ellie.'

'Then a trip to Virginia might be exactly what you need right now.'

'Oh, it's not a trip.' I shook my head. 'Well, it is and isn't. I'm thinking of moving back permanently once I know Ellie's going to be okay. I'm going to shop around for a place when I get there and come back to Edinburgh and sort out my affairs . . .'

Dr Pritchard shook her head. 'I don't understand. I thought Edinburgh was your home. I thought Ellie was your family.'

'Ellie is my family. She always will be.' I smiled sadly. 'I can't watch him be with someone else,' I admitted. 'He was wearing me down, all right. You, Ellie, him – all of you were wearing me down about it. You don't think I know chasing him off is irrational?' I found myself raising my voice. 'I know it's irrational. I couldn't stop myself – it was like someone else was inside me, pushing him away because I was so terrified of losing him.'

'Joss' – the good doctor's voice was soft, soothing – 'irrational, yes, but understandable. You suffered a lot of loss as a young girl. Braden knows exactly what you were doing. That's why he wasn't giving up.'

'He gave up at the sight of the first long pair of legs that came along.'

'That's really why you're leaving?'

'I know I sound like a crazy person. One minute I'm adamant I don't want to be with him, and as soon as I find out he's with someone else, I freak out. Thing is, nothing's changed. Except now I don't want to be with him because he clearly doesn't love me the way I love him. It's always been the thrill of the chase with him.'

'Well, I'd have to have Braden in to speak with him to have an opinion on that, but I do think you need to communicate with him. You need to tell him this before you leave for Virginia, or you'll always wonder, Joss. Do you know what's scarier than taking a risk and losing?'

I shook my head.

'Regret, Joss. Regret does awful things to a person.'

We all went to the hospital for Ellie. Even Hannah and Dec. When they came to take her down for her surgery we all took turns reassuring her. Last, Adam gave her a long, sweet kiss that would have melted even the most unromantic heart. It sucked that something as major as brain surgery had finally made him step up to the plate, but life was like that sometimes. Some of us needed a swift kick in the ass.

We sat in a waiting room even though the doctors told us we should probably go home and come back in a few hours. None of us wanted to leave. I sat next to Elodie, Hannah on my other side. Clark sat across the room, watching Dec play his Nintendo on silent mode. Braden sat on Clark's other side with Adam on his right. We barely spoke. I got coffee for everyone and soda for the kids. I took Hannah on the hunt for some sandwiches and tried to ask her about the latest book she was reading, but neither one of us was feeling it. Dec was the only one who ate all of his sandwich, while the rest of us just nibbled, our stomachs too full of nerves to make room for anything else.

Did you know that time stops in a hospital waiting room? No joke. It just stops. You look at the clock and it says 12:01; you look back at it in what feels like an hour and it's only freaking 12:02.

Ellie had painted my fingernails last night when she'd needed something to do to take her mind off surgery.

By the time the surgeon came out to us hours later, I had picked every last bit of the polish off.

We shot to our feet when Dr Dunham finally entered the waiting room. He smiled at us, looking tired but perfectly calm. 'Everything went really well. We removed all of the mass and have sent the tumors for biopsy. Ellie's been taken to the post-op wing but it'll be a little while yet before she comes out of the anesthesia. I know you've been here all day, so I suggest you go home for a while and return for tonight's visiting hours.'

Elodie shook her head, her eyes bright with worry. 'We want to see her.'

'Just give her some time,' Dr Dunham replied kindly. 'I promise she's fine. You can return tonight. I'll warn you now, she'll probably still be very groggy, and the right side of her face is swollen quite badly from the surgery. That's perfectly normal.'

I squeezed Elodie's arm. 'Come on. We'll go get the kids some dinner and come back later.'

'Yeah, Mum, I'm hungry,' Declan complained quietly.

'Okay,' she whispered, still sounding unconvinced.

'Thank you, Dr Dunham.' Clark held out his hand and the surgeon took it with a kind smile. After Adam and Braden shook his hand and Elodie and I offered him a grateful smile, Dr Dunham left us to gather ourselves. A tension had eased between us all, knowing that Ellie had come through surgery safely, but we were still anxious to see her.

It wasn't until we were leaving the hospital and

Braden edged up to me and drew me into his side for a hug that I realized for once in God knows how long that I hadn't been thinking about my drama with him. I'd just been thinking about Ellie.

As soon as he touched me, though, I remembered Isla and tensed.

He felt it, his body turning hard against mine. 'Jocelyn?' he asked.

I couldn't look at him. I shrugged out of his hold, taking advantage of his surprise, and hurried to catch up with Hannah.

That night the nurse led us to the post-op wing, and we were allowed in to see Ellie. Her curtains were drawn around her, and Elodie and Clark were in front of me so I didn't see her at first. When they greeted her quietly and stepped back I flinched.

I hadn't expected to feel so scared.

Dr Dunham was right – her head was pretty swollen and kind of misshapen on the right side, and her eyes were still glazed from the anesthesia. White padded bandages were wrapped tightly around her head, and I felt my stomach lurch as I thought about the fact that her brain had been cut into today.

She gave me a lopsided quirk of a smile. 'Joss.' Her voice was hoarse, barely audible.

I wanted to run. I know – that's horrible. But I wanted to run away from this part. People ending up in the hospital had never concluded well in my life, and seeing her there, so vulnerable, so exhausted, just reminded me of how close we could have come to losing her.

I felt a hand squeeze mine and turned my head to see Hannah watching me. She looked as pale as I felt, and her fingers were trembling between mine. She was scared, too. I smiled reassuringly at her, hoping I was pulling it off. 'Ellie is okay. Come on.' I tugged on her hand and pulled her with me to Ellie's bedside.

I reached out for the hand Ellie had held out for her mom and slid mine into it, feeling relief and love as she gave me a gentle squeeze. 'Am I pretty?' she asked with a little slur, and I laughed softly.

'Always, honey.'

Her eyes dropped to Hannah. 'I'm okay,' she whispered.

'Are you sure?' Hannah pressed in close to the bed, her frightened eyes glued to Ellie's bandaged head.

'Mmm-hmm.'

She was still tired. I knew we shouldn't stay long. I gently eased Hannah back so Braden and Adam could get in with Declan. Declan thought she looked cool, of course. Once Braden said hello, Adam wouldn't leave Ellie's side.

Her eyes started to flutter closed.

'We should leave her to rest,' Clark ordered in a hushed voice. 'We'll come back tomorrow.'

'Els,' Braden murmured, and her eyes fluttered back open. 'We're going. We'll be back tomorrow.'

'Okay.'

Adam grabbed a chair from the side of the room and put it beside her bed. 'I'm staying.'

We nodded, not really wanting to argue after seeing the determined clench of his jaw.

With soft good-byes we left them, Braden and I trailing at the back as we walked in a solemn fog through the hospital.

'She looked tiny,' Braden observed hoarsely. 'I wasn't expecting her to look so bad.'

'The swelling will go down.'

He shot me a careful look. 'Are you okay?'

'I'm fine.'

'You don't seem fine.'

'It's been a tiring day.'

We stopped at – actually, I didn't know where. The hospital was kind of confusing, with lots of a little parking lots and different entrances and yellow barricades. I didn't know where the hell I was. We were standing at an entrance, anyway, and Elodie sighed. 'Are you two getting a taxi back?'

Clark's car wasn't big enough for everyone to get a ride in. I'd gotten a ride going to the hospital, but Adam and Braden had gotten a cab. I supposed it would be rude to suggest Braden take a cab and I get a ride.

'I'll get a cab. Braden, you should go with them.'

He smirked knowingly. 'We'll get a taxi together.'

Shit.

I reluctantly let Ellie's family go and waited as Braden

called for a cab. I then stood at the entrance doors, keeping an eye out.

I smelled his cologne as he pressed close to my back. I shifted uncomfortably, trying to block out the fact that even though I'd ripped the bedsheets off my bed, I hadn't washed them because I could still smell Braden on them. I really was *that* girl.

'Do you want to tell me why I'm getting the silent treatment?' he asked gruffly, his breath hot on my ear.

I hunched up my shoulders, pulling away. His voice had an effect on my body that I didn't want him to know about. 'I'm talking to you.'

'Barely.'

'I've got a lot on my mind.'

'Do you want to talk about it?'

'When have I ever wanted to talk about it?'

I felt the heat in my blood grow hotter as he stepped closer, his hand sliding down my hip. 'You used to talk to me, Jocelyn. Don't pretend you didn't.'

Seeing the familiar black cab of the city turn the corner into our part of the building, I pulled away quickly. 'Cab's here.' And I started off toward it.

When we'd settled in the cab I could feel he was annoyed. I also knew him well enough to know that he was going to try to talk to me about it even if it meant following me home. I gave the cab driver Jo's address in Leith.

Braden shot me a look.

I shrugged. 'She asked me to come over.'

After a few more inane questions and a few more one-word responses from me, Braden gave up but not before sending me a lethal *this isn't over* warning look.

I got out at Jo's without a good-bye and watched the cab drive away. I called Jo to make sure she was home and went up to her apartment and spent almost all night there.

Avoiding Braden took skill. Well, no, it just involved me not spending any time at the apartment. It also meant getting a cab out alone to visit Ellie. Every day, without fail, Braden sent a text asking if I wanted him to swing the cab by my place to pick me up for visiting hours at the hospital. I sent him a polite *No, thanks* back each time. Visiting hours were all about Ellie, so I was safe. She had a private room, was bored out of her mind and desperate to get home, but she had a whole week there. The swelling was going down more each day, but I could tell she was exhausted. She let us all – and by all, I mean Elodie – chat around her, smiling and taking it in. Thankfully, I didn't see the sad part, when her eyes would inevitably get all weepy as we left her. I didn't get to see that part because I always left before everyone else. I saw not only the questions in Ellie's eyes when I did this, but in everyone else's, too. I tried to make up for it by bringing her a silly present each time I visited, but I knew she was dying to ask me what was wrong.

I wasn't at all surprised that Braden didn't chase me out of there.

370

He had moved on, so he didn't *really* need to know why I was avoiding him.

Or so I thought.

New Year's Eve I spent with Jo. I got a call from Rhian. Texts from Craig, Alistair, Adam, Elodie, Clark, and the kids.

I got a text from Braden: *Happy New Year, Jocelyn. I hope it's a good one for you. x*

Who knew a text could be so heartbreaking? I texted back . . . wait for it . . .

Back at ya.

Yeah, I did. I did do that. I'm an idiot.

As I began staying away from the apartment, swimming at a different pool, and avoiding the gym we shared, I think it must have begun to dawn on Braden that I knew about Isla.

Four days into Ellie's recovery at the hospital and only a few days before she was to come home, I got another text from Braden.

We really need to talk. I've come by the flat a few times but you're never in. Can we meet up? x

I didn't text him back. Obviously he wanted to tell me about his new manager.

It didn't matter that I didn't text back. Fate already had plans for us to meet. Two days after the text, I was dodging the apartment and having lunch at this great pub on the Grassmarket. I was going to head up to George IV Bridge and head south toward Forrest Road, where there was this kitschy little store that Ellie loved. They sold these umbrellas that were like old-fashioned parasols and she'd been going on and on about buying one but never had. So I was going to buy it for her as a little present for her return to the apartment the next day.

I had just finished my lunch and stepped out onto the Grassmarket, trying to shove my wallet back into my bag, when I heard, 'Jocelyn?'

My head snapped up and my heart did that thing where it beat so hard it unhooked itself from my chest and took a swan dive into the pit of my stomach. Braden was standing before me and at his side was this tall, stunning blonde. She was wearing a pencil skirt, a Victorian-style suit jacket, and sexy stiletto heels; her long blonde hair was perfectly tousled, and her makeup was as flawless as her face.

Was she for real?

I hated her instantly.

'Braden,' I murmured, my eyes flying anywhere and everywhere to avoid his gaze.

I should mention that I was wearing my jeans with the worn-out knee, a ratty T-shirt that advertised a famous beer, and my hair was in its usual knot on my head. I wore no makeup.

I looked like hell.

I'd really made his choice easy, huh?

'I texted you,' he said in an annoyingly stern tone.

My eyes flew to his. 'I know.'

His jaw clenched.

Isla cleared her throat politely, and he tried to relax, although his penetrating gaze didn't leave mine as he said, 'Isla, this is Jocelyn. Jocelyn, this is Isla, the new manager of Fire.'

Putting on my best acting skills, I smiled politely and held out my hand for her to shake. She smiled back at me curiously. 'I've heard all about you,' I told her meaningfully.

Braden's whole body froze, and I gave him a bitter smile, my eyes sending their own message – *Yeah, I know all about her, asshole.*

Isla turned to Braden with an attractive and exceptionally flirtatious tilt to her mouth. 'You've been telling people about me?'

He didn't answer. He was too busy killing me with his eyes. 'Isla, can you give us a moment, please?'

Uh-oh.

And then miracle of miracles: Bon Jovi saved the day. I'd reset my ringtone. *'Shot through the heart, and you're to blame. You give love a bad name.'*

Yeah, I hadn't been feeling subtle that day.

Braden raised an eyebrow at the song, a stupidly amused smile curving his lips as I pulled my cell out. Rhian. Thank God. 'I have to take this. I'll catch you later.'

His smile quickly turned into a glare. 'Joce—'

'Rhian,' I answered with affected cheer, giving Isla a little wave good-bye, one she returned obliviously.

Rhian snorted. 'You sound wired.'

I hurried past the pubs, heading for Candlemaker Row, a shortcut down to the bridge and Forrest Road. 'I didn't give you a good enough Christmas present, do you know that?'

'Uh, why?'

'Because you just saved my ass. I'm sending you a little something as a thank-you.'

'Ooh, chocolate, please.'

'Done.'

I let her talk to me about everything and nothing for ten minutes in a desperate attempt to dull the excruciating ache in my chest at seeing Braden. It didn't last long. I went home, curled up with the unwashed bedsheet that smelled like him and cried for three hours before I finally got up the courage to put it in the wash.

25

Perhaps I was still feeling guilty about flaking out on Ellie that first night, so I went a little overboard on getting the apartment ready for her return. It was clean from top to bottom, but I'd held back my own inclination to tidy and left her clutter out, as I knew it made her feel at home. I ordered this gorgeous pale-green luxury bed set online because she loved green, bought a few decorative cushions, and made her bed up into something fit for a princess. I bought a breakfast-in-bed table that rolled up to the side and swung over so she could eat in bed. I bought flowers. Chocolates. I packed the fridge with her favorite Ben & Jerry's ice cream. There was a pile of the latest issue of every magazine I'd ever seen her reading on her bedside cabinet. A couple of Sudoku and crossword puzzle books. And the most extravagant . . . a small flat-screen television with a built-in DVD player. It was probably a little much for a patient who was only supposed to be on bed rest for two weeks, but I didn't want her to get bored.

'Oh my God.' Ellie's eyes widened as she walked into her room. She was standing with her arm wrapped around Adam's waist, and Elodie, Clark, and Braden were already in the room, smiling at everything. The kids were back at school, so they'd missed out on 'Joss goes overboard.' Ellie's eyes swung to me. 'You did all this?'

I shrugged, suddenly feeling very uncomfortable. 'It's not much.'

Ellie laughed and came over to me slowly. 'You're a little bit awesome.'

I huffed. 'If you say so.'

'Come here.' She wrapped her arms around me, and I hugged her, as always feeling like a little girl hugging her mother because she was so tall. 'I love it. Thank you.'

'I'm glad.' I gently eased her back and frowned. 'Lie down.'

Ellie groaned. 'This is going to be fun.'

As Adam helped Ellie off with her shoes and into bed, Elodie came over to me. 'The doctor says you need to make sure her bandages don't get wet when she's showering.'

'She can take baths for now.'

'Good. And she's to rest. She's allowed to walk about but not constantly.'

'Got it.'

'She's to go back in two weeks to get the bandages off.'

'Okay.'

'And then she has a checkup three months after that. If everything's fine, it'll be a year after that.'

I frowned. 'Wait.' I shot a hopeful smile Ellie's way. 'You got your biopsy results?'

'No one told her?' Ellie's brow puckered as she stared accusingly around the room.

Braden sighed. 'Maybe if she would stop avoiding everyone someone might have.'

'Hello!' I waved my hand. 'Results, please?'

Ellie grinned. 'Benign.'

I sagged in relief to hear confirmation of Dr Dunham's prediction. 'That really should have been the opener.'

'Sorry.'

'Uh-huh.' I quirked an eyebrow at Elodie. 'PS, I'm going to take good care of her.' My eyes flicked to Adam, who had climbed on top of the covers on Ellie's other side. 'That's if Lover Boy let's me.'

Adam grimaced. 'I'm too old to be called Lover Boy.'

'I quite like it.' Ellie smiled mischievously.

'Then Lover Boy it is.'

'Well, I think I'll go make us all some coffee before I throw up on Ellie's new bedspread,' I cracked and made to move toward the door.

Braden stepped in front of it, his face expressionless. 'We need to talk.' With that he turned on his heel and walked out of the room, leaving me no choice but to follow.

I found him in my room, and as soon as I walked in, he strode past me to shut the door.

'We could talk in the sitting room,' I told him irritably, hating him in there, where so many memories lived. Plus his presence in my room had always been overwhelming.

In response, he prowled toward me, coming to a stop when there was only an inch of space between us.

I wanted to back up but didn't want to give him the satisfaction. I stared up at him defiantly, and he bent his head a little so he could look me directly in the eyes.

'I've been trying to give you space, but this is ridiculous.'

My head snapped back. 'Uh, what?'

I watched his gorgeous and furious eyes narrow into slits. 'You're never here. Are you seeing someone else? Because I swear to God –'

Furious didn't even cover it. 'Are you kidding me?' I yelled, forgetting there was an audience down the hall.

'Well, what the hell is going on?'

I drew in a shuddering breath, trying to calm down. 'You're an asshole. Coming in here and accusing me of messing around behind your back when you're the one who's screwing his new nightclub manager.'

Now Braden jerked his head back in shock – and the look he gave me? Well, let's just say it was not a polite way of expressing that he thought I had a screw loose somewhere. 'Isla? You think I'm fucking Isla? I don't believe this.'

Okay. I was completely confused. I crossed my arms over my chest in an attempt to look as if I was in control of this conversation. 'Ellie told me everything.'

His mouth actually fell open. It would have been funny if the situation hadn't been like a knife in my gut. 'Ellie? What exactly did Ellie tell you?'

'She met you for lunch. The two of you met her and Adam for lunch, and she said that you were all over each other.'

Now Braden crossed his arms over his chest, the soft fabric straining against the muscles of his biceps. I had a flashback of him above me, his hands pressing my wrists into the mattress, the muscles in his arms moving as he thrust hard into me over and over again.

I flushed, shaking the image out of my head.

Crap.

'Ellie told you she had lunch with me and Isla, and that I was all over Isla?' he asked me slowly, as if I were a mental patient.

I answered through gritted teeth. 'Yes.'

'If she hadn't just had brain surgery, I swear to God, I'd kill her.'

I blinked. 'What?'

Braden took another step forward, which meant I had to step back if I didn't want my boobs mashed up against him. 'I never had lunch with Isla and Ellie. They met when she and Adam stopped by the club to drop off a USB stick I left at the flat. They met for two seconds.'

I scratched behind my ear, not liking at all where the new information put me in this conversation. 'Why would she tell me that?'

Braden sighed heavily and turned away, running a hand through his hair in frustration. 'I don't know. Probably because I told her I was giving you space as part of the next stage in my plan to get you back, and Ellie didn't agree it was a good idea. Apparently Ellie thought jealousy was the next step.' He shook his head and shot me an unfathomable look. 'Apparently she was wrong.'

I watched him as he wandered around my room, clearly trying to put his thoughts together as much as I was trying to come to terms with the idea that Braden hadn't moved on at all. But I still couldn't understand why Ellie would hurt me like that. I also wondered when the hell she'd started getting so good at lying. She couldn't lie for shit when I first met her.

Oh.

My fault?

'I still don't understand. I met Isla, buddy, and she's exactly your type. She was definitely flirting with you.'

'Why do you care?' He grinned, running his hands along my bookshelf. 'You said you don't want – 'He stopped, his body tense with a sudden alertness.

'What?'

He pulled at something on my bookshelf, his head bowed, and then he turned to me, eyes accusing. 'Going somewhere?' He held up my e-ticket printout for my flight to Virginia.

My brain and emotions were still trying to decide whether this new information affected my plans, so my brain just told me to say the first thing that was technically true. 'I'm going home.'

I knew it was bad. I knew it was bad because Braden didn't say anything. He seared me into my walls with a look I never wanted to see in his eyes again, and then he spun on his heel and slammed out of my room.

No argument. No discussion.

I wanted to cry again. Once I'd started down that path of giving in to tears after years of holding them back, there seemed to be no stopping them. My mouth trembled and I hugged my arms around my body to still the tremors running through the rest of me.

Ten minutes later I felt calm enough to make everyone coffee and take it into Ellie's room. Braden sat in the corner and didn't even look at me.

Suffice to say we created a horrible tension in Ellie's bedroom. Everyone had heard us arguing and everyone had heard Braden nearly splinter my wooden bedroom door when he slammed it. It was awkward.

Finally realizing his mood was poisoning Ellie's triumphant return home, Braden got up, kissed her forehead, and told her he'd check in later. Ellie nodded, biting her lip in worry as she watched him walk out. She cut me a look, and like a guilty school child, I quickly glanced away.

Elodie and Clark left soon after, and I was just getting up to leave her and Adam alone when Ellie stopped me.

'What's going on with you and Braden?'

'Ellie, I'm not dragging you into our drama when you're still in recovery.'

'Is it about that tiny white lie I told you about Isla?'

I spun around, my eyebrow raised at Ellie's shamefaced expression. 'Yeah. I just found out about that.'

Ellie glanced at Adam, who was frowning, clearly confused. 'I did a bad thing.'

He nodded. 'I'm getting that. What happened?'

'I told Joss that you and I had lunch with Isla and Braden and they were all over each other.'

Her boyfriend reared back just like Braden had. In fact, I'd noticed the two of them had quite a lot of similar mannerisms. They spent far too much time together. 'We never had lunch with them. We stopped in for two seconds at the club.'

'Okay, this game isn't fun anymore,' I snapped, forgetting that I was snapping at a patient. 'Why would you lie to me?'

Ellie's eyes were pleading and pitiful. Girl could get herself out of murder, she was so damn cute. 'Braden told me that since getting in your face all the time wasn't working, he'd come up with this stupid plan to back off and make you miss him so much you came back to him. I told him you were too stubborn to fall for it.'

Actually, I *had* been missing him. Bastard knew me too well. 'Mmm,' I answered noncommittally.

'You were being really obstinate, Joss. I thought if I provoked your jealousy, you'd get scared and go running off to get him back.' Her face was pale as she looked into Adam's eyes. 'It really backfired.'

'I can see that,' he murmured, trying not to smile.

This was not funny!

'You are so lucky you just had brain surgery.'

Ellie winced. 'Sorry, Joss.' Then her eyes turned hopeful. 'I meant to tell you before the surgery, but I was so scared that day, I forgot. Now you know the truth, though. You can just stop fighting and go get him back.'

It was my turn to sigh. '*He's* mad at *me* now.'

'For not trusting him?'

'Something like that,' I mumbled, wondering what the hell I was going to do next.

'Am I forgiven?' Ellie asked quietly.

I rolled my eyes at the question. 'Of course. Just . . . quit the matchmaking business. You suck at it.' I gave them a forlorn little wave and left the room, closing the door quietly behind me.

I sat down at my typewriter, staring at the latest page, trying to figure out what this meant to me now. Dr Pritchard said I'd regret not being honest with Braden. And the truth is, all the things that I'd worried about – me not being good enough, Braden being so intense, what could happen to us in the future – seemed like small change after discovering a little taste of what it felt like when I thought he didn't love me.

I should talk to him.

I was still going to Virginia to face up to my family's death.

But I knew I should talk to him.

Wait a minute. I jerked around in my chair to look at the bookshelf where my ticket had been. It wasn't there. And now that I thought about it, I hadn't seen Braden put it back.

Oh my God, he'd stolen my ticket!

My ire fueled me into hyperenergy. Intense! Braden, intense? He was a freaking overbearing asshole! I shoved my feet into my boots, shrugged into my coat, buttoning it up wrong and then screaming under my breath in exasperation. I grabbed my keys and my purse and attempted a little bit of calm as I told Adam and

Ellie I was going out. They called, 'Okay,' back to me through the door, and I slammed out of there, my hand in the air for a cab.

I couldn't think. I couldn't breathe. I mean, that took the cake. Stealing my plane ticket!

He was such a caveman!

I practically threw my cab fare at the driver and hopped out, running down Quartermile to the entrance to his apartment. I knew I was on camera when I buzzed, so I glared up into it, half expecting him to not let me in.

He let me in.

It was longest elevator ride of my life.

I got out to find Braden standing at his door looking casual and unaffected in his sweater, jeans, and bare feet. He stepped back quickly to hold the door open for me as I stormed past him.

I spun around, almost losing my balance, I had such an angry momentum going for me.

The idiot was smirking at me as he closed the door and strolled toward me, into the sitting room.

'This isn't funny,' I bit out, probably overreacting . . . but I was dealing with a whole mess of emotions that *he* had put me through the last few weeks.

Okay, I had maybe put myself through half of them, but I was angry at me, too. I couldn't have an argument with myself, though, so *he* was getting it!

The smirk dropped from Braden's face, the scowl reappearing. 'I know it's not bloody funny. Believe me.'

I stuck out my hand. 'Give me my ticket back, Braden. I am not even kidding.'

He nodded and pulled the ticket out of his back pocket. 'This ticket?'

'Yes. Give it to me.'

Then he shot me into volcanic rage. Braden tore up my ticket, letting the pieces flutter to the floor. 'What ticket?'

Despite the thought that was tucked somewhere in the back of my brain that told me I could print out another one . . . I lost it.

With an animalistic growl I didn't even know I was capable of, I threw my body toward his, my hands out as I shoved at him with enough might to make him stumble. Suddenly it was all there in my gut, the last six months of emotional upheaval, the dramatic changes he'd brought into my life – the uncertainty, the jealousy, the heartache. 'I hate you!' I yelled, the words tumbling out of my mouth with a mind of their own. I spun away from him. 'I was fine until you!' My eyes started to sting as I stared back at his stony face. 'Why?' My voice broke, and the tears spilled down my cheeks. 'I was fine. I was safe and I was fine. I'm broken, Braden. Stop trying to fix me and just let me be broken!'

He shook his head slowly, his own eyes bright, and I stood frozen as he came to me. I closed my eyes at his touch, his hands wrapping around my arms to tug me close to him.

'You are not broken.'

My eyelashes fluttered open, and I stared up into his beautiful face, his anguished, beautiful face. 'Yes, I am.'

He gave me an angry shake now. 'No, you're not.' He

leaned his face into mine and I found myself caught in his pale-blue eyes, mesmerized by the glitter of silver striations in them. 'Jocelyn, you're not broken, baby,' he whispered hoarsely, his eyes pleading with me. 'You've got a few cracks in you, but we all have some.'

More tears spilling, my mouth trembled as I whispered back, 'I don't hate you.'

Our eyes locked. So much emotion, so much uncertainty, so much of everything had built up around us in this thick tension that the air felt charged, desperate. Braden's expression changed, his eyes burning as they dropped to my mouth.

I couldn't tell you who reached whom first, but seconds later my lips were crushed under his, and his hand was tugging almost painfully at my hair as he took out my clip to let the mass of it fall around my shoulders. And then I felt his tongue slide against mine, and I could taste him, smell him, feel his strength all around me.

I had missed him.

But I was still angry, and from the bruising kiss that I wasn't pulling away from, I felt how angry Braden was, too. That didn't stop us. We broke from the kiss for two seconds so Braden could pop the buttons on my coat and rip me out of it. I tugged at the hem of his sweater, my hands frantically chasing it off him and then coming back to roam his hot, hard chest and abs. I threw my body against his for another kiss, but Braden wasn't done ridding me of clothes. Impatiently I pulled back to help him whip off my sweater, but I wasn't waiting any longer after that.

My hands on his nape brought his head down to mine, and I kissed him for all the days I hadn't been kissing him. It was a desperate, sexual tangle of tongues and hot breath, my sex pulsing readily just from the wet hardness of that one kiss.

I was so into it, I barely felt Braden haul me none-too-gently against a wall, his mouth breaking from mine as he trailed kisses down my neck, his strong arms hooking under my thighs to wrap my legs around his waist. My body slid up the wall, his hard cock nudging against my crotch, jeans to jeans.

'Fuck,' Braden murmured hotly, his mouth dipping to the rise of my breast. He held me up with one hand on my backside, the other peeling my bra down, letting the cool air whisper across my nipple. It puckered up for Braden's kiss, and I gasped at the bolt of pleasure that shot between my legs as he sucked it into his mouth. I jerked my hips, rubbing against Braden's erection.

'I can't wait,' I breathed, gripping at his shoulders.

As if to test that, Braden unbuttoned my jeans and slid his hand inside my panties. I whimpered, pressing up against his fingers as they dipped inside of me.

'Christ.' His head fell against my chest as he slid them in and out. 'So wet and tight, babe. Always.'

'Now,' I growled, my nails digging into his skin. 'Braden.'

And then we were moving, me holding on to him as he turned us and brought us down onto the couch, his hands quickly tugging my jeans down my legs. I unhooked my bra as he returned for my panties, my foot giving a little flick to get them off me. Panting with anticipation, my skin on fire, I fell onto my back, my legs parting for him. 'Braden, now.'

He had stopped, frozen as he looked down at me lying naked beneath him, my chest rising and falling with short, excited breaths, my hair spread out all around me. I watched his expression change; he was no less turned on, but he looked softer somehow. He pressed a hand to my quivering belly and coasted it gently up my stomach, between my breasts, to my jaw as he moved over me, his jeans abrading my bare legs. 'Ask for it,' he whispered gruffly against my lips.

I glided my hand down between us, pulling down the zipper on his jeans. My fingers slid under his boxer briefs, curling around his dick. I tugged it out of his jeans and watched his eyes close, his breath stutter. 'I want you to fuck me.' I gave a little lick at his lips that made his eyes shoot back open, blazing down at me. 'Please.'

With the growl that I had missed, Braden shucked his jeans down a little, then wrapped his hand around mine so that we both guided him between my legs. At the slightest brush of him against me I grew even wetter. I let go, my hands moving around to grasp his ass as he slid slowly into me. I squeezed his backside, urging him to go faster.

Which he did – with pleasure.

'Harder,' I moaned. 'Harder, Braden. Harder.'

Asking for it hard never failed to spur Braden on. He

kissed me and then slammed home. Pleasure coiled tight in me as his cock kissed me so deep, and I threw my head back to cry out, my cries getting louder as he pounded delicious strokes into me. What he was doing to my insides, the sight of him straining above me, the sounds of our excited pants and groans and the wet, primal noise of sex – all of it surged me toward satisfaction, and fast. I blew apart, screaming his name as I came. I came so hard, my sex pulsing around Braden, that I milked him into his own orgasm, his body tensing as it shot through him, his hips continuing to jerk him in and out, prolonging both our releases.

Best. Sex. Ever.

Braden groaned and collapsed against me. I stroked my hands against his ass soothingly before gliding them up his back to hold him close.

He turned his head against my neck and pressed a familiar kiss there.

'You still mad at me?' he murmured.

I sighed. 'I was going home to do what I should have done eight years ago. I was going home to say good-bye to my family.'

Braden grew still and then he pulled back to gaze down into my face, his eyes full of remorse. 'God, I'm so sorry, babe. About the ticket.'

I bit my lip. 'I can reprint it. And . . . I was thinking about staying in Virginia permanently after Ellie is back on her feet.'

The remorse fled quickly. 'Over my dead body.'

'Yeah, I thought you'd say that.'

He frowned. 'I'm still inside you.'

'I can feel that.' I smiled, bemused.

'Well, at least let me get out of you before you tell me you're attempting to leave me.'

I leaned up and kissed his lips. 'I don't know if that's what I'm doing yet.'

Used to nothing being straightforward with me, Braden exhaled slowly and withdrew. He tucked himself back into his jeans and sat up, holding out his hand. Deciding to trust him again, I let him pull me to my feet and followed him up the stairs to his room. He nodded at the bed. 'Get in.'

Since I was naked and sated and really in no mood to argue, I scrambled onto his bed and got in. I watched with pleasure as Braden stripped down to nothing and got in beside me. I was immediately settled into his side, my head on his warm chest.

'So, what are you doing?'

That was some question. And where to begin?

'I had a really good family, Braden,' I told him softly, pain I'd been hiding for too long threaded in every word. Braden heard it and his hold on me tightened. 'My mom was an orphan. She grew up in foster care here, and then moved to the States on a work visa. She was working at the college campus library when she met my dad. They fell in love, they got married, and for a while they lived happily ever after. My parents weren't like my friends' parents. I was fourteen and they were still sneaking around, making out when they didn't think I could see them. They were crazy about each other.' I felt my throat close up but tried to hold it together.

'They were crazy about me and Beth. My mom was overprotective and a little overbearing because she didn't want us to ever feel as alone as she had felt growing up.' I smiled. 'I thought she was cooler than all the other moms because, well, she had a cool accent, and she was kind of blunt, but in a really funny way that shocked some of the preppy housewives who lived in our town.'

'Sounds like someone I know,' Braden murmured, amusement in his voice.

I grinned at the thought that I might be a little like my mom. 'Yeah? Well, she was awesome. And my dad was just as great. He was the dad who checked in with you every day to see what was up. Even as I got older and became this entirely new creature called a teenage girl, he was still always there.' I felt a tear fall. 'We were happy,' I whispered, just managing to get the words out.

I felt Braden kiss my hair, his grip on my arm so tight it almost hurt. 'Babe, I'm so sorry.'

'Shit happens, right?' I swiped quickly at the tears. 'One day I was sitting in class and the police came to tell me that my dad had swerved into a truck to avoid a motorcyclist who'd come off his bike. Gone. Mom. Dad. Beth. I lost my parents and I lost a little girl I hadn't really had a chance to get to know. Though I knew enough to know that I adored her. I knew she would cry if she couldn't see her favorite teddy bear – this ratty old brown bear with a blue ribbon around his neck that used to be mine and still smelled like me. His name was Ted. Original, I know. I knew that she had a sophisticated taste in music because all you had to do to stop her from crying was play "MMMBop" by Hanson.' I laughed sadly at the memory. 'I knew that when I was having a bad day, all I had to do was pick her up, hold her close, smell her skin, and feel her tiny warmth against me to know that everything was okay . . .

'I went off the rails when I lost them. My first foster home was full of other kids, so my foster parents barely even noticed I was alive, which was fine by me since it meant I could do whatever I wanted. The only thing that numbed everything was doing stupid shit that made me feel like crap about myself. Lost my virginity too young, drank way too much. Then after Dru died, I just stopped. I was moved to another foster home on the other side of town. They didn't have much, but there were fewer kids there and one kid in particular who was pretty cool. She wanted a big sister, though . . .'

I sucked in a breath, feeling the guilt wash over me all over again. 'I didn't want to be anything to anybody. She needed someone, and I didn't give it to her. I don't even know what happened to her after I left.' I shook my head regretfully and sighed. 'When I was there, I went to a couple of parties over the years, not a lot. Always ended up with some guy I didn't know or care to know.' I heaved a sick sigh. 'Truth is, I went out on the same night every year. To a party, to a bar. It didn't matter as long as it helped me forget. I've spent eight years burying my family, pretending they never existed, because, yeah – like you said – it was easier to pretend I'd never had them than to deal with how much it hurt to lose them. I realize now how unfair that was to them. To the memory of them.'

I clenched my jaw to stem the tears, but they spilled over anyway, dripping onto Braden's chest. 'The one night I went out was the anniversary of their deaths. But I stopped doing that when I was eighteen. I went out that night and I went to a party and I can't remember anything that happened after I arrived. I woke up the next day and I was naked in bed with *two* guys I didn't know.'

Braden cursed low under his breath. 'Jocelyn.'

He was belatedly angry, I knew. 'Believe me, I've been there. I was furious at myself, violated, scared. Anything could have happened to me. And sexually . . .'

'Don't.'

I stopped at his scary tone. 'I got checked out and those guys hadn't given me anything, thank God. But I never slept with anyone again. Until you.'

Another tight squeeze for that one.

'I might never stop fearing tomorrow, Braden,' I admitted calmly. 'The future, and what it can take from me, scares me. And sometimes I freak out, and sometimes my freak-outs hurt the people closest to me.'

'I understand that. I can deal with it. You have to trust me.'

'I thought you were the one with the trust issues,' I grumbled.

'I trust *you*, babe. You don't see yourself the way I see you.'

I traced a little 'J' on his chest. 'I do trust you. I just didn't expect Ellie to lie to me, so I took her word as gold. I'm sorry.'

Braden let go of his breath. 'I love you, Jocelyn. These last few weeks have been a nightmare for more reasons than one.'

I thought of the long-legged blonde that had put me through hell. 'And Isla?'

'I swear I never slept with her.'

'Did anything happen?'

His chest froze beneath me.

'Braden?'

He sighed heavily. 'Yesterday she kissed me. I didn't kiss her back. I pushed her off and told her about you.'

I was silent a moment, and then I replied decisively, 'You have to fire her.'

Braden snorted. 'Are you finally admitting you love me?'

'I can't promise it'll be easy, Braden. I'll probably always be a little irrational about the future. I'll worry a lot.'

'I told you I can handle it, babe.'

'Why?'

'Because' – he sighed – 'you make me laugh, you challenge me, and you turn me on like no else can. I feel like I'm missing something really important when you're gone. So important I don't feel like myself. I've never felt like someone was mine before. But you're mine, Jocelyn. I've known that from the moment we met. And I'm yours. I don't want to be anybody else's, babe.'

I leaned up on my elbow so that I could look him in the eye; then I pressed a soft kiss to his lips and fell against him. His arms came around me to hold me close as he deepened the kiss. When I finally came up for air I was panting a little. I touched my finger to his lips, determined that one day I'd enjoy this contentment without worrying it would be taken from me. 'Do you think you might be able to come to Virginia with me? To go through my parents' things?'

His eyes smiled, and I can't tell you what it did to me that I could make him that happy. 'Of course. We'll go whenever you want. But we're coming back.'

I nodded. 'I was only moving to Virginia because I thought you were moving into Isla.'

Braden grunted. 'Nice.'

'You're firing her, right?'

He narrowed his eyes. 'You just want me to fire her?'

'If I told you that Craig kissed me last night would you make me quit?'

'Point taken. I'll find her a job elsewhere.'

'Elsewhere as in nowhere you work.'

'Christ, you're bossy.'

'Uh, do you not remember dry humping me against a desk after Craig kissed me?'

'Again, point taken.'

I buried my head against his chest. 'I thought I'd really fucked up.'

He squeezed my nape. 'We both really did. But that's over now. From now on I'm completely in charge. I think we'll have a lot less drama, and definitely no more breakups, if I'm in control of this thing.'

I patted his stomach. 'Whatever you need to tell yourself to get through the day, baby.'

'You still haven't said it, you know.'

I turned my head and smiled up at him. I took a big inner breath. 'I love you, Braden Carmichael.'

His grin made my chest swell. 'Say it again.'

I giggled. 'I love you.'

He sat up quickly and then swung out of the bed, pulling me with him. He pushed me toward the en suite. 'You're going to say it again while I fuck you in the shower.'

'This whole taking control thing is kind of hot.'

'It's about to get hotter, babe.' He smacked me lightly on my ass, and I gave a little squeal, his laughter and mine filling the bathroom as we stumbled together into the shower.

26

'Now, you're sure you're going to be okay?'

Ellie crossed her arms over her chest and blew air out between her lips. 'If you ask me that again, don't bother coming back.'

I shot Braden a look and he shook his head slightly. 'Don't look at me. She didn't have attitude until you moved in with her.'

That was fair.

Ellie giggled at my faux wounded look and threw up her hands. 'Guys, come on. It's been a month. I'm fine. Adam's practically living here, and you have a plane to catch.'

Braden kissed his sister's cheek before turning to open the front door with our suitcase in hand. In the end it had been a good thing Braden ripped up my plane ticket, because inviting him to come to Virginia with me had meant rearranging his schedule and changing the flight dates. And, well, to be honest, we wanted to make sure Ellie was back on her feet before we left.

After a month of being mothered by me, Adam, Braden and her actual mother, Ellie was probably glad to be rid of us. She was still trying to get her energy level back up and was often exhausted. And she was still very much shaken by the experience. I'd suggested she start seeing Dr Pritchard, and Ellie had her first appointment in a few days. Hopefully the good doctor would help her out. I wondered if the good doctor would help me out. I was feeling a little separation anxiety.

'Joss, the taxi is waiting.' Ellie shooed me toward to the door.

'Fine,' I grumbled. 'But if you let anything happen to yourself while we're gone, I will kill you.'

'Noted.'

'Tell Adam the same goes for him.'

'I will warn him. Now will you go and do this very important thing?' She hugged me tight. 'I wish I could come with you.'

I gave her a squeeze and pulled back. 'I'll be fine. I've got a bossy businessman watching my back.'

'I heard that,' Braden called from the other side of the door. Damn. I'd thought he was already in the cab.

'I better go before I end up taking this flight alone.'

'Call me when you land.'

'Will do.'

We said good-bye, and I let Braden bundle me into the cab. It had been a long month, worrying about Ellie – and we were still worrying – but the tons of make-up sex Braden and I were having definitely took a load off.

Pun intended.

We were still finding our way back after the whole breakup mess but this new 'us' was kind of hot. Oh, and this new us involved no Isla. Braden fired her but got her a job at a nightclub he didn't own through a friend. I think she could have gotten another job by herself – she was annoyingly beautiful – but Braden felt guilty. Technically his manager had come onto him, so he had nothing to feel guilty about, but Braden wasn't comfortable with the idea that his manager had somehow tried to take advantage of him. That didn't go down well in caveman world.

I for one was still feeling guilty about the emotional mess I had turned into. In an effort to make up for it, I cleared out one of my bedside cabinets and two drawers in my dresser for Braden's use. I still couldn't get the image of his stupid grin out of my head when I'd told him that. He'd jumped out of bed – mid-make-out, I might add – to unpack his overnight bag into the drawers.

He was like an excited little kid on Christmas morning.

Braden had to one-up me, though, and gave me a key to his apartment the next day. I would have given him a key to ours, but he already had one.

I was pretty quiet on the way to the airport and pretty quiet when we got there. My head was already in Virginia with my family. We were flying into Richmond and staying at the Hilton. The storage facility where the lawyers had put all of my family's belongings for me until I inherited them was in the city. Rather than taking it all out, I'd continued to pay rent on the storage unit. Once I'd sorted through everything and decided what to do with it, Braden and I were heading out to the small town where I grew up in Surry County. It was just a little more than an hour outside Richmond and driving would be an experience for both of us since neither of us had driven in a really long time. And Braden had never driven on the right-hand side of the road before.

I mused over this as Braden guided us through check-in and security.

'I know you've got a lot on your mind,' he said as he took a seat outside our gate. 'But if you start to freak out, you have to tell me, okay?'

'Okay.' I nodded.

'Promise?'

I sat down beside him, pressing a soft kiss to his lips as I did. 'Promise.'

We were quiet a moment, and the silence between us was nice.

And then . . .

'You fancy joining the mile-high club?' I turned my narrow-eyed gaze on him, and he gave me that slow, sexy smile that had gotten me here in the first place. 'It could be fun.'

I shook my head at him, smiling despite myself. 'Baby . . . with you it's always fun.'

'Mmm.' He dipped his head toward mine and whispered across my lips before giving me a searing kiss, 'Good answer.'

Richmond, Virginia
Three days later

'Oh, baby, don't stop,' I begged, my hands curling into the sheets in front of me.

Braden gently squeezed my breast before pinching my nipple between finger and thumb. He did that at the same time as he circled his hips as he thrust into me, and I panted harder.

I'd woken up that morning on my side to feel his heat at my back, his arm around my waist and his cock already buried deep inside of me.

'Come for me, babe,' he demanded breathlessly, his strokes grow-ing faster. 'Come for me.' He slid his hand down my nightie and between my legs, his finger slip-ping through my sex to circle my clit.

Oh . . . Goooodddd!

I threw my head back, crying out his name as I came around him.

Braden slammed inside me one last time, burying his shout in my neck as his body shuddered against me as he climaxed.

I fell limpid against him. 'Good morning.'

His mouth smiled against my skin. 'Morning.'

'If you wake me up like that at least once a week, I will be a very happy girl.'

'Good to know.' He eased out of me gently, and I turned around to face him, my hand reaching to cup his cheek so I could pull him down for a deliciously soft kiss.

When Braden pulled back, he was frowning. 'No more stalling. Today we do this.'

I swallowed but nodded. We'd arrived in Richmond two and a half days ago, and I'd not been able to leave the hotel room, insisting on having sex constantly with my boyfriend. Now, this was difficult for Braden because he really, *really* didn't mind the constant sex, but he was worried that I kept putting off what we were here to do.

Obviously my time was up.

The self-storage facility was just over twenty minutes away from the hotel, on a street not too far from Three Lakes Park. I saw Braden taking in the city as we got a cab out to the facility – we'd rent a car for the drive to my hometown later – but I wasn't really in the mood to reminisce about the state in which I'd grown up. I was about to do plenty of that, and I was pretty scared, if I were honest with myself.

The guy was friendly at the storage place. I gave him my ID and storage-unit number, and he took us around what looked like normal car garages with bright red doors. He stopped in front of one of them abruptly. 'Here you go.' He smiled and left us to it.

Braden rubbed my shoulders, sensing my hesitation. 'You can do this.'

I can do this. I keyed in the code on the key pad next to the door, and the metal doors started to rise. When they'd finally rotated up along the ceiling, I let my eyes take in the sight before me. There were boxes and boxes of stuff. Suitcases. A jewelry box. Trembling, I took a step inside and tried to calm my heart before it rocketed me into a panic attack.

I felt Braden's cool, large hand slip into mine, and he squeezed. 'Breathe, babe. Just breathe.'

I smiled up at him, a wobbly kind of smile.

I could definitely do this.

Epilogue

Dublin Street, Edinburgh
Two years later

At the sound of a throat clearing I glanced up into the mirror and saw Braden leaning against the doorjamb of our room. I whirled around, my hands immediately going to my hips. 'What are you doing here? You're not supposed to be here.'

Braden smiled softly, his eyes drinking me in, and the look in them made me feel all mushy. Damn him. 'You look beautiful, babe.'

I glanced down at the dress and sighed. 'I can't believe you managed to talk me into this.'

'I can be very persuasive when I want to be.' He was grinning smugly now.

'Persuasive is one thing. This . . . this is a miracle.' I eyed him carefully. 'Wait, is that why you're here? To make sure I leave?' That bothered me. A lot. I actually felt my heart stop.

Braden grimaced. 'No. I have every faith in you, and I know you're going to walk out that door.'

'Then why are you here?'

'Because I haven't seen you in a few days and I missed you.'

'You're about to see me in half an hour. You couldn't wait?'

'There will be other people there though.' He made a step toward me, giving me *that* look.

Oh, no. No!

'That can wait.' I held up a hand, holding him off. 'Now, *you* got me into this. I wasn't sure I wanted to do it, but you got all persuasive, and then you got me all into it. And I want it to be kind of perfect – as in . . . done right. So get your ass out of here, mister.'

He was grinning broadly now as he backed up. 'Okay, you're the boss.' I snorted at that one. 'I'll see you in half an hour.'

'Braden!' Ellie fell into the doorway in a champagne silk floor-length gown. 'It's bad luck to see the bride before the wedding. Get out!' She pushed him up the hallway and out of sight.

'See you soon, babe!' he called back, laughing.

I shook my head, trying to calm the nerves and the warring giddiness as I looked into the cheval mirror. I was almost unrecognizable in my ivory wedding dress.

'Ready, Joss?' Ellie asked, out of breath from beating her brother out of the apartment.

Rhian appeared at her side, wearing a teasing grin and the same champagne dress Ellie had on, a gold wedding band beside the diamond engagement ring James had given her years earlier. They'd been married for eight months. 'Yeah, you ready, Joss?'

We were standing in the master bedroom, what used to be Ellie's room but which was now mine and

Braden's. In Virginia I'd found some things – my mom's jewelry; Beth's favorite teddy bear, Ted; a few photo albums; and a painting – that I'd wanted to keep. Everything else we gave away or threw out. It took us a couple of days, and a lot of tissues for me, but we did it, and then we took off to say good-bye to my family at their graves. That was hard. I couldn't stop the panic attack that caused and for a while Braden just sat in the grass with me and held me as I tried to apologize to my mom, my dad, and Beth for my eight years of trying not to remember them.

Going through that with me had made Braden and me closer. When we got back to Scotland, we were pretty much inseparable. Ellie and Adam were inseparable, as well, and there had been too much awkwardness with the four of us living together with Braden and Ellie being brother and sister. Neither of them wanted to hear the sex stuff. So Ellie had moved into Adam's place a few months after her surgery, and Braden had put his apartment up for rent and moved into Dublin Street with me.

A year later he'd actually prearranged with a cabdriver to stop outside the Bruntsfield Evangelical Church, where he proposed to me in the cab, in remembrance of how and where we'd first met.

Fast-forward to now. After the wedding we'd be flying off to Hawaii for our honeymoon, and when we came back it would be to Dublin Street as Mr and Mrs Carmichael. My chest squeezed, and I took a deep breath.

Braden had been talking about having kids lately. *Kids. Oh, wow.* I glanced at my completed manuscript lying on my desk. After twenty rejection letters I'd gotten a call from a literary agent who wanted to read the rest of it. I'd just mailed the full manuscript out two days ago. For two years that manuscript had been like a kid to me, and I'd had plenty of freak-outs about publishing my parents' story. And now Braden wanted real kids? I'd freaked out when he'd first mentioned it, but he just sat there sipping his beer while I silently spiraled. Ten minutes later he'd looked back at me and said, 'Are you done?'

He was used to my freak-outs now.

I shot a look at the photograph I had of my parents on my desk. Like me and Braden, Mom and Dad had been passionate about each other, had argued a lot and had their issues, but they always got through it because of how deeply they felt for each other. They were everything they couldn't be without the other. Sure it could get rough sometimes, but life wasn't a Hollywood movie. Shit happened. You fought, you screamed, and somehow you worked like hell to get out on the other side still intact.

Just like me and Braden.

I nodded at Ellie and Rhian.

Sometimes the clouds weren't weightless. Sometimes their bellies got dark and full. It was life. It happened. It didn't mean it wasn't scary, or that I wasn't still afraid, but now I knew that as long as I was standing under the sky with Braden beside me when those clouds broke, I'd be all right. We'd get rained on together. Knowing Braden, he'd have a big-ass umbrella to shelter us from the worst of it.

That there was an uncertain future I could handle.

'Yeah. I'm ready.'

Acknowledgements

I can't begin to thank my readers enough. *On Dublin Street* was an entirely new venture for me into adult contemporary romance, and I was not prepared for the wonderful reception it received. I am truly overwhelmed and blown away by the positivity and love *ODS* has been given. The success of its release has opened so many new doors for the series and introduced me to some wonderful new people.

I'd firstly like to thank Lauren E. Abramo, my phenomenal agent at Dystel & Goderich Literary Management. You have been tremendous, Lauren! I can't thank you enough for championing me and *ODS*, and for bringing such amazing new developments into my life.

This leads me to my editor, Kerry Donovan, at New American Library. Kerry, thank you for believing in *On Dublin Street* and in me. Your enthusiasm for the world and characters I've created brings me no end of happiness and I can't wait to see what we can do together in the future.

I'd also like to thank Ashley McConnell and Alicia Cannon, my original editors on the self-published edition of *On Dublin Street*. You're awesome, ladies! Thank you for all your hard work (and comments that made me laugh). Also, a massive thank-you to Claudia McKinney (aka Phatpuppy Art) for your talent, for creating art that speaks to me, and mostly for being an unbelievably lovely person to work with.

I also want to thank a few fantastic book bloggers who have not only been incredibly supportive of *On Dublin Street* since the moment I announced my plans to publish adult contemporary romance, but have supported me almost from the beginning of my writing career: Shelley Bunnell, Kathryn Grimes, Rachel at the blog Fiktshun, Alba Solorzano, Damaris Cardinali, Ana at the blog Once Upon a Twilight, Janet Wallace, Cait Peterson, and Jena Freeth. You guys always astound me with your unbelievable support, enthusiasm, and kind words. You make me smile on a daily basis.

I can't forget to say a huge thank-you to my fellow authors: Shelly Cranc, Tammy Blackwell, Michelle Leighton, Quinn Loftis, Amy Bartol, Georgia Cates, Rachel Higginson, and Angeline Kace. I cannot tell you how much your friendship these past few months has meant to me, and how wonderful it is to have such awesome, kind ladies to turn to for help, advice, and a giggle. There are no words to describe how brilliant you all are.

A rather HUGE thank-you to my readers for taking a chance on me, for encouraging me, and for filling my days with big cheesy grins caused by reading your e-mails and Facebook, Twitter, and Goodreads comments. You've no idea how much I appreciate those. :)

And finally, a special thank-you to my mum and dad; my brother, David; Carol; my closest friends, Ashleen (congratulations, Mrs Walker!), Kate, and Shanine; and all my family and friends for being there and for being you. Some elements of *On Dublin Street* are personal to me, and personal to you. Sometimes it takes a lifetime to learn the important lessons; for us it seems to have come upon us all too quickly.

Grief and loss are probably the most fearful creatures that exist. They can teach us to worry about the future and question the longevity of contentment, and prove us unable to enjoy happiness when we have it. But loss shouldn't be a fearful creature. It should be a creature of wisdom. It should teach us not to fear that tomorrow may never come but to live fully, as though the hours are melting away like seconds. Loss should teach us to cherish those we love, to never do anything that will result in regret, and to cheer on tomorrow with all of its promises of greatness.

Sometimes strength and courage aren't in the big things. Sometimes the bravest thing we can do is enjoy what we have and be positive about what makes us lucky. It's easy and unextraordinary to be frightened of life. It's far more difficult to arm yourself with the good stuff despite all the bad and step foot into tomorrow as an everyday warrior.

To my family and friends: You're the strongest warriors I know.

He just wanted a decent book to read ...

Not too much to ask, is it? It was in 1935 when Allen Lane, Managing Director of Bodley Head Publishers, stood on a platform at Exeter railway station looking for something good to read on his journey back to London. His choice was limited to popular magazines and poor-quality paperbacks – the same choice faced every day by the vast majority of readers, few of whom could afford hardbacks. Lane's disappointment and subsequent anger at the range of books generally available led him to found a company – and change the world.

'We believed in the existence in this country of a vast reading public for intelligent books at a low price, and staked everything on it'
Sir Allen Lane, 1902–1970, founder of Penguin Books

The quality paperback had arrived – and not just in bookshops. Lane was adamant that his Penguins should appear in chain stores and tobacconists, and should cost no more than a packet of cigarettes.

Reading habits (and cigarette prices) have changed since 1935, but Penguin still believes in publishing the best books for everybody to enjoy. We still believe that good design costs no more than bad design, and we still believe that quality books published passionately and responsibly make the world a better place.

So wherever you see the little bird – whether it's on a piece of prize-winning literary fiction or a celebrity autobiography, political tour de force or historical masterpiece, a serial-killer thriller, reference book, world classic or a piece of pure escapism – you can bet that it represents the very best that the genre has to offer.

Whatever you like to read – trust Penguin.

read more
www.penguin.co.uk